PURE TERROR

As he approached the rear wall of the cave, Troy stopped in confusion. In a far corner lay a pool of dark shadow . . . or what he thought was shadow. Upon further inspection, he found it to be something much more solid. It was jet black, and the glow of the candle seemed to glisten off it.

He could hear the thing breathing now, low and husky. The smell of a serpent was so cloying that it was nearly overpowering.

Abruptly, Troy recalled the stories that had circulated around the county during the past week; stories of farm animals being ripped apart by some strange animal.

A dry rustling filled the cave. The creature was rising slowly to its feet. Troy could feel the gust of its breath. As it engulfed him, it hit the flame of the candle. *God help me . . . no!* he thought.

An instant later, the cave was plunged into pitch blackness. The boy screamed, but no one heard his cry.

He could do nothing but stand there as he listened to the sound of clawed feet scampering through the darkness toward him.

FEAR

RONALD KELLY

ZEBRA BOOKS
KENSINGTON PUBLISHING CORP.

ZEBRA BOOKS are published by

Kensington Publishing Corp.
850 Third Avenue
New York, NY 10022

Copyright © 1994 by Ronald Kelly

Zebra and the Z logo Reg. U.S. Pat. & TM Off.

First Printing: September, 1994

Printed in the United States of America

In memory of my grandparents

John Alexander and Clara Spicer
Alfred and Ora Kelley

*who taught me to appreciate
the old ways and blessed
me with the gift of
storytelling.*

Prologue

John Haskel awoke to the sound of his finest Holstein, Buttercup, screaming in the dead of night.

It wasn't a moo that she uttered; not even the long, mournful sort that cows bellow when something spooks them particularly bad. No, this was screaming, startlingly shrill and full of terror.

John sat up in his bed. His fifty-year-old heart pounded in his lean chest as he listened to the milk cow shriek at the top of her lungs. Then the godawful sound stopped cold. That caused John's heart to beat even faster . . . the abruptness with which Buttercup's horrified cry had been cut short.

The farmer sensed his wife, Doris, stir in the brass-framed bed next to him. "John," she muttered sleepily. "What was all that commotion?"

John started to answer, but found that his mouth was drier than cotton. He swallowed and tried again. "I don't know, hon. Kinda sounded like ol' Buttercup. Whatever it was, it came from out in the barn."

He kicked the covers aside and left his side of the bed. The hardwood boards of the bedroom floor felt cool against his bare feet, but that was the only comfort he experienced as he crossed to the open window. It was late June and even at that late hour—nearly half-past midnight—it was still warm and uncomfortably humid. By the time he reached the window, a sticky sweat slickened his armpits and the small of his back, causing the cotton material of his nightshirt to adhere to his body.

John stared through the window screen, but he could see nothing. There was no moon that night, so, at first, all he could detect was pitch darkness. He stood there for a long moment, letting his vision grow accustomed to the gloom. He noticed the scattered winking of fireflies in the yard out back, then the dark structure of the big barn that stood a hundred feet or so from the two-story farmhouse that the Haskels called their home.

"See anything?" asked Doris from the bed. Her voice held a tone of groggy disinterest. John could tell that his wife was still half asleep.

"Hell no," grumbled the farmer. "Too damn dark." He strained his ears, listening for noises, but none came from the vicinity of the barn. "Can't hear a dadblamed thing, either. Reckon I'd better go down and check, just to make sure."

"Maybe that weasel is messing around in the henhouse again," offered Doris.

John shook his head. "Weren't no weasel that caused that sound. It was Buttercup. I'd swear to it."

He felt his way through the darkness to the closet next to the chest-of-drawers. John rummaged through the clothes that hung there until he found what he was looking for, leaning in the far corner. He took out the twelve-gauge shotgun and broke open the twin breeches. He recalled the cow's terrified scream, as well as its abrupt ending, and decided that rocksalt might not be enough that night. He shucked the loads from the chambers and replaced them with shells packed with double-aught buckshot. John closed the scattergun with a snap, then started back to the foot of the bed where his work boots were parked. It took him a moment of fumbling, but he finally got the boots on and the laces tied.

"You be careful," mumbled Doris. She was back in her usual position, lying on her stomach with her face partially buried in her duck-feather pillow.

John leaned down and kissed her on the left ear. "Be back directly," he told her. He was answered by the soft purr of his wife's snoring.

A moment later, he was making his way down the stairway to the lower floor. Except for John and Doris, the farmhouse was unoccupied. Their five children had long since grown up and moved on to lives of their own. John had bought the farm in 1922 and made a meager living growing corn and taters ever since, even through the hard times brought on by the Depression. It was now 1946 and, even with the prosperity that had seemingly followed the Second World War, John and Doris still found it difficult to pay the mortgage and keep a decent meal on the table come suppertime.

He reached the kitchen downstairs, then stepped into the pantry and found the lantern he kept on the top shelf just above his wife's jars of canned preserves and green beans. John shook the lantern and heard the faint swish of kerosene in the base. There wasn't very much left, but hopefully enough to shed some light on whatever had happened in the barn . . . or was still taking place, for all he knew.

John set the lantern on the kitchen table, found a book of matches in a Tampa Nugget cigar box underneath the potbelly stove, then struck one. He raised the cloudy chimney of the lantern, lit the wick, and turned up the flame. It faltered weakly, due to the lack of coal oil in the lamp's reservoir. He just hoped it would stay lit while he was exploring the barn.

He unhooked the back door screen and stepped onto the rear porch. John stood there for a moment, feeling more than a little uneasy. The recollection of the screaming cow wasn't all that preyed on his thoughts. Another thing that bothered him was the absence of sound in the grassy yard that stretched between the house and barn. Usually, the night was alive with the chirping of crickets, as well as the lonely call of a whippoorwill every now and then. But, at that moment, John Haskel heard nothing. The warm summer night was completely silent.

Slowly, he started toward the dark structure of the barn. He passed the clothes line where Doris hung their laundry to dry, as well as the outhouse and the tool shed. As he approached the chicken coop, the unnatural silence of that night unsteadied his nerves once again. There was well over three dozen laying hens inside the coop, but they made no noise. He could imagine them burrowed into their nests, cowering in the darkness, afraid to make a sound.

John paused next to the henhouse and took a moment to check his shotgun again, then continued on. He walked toward the single door that led into the barn and spotted something peculiar before he reached it. He lifted the lantern, casting its muted glow on the structure's main entrance. "What the hell happened here?" he whispered to himself.

The lower half of the door sported a jagged hole that was roughly two feet in diameter. As he crouched next to the opening and ran his fingers along its splintered edges, John found that the sturdy lumber of the barn door had not been kicked or battered in. Rather, it had been *gnawed* completely through. He pulled his fingers away from the opening and found them coated with wetness. The dampness that clung to his fingertips was slick and foamy, like the slobber from some kind of animal.

He lowered his head to the hole in the door and listened. This time he heard something. It was an ugly combination of sounds; ripping and tearing, as well as the soft patter of liquid dripping onto the barn's earthen floor. Two distinct smells also drifted from within the building. One was a scent that he recognized from years of hunting and field-dressing in the Tennessee woods. It was the rich, coppery odor of freshly let blood, and apparently quite a bit of it. The other was a musky, sour stench that was even more unnerving than the smell of blood. John had killed too many chicken snakes in the corn crib during his lifetime not to recognize the rancid odor that was common of a serpent.

John leaned the shotgun against the weathered wall of the barn and fumbled with the latch of the barn door. After it was disengaged, he retrieved the twelve-gauge and pushed at the door with his foot. Lazily, it swung inward with a squeal of unoiled hinges. He expected the strange noises to stop at the sound of his entrance, but, strangely enough, they didn't. The ripping and tearing continued, as well as a noise that John could only describe as the coarse grinding of something incredibly sharp against raw bone.

The farmer said nothing. He didn't call out in warning or attempt to scare the intruder away by making a lot of noise. No, he simply made his way as quietly as possible toward the rear of the barn and the place where the sickening sounds of feeding came from. It was the last stall near the back wall . . . the stall that Buttercup normally occupied.

The closer John came to the stall, the stronger the scents of blood and snake grew. He stared down at the ground. The lantern light revealed dark rivulets trickling across the floor of earth and manure, seeping from underneath the gate of Buttercup's stall. John balanced the shotgun in his right hand and curled his index finger through the triggerguard. As he neared the stall door, he saw that deep grooves had been gouged into the wood along the top, as if something with extremely sharp claws had scrambled over the hinged partition in its haste to get to the cow.

John hesitated for a moment. The sounds of ripping and tearing and grating ceased to let up, and the farmer found himself wondering just what sort of creature could possess such an insatiable hunger. There seemed to be no pause in the intruder's appetite. The ugly noises failed to slow down for even a second, instead growing in their ravenous fury.

The farmer took a deep breath, bracing himself for the worst. But, when he finally gathered the nerve to step up to the gate and illuminate the stall with the glow of the kerosene lantern, John Haskel was still not prepared for the horrible scene he lay witness to.

Buttercup was no longer the healthy Holstein that had provided milk, butter, and calves for the Haskel family for the past seven years. Now she was only a torn and bloody carcass that had been ripped open and disemboweled. John glanced over at the cow's head, which lay a good five feet from its mutilated body. Buttercup's glassy eyes stared dumbly at him, bulging from one final moment of shock and agony, but blinded by death.

John then turned his startled gaze to the horrid thing that had been responsible for the slaughter. At first, he was certain that it was some sort of monstrous dog, but the flickering light of the lantern dispelled that first impression. The creature was about as tall as a year-old calf, yet long and lean of body and limb, perhaps seven feet from snout to tail. Its neck was serpentine, as was its triangular head, which dove deeply into the cow's open belly like a piston, pulling and tearing with powerful jaws. And there was one other point that John couldn't ignore. The creature that had killed Buttercup was not covered with fur or hair, but with a gleaming coat of jet black scales. Looking at it, John Haskel was reminded of the sleek and fluid body of a black racer.

The farmer swallowed dryly, feeling a little dizzy at the sight of so much blood. It was that insignificant sound that finally alerted the creature to his presence. With a cross between a snarl and hiss, the monster withdrew its head from the carcass and turned its attention toward the man at the gate. It regarded him silently for a moment and that was when John saw the thing's eyes clearly for the first time. They were greenish-gold in color and the pupils were narrow slits like those of a snake, rather than round like a warm-blooded animal's. Contempt burned in those reptilian eyes—a contempt that was plainly evil in nature—and it snapped its jaws as it drew a ragged string of bloody tissue down its gullet. Something that looked like a mixture of saliva and snot dripped from its yellowed fangs, which were razor-sharp and a good three to four inches in length.

John simply stood and stared at the creature, paralyzed for an instant by the dark malice that flared in its golden eyes. The double-barreled shotgun felt heavy in his hand and he considered putting it to use, but secretly knew that such an action would be in vain, as well as downright foolhardy. Just looking at that coat of black armor, John knew that a blast of buckshot would rattle right off it with about as much effect as spring rain on a tin roof. The load of double-aught would scarcely be out of the barrel before the creature would react, leaping over the gate of the stall after him.

Carefully, John stepped back a couple of paces. The monster continued to glare at him, its toothy jaws curling into a sinister grin. "You just go on back to your eating," the farmer said softly. "Finish what you came to do and then git." But, even as he said it, John knew that the creature would "git" when it was good and ready to, and not a moment before.

The glow of the lantern began to falter, its supply of kerosene dwindling down to nothing. The light began to dim and, suddenly, John knew that he had to leave right then. He shuddered at the thought of being trapped inside the barn with only pitch darkness between him and the monster.

John watched as it growled at him one last time, then turned its attention back to the dead cow. Slowly, he backtracked to the barn door, his heart thundering in his chest. He reached the entrance just in time. The lantern's flame winked out a moment before he ducked through and shut the door behind him.

As if in a daze, John Haskel walked through the dewy grass, back toward the farmhouse. He strained his ears and, faintly, heard the sound of bones being cracked for the marrow.

He reached the house and let himself inside. John closed the back door and locked it, but knew that it would be little security against the thing in the barn if it had a notion to come in. He just hoped that poor Buttercup would fill its belly and satisfy its hunger that night, and that it would go its way afterwards.

John mounted the stairs, walked down the hallway, and returned to his bedroom. Doris was fast asleep and he was careful not to wake her. He leaned the shotgun against the bedpost, then shucked the workboots from his feet. Gently, he climbed into bed and slid beneath the covers.

He lay there for a very long time, unable to sleep. Trembling, he listened for sounds, but heard nothing. He had always considered himself to be a brave man who was afraid of nothing but the good Lord above. But his trip to the barn that night had given him something else to fear. He thought he had known evil, but he was mistaken. For nothing that he had come across in fifty years of hard-living could hold a candle to the abomination he had just encountered in Buttercup's blood-splattered stall.

Part One
Menace

One

Barber Shop Talk

"I reckon you're next, young man."

At the sound of Mr. Drewer's voice, Jeb Sweeny pried his eyes from the pages of a Captain America comic book and looked up. Amos Parnell was stepping down out of the barber chair, freshly clipped and smelling of hair tonic, while Mr. Drewer flapped the striped barber's sheet, sending twigs of curly brown hair falling to the floor. The barber stood there, holding the cloth in his liver-spotted hands like a bullfighter holding a cape, his eyes appraising the challenge of Jeb's shaggy head.

Reluctantly, the boy closed the comic book and laid it on top of a stack of magazines, mostly *Life* and *Saturday Evening Post*. Jeb had only been halfway through the story, in which Captain America and his sidekick Bucky were in the heat of battle against a troop of stormtrooping Nazis. He wanted to finish the comic and find out what happened, but Mr. Drewer was not a man to be kept waiting, especially on a Saturday afternoon with a shop full of customers.

"Yes sir," he said politely, then approached the chair. It was a sturdy piece of equipment, all stainless steel and padded black cowhide leather. As the ten-year-old hopped up into the seat, he wondered if the electric chair at the state penitentiary in Nashville held any resemblance to Mr. Drewer's own throne of torture.

Jeb parked himself in the chair and, a moment later, was wearing the striped sheet. He grimaced when the barber tied the strings a little too tightly around the back of his neck, but didn't complain. Mr. Drewer jacked the chair up a few extra inches using a foot pedal at the circular base. Jeb felt the elderly man's breath blowing warmly on the nape of his neck and pictured him standing at the ready, stainless steel scissors in one hand and skinny, black comb in the other.

"Heavy off the sides and light on the top, I recall," said Mr. Drewer with the all-knowing tone of a mind-reader.

"Aw, stop showing off, Howard," Cy Newman snapped good-naturedly from his usual seat by the front window. "You've been cutting the boy's hair since he was a tadpole." The old man sent a spritz of tobacco juice into a tarnished brass spittoon, then turned his attention back to his checker game against Bill Brownwell.

Mr. Drewer ignored the critic and patted Jeb gently on the shoulder. "Am I right, son?" he asked.

"Right as rain, Mr. Drewer," said Jeb, knowing what the reward for his loyalty would be. It came a moment later with the rattle of a glass jar and the crinkle of cellophane being peeled away. Jeb's mouth hungrily accepted the lollipop the barber deposited there. The boy bit down on the sucker with a crunch. It was grape; his favorite flavor.

Cy grunted sourly, his wrinkled face looking a lot like Karloff's Mummy. His frown deepened even more when Brownwell chuckled softly and jumped him three times in a row.

Jeb tried to settle back and relax, but even with the benefit of free candy, the barber chair was still one of his least favorite places to spend a Saturday afternoon. He sat ramrod straight and froze as Mr. Drewer's scissors went to work at breakneck speed. Bits of sandy blond hair littered Jeb's covered shoulders and, every now and then, he could feel the cold steel of the scissors against his skin. It hadn't happened yet, but Jeb was sure that one day Mr. Drewer's aim would slip and he would cut one of his ears off, clean as a whistle.

Instead of contemplating possible mutilation, Jeb turned his attention elsewhere. The barber shop was packed. Patrons lined the walls, some sitting and reading, while others stood around chewing the fat. The place was the same as it had been since Jeb's first visit when he was two years old. The hardwood floor was covered with that day's clippings—a hairy mosaic of blond, black, red, and gray—and, overhead, spun a ceiling fan that could have used a drop or two of oil in its inner workings. Behind the single chair, stretched a long counter with a big oval mirror hanging over it. The counter boasted bottles of colorful liquid and alcohol jars holding disinfected combs and scissors. The barber shop smelled strongly of bay rum, witch hazel, and talcum, so much so that you could nearly taste it.

Jeb settled his gaze on a calendar from Holt's Feed and Farming Equipment that hung on the wall opposite the chair. The picture for the month of June was a pleasing one to his youthful eyes; a leggy photo of a winking Betty Grable that made Jeb squirm a little, although he couldn't figure out exactly why.

"Stop your wiggling, boy, before I end up scalping you," said Mr. Drewer.

"Yes sir," replied Jeb. His eyes moved along the seams of Betty's stockings, from ankle to butt, and then back again.

"Jeb, how's your grandmother feeling these days?" asked Benny Saunders, who owned the sawmill south of town.

The farmboy turned his eyes from the pin-up and looked at the burly man with the U.S. Navy tattoos on his forearms.

"She's been feeling rather poorly lately," was all he said, not wanting to elaborate.

Several men in the barber shop traded sad but knowing glances, Benny among them. "Well, you just let her know that our prayers are with her, will you?"

Jeb nodded solemnly. "Yes sir, I surely will."

As Mr. Drewer worked, a conversation started up, involving the barber, Cy Newman, and Bill Brownwell. The subjects discussed included the drought that had plagued Tennessee so far that summer, what a good or lousy job President Truman was doing in the White House—depending on who was talking—and whether the town council would vote to have the bricks pried up out of Main Street and replace them with modern asphalt. Cy and Bill approved of the arrival of progress, while Mr. Drewer claimed that the town of Pikesville would lose what little innocence and charm it had left if even one brick was removed from its cobbled streets. Although he had no say in it, Jeb hoped that the town did vote for the paving. He had heard that you could leave your handprint in asphalt if it was warm enough and hoped to test that theory out if given half the chance.

Jeb's attention drifted away from the talking, again returning to the calendar. His gaze centered on those fishnet hose again and he wondered how it would feel to actually touch a woman's leg.

Then the gab turned toward other subjects and Jeb found himself regaining interest. "I ran into John Haskel over at the grocery this morning," said Cy, crowning one of his checkers king with a gloating smile of toothless gums. "Seemed mighty shook up about something, so I asked him what was ailing him. And, Lordy mercy, you wouldn't guess what he had to tell me!" Cy worked his jaws, draining every bit of juice from his chaw and then spitting the wad of tobacco into the spittoon with a metallic *clang*.

"Well, don't leave us hanging," complained Mr. Drewer. "Tell us what he said."

Cy laughed, his rheumy eyes sparkling with humor. "Said that something broke into his barn last night and killed his cow. Claimed that it gutted the animal and stripped it clean down to the bone."

"Bear?" asked Bill Brownwell as he reviewed the options for his next move.

"Nope," said Cy with a smug grin.

Mr. Drewer finished his work with the scissors. He deposited them back into the alcohol jar, then plugged in his electric clippers. "Come on, Cy. Why don't you just spit it out?" He turned on the clippers and began to run it along the back of the boy's neck and around the edges of his freckled ears.

Jeb strained to hear over the loud burr of the clippers, wanting to find out just what John Haskel had told Cy Newman. Presidents and droughts were of no interest to him, but murdered cows were right down Jeb's alley.

"You won't believe it, but he claimed it was some kinda monster," laughed Cy. A drop of tobacco juice trickled down the man's wrinkled chin and he wiped it away with the back of his hand. "Said it was sort of a cross between a snake and a hound dog."

"You're joshing!" said Mr. Drewer. He finally finished with the clippers and, much to Jeb's delight, cut them off and returned them to the counter.

"I swear on a stack of Bibles, that's what he told me, word for word," proclaimed Cy Newman. "Said it was all covered with black scales and had a mouth bristling with sharp teeth. Said he seen it with his own eyes."

"Aw, that's a load of bullsh—" began Bill, but altered his statement at the sight of the boy in the chair, "—shingles! John didn't see no such thing!"

"Claims to have the proof," said Cy. "Said he went back down to his barn this morning and all that was left of his cow was bones. Every shred of meat and hide had been stripped clean off."

"Could've been some sort of circus freak," allowed Mr. Drewer. "Maybe a deformed animal that got loose somehow. I hear tell there's a carnival going on over in Bedloe County."

"Wasn't no freak!" balked Bill Brownwell. His eyes drifted around the checkerboard, but the prospect of him winning that afternoon's game was slim. "John was just having a nightmare. Or, else, he was a little too free with the bottle last night. He wasn't above taking a swig every so often in his younger days and that's a fact!"

Jeb knew his torturous time in the barber chair was reaching its end when he caught the dusty scent of talcum. The bristles of Mr. Drewer's brush tickled the back of his neck an instant later, brushing the stray hairs away and coating his skin with the fine, white powder.

"Anyway, he said he was going over to the sheriff's office and have Ed North come out and take a look at it. Don't know what Ed would do about it, though. He's better at working crossword puzzles and polishing a chair seat with his butt, than chasing cow-eating critters across Mangrum County."

Bill kicked Cy in the shin beneath the checker table. "Ain't proper to be talking about the law like that in front of the young'un."

A wounded look crossed the elderly man's face. "Ain't saying nothing that ain't already been said a dozen times before," he grumbled as he moved another checker.

Jeb felt the strings around his neck loosen, allowing him to breathe freely again. Soon, the sheet was off him and he was hopping down out of the chair. By the time he turned around, Mr. Drewer's hand was outstretched, his palm resembling a collection plate at Sunday services. Jeb dug into the right pocket of his Duckhead overalls and withdrew seventy-five cents. He laid the three quarters in the man's hand and peered at himself in the oval mirror. Mr. Drewer had really given him a shearing this time. He felt absolutely naked, so much so that he had to look down to make sure he was still fully clothed.

After the transaction had been completed, the next customer was called and the barber chair was occupied once again. Jeb lingered beside the shop's open door, reluctant to leave before he heard the rest of the story concerning John Haskel's dead cow.

"You know," mused Mr. Decker as he snapped Jeb's blond hairs from the folds of the sheet and tied it around Benny Saunder's sunburned neck, "If something odd did break into Haskel's barn and did eat his cow . . . and if this thing did look like he said it did . . . well, then, I reckon we all have a pretty good notion where the critter came from. And, I'll give you a hint. It wasn't from no traveling carnival, either."

An uneasy silence hung in the barber shop for a moment. Then Cy Newman arched his snow-white brows. "You mean . . . Fear County?"

Mr. Decker opened his mouth to reply, but clammed up when he saw Jeb still standing in the doorway. "You'd best head on downtown, Jeb," he said with a flourish of his comb. "Sam's probably done with his business at the feed store. It wouldn't do for him to get into trouble while waiting for you."

Jeb knew the barber was right. "Yes sir," he said, then left, stepping outside into the bright sunlight. The sun-baked sidewalk scorched the bottoms of his bare feet and he hopped off the curve and into a patch of cool shadow that stretched in the alleyway next to the barber shop. Standing there, he attempted to hear more of the conversation between Mr.

Drewer and the checker players, but all he could detect was a low mumbling.

With a sigh, Jeb finished the rest of his sucker. He stripped the last crystals of grape candy from the stick, then tossed it into the gutter. He looked out into the street and spotted a familiar form stretched out in the shade beneath the apple bin in front of the grocery store. "Buckshot!" he yelled. "Git over here, boy!"

The bluetick hound opened his eyelids and stretched his speckled legs. Reluctantly, he rolled over and crept out from beneath the fruit stand, looking none too happy about being roused from his nap. As the dog made its way carefully across the street, waiting for a tan Buick to pass before continuing on, Jeb smiled at his best friend in the whole world. Buckshot had been his constant companion since he was four years old and, since that time, both had gone on their share of coonhunts together. On one such hunt a couple of autumns ago was where Buckshot had received some of his more interesting features. The hound was blind in his right eye and was missing most of his left ear. The injuries had come from an unexpected tangle with an angry she-coon that Buckshot had been trying to tree. The raccoon—which had been nearly twice the size of the bluetick—would have more than likely killed Buckshot if Jeb hadn't gotten there in time to run the feisty animal off into the dense woods along the winding channel of Mossy Creek.

When the dog finally reached the mouth of the alleyway, Jeb crouched down and ran an affectionate hand along his back. "You're a good ol' boy, ain'tcha?"

Buckshot replied with a yawn and a burst of bad breath in his master's face.

"I do declare, Buckshot," said Jeb, rocking back on his heels. "Smells like you fell head-first into an outhouse and swallowed yourself a bellyful." He rummaged through his overall pockets, sorting through an assortment of treasures common of boys his age: a lucky buckeye, coins flattened by train wheels, a Case pocketknife with a dull blade, and a flint arrowhead he had unearthed in a creekbed. Finally, he found what he was looking for. He withdrew an unwrapped stick of King Leo peppermint candy, picked the pocket lint off it, and broke it in half. He gave one piece to Buckshot, while keeping the other. "Here, this oughta help. But don't go too near Grandma. If she smells it on your breath, she'll tan my hide and give me a talking to about giving you the worms."

Buckshot gobbled up the candy swiftly, chewing it only twice before swallowing the rest of it whole. Jeb savored his more slowly, even though the mixture of grape and peppermint left a bitter taste in his mouth.

Jeb stared out into the street again, wondering if he could make it to the other side of Pikesville without burning the soles of his feet. It was nearly two in the afternoon. The sun was hot and the streets and sidewalks of the little town could have fried eggs. He gauged the amount of shade provided by the awnings of various shops along Main Street and decided that there simply wasn't enough islands of relief between there and the feed store. He decided to take the long route and enjoy the shadows that the back alleyway provided.

"Come on, boy," he called to the dog. "Let's go find Sam."

As Jeb rounded the back of the barber shop and started down the alleyway that was choked with smelly trash cans and empty boxes and packing crates, Buckshot gave the cool spot beneath the apple bin a last, longing glance, then faithfully followed his young master.

Two

Three Against One

Jeb headed north across town, skirting the rear walls of Drewer's Barber Shop, the Fashion Boutique, and the Pikesville Five & Dime. The bright humidity of that June afternoon was left behind on the main thoroughfare. There in the alleyway, the shadows were thick and plentiful. There was even something of a breeze blowing from the south, if only a small one. The boy grinned as the air fluttered through the stubble of tiny hairs on the back of his freshly trimmed neck. It felt deceptively cool for a day that was topping the upper nineties.

As he walked, swirling his tongue around the peppermint stick, Jeb's thoughts turned back to the topic that had been discussed during his departure. The story about the devoured cow in John Haskel's barn was interesting to be certain, but something else intrigued his youthful curiosity even more. And that was Fear County.

Jeb had heard about the place all his life, but, strangely enough, knew absolutely nothing about it. All he knew was that it had been named Fear a hundred years or so ago because that was the emotion the dark and desolate county conjured the most, and the name had stuck, even on the state maps. He also knew that it was located sixteen miles due south, bordering their own rural county of Mangrum. Jeb tried hard to recall any other information he had gathered about the county during his ten years, but found that there was very little to remember.

As the peppermint reached its end and his fingers grew red and sticky, Jeb suddenly came up with something, although the incident came across a little hazy and unfocused at first. He studied on the event for a moment, trying to remember it as clearly as possible.

When he was five years old, there had been a Saturday morning when he came to town with his Grandma Sweeny to shop for new Sunday shoes. He remembered that part plainly at least—the way the patent-leathers had pinched and cramped feet that were accustomed to fresh air and the feel of gravel and grass. In any case, they were leaving Thompson's Shoe Store, when they noticed that Main Street had been cleared of weekend shoppers. In the center of the avenue was the patrol car of the then sheriff of Mangrum County, Jake Anderson, parked crossways, blocking all traffic from either north or south. The sheriff stood behind his blue Ford, holding a Winchester shotgun, the kind you pump the foregrip to load. Along with him were several other men, all men Jeb knew on sight, but oddly enough wearing deputy badges. They also carried guns, mostly their own hunting rifles.

Jeb remembered him and Grandma standing in the doorway of the shoe store, confused about what was going on. Then Sheriff Anderson looked over at them. The expression on his face looked about as cheerful as a funeral. "I'd advise you and the boy to step back inside, Miss Lucille," the constable had said. "There's trouble coming."

They had done as they had been told. Henry Thompson came over and closed the open door, then stood next to Jeb and his grandmother as they curiously stared out the front window at the sheriff and his sworn-in deputies. Anderson had been right, for a moment later trouble did, indeed, arrive in Pikesville. It came in the form of a sleek, black sedan, heading at a high rate of speed down the center of Main Street. It was heading from north to south . . . heading straight for the Fear County line.

Jeb had watched as Sheriff Anderson left his place behind his car and stepped out into the center of the street, looking more than a little scared. When the car kept on coming, giving no evidence of intending to slow down, Anderson had lifted the shotgun to his shoulder and fired. The load of pellets hit the sedan's right front tire, blowing it out. The black car slowed a little, but not nearly enough. The sheriff jumped out of the way and the sedan slammed forcefully into the side of the patrol car with a buckling of metal and a crash of broken glass.

A moment later, the sedan's passenger door popped open and a man jumped out. All that Jeb remembered about the fellow was that he was bearded and as skinny as a rail, and that he held a butcher knife in his hand. A bloody butcher knife. "Drop that blade, Jack Gallow!" the sheriff had demanded. But the man had merely laughed, his eyes bright and crazy as he tightened his grip on the carving knife and kept right on coming.

The Winchester had boomed for a second time. Jeb saw the man go down, shot in the left leg, a second before Grandma's meaty hand had clamped firmly over Jeb's eyes, cutting off his view. He had managed to pry one of her fingers loose, though, long enough to see Anderson's temporary deputies rush to the trunk of the car. Jeb heard the muffled crying of a child as the men worked at the trunk lid with a crowbar. Then it was open and the crying grew louder. The faces of the deputies grew as pale as lard and one of the men even turned and puked, right there in the center of Main Street.

Then Jeb heard one of the deputies say something that had stuck in the boy's mind for the past five years of his life. He had said "The dirty son of a bitch . . . he's done taken the young'un's *arm!*"

Jeb didn't know exactly what that had meant back then, and he still wasn't exactly sure. He just remembered them hauling Jack Gallow, laughing wildly, toward the courthouse, while Sheriff Anderson followed, carrying a squawling baby that was wrapped in a blood-drenched blanket. Jeb thought of poor Jake Anderson. The sheriff had never quite been the same jovial man after that. In fact, it was only a year and a half later when Anderson had locked himself in a cell of the Mangrum County jail, put the barrel of his service revolver against the roof of his mouth, and blown his brains out.

Jeb recalled the talk that had circulated following the arrest of Jack Gallow and one of the things that had been said was that the knife-wielding madman had been born and bred in Fear County. Jeb knew that Gallow had been convicted and sent to the state pen, but he had no idea what had happened to the infant that had been delivered from the trunk of Gallow's black sedan. Sometimes Jeb dreamt about that Saturday morning and woke in a cold sweat, swearing that he heard the crying of that kidnapped baby in the bloody blanket.

The boy continued on down the rear alleyway, feeling goosebumps prickle the flesh of his freckled arms. The mere thought that the critter that had killed John Haskel's cow had also been from Fear County sent a delicious thrill of spooky excitement through Jeb. He could imagine it crouching over the gutted Holstein, grinning wickedly and looking, for all the world, like the reptilian kin of Jack Gallow himself.

Jeb nearly jumped out of his skin when a shrill yelp came from behind him. He swallowed the last piece of his peppermint and stopped, dead still in the alleyway, afraid to move. He heard the pad of quick feet and, at first, was certain that it was the snake-critter, running straight for him. But, a moment later, his fear turned to relief. Buckshot shot past him, a wounded howl barreling up out of his throat. The hound dog ran a couple more yards, then stopped. With a hurt expression in his eyes, Buckshot tenderly licked at his haunches.

"What in tarnation's wrong with you, boy?" asked Jeb. He took a couple of steps forward, then let out a yell himself as a rock the size of a walnut struck him squarely between the shoulder blades.

"That's what's wrong with your mangy mutt, you little bastard!" came a voice from behind a stack of wooden crates Jeb had passed only a second ago.

Instantly, Jeb's relief dissolved. It sped past the emotion of fear and became a mixture of panic and pure terror. He recognized that voice, as well as the snickering laughter that accompanied it.

He didn't want to turn around, but he did anyway. They were there just as he expected them to be. It was Troy Jenkins and his buck-toothed cronies, the Boone twins. Troy was two years older than Jeb and a notorious bully to him and his fellow classmates at Pikesville Elementary School. Troy was well known for the suffering and humiliation he subjected the local children to on a daily basis, as well as his much-dreaded "Indian rope burn." Danny and Donnie Boone pretty much tagged along in order to brown-nose and stay in Troy's good graces, flanking him on both sides like a pair of human bookends. But, sometimes, they too got in on the action, holding down helpless victims, while Troy inflicted whatever torment popped into his demented head at the time.

"You'd best stay away from me, Troy Jenkins," said Jeb, trying his best to sound brave, despite the tremor in his voice. "And leave my dog alone, too."

"Aw! And what if I don't, bastard?" leered Troy. His grin revealed that horrifying mouthful of missing and broken teeth that gave him the appearance of a hungry gator every time he smiled. "What're you gonna do then? Huh?"

In spite of his fear, Jeb bristled at the name he had been called. "You take that back, Troy. I ain't one and you know it!"

The twelve-year-old's green eyes sparkled cruelly. "What? A bastard? Well, now, that's what you are. You ain't got no mama, do you?"

Jeb's face turned hot and red. "Sure, I do."

Troy laughed. "That's funny, 'cause I sure ain't never seen her. Have you, boys?"

"Never have," agreed Donnie Boone.

"Can't rightly say that I have either," matched Danny Boone.

"Well, I do have one," proclaimed Jeb defensively. "It's just that she's been gone for a long time."

"Yeah," said Troy with a smirk. "Since you were a little baby. Way I heard it, she got the hots for a traveling preacherman who did a revival here and ran off with him."

Jeb said nothing, feeling a sudden attack of shame grip him. There was nothing he could say to dispute what Troy had just said. After all, like it or not, it was the truth. Everyone in Pikesville seemed to know about his runaway mother and the sinful way she had up and left her husband and newborn child, although they were tactful enough not to mention it. That was, everyone except Troy Jenkins.

"Okay," Jeb finally allowed, "So my mama ain't around. That still don't make me a bastard. You're only a bastard when you don't have a daddy."

Troy spat into the dirt of the alleyway and laughed. "That's a joke. You've gotta be a bastard, 'cause you sure as hell don't have much of a daddy, do you? Came back from the war with his brains all scrambled, acting like a dadblamed baby. Tell me something, bastard. Do you change your daddy's diapers?"

Jeb felt anger creep up the back of his neck. He clenched his fists into hard balls, but didn't advance toward the bully. Troy had six inches of height on him and a good twenty pounds, and Jeb knew that it was unwise to buck such odds, especially when there was a hefty dose of pure meanness to go along with everything else.

"I said for you to stop calling me that," he repeated. "You know what my name is, so why don't you use it?"

"Yeah," said Troy in a mocking voice. "I know your damned name. It's Jeb Sweeny. Jeb! What kinda stupid name is that to have?"

Again, Jeb was at a loss for words. He too had wondered why he had been given such a name at birth. He had come up with two plausible explanations. Either he had been named after the Confederate hero, J.E.B. Stuart, or his mother, who Grandma said had suffered from a lisp, had intended to call him Jed but had mistakenly called him Jeb instead.

"You said it, Troy," said Donnie eagerly. "Jeb is a dumb name."

"Jeb!" groaned Danny, pretending to stick his finger down his throat.

Troy Jenkins looked over at his two pals, a little irritated. "You know, I'm sick and tired of all this talking," he said, staring the Boones into obedient silence. Then he turned his mischievous eyes back to Jeb. "Been a while since I've given you a sound thrashing, ain't it, Sweeny?"

Jeb's anger began to falter and he felt the familiar sensation of fear resurface. He shot a quick glance over his shoulder and gauged the distance between where he stood and the far end of the alleyway. A good sixty or seventy feet lay in between and he knew he would never make it to safety, even if he had a headstart. It looked as if he would have to take the punishment that Troy and the Boones seemed determined to inflict on him, whether he liked it or not.

Troy took a menacing step forward, grinning like some sort of deranged circus chimp. He hadn't gotten five feet, when Jeb heard a low growl rumble closely behind him. The farmboy couldn't help but smile to himself. Buckshot was a good, easy-going dog . . . except when those he loved were threatened somehow. Then he quickly bared his teeth and stood his ground, like an ornery ol' grizzly bear wrapped tightly in dog skin.

The bully stopped and glared at the bluetick hound. Behind the meanness in his eyes, Jeb could detect a glint of apprehension, if only a little. "Donnie," he called to one of the twins. "Keep that flea farm outta our way, whilst we get down to brass tacks, okay?"

Donnie Boone swallowed with a low bobbing of his Adam's apple. He looked at Buckshot. The dog's lean body trembled as he stood poised, ready to leap forward, his dark lips curled away from a wolfish grin of yellowed, canine teeth. Then Donnie looked back over at Troy and decided that he feared the bully even more than he did the dog. He bent down and, finding a length of splintered two-by-four close by, hefted it threateningly in his hand. "All right, boss. I've got 'im covered."

Suddenly, without any farther warning, Troy and Danny attacked. They came at Jeb at different angles, Danny diving for his feet, while Troy swung a fist straight toward his head. Jeb, of course, attempted to dodge the blow, but, like always, he was just a shade too slow in moving. Troy's knuckles glanced off his left cheekbone and the tip of his nose, bringing a burst of burning pain. A second later, Danny tackled him around the shins, putting all the force he could muster behind it. Jeb fought to keep his balance, but to no avail. Soon, he was slamming to his back on the dusty ground with enough impact to drive the breath completely from his lungs.

As Troy and Danny pounced on him, Jeb turned his head and saw Donnie Boone run toward Buckshot with the board fisted in both hands like a Louisville Slugger. The hound dog barked and growled, but was sensible enough to back away and stay clear of the two-by-four. Donnie looked scared at first, but when the dog refused to come closer, he grew cocky and began to taunt Buckshot, daring him to try something.

Just when Jeb began to regain his lost breath, he felt Troy's weight descend on him, the patched knee of his blue jeans landing squarely in the center of his stomach. The pain that shot through his belly was so strong that he nearly lost the lunch of baloney sandwiches and buttermilk that Grandma had packed for his and Sam's trip to town that afternoon. He swallowed hard, however, and managed to keep from throwing up.

"Hold his arms!" Troy told Danny. A moment later, Danny was standing over Jeb, his filthy bare feet bearing down on the farmboy's wrists. Jeb struggled to break loose, but he simply couldn't gain the leverage to do so. He looked up at the sparkle of sadistic cruelty in Troy's eyes as the bully sat on top of his chest. Something about the ugly expression in Jenkins's eyes told him that his infamous Indian Rope Burn was the furthest thing from his mind at the moment. No, he had something much more humiliating in store for his latest victim.

"I know it's past dinnertime, Sweeny," said Troy with a snaggle-toothed grin. "But, I do declare if you don't still look a little hungry." He glanced at each Boone brother. "What do you think, boys? Don't he look hungry to ya'll?"

Danny nodded. "Sure does. Real hungry."

Donnie refused to pry his eyes from the dog that still snapped and snarled nearby. "Yeah, boss. Whatever you say."

Troy returned his gaze back to the ten-year-old beneath him. Jeb stared back and noticed that the color of Troy's eyes was the same as algae floating on top of a stagnant pond. "Is that right, Sweeny? Are you still hankering for something to eat? Well, if you are, I'll sure oblige you."

Terrified, Jeb watched as Troy reached into his shirt pocket and rummaged around for something that seemed to allude his probing fingers. A myriad of nasty creatures danced through Jeb's thoughts, but none could compare to what Troy finally produced. For, held between his thumb and forefinger, was a fat black bug that wiggled and squirmed in his grasp. It was a dung beetle, or, as most kids called it, a doo-doo bug. Jeb saw that its bulbous hindquarters was crusted with something brown that, more than likely, wasn't Tennessee clay mud.

"A beauty, ain't it?" asked Troy proudly. "Know where I found it? It was crawling on top of a stinky ol' cowpie out in Fletcher Howell's pasture. It was busier than a bee, rolling up them little balls of shit, getting ready to lay its eggs in 'em. But I just couldn't resist picking up the little critter and taking it with me . . . in case I found someone hungry enough to want it."

"This ain't funny, Troy Jenkins," said Jeb. He tried to cock his head away from the squirming beetle, but the ground wouldn't allow his retreat.

Troy snickered. "Don't mean it to be funny," he said. "Danny, do me a big favor. Reach down and open his mouth for me. I've got my hands full with this bug here."

"You got it," said Danny Boone. The buck-toothed boy squatted down and, using both hands, pried Jeb's jaws apart.

"Get ready, Sweeny," said Troy, lowering the doo-doo bug,

inch by inch, toward Jeb's open mouth. "'Cause here it comes."

Jeb attempted to close his mouth, but Danny's hands were much too stout. He caught the sickening scent of cow manure and felt one of the beetle's oily black legs tickle his upper lip. Seemingly at the point of defeat, Jeb closed his eyes and waited for the insect to fall, kicking and flailing, past his tongue and down his throat.

But just when the humiliating act seemed on the verge of being completed, a reprieve came from clear out of the blue.

"Now, ain't that a nasty thang to do to somebody," came an adult voice that sounded like rusty nails grating against sandpaper. "Just plain, downright nasty!"

Three

Roscoe Steps In

Immediately, the dung beetle was lifted away from Jeb's mouth. The boy breathed a sigh of relief, but knew very well that he wasn't out of the woods yet. The appearance of a grown-up didn't mean much to Troy Jenkins. The bully wasn't the type to back down, even in the face of authority. After all, he had spit chewing tobacco in Principal Garton's face last year and stamped the instep of his foot so hard that the man was forced to wear a cast for nearly three weeks. Troy had been suspended from school for his shenanigans, but had come back even meaner and more rebellious toward his teachers than before.

Danny Boone stepped away, freeing Jeb's aching jaw and wrists, but Troy stayed where he was, perched on top of the farmboy's chest. "What the hell do you want, nigger?" he asked. Jeb sensed the bully's emotions shifting gears, clutching from sadistic mischief to flat-out hatred.

Jeb twisted his head around and saw exactly who his savior was. It was an elderly black man, perhaps sixty years of age. The Negro was tall and as bony as a skeleton. He wore a dusty fedora hat, threadbare traveling clothes, and wire-rimmed spectacles with lenses as thick as the bottoms of soda pop bottles. Slung across his slightly hunched back was an old flattop Fender guitar with a worn shaving strop as a makeshift strap.

The black man stared at Troy Jenkins, frowning sourly. "What I want, son, is for you to stick that ol' shit bug back in your pocket and leave this poor boy alone. Ain't a nice thang you're a-doing to him, you know."

Jeb detected Troy's animosity suddenly center on a different victim. "Oh, I get it," said the bully. "You're more hungry than Sweeny here is. Well, I ain't one to deny a man a square meal." Troy left his seat on Jeb's chest and stood up, dangling the dung beetle toward the elderly man. "I reckon I'll feed it to you instead."

The Negro grinned, displaying a mouth that shared equal space between God-given ivory and dentist-given gold. In fact, Jeb figured you could probably melt down all those gold teeth and come up with a solid ounce or two of the precious metal. "You've got balls, boy," said the black man. "But that don't mean you've got a bit of brains in your head. I suggest you and your buddies move on along."

Troy Jenkins laughed loudly. "Uh-uh. Not until I cram this bug down your skinny throat, old nigger." He motioned to the two Boone brothers. "What do you say, fellas? Why don't we wrestle the peckerwood down and feed it to him?"

Danny grinned broadly, his protruding teeth making him look a lot like Edgar Bergen's Mortimer Snerd. "Sounds good. Let's do it to him!"

Donnie, however, wasn't as enthusiastic. "I don't know, Troy," he said, looking a little doubtful. "I've heard about them niggers. Some of 'em know black magic. You know, voodoo and conjuring and stuff like that."

"Bullshit!" said Troy, taking a threatening step toward the old man.

The Negro's eyes glinted shrewdly. "He ain't joking, son. Our kind do know of such things and some of us even practice 'em. Take me, for example. I come from a long line of black sorcerers. My grandpappy was an African witch doctor and my pappy before me was a mojo man from down Louisiana way. Just natural that I'd follow in their footsteps as well."

Troy stopped a few yards from the black man and studied him for a moment. He grinned as he stuffed the squirming beetle back into his shirt pocket. "Okay, old nigger," he taunted. "Why don't you just show me some of that black magic of yours. Come on, turn me into a frigging toad or some such thing."

Donnie Boone looked horrified. "Don't, Troy! He might just up and do it."

The Negro smiled. "Best listen to your friend, boy. Wouldn't do to tempt me."

"Aw, you're full of it," snapped Troy. "Come on, Danny. Let's give this old nigger the Indian Rope Burn. Or are you just as chickenshit as your brother?"

A trace of reluctance shone in Danny's eyes, but only for a second. "Of course not, Troy. Let's get the old son of a bitch."

Jeb sat up from his prone position and watched as Troy Jenkins and Danny Boone started toward the man who had saved him from having to swallow a doo-doo bug. They were almost upon the lanky Negro, when the man reached inside the open collar of his shirt and withdrew something that was attached to a length of beaded rawhide around his neck.

It was a dried chicken foot, hacked cleanly off just above its skinny ankle.

"Oh, Lordy, Troy," moaned Donnie Boone dropping his two-by-four. "Now you've done gone and done it!"

"Done what?" asked Troy harshly. "Ain't nothing but an old chicken's foot."

The old black man flashed his golden grin. "You are stupid, ain't you, boy? Don't you know a mojo charm when you lay eyes on one?"

"That ain't no charm," said Danny, although there was a definite lack of conviction in his voice.

"Yes, it is, son," said the old man. "And the things it can do to a soul . . . well, if I told you, it'd sure enough curl your hair."

"I ain't gonna listen to your bull," said Troy. He glanced over at Danny. "Well, are you with me? Are we gonna give him the Burn or not?"

"Uh, sure," said Danny. "I reckon so."

When they took a couple more steps toward the old man, he raised the chicken foot and began to move it in an odd circular motion, rattling the beads on the thong at the same time. "Well now, I reckon ya'll just won't give me no choice but to put a curse on you. Can't say I'll be too sorry about it, either, considering the no-good ya'll were up to when I arrived."

Troy laughed. "Curse! What kinda curse are you gonna put on us, nigger?"

The black man's smile gleamed like yellow fire. "Let me see. I could hex you with several that I could think of off hand. But it's gotta be something really special. Something that'll teach you a lesson."

"What?" asked Donnie Boone, his eyes as wide as silver dollars. "Whatcha gonna do to us?"

"I know," said the Negro with a sinister grin. "I think I'll put the hoodoo on your private parts. Maybe shrivel your peckers till they fall plumb off. Then you won't have nothing to play with in your beds at night."

It was at that moment that Jeb Sweeny saw something that he thought he would never witness in his lifetime. The expression of smugness in Troy Jenkins's face slipped away and, in its place, bloomed a look of growing terror. Apparently, the old Negro had found Troy's Achilles heel, so to speak.

Then, without another word, the elderly man began to buck and dance. His eyes rolled up into his head until only the whites showed and he waved the disembodied chicken foot back and forth. "Ungalla-chilla-changa!" he shrieked, moving toward Troy and his cohorts. "Megella-hebba-debba-magoolla-banga!"

Donnie Boone's face turned pale and his eyes bugged from his head. "I feel it happening!" he moaned. "I can feel mine starting to shrivel!"

Danny was also caught up in the same fit of hysteria. "Me, too!" He stared down at the crotch of his overalls and was shocked to see a wet spot spreading across the denim material.

Troy suddenly knew when he had met his match. His genitals began to tighten in fear, but he wasn't about to take any chances, especially not where his favorite appendage was concerned. "Come on, fellas!" he yelled. "Let's git the hell outta here!"

Jeb sat on the ground and watched as Troy Jenkins and the Boone brothers turned tail and ran, heading back down the alley toward the southern end of town. Jeb savored that sight, committing it to memory so he could relay it, detail by precious detail, to his classmates when school started back that following September.

The lanky black man stopped his chanting and dancing. He waited until the boys were out of sight in a cloud of churning dust, then sat down on an apple crate nearby and cackled to the high heavens. "Lawdy mercy!" he shrilled, tears coming to his eyes. "Never in my born days have I seen a pack of white boys run so fast!"

Jeb left his spot on the ground and stood up. He slapped the dirt off the seat of his overalls, then walked over to the old man. The Negro was laughing so hard that Jeb was afraid that he would suffer a heart attack and fall over dead at any moment. Eventually, though, the humor of his prank diminished and, wiping his aged eyes with a grungy red bandanna, the black man finally settled down.

The farmboy with the sandy blond hair stood with his hands in his pockets for a long moment, studying the man who sat before him. Gradually, he grew more and more convinced that the old Negro was not really a stranger to him at all. "I know you, don't I?" he finally found the nerve to ask.

The elderly man nodded. "More than likely. Name's Roscoe Ledbetter."

Suddenly, it dawned on him. "Yeah, that's right," said Jeb. "I thought I knew you from somewhere. You're that bluesman who sets up shop down on the corner of Willow and Main every summer. You pick guitar and beg for pocket change."

Roscoe removed his hat and, taking the bandanna, blotted the sweat from the top of his head, which was as shiny and naked as a billiard ball. "Never begged a day in my life, son," corrected the black man. "No, I've always given a fair share of entertainment in return for a man's nickels and dimes. If they were down in New Orleans, they'd have to pay a dollar or two to hear blues the likes of mine. Here, let me play you my latest and you tell me what you think. It's called the 'Roaches-in-my-Shoes Blues.' "

"All right," said Jeb. He sat down on a crate next to Roscoe and watched as the old man laid his hat at his feet and pulled the guitar from over his back. Roscoe took a small glass bottle from his vest pocket and stuck it on the end of his index finger. Then, cradling the beat-up instrument lovingly in his arms, he began to play and sing.

"Well, I woke up early this morning . . . and I climbed right outta bed . . . Yes, Lawd, I woke up bright and early

this here morning . . . yes, I climbed up outta bed . . . stuck my feet down in them empty shoes . . . wished I'd stayed in bed instead . . ."

Jeb watched as the black man's hands fluttered across the guitar. He slid the bottled finger up and down its neck of inlaid mother-of-pearl, making the strings hum and twang, squeal and squawl. Then Roscoe sang the second chorus.

"Well, I got them roaches-in-my-shoes blues . . . feel them crawling thro' my toes and 'round my heels . . . Say I got them ol' roaches-in-my-shoes blues . . . feel them dancing across my arches . . . Lawd, I hate just how that feels!"

After the song was finished, Roscoe grinned his ivory and gold smile. "So, what do you think, son?"

Jeb dug into his pocket and brought out one of his flattened pennies. He tossed it into the man's sweat-stained fedora. "Does that answer your question?"

Roscoe laughed. "Much obliged to you," he said, picking up his hat. He extracted the penny and studied it for a moment. "You know, I used to do the same thing when I was your age, excepting the penny had an Indian's head on it instead of ol' Abe Lincoln."

"I'm afraid it's all I really have," said the boy.

Roscoe grinned and pocketed the coin, along with the little glass bottle. "Wouldn't trade it for anything in the world," he said sincerely. He eyed the freckle-faced boy through the thick lenses of his eyeglasses. "I've introduced myself. Now exactly who might you be?"

"Name's Jeb," said the ten-year-old. "Jeb Sweeny."

Roscoe's eyes widened. "Would you be the son of Sam Sweeny?"

"Yes sir, I would."

"Well, shut my mouth!" proclaimed the bluesman. "I've known your papa from way back, son. Why, nearly every time I come to Pikesville, he comes around and listens to me play for hours at a time. I recall that he could pick pretty good himself, too."

Jeb thought back to his father's prowess with a guitar or banjo, and how he used to play songs like "Cotton-Eyed Joe," "The Wabash Cannonball," and "Cumberland Gap." Sadly enough, though, those times were gone forever.

The thought of his father made Jeb realize how late it was getting and that he needed to get to the feed store as soon as possible. "Well, Mr. Ledbetter," he said as he stood up, "I reckon I'd best be going. Really did like the song. Oh, and I'm really obliged to you . . . for running off Troy Jenkins and the Boones like you did."

"It was purely my pleasure, son."

Jeb eyed the old man curiously. "Tell me something. Are you really a mojo man?"

Roscoe winked at the boy. "You never know. I'll be seeing you around, Jeb Sweeny."

"Yes sir," agreed Jeb. "I certainly hope so."

The farmboy called to Buckshot and, for the second time that afternoon, the dog pried himself lazily from a patch of cool shade and followed his roaming master. The hound panted thirstily, his tongue yearning for a drink of cool water and his speckled body anxious to find the next oasis of peaceful shade that he could resume his interrupted nap in.

Jeb walked to the far end of the alleyway, where Willow Drive met Main Street and gave way to the sun-drenched brick once again. When he turned around to see if the elderly bluesman was still sitting on the apple crate, he was surprised to find the man gone.

There had been no sound of footsteps, no swishing of the guitar against the back of the Negro's vest as he walked.

For all outward appearances, Roscoe Ledbetter had simply vanished into thin air.

Four

Baby Mouses

Perplexed, Jeb scratched his freshly trimmed head and stared down at Buckshot. "Pretty strange, huh, boy?"

The hound dog paid his master no mind. He stood in the mouth of the alleyway, appraising the lofty structure of the courthouse across the intersection of Willow and Main, or rather its grassy yard with its multitude of tall shade trees. In Buckshot's eyes, it was a pleasant oasis amid a hazy June desert.

As Jeb made his way quickly across the hot brickway of Willow Avenue and then even swifter across the bustling stretch of Main Street, he assessed the extent of his injuries. They weren't too severe. After all, he had suffered worse. His cheek felt swollen from its clash with Troy's knuckles and his stomach still ached a little where the bully's knee had landed. Jeb couldn't believe his bad luck. A close call with the Hitler of Pikesville *and* a haircut . . . all in one day!

Just when the boy was sure that the hot street would blister every bit of hide off the soles of his feet, he reached the opposite side. There awaited the cool comfort of green grass. Jeb stood there for a moment, wiggling his toes in a patch of soft clover, allowing the heat in his feet to slowly subside.

While he enjoyed the feeling of relief, he took a long look at the heart of his hometown.

Geographically, the town of Pikesville was located in the middle of Mangrum County, which was located just a little northwest of the center of the state of Tennessee. It was the county seat and the proud boaster of the largest shirt factory in the Volunteer State, even though that facility had temporarily been used to make paratrooper parachutes during the War. The town had nine hundred and fifty citizens in its combined population, both living within its central community and on the bordering farmland, which stretched an even twelve miles on all four sides. The immaculate courthouse of whitewashed wood and brick stood to the west of Main Street, while to the east were the elementary and high schools. Past the intersection of Main and Willow with its one and only traffic light, lay the double row of shops and small businesses that stretched southward toward the end of town. Anything you might imagine could be purchased along Pikesville's Main Street; everything from hardware, clothing, and groceries, to a yank of the pliers from Doc Hayes at the dentist office or a trim and a shave from the able hands of Howard Drewer. Jeb ran his hand along the contours of his shorn head and was thankful that it would be a whole month before he was sentenced to another visit to the barber shop.

As the town's business district thinned out, it was followed by the residential section. Homes, both fine and modest, stood on shady, maple-lined streets with names like Oak, Elm, and Birch. Further on stood the saintly and steepled structures of the town's various churches. They ran a gambit of denominations—Baptist, Methodist, Presbyterian—and each were smug in the conviction of their faith, as if only they held the key to heavenly salvation. Jeb, Sam, and Grandma Sweeny attended the Pikesville Baptist Church every Sunday morning, even though Jeb would have sometimes rather been sitting on the riverbank fishing, than confined to a hard pew, listening to how many ways a person could sin and how many horrible ways an immortal soul could suffer in the fiery bowels of Hell.

Beyond the church houses, lay the broad stretch of rich farmland that served as the true basis of Pikesville's prosperity. On the far side of the Cumberland River and its long steel and concrete bridge, spanned acre upon acre of grassy pasture and furrowed field. All manner of crops were planted in the dark brown earth—tobacco, corn, beans—while every breed of livestock imaginable grazed and grew fat on cut hay and alfalfa. On the edges of those agricultural landscapes stood the farms. Some were huge and almost citylike in the extent of their activity, such as York's Dairy on Crabapple Road. Others, like the Sweeny place near Mossy Creek, were much smaller, owned and operated by family alone. The Sweenys had planted few crops since the end of the War and Sam's tragic return home, but they did make a modest living selling eggs and raising prized China white hogs. In fact, one of their hogs named Old Jack had won the blue ribbon at the Mangrum County Fair three years in a row.

Jeb thought about what lay beyond the twelve-mile stretch of farmland. Rolling pastures gave way to dense forest where the railroad swung gently northwest to southeast. Jeb had no idea what lay beyond the woods. All he knew was that, four miles farther on, lay the Fear County line. The boy had never ventured that far south of Pikesville in his young life and, oddly enough, he couldn't rightly think of anyone in town who claimed that they had, either.

The ten-year-old looked up at the big clock that was set in the front wall of the courthouse, just above the eaves of the columned porch. The great iron hands pointed the time as being twenty past two. "Come on, boy," he called to Buckshot, who was heading toward the shade of a black oak tree. "We've gotta get on to the feed store."

Buckshot gave his master a baleful look and, if he could have cussed beneath his breath, he would have. Obediently, he veered away from the inviting patch of shade and followed Jeb across the grassy courtyard.

Jeb waved to a couple of elderly farmers who sat on a park bench next to the courthouse's brick walkway. They nodded to the boy and waved back, smiling as Jeb leaped nimbly over the hot bricks and landed well onto grass on the other side. The bluetick hound wasn't quite as energetic, however. It sauntered lazily across the walkway, twitching its good ear at a horsefly that divebombed him in the humid, summer air.

As he walked across the grass, Jeb was surprised—and pleased—to see a pretty, dark-haired girl of his own age sitting in the white gazebo on the western side of the lawn. He threw up his hand and grinned. "Hi, Mandy!" he called out cheerfully.

The girl simply turned up her nose at him, as if saying "My name is *Amanda!*" and continued to pet the animal in her lap, a fluffy white cat named Queenie. Jeb was discouraged by the snubbing he received since, secretly, he had a huge crush on the girl. Jeb had sat behind Mandy Rutherford in Miss Winston's class at school the previous year, but no matter how hard he tried, he simply couldn't get the girl to take a liking to him. He figured it had something to do with her father being the president of the Mangrum County Bank. Even as young as he was, Jeb Sweeny was painfully aware of how wide the gap between rich and poor could stretch, and it was that gap that apparently separated him from the girl with the long black hair.

Reluctantly, Jeb left the cool greenery of the courthouse yard and stepped back onto the hot cement of the sidewalk that ran westward along Willow Drive. He lifted his toes, raised his heels, and tried walking on the balls of his feet like a cat for a while, thinking that it would be better to burn only one part of his feet and save the others. But, after a while, he tired of walking that way. He left the sweltering concrete and ducked past a loose board in a fence, taking a detour through a vacant lot. Unlike his carefree romp across the grassy courtyard, Jeb was careful where he stepped this time. The lot was littered with rusty nails and broken bottles; things that could cripple a free-roaming country boy and inflict the dreaded affliction of lockjaw as well, although Jeb had never come across anyone who had ever suffered from the mysterious malady.

When the vacant lot came to its end, Jeb pulled himself up over the board fence and landed lightly on the other side. Buckshot was waiting for him at the curb, having relieved himself on the tire of a Chevrolet pickup truck. The dog lowered his leg and followed closely at his master's heels. A few last drops of pee dotted the hot sidewalk like the trail from a leaky fuel pump, then quickly evaporated.

Making his way briskly from one patch of shade to another, Jeb walked down Willow Drive. He passed Pile's Texaco with its greasy repair bays and Fire Chief gasoline pumps. Up ahead was the big gray building that housed the Pikesville shirt factory on one side of the street, while his destination, Holt's Feed and Farming Equipment set on the other, with its two grain silos and a fenced-in yard of tractors, sowers, and other equipment. Further on, where Willow petered out into a deadend, stood the train depot next to the railroad tracks. It had been nearly two years since Jeb last stood on its boarded walkway. That was when his father had returned home, prematurely, from the War. Jeb remembered that day clearly; the coal-burning L&N locomotive, Grandma holding his hand a little too tightly, and his father stepping down out of a passenger car, his duffel bag slung over his broad shoulder. Jeb also recalled the moment when Sam Sweeny had grinned goofily and stared straight at him with big, dumb eyes, recognition failing to surface when he looked at his one and only son.

Jeb drove the sad memories from his mind and continued on. Up ahead, next to the loading dock of Holt's, was parked the Sweenys' flatbed wagon, with a single, gray mule tethered to the front. The Sweenys were one of the few farm families in Pikesville that still used a wagon for doing chores and taking trips to town. There were several good reasons for that. Grandma had never learned to drive a car, Jeb was much too young to handle a vehicle, and Sam had lost whatever ability he had possessed for driving in that foxhole on the German front.

"Hey, Jeb!" called a rumbling, childlike voice from the direction of the wagon. "Hey there!"

Jeb looked to where a big, lumbering man of thirty-eight sat on the open tailgate of the wagon. He wore a blue chambray shirt, denim britches, and scuffed army boots. He waved excitedly at the boy and hopped down off the flatbed, grinning benevolently as usual. Jeb smiled back, although it was hard to do so sometimes. His father's features were the same as they had been before the War—wavy black hair topping a handsome, tanned face. It was the eyes that were strikingly different. The intelligence, rural savvy, and plain old common horse sense that had sparkled there before his return home were gone. Now the childlike innocence of a five-year-old gleamed from those soft brown eyes.

"Sorry I'm late, Sam," said Jeb. "But Mr. Drewer had a shop full of folks today and I had to wait for a spell." It made Jeb ache a little inside to call his father by his first name, but he knew that it was much less confusing for Sam that way. Jeb understood what had happened to his father while he was fighting the Nazis back in Germany; how an enemy shell had landed in the middle of a foxhole, killing most of the men in his father's infantry unit and giving Sam something called "shell-shock." The concussion from that explosion had damaged his father's brain somehow and erased all he had known before that fateful moment. Therefore, upon his arrival home, Sam Sweeny had regarded Grandma and Jeb more as friendly strangers than family. His love for them was genuine, but he regarded Jeb more like his little brother than his son. Although it hurt Jeb, he had finally learned to accept Sam on similar terms. Two years had passed and Sam had not improved during that time. It was clear to see that the man that had been his father was lost forever.

"I've been waiting for you, Jeb," said Sam. "See, I loaded the wagon up with the chicken feed, just like you told me to. I even paid Mr. Holt and got the right change back this time, I surely did!"

"That's real good, Sam," said Jeb. "I'm right proud of you."

Those few words of encouragement made Sam Sweeny grin even more broadly, if that was humanly possible.

Jeb regarded the big man curiously. "Now, I ain't never seen you so fired up about loading feed sacks before. Is there something else you're excited about? Maybe something you wanted to show me?"

Sam nodded enthusiastically. "Yeah, Jeb! Yeah, something really swell! It's 'round back here. Come on, Jeb. Follow me!"

"Okay, Sam," said Jeb. He looked up at the open door of the loading dock and saw a couple of Holt's workers standing there, chewing toothpicks and making snide comments to one another. Jeb felt the heat of shame begin to creep up the back of his neck, but he quickly fought the emotion off. He shot the snickering men a dirty look, then, leaving Buckshot in the shade beneath the wagon, followed Sam to the rear of the feed store.

Behind the building lay a clutter of stray boards, empty

nail kegs, and empty packing crates. When Jeb turned the corner, he found Sam kneeling next to one of the open crates, which had "40-WEIGHT MOTOR OIL" stenciled across the side in black ink. "What is it, Sam?" he asked. "What've you got there?"

"Something swell, Jeb," said Sam excitedly. "Come and look!"

Jeb stepped up and looked over Sam's shoulder. Inside the wooden crate, nestled in a bed of brown grass and chewed paper, lay a nest of baby mice. There were perhaps seven or eight of the newborn rodents. They squirmed and peeped, tiny things about as big as Jeb's thumb, bright pink with a light coat of gray fur on their heads and backs. The mice were blind, their eyes not yet open to the world around them.

"Look, Jeb!" said Sam with a big grin. "It's mouses! Baby mouses!"

"Mice," corrected the ten-year-old, although he knew it was pointless to do so. Sam tended to forget almost anything you tried to teach him. He might remember for ten or fifteen minutes, but after that he would be saying or doing the same old thing again.

"Yeah," said Sam. "Ain't they pretty?"

Jeb couldn't help but smile. "Yeah, Sam, they are." He watched as the man reached out with a calloused hand that was strong enough to crush walnuts between thumb and forefinger. "Now, don't go touching them, Sam. It ain't right to."

Sam looked over his shoulder at Jeb, perplexed. "But why not, Jeb? I just wanted to pet 'em a little while."

"I know that, but remember what I told you about baby animals? If you touch them after they're first born, you'll leave a man-scent on them. Then their mama will smell it and won't have nothing to do with them. She'll stop suckling them and they'll starve to death. Either that or she'll end up eating them."

"But why would their mama do something awful like that?" asked Sam.

Jeb shrugged. "I don't know. It's just a critter's way sometimes."

Sam stared at the baby mice for a moment, then looked back at Jeb, his brown eyes pleading. "Jeb . . . can we take 'em home with us? Please, Jeb, can we?"

Jeb hated it when Sam asked something of him that he couldn't possibly agree to. "Afraid not, Sam," he said. "I don't think their mama would like that. And I don't think Grandma would like it much, either, do you?"

Sam's brow creased as his weakened mind tried to find a plausible solution. "We could find their mama," he said slowly. "Yeah, we could find 'er and take 'er with us. And when we got home, we could hide 'em from Grandma."

"That wouldn't be right, Sam," Jeb explained. "If you hid them from Grandma, you'd be doing something dishonest. And remember what happens if you make a habit of that."

Sam thought hard, recalling what he had learned in church the previous Sunday. "When I die, I won't get to go to heaven to see Jesus. I'll have to go down to the bad place and burn and scream and gnash my teeth forever, right?"

"That's right," said Jeb. He laid an affectionate hand on his father's shoulder. "Now, come on and leave them mice alone. We gotta get on back to the farm. Won't be long till suppertime."

"All right," said Sam. "But just let me look at 'em a minute more, okay?"

"Sure," said Jeb. "But just for a minute."

The boy stood there for a moment. He ignored the squirming mice in the crate, instead looking at Sam's face. It was so full of joy and wonder that it pained Jeb just to look at it, almost to the point of bringing him to tears.

Jeb was about to pull Sam away from the nest of mice

and lead him back out front to the wagon, when he sensed that someone was behind them. The boy turned to find the owner of the feed store, Harvey Holt, standing there. His beefy face was red and angry, and his shirtsleeves were rolled to his elbows. At first, Jeb was certain that Holt's rage was focused on him and Sam. But a moment later, he discovered that was not the case.

"Where are the filthy things?" he demanded to know.

"What?" asked Jeb.

"Those damned mice!" growled Harvey, his eyes livid. "One of my men said there was a nest of 'em back here!"

Before Jeb could answer, the man was stalking toward the crate that Sam crouched next to. As he grew near, Jeb saw that he held a garden hoe in one burly hand. The implement was straight off the store rack, its price tag still dangling from the crooked neck above the hickory handle.

"There they are, the little bastards!" said Harvey Holt. Roughly, he pushed past Sam with enough force to knock the kneeling man over. Sam landed on his butt in the sawdust and, confused, looked up at the fuming store owner.

"Whatcha gonna do?" he asked breathlessly when Harvey raised the hoe. "Whatcha gonna do to the mouses?"

"Gonna kill them, that's what!" snapped Harvey. "Can't let them grow up and get fat off my grain, now can I?"

Sam Sweeny's face drained deathly pale and his eyes widened in horror as Holt swung the hoe overhead, then brought it down upon the empty crate. The flat blade smashed through the flimsy wood and bore down upon the mewing tangle of tiny rodents. The edge of the hoe sliced into the bodies of the baby mice, snapping small bones and rending tender flesh. A low moan sounded in Sam's throat as droplets of blood speckled the legs of Harvey's cotton pants. A couple more whacks of the hoe finished the job.

"There!" said Harvey, stepping back and eyeing his handiwork proudly. "They won't be no bother now. No sirree!"

Jeb was a little shocked at the brutality shown by Harvey Holt, but not nearly as much as Sam was. The boy watched as his father's face, which had turned as pale as Grandma's biscuit dough during the attack, slowly shed its expression of distress. Sam's cheeks suddenly turned tomato red and the look of confused hurt in his dull eyes abruptly changed into hard anger. Jeb recognized that look. Sam rarely got mad about anything, but when he did, it was a frightening thing to see. It was like watching a six-foot-three, two hundred and sixty pound youngster throwing a temper tantrum.

"You shouldn't have done it!" said Sam as he rose to his feet. "Them poor mouses . . . they didn't harm you none!"

Jeb took a step forward. "Just calm yourself down, Sam. Please."

Harvey Holt retreated a couple feet, raising the hoe in front of him. "You stay away from me, you dadblamed simpleton!" he warned. "I swear, stand clear or I'll hit you with this hoe!"

Sam didn't stand clear, though. Puffing like a steam engine, the man kept on coming, his eyes full of dark rage. "You killed 'em! Cut 'em all into little bitty pieces!"

Jeb opened his mouth to speak again, but the words lay frozen on his tongue just as Sam reached the owner of the feed store. Holt swung with the hoe, but it was like swatting at a red-eyed bull with a bamboo fishing pole. Sam reached out his big right hand and, pretty as you please, caught the hickory handle of that garden hoe. A second later, it was wrenched clean out of Harvey's hands. The storekeeper let out a little yelp, then grew fearfully silent as Sam tossed the hoe aside and grabbed a fistful of the man's shirt, starched white collar and all.

Harvey Holt was a big man; the kind whose shadow you

could take a nap in if he had a mind to stand in one spot long enough. But Sam Sweeny was bigger and stronger, his muscles hardened from day after day of working the dusty acres of the Sweeny farm. With little effort, Sam tightened his grip on Harvey's shirt and hauled him upward until his feet were dangling a good two inches from the sawdust-covered ground.

Jeb ran up to Sam, his heart beating wildly. "Now you stop that, Sam! Come on . . . put him down!"

Sam wasn't listening, though. His attention was rooted to the face of the man he held at the end of his arm. "It was mean for you to do 'em like that!" he growled. "Just plain mean! I think you oughta say you're sorry . . . right now."

"Damned retard!" sputtered Harvey Holt. "Let me go!" The store owner's face grew beet red, then took on a shade of deep purple as the hold on his collar grew even tighter. Harvey shifted his eyes to Jeb. "You'd best get this half-wit to let me go, Jeb Sweeny, or I swear I'll go straight to Sheriff North and have him thrown into the state asylum! Don't think that I won't, either!"

Jeb knew that Harvey Holt was a man of his word, but still he knew only one thing would guarantee his release. "I can't do much about it, Mr. Holt. I reckon you'd best tell him you're sorry."

"I'd rather rot in hell first!" gasped the man.

Sam's outrage was stoked by the man's cursing. "Ain't right for you to say that word out loud, not in front of Jeb!" Sam shook his arm violently, jerking Harvey back and forth like an oversized rag doll. "Now, you do like I said. You say you're sorry for killing them mouses *and* cussing in front of Jeb!"

The defiance abruptly left Harvey Holt and, suddenly, all he wanted was to be clear of the angry farmer. "All right, dammit! I'm sorry! Now let loose of me!"

Satisfied, Sam relinquished his hold on Holt's collar. An instant later, the storekeeper landed on his butt in the sawdust with a loud grunt. As Jeb rushed to Sam's side, the owner of Pikesville's only feed store glared at the two. "You'd best keep a leash on that imbecile, Jeb Sweeny, before he goes and hurts someone! And you keep him clear of me, too. If he lays a hand on me again, I'll go straight to the sheriff. I promise you that!"

"He wouldn't have really hurt you, Mr. Holt," assured Jeb, although he wasn't at all sure that what he said was the truth. "He's just like a big ol' kid when he gets riled up. He was just throwing a little fit, that's all."

Harvey tugged at his shirt collar, allowing his face to return to its normal hue. "Well, I don't rightly believe that, but I'll let it pass . . . this time. Next time, I'll have the idiot locked up!"

"Come on, Sam," said Jeb, taking his father by the hand. "Let's go home."

His anger depleted, Sam nodded dumbly and allowed the ten-year-old to lead him back around the store to Willow Drive. A moment later, they were sitting on the seat of the wagon. Jeb took hold of the reins, disengaged the brake, and called for Buckshot. The dog awakened from his slumber and, seeing the wagon lurch above him, darted from underneath and jumped up into the bed. As the hound perched atop a sack of chicken feed, Jeb snapped the reins and, jerking them sharply to the right, made a U-turn in the middle of the street.

As they approached the intersection of Willow and Main, Jeb finally released a sigh of relief. Once again, Sam had escaped the threat of the county sheriff by the grace of God and the skin of his teeth. "I do declare, Sam!" he said scoldingly. "Can't you ever stay clear of trouble when we come

to town? You'd best learn to curb your temper or, I swear,
I'll leave you at home next time!"

When Sam refused to answer, Jeb turned his head and felt
his heart drop a couple of inches in his chest. His father
was crying. The thirty-eight-year-old man was blubbering like
a baby. At first, Jeb thought he was upset over the harsh
words he had just spoken. But he knew that wasn't the case.
It wasn't shame and hurt that creased Sam's rugged features,
but sorrow and grief.

"Why'd he have to do it, Jeb?" sobbed Sam, tears streaming down his cheeks. "Why'd he have to kill them mouses?
Chop 'em up and kill 'em like that?"

Jeb wanted to tell him that Holt had exterminated them
in order to protect his grain; a fact that the old Sam Sweeny
would have certainly understood. Jeb recalled how his father
had once acted just as Holt had, killing meddlesome weasels
that preyed upon their chickens or snakes that crept into the
barn and spooked the hogs. But that part of Sam was gone.
Now his eyes innocently saw such scavengers as nothing
more than cuddly critters to be petted and cherished.

"I don't know, Sam," Jeb finally said as he steered the
wagon southward along Main Street. "I reckon he just don't
like animals the way you do. He saw them as something
harmful, instead of a nest of baby mice."

"That still didn't give him the right to kill 'em!" weeped
Sam, snot dribbling down his upper lip. "They were just
babies! They couldn't even eat his ol' grain! They didn't even
have any teeth yet!"

"I know, Sam," said Jeb soothingly. As he urged the mule
along Main Street, the boy was aware of the attention that
his father was drawing. He could feel eyes watching them
as they passed, some sympathetic, while most were merely
amused. Jeb began to feel his discomfort turn into embarrassment, but he remembered what Grandma Sweeny had told

him; that his father's injury was something that couldn't be helped and wasn't anything to be ashamed of. Jeb fought hard to convince himself that what she had said was true, but sometimes, with the whole town of Pikesville watching, it was a mighty hard thing to do.

Jeb passed the crowded shops that lined both sides of Main Street, then pulled back on the reins when they reached the grocery. "Whoa, Nellie!" he yelled out and, reluctantly, the mule sauntered to a halt. The boy turned to the man next to him and held out his hand. "Where's that change that was left over from the chicken feed?"

Sam continued his crying, but managed to dip his hand into his shirt pocket. He gathered the contents and deposited fifty cents in dimes and nickels in the boy's cupped palm.

"I'll be back directly," promised Jeb. He engaged the wagon's brake, hopped down to the street, then disappeared into the store.

A moment later, he returned and, again, took his place on the seat. He held out two items that were sure to take Sam's mind off the murdered mice. One was a frosty bottle of Royal Crown Cola. The other was a chocolate moon pie.

Jeb couldn't help but grin when Sam's tears ceased to flow and he snatched the soda and pie out of the boy's hands. "Thanks, Jeb!" beamed the man gratefully. "Thanks a bunch!"

"Just don't mention it to Grandma, okay?" said Jeb with a wink. "If she found out I let you have sweets so close to suppertime, she'd nail both our hides to the barn door."

Sam frowned a little. "That'd hurt, Jeb."

The boy laughed. "Yeah, it surely would, wouldn't it?"

As Jeb released the brake and put the mule in motion again, he looked over at his father. The big man sat there, now completely content, alternating between bites of moon pie and swallows of soda pop. At that moment, he had an overwhelming urge to reach out and hug his father, perhaps tell him how much he loved him.

Before Jeb could act on the impulse, Buckshot appeared between the two, having gotten a sniff of the marshmallow and chocolate pie. The dog lunged forward, hoping to steal a bite, even though Sam held it away, teasingly. But all it took from Buckshot was a pitiful whimper and one look from those sad, hound dog eyes to melt Sam's big heart. "Go on, boy," he said, lowering his hand. "Help yourself." Buckshot wasted no time. He chomped down on the pie, taking away half the wrapper with his first bite.

Jeb smiled and urged the mule onward. Soon, they passed the rolls of fancy houses and the stately churches with their manicured lawns and stained-glass windows. The boy had eagerly anticipated their trip to town all that week, but that Saturday afternoon, Pikesville had proven to be more of a bother than anything else. Jeb was glad to be away from the town limits and on the road back home again. And, from the way Sam and Ol' Buckshot had suddenly cheered up, he could tell that they were, too.

Five

Another Shadow

In the high grass, crickets sang along with the rapid-fire picking of banjo and mandolin that drifted from the speaker of a tube radio. Like the country band that played over the airwaves, the insects were unseen but certainly vocal that summer night.

The heat of that day hadn't subsided with the arrival of sundown. If there was any variation in the temperature it was a small one. Even the breeze that Jeb had enjoyed in the alleyway behind Drewer's Barber Shop was noticeably absent. The night air hung heavily around the single-story farmhouse, muggy and uncomfortably warm.

The Sweeny family listened to the radio, just like they did every evening after suppertime. Since it was too hot to sit in the parlor, they had placed the radio on the sill of the open window and retired to the front porch. As they listened to the Grand Ole Opry broadcast from Nashville, each one settled into their usual spots on the porch, staring quietly into the night as if imagining the cathedral-like chamber of the Ryman Auditorium. In their minds, they pictured the singers in their fringed shirts and cowboy hats, stepping up to the microphone to sing a well-known song or two, then moving on to let another artist have their turn.

Jeb sat on the edge of the porch, near the steps, his back

to one of the four posts that supported the eaves overhead. Buckshot lay nearby. The boy scratched the sleeping dog behind the ears with his bare toes, while he worked on something he had given much thought to since his unexpected encounter with Troy Jenkins and the Boones that afternoon. Meticulously, he tied a length of rubber he had sliced from an old innertube to the ends of a forked hickory branch taken from a tree out back of the barn. He tied and untied the length of innertube several times, trimming it down with his pocketknife and searching for just the right tension.

Sam was stretched out on the porch swing, his boots off and his sock feet resting on one of the armrests. He snored softly, his chest rising gently to the same level as his bloated stomach. Despite the snack of RC Cola and moonpie, Sam had stuffed himself at the supper table that night, feasting on white beans, taters, cornbread muffins, and iced tea. Every so often, he would fart in his sleep, drawing a giggle from Jeb and a disapproving look from Grandma Sweeny.

The elderly woman sat in her straight-back rocking chair, slowly swaying to and fro, while tapping her right foot to the music. She cooled herself with a pasteboard fan given to her by the Baptist church—depicting the Last Supper in muted colors—and stared off into the darkness. It was almost as if she were expecting someone to come visiting, whether they were invited or not.

As Roy Acuff and his Smoky Mountain Boys began to play "The Great Speckled Bird," Jeb turned his attention from his project and looked over at his grandmother. Lucille Sweeny was known throughout the county as a devout Christian and a woman not afraid to speak her mind. She was a master quilter and canner of preserves, as well as a shrewd businesswoman when it came down to haggling over the price of eggs or hogs. In fact, Grandma was about the strongest woman Jeb had known in his young life. She was good at scolding him for wrongs he was guilty of and could make a willow switch sing a wicked tune at the seat of his britches, but then again, she had her soft side, too. He saw that side now. Grandma rocked gently in her chair, her eyes closed behind the thick lenses of her spectacles and her mouth silently uttering the words of the gospel hymn that drifted from the radio.

Just looking at her made him feel a little sad and the "Speckled Bird" sure didn't help matters any. Brother Oswald's dobro sounded particularly mournful that evening, but that wasn't exactly it. Rather, it was Grandma herself that filled Jeb full of sorrow. Staring at the loose and yellowed flesh of her face, and the deep sockets of her eyes, he could picture the woman's skull hidden not far underneath. It was a picture he didn't rightly wish to hold in his mind for too long a period of time.

As he turned his attention back to the slingshot he was making, Grandma spoke. "So, how'd the trip to town go today?" she asked.

Jeb frowned. It was a question she had already asked at the supper table and it took him a moment to remember the answer he had given scarcely an hour before. "Uh, just fine, Grandma," he lied.

He could feel the old woman's eyes appraising him from the lofty perch of her rocker. "All right," she allowed. "So where did you get all them scrapes and bruises?"

Jeb swallowed dryly. "Wasn't looking where I was walking and walked smack dab into the door of Mr. Drewer's barber shop," he fibbed once again.

He sensed Grandma's expression of amusement, rather than saw it. "Then that door must've sprouted a right hard pair of knuckles, I'd say," she said. "What's that you're working on, son?"

"A slingshot. You know, like the one David used against

Goliath." He hoped maybe that a reference to the Bible would satisfy her curiosity and she would abandon the subject of his eventful afternoon in Pikesville.

But, apparently, it only fueled the fire. "Is that what you're aiming to do with that there slingshot, Jeb?" asked Grandma. "You looking to bring down a Goliath of your own?"

"No, ma'am," he said. His ears reddened slightly as lie piled upon lie. "Just soda bottles and tin cans."

Grandma chuckled. "At first maybe. Then you'll likely go after birds and critters. I don't want you killing squirrels and songbirds, but you can knock blackbirds out of the sky till your heart's content. Those pesky devils have been pecking holes in my tomatoes out in the garden, trying to get to the seeds inside, and I have no great love for 'em."

Jeb grinned, his ears cooling. "Yes, ma'am. I'll sure do what I can." He finished tightening the knots of the innertube and tested the length of rubber again. It was just right. He dug into the side pocket of his overalls and withdrew a single marble from the clutter inside. He cradled the glass ball in the center of the sling and stretched the innertube until his hand was nearly touching his shoulder. He aimed off into the darkness, toward the dusty stretch of Mossy Creek Road. He could barely see the pale head of the metal mailbox sitting atop its post of knotty pine. He squinted and pulled back the sling just a hair further, imagining that it was Troy Jenkins standing out there, hankering for another fight. Jeb grinned and released his hold. The length of rubber slapped air and the marble arched off into the night. He waited for a second, thinking that he had misplaced his aim, then heard the faint clang of the missile putting a dent in the rear of the metal box. Satisfied, he stuck his new weapon in his back pocket and smiled proudly to himself.

On the radio, the King of Country Music left the stage and Ernest Tubb stepped up to the mike. Soon he was belting out "I'm Walking The Floor Over You" in high, nasal tones. Halfway through it, Jeb heard the brittle creak of the rocker. He looked around to see Grandma lifting herself out of the chair. It took her a moment or so longer than it normally did, which, for some reason, sent a bell of alarm ringing in the youngster's head.

"Grandma?" he asked, his face worried.

The elderly woman forced a smile. Now it was time for her to lie. "Don't fret none over me. I'm all right."

Jeb watched as she laboriously made it to her feet and walked slowly to the front door. As she opened the screen and paused in the light of the inner hallway for a long moment, Lucille Sweeny's silhouette stood out starkly against the glow. It was a silhouette that was a good thirty pounds lighter than it had been the same time the previous month. Jeb felt his heart quicken at the sight of her flower-print dress hanging like a loose tow sack upon her dwindling form. Grandma had always been a healthy, big-boned woman that rivaled Sam in height and weight, but lately she seemed to shrink with each passing day. And that wasn't all. Her strength and sassiness had seemed to diminish, too. She was beginning to look like some of the old folks who sat in wheelchairs on the porch of the Pikesville Nursing Home next to the Baptist church. Those who had lost all the spunk and cheer in their lives and were no more than hulls of flesh and bone, waiting to go to sleep one night and never wake up again.

The screen door slammed and, for a moment, Jeb simply sat there, uncertain about what he should do next. The announcer on the radio vocalized the virtues of Martha White's Self-Rising Flour, while Sam lay in the swing, mumbling something about "damned Nazis." Buckshot, too, was in the depths of a dream, his feet twitching as he ran a coon through an imaginary thicket.

Finally, a sound from inside roused Jeb from his spot on the porch. It was a low groan—a groan of pain—followed by a whimpering plea of "Lord Jesus, have mercy!"

Careful to make no noise, Jeb crossed the porch and slipped past the screen door. He made his way down the hallway that led through the center of the farmhouse to the rear kitchen. When he reached the kitchen doorway, he paused, standing just out of view. He peeped past the edge of the doorframe and saw his grandmother standing at the counter that ran along the far side of the room. She stood there feebly, one hand on the counter to steady herself, while the other pressed against her lower abdomen, where her female parts were. Her wrinkled face was even more wrinkled than usual, and Jeb realized that those lines had been etched there by some horrible agony that she was experiencing at that moment.

Jeb felt his heart sink in his chest like a heavy stone. Once again, the ugly shadow of his grandmother's illness was showing itself, casting its darkness across the Sweeny household. Jeb trembled in the doorway as he watched Grandma breathe deeply and reach for the door of a cupboard on the wall. He knew what she was looking for. Soon, she had found it. It was a tall skinny bottle of brown liquid nearly as thick as sorghum molasses. Even from where he stood, he could see the letters on the label in bold print: LAUDANUM.

As Grandma shakily uncapped the bottle and took a tablespoon from a silverware drawer, Jeb thought about the events that had led up to the sorrowful discovery of the woman's hidden condition. First there had been Grandma's secretive trip to Nashville with her best friend, Miss Claudine Johnson, a skinny spinster who owned the farm next to theirs. He recalled their return and the long expressions on their faces; expressions of fear and worry. Secondly, there had been his grandmother's startling loss of weight and energy; something that he had first attributed to old age more than anything else. Then, third and last, came the hard slap of truth in the form of a letter Grandma had left, opened and forgotten, atop her sewing box in the parlor. It was a letter Jeb had no business reading and one that he wished he never had. It had been a letter from a Nashville doctor, one with too many big words and not nearly enough compassion. But there had been several phrases that Jeb had understood; phrases that had seemed to have been penned by the hand of the Grim Reaper himself.

Result of biopsy: ovarian cancer. Advanced and inoperable.

That awful word filled his head now, refusing to be chased away by even the most joyous thoughts of summer. Cancer. Two mere syllables, but, oh, what weight and finality they possessed. Enough to make the strongest man weep and chase the glimmer of hope from the eyes of the most cheerful soul. Jeb felt that familiar ache of helplessness run through him from head to toe. He hated that word most of all, even more so than others like homework, castor oil, and, of course, Troy Jenkins.

Breathlessly, he watched as Grandma carefully poured the nasty potion into the cradle of the spoon. She downed the medicine, then paused for a moment and poured another spoonful.

Jeb was shocked and disheartened. He had never seen Grandma take that much before. He knew what the medicine was and what it was for, because he had looked up the word *laudanum* in the big dictionary at the Mangrum County library. It was a powerful painkiller that was a combination of opium and alcohol. Jeb didn't rightly understand all of what he had read, but he did know one thing. Grandma thought the drinking of liquor was a sin, plain and simple. So she had to be hurting mighty bad to be drinking something that had even the smallest amount of alcohol in it.

Grandma grimaced as if she'd just downed a dose of poison. She returned the bottle to the cupboard, then stood stone still and cocked her head slightly to the side like Buckshot did when he heard something interesting. "I know you're standing there, Jeb. I can hear you breathing."

As she turned around, Jeb stepped through the doorway into the kitchen. He was shocked at how very pale and bloodless his grandmother's face looked. "Grandma?" he asked ". . . are you all right?"

The woman forced a smile. "If you were a few years younger, I'd be tempted to grin and say yes." she told him. "But, I can't do that. You're too smart to be fooled." Her smile waned a bit. "I'm sick, child. Bad sick."

Jeb felt his eyes grow hot and moist. "I know," he said softly.

Grandma's expression darkened a shade. "I reckon you heard it from one of those tongue-wagging gossips in town. Dadblamed busybodies!"

"No, ma'am," said Jeb. "I found the letter. The one you got from Nashville."

"And you read it?"

Jeb nodded.

Grandma sighed, whether in relief or in regret, the boy could not tell. "Then you know that your grandmother's dying?"

The tears came then, spilling down his freckled cheeks. "Yes, ma'am."

A moment later, he was across the kitchen and in his grandmother's embrace. Grandma gently ran her fingers through his freshly trimmed hair as he sobbed quietly. "It ain't as bad as it seems," she whispered down to him. "You've had enough Sunday schooling to know that death ain't the end to life. I'll just be leaving ya'll to live with Jesus, that's all. Sometimes a person just don't have no choice but to accept it, no matter how bitter a pill it might seem."

Jeb tried to find comfort in his grandmother's calm reasoning, but he simply couldn't. "I don't want you to die, Grandma," he moaned softly. "I love you."

"And I love you, too, Jeb," she replied, her voice breaking. "But you've gotta be strong for me, be a man and hold your head up high." She paused for a moment, then continued. "And, another thing. I think it'd be best if we didn't tell Sam about this. The way your pa's mind is, well, I don't think he'd be able to handle it as well as you are. Will you promise me that we'll keep this just between you and me, if only for the time being?"

Jeb looked up and saw that tears also brimmed in Grandma's eyes. "Yes, ma'am. I promise. I won't tell him."

Grandma hugged him close. "That's my boy! Now you go to your room and get ready for bed. I'll go out to the porch and rouse Sam. He'd sleep all night long on that swing if I'd let him."

Reluctantly, Jeb pried himself from his grandmother's embrace and left the kitchen. He walked down the hallway to the door of his and Sam's bedroom. Jeb didn't turn on the light when he entered, instead crossing the dark room to his bed. Pictures of Roy Rogers and Gene Autry that Jeb had cut from magazines hung on the walls above his bed, along with a couple of tanned raccoon hides that he and Buckshot had netted the autumn before. Silently, he undressed, hanging his overalls on the edge of the headboard, then climbed into bed, wearing only his underwear. As usual, the sheets and pillowcase felt soft and smelled fresh, thanks to Grandma's daily routine of tub washing and sun drying. Even that small consideration on his grandmother's part made Jeb's heart ache. Before, he had taken such little things for granted. But now, knowing what he knew, they seemed like God-given blessings.

He lay on his side in the darkness, willing the tears and

the pain in his soul to go away, but it was an impossible task. He simply couldn't drive the fearful prospect of losing his grandmother from his thoughts. It was there like an ugly tattoo that couldn't be scrubbed away with soap and water; etched there in the gray flesh of his brain in dark, grievous strokes too bold to be ignored.

Jeb thought of the Sweeny family and the long string of shadows that had loomed over them during the past few years. Shadows of sadness and pain. First there had been Grandpa Sweeny's death two years before Jeb's birth; he had neglected to wear a hat as he toiled in the tobacco patch one sweltering August afternoon and paid for it with a heat stroke from which he had never recovered. Secondly, there had been the shameful matter of Jeb's mother running off with a traveling preacherman when the boy was scarcely one year of age. After that came the tragedy of Sam Sweeny's injury in wartime and the mental loss he had sustained.

All had been shadows that had come and gone; tragedies the Sweenys had endured and learned to live with. But this latest shadow, in Jeb's mind at least, seemed to be the darkest and most devastating one yet.

As he lay there, trembling, his tears dampening the cloth of his pillow, Jeb heard his father enter the room. Mercifully, the room remained dark as Sam made his way sleepily across the bedroom. Jeb listened. He heard the squeak of rusty springs as his father sat on the edge of his bed and began to undress.

Then Sam spoke, barely able to suppress a yawn as he did so. "Oh, Jeb? You awake?"

Jeb fought hard to steady his voice. "Yep."

There was a tone of puzzlement in Sam's deep voice. "Jeb, what's wrong with Grandma?"

The boy's heart leapt in his chest. Could Sam possibly

suspect something? Had someone in town told him? "Nothing," he said. "Why do you ask?"

"When she woke me up, her eyes were all red . . . like she'd been crying or something."

"It was just a song she heard on the radio, that's all," Jeb lied. "You know how those old hymns make her sad sometimes."

"Okay," replied Sam, seemingly satisfied by the boy's explanation. "Goodnight, Jeb."

"Good night, Sam," he said softly.

A moment later, Jeb's father was asleep once again. But slumber came much harder for the boy. He lay awake in his bed, listening to Sam's snoring, as well as the nocturnal symphony of crickets and toads in the darkness just beyond the bedroom's open window. Again, the thought of Grandma's illness preyed upon his youthful mind. This time it was not sorrow or grief that gripped him, but cold, inescapable fear. The fear of the unknown.

Jeb had never known his real mother. Grandma Sweeny had been the only real mother the boy had ever known. She had taught him to read from the Bible when he was five years old, had taught him the difference between right and wrong, rewarded him when he was good and punished him when he was bad. And now the threat of losing her had presented itself. The inner workings of her body had somehow gone haywire and cancer was taking her away from him, pound by pound, day by day.

He tried hard to accept that fact and be brave about it, just like Grandma hoped he would, but it was difficult. Not that he was afraid of what would happen to Grandma after death. She was a good Christian woman and Jeb knew that God would reserve a place for her in heaven; he was certain of that. No, what scared Jeb the most was what would become of him and Sam. The mere thought of what might take

place mortified the farmboy to the very depths of his soul.
Neither he nor Sam had any other living relatives. More than
likely, his feeble-minded father would be sent to the state
asylum in Nashville and Jeb would be condemned to some
dark prison of an orphanage. If Sam had possessed the presence of mind to capably take care of the farm and Jeb, such
a grim prospect would have never entered the boy's mind.
But the truth of the matter was that Sam was not able to
take on such a responsibility. He could hardly tie his boot-
laces in the morning without Jeb helping him do it.

Fear turned into despair and, eventually, the weight of Jeb's
thoughts exhausted him and he drifted into a restless sleep.
Later that night, he dreamt that he was flying over the sunny
pastures of Mangrum County on the wings of a shadow.
Soon, it had taken him away from the safety and familiarity
of the home he had known all his life and dropped him into
the dark heart of a land that reeked of pure evil. A land
choked with shadows so horrible that they made that of
Grandma's cancer seem mercifully welcome in comparison.

Six

Visitors In The Night

Roscoe Ledbetter sat in front of a small campfire, despite the warmth of the evening. He was perched atop an empty nail keg he had liberated from the trash pile behind Holt's supply house, his aged eyes peering through the lens of his spectacles at the meager meal that was assembled before him.

Monday was always a poor day for picking up spare change. The weekend tended to drain pockets and purses alike and folks just naturally hung onto what they had left until the following payday. By the time he'd slung his guitar over his back and deserted the corner of Willow and Main that evening, Roscoe had netted a grand total of forty-three cents. Still, it had been enough to buy him a modest feast consisting of a can of pork and beans, a pack of saltine crackers, and a frosty bottle of Nehi Orange.

The black man poked at the guts of the fire with a stick, then began to prepare his supper. He reached into his pants pocket and withdrew an old Swiss Army knife. Roscoe unfolded the can opener and meticulously went to work. Soon, he had the top cut away. He peeled away the paper label, then placed the tin can into the flames. As the beans cooked, he opened the crackers and uncapped the bottle of soda pop.

Roscoe sat there on the keg for a moment breathing in the heavy scent of honeysuckle blossoms and the tangy scent of the pine grove that stood around him. To the west stretched miles of similar woodland, as well as numerous hills and hollows. To the east, across the railroad tracks that lay scarcely fifty feet away, was the town of Pikesville. The June night engulfed the patch of thicket Roscoe had set up camp in, humming with the steady rhythm of cicadas and crickets that sang, hidden from view, in the trees and bramble. It was a noise Roscoe had grown accustomed to during his rambling across the state of Tennessee. Many a night he had lain awake, staring at the stars and listening to the reedy chorus of the insects, as well as the distant baying of a hound or the inquisitive hooting of a white-faced owl.

The old bluesman turned his attention back to the meal at hand. He returned the can opener to its rightful place and unfolded the spoon from the body of the knife. He was about to fish the can of bubbling beans from the fire, when he heard the rumbling of a car engine and the crackling of tires on gravel nearby.

Roscoe peered through the tangle of the thicket, trying to make out the vehicle that approached. The glow of the moon overhead shone softly on the sleek body of a navy blue sedan. He watched as it climbed the hump of the railroad tracks and, straddling the gravel bed, parked there.

The headlights winked out and the engine grew silent, followed by the slamming of a door. "Ledbetter?" someone called out. "Roscoe Ledbetter . . . are you out there?"

Roscoe grunted and turned his attention back to his supper. He recognized the voice. It belonged to Ed North, the sheriff of Mangrum County. Roscoe had half expecteded the constable to pay a visit to his makeshift campsite. It was a testament to the lawman's laziness that it had taken him three whole days to make his appearance.

"I'm here," Roscoe replied. "By the fire."

He took a swig of the Nehi and smiled as he heard North

struggle his way past the edge of the thicket, cussing as he tripped and stumbled.

A moment later, the man stepped out of the darkness and into the flickering glow of the campfire. Ed North was a short, stocky fellow with rusty red hair and a pair of droopy hangdog eyes. He wore a brown fedora, tan trousers, and a wrinkled white shirt with the sleeves rolled up to the elbows. Both the brass badge pinned to his breast pocket and the Colt .38 holstered at his hip looked tarnished and neglected. Likewise, North himself had a slow, reluctant pace to his movements, like a man who knows the duties of his job, but was none too enthusiastic about expending the time and energy to perform them properly and punctually.

"Howdy, Sheriff," greeted the black man.

North nodded. "Heard you'd blown into town, Ledbetter. Just thought I'd stop by and see what you were up to."

Roscoe stirred the can of hot beans and withdrew a steaming spoonful. "Well, right now, I'm fixin' to chow down on beans and crackers. I'd offer you some, but I ain't Jesus and this ain't the loaves and the fishes."

Ed North patted his ample stomach. "Already had supper myself. Mrs. North cooked up a mess of corned beef and cabbage. It was mighty good."

Roscoe stared down at his can of beans. Its tiny slab of white pork sat there like a lifeboat atop a bumpy, brown sea. "Yeah, I reckon that was good eating. Well, no need to wear out your leg joints, Sheriff. Sit down for a spell if you have a mind to."

North glanced around and finally settled for the exposed root of a big pine tree. He sat down and, taking a bag of Our Advertiser tobacco from his shirt pocket, began to roll himself a cigarette. "So, how've you been, Ledbetter?"

Roscoe blew on the spoonful of hot beans before shoveling them into his mouth. "Oh, fair to middlin', I suppose," he replied. "Getting too dadblamed old and my arthritis gives me fits when the days are rainy. But other than that, I'm doing fine."

"That's nice to hear," said the constable. With apparent frustration, North labored over his smoke, his fingers clumsily attempting to curl the paper without losing most of the tobacco. "How's business been? Made a million with that guitar yet?"

The bluesman grinned. His teeth—genuine and otherwise—flashed in the firelight. "A million pennies perhaps. Spent 'em just as quickly as I fetched 'em, though." Roscoe eyed the lawman carefully. "But that ain't why you came out here tonight, is it? You got something else on your mind."

The sheriff looked up from his work and chuckled. "Saw right through me, huh?"

"Like a ghost."

North finished his cigarette—which looked like it had been rolled by a blind, one-armed monkey—and, pursing it between his lips, lit it with a match. "Well, to tell the God's honest truth, the reason I came looking for you, Ledbetter, is because of a complaint I received."

"Oh?" asked Roscoe. "Don't tell me somebody didn't like my picking and singing."

"No, that ain't it," said North. "Matter of fact, it was Albert Jenkins who came to my office, madder than a wet hen."

"Jenkins?" said Roscoe, his dark brow furrowed. "Can't say I know of the man."

"He's the janitor over at the elementary school. What he said was that you bothered his son, Troy, and his friends, the Boone brothers."

Roscoe smiled as he took a swallow of the Nehi Orange. "Bother 'em? No, sir. I simply prevented 'em from doing a wrong to a child they outnumbered, three to one."

"And who was that?" asked the lawman.

"Jeb Sweeny," said Roscoe. "Blond-haired boy with freck-les. Had a one-eyed bluetick hound dog with him."

North nodded and exhaled through his nose. "I know the boy's family. Poorer than Job's turkey, but they're good folks."

"Well, this Troy Jenkins and his buddies, they had Jeb on the ground and was trying to cram a shit bug down his throat," explained the Negro. "I just chased 'em off, that's all."

"Scared 'em off is more like it," corrected the sheriff. "Al-bert claimed that you put some kinda nigger curse on 'em."

Roscoe laughed heartily. "Made out that I did, anyhow!" He withdrew the chicken foot from inside his shirt. "I just waved this around and chanted a few conjure words and them young'uns lit out like scalded hogs!"

"Well, in any case, Ledbetter," he said. "I'm gonna have to insist that you stay clear of those boys. If you see 'em getting into mischief again, then you'd better just look the other way."

"I just evened up the odds, that's all," claimed Roscoe.

"I know, but that don't make no difference," said the sher-iff. "Don't fool around with those boys again or I'll be forced to ask you to leave Pikesville . . . and never come back."

A look of distress crossed the Negro's aged face. "Sheriff, do you know why I come to this town every June and July? It's 'cause of the Fourth of July celebration ya'll put on. No county in the state of Tennessee can hold a candle to the fireworks that Mangrum shoots off every year. Why it's purely a sight to behold!"

"Yeah, it'd be a shame to run you off, Ledbetter," said Ed North. "Folks here in town like to hear you play that guitar and some even enjoy your caterwauling. But I ain't joking. I'll send you on your way if I have to."

Roscoe stared at the fire before him and said nothing in

reply. He took another bite of beans, then took a hold of a gold chain and fished an old pocketwatch from the front of his vest. He peered at its face through the thick lens of his spectacles. "I'd say your visit is over with, Sheriff. It's about time for you to go."

Puzzlement shown in the lawman's eyes, followed quickly by mounting anger. "What the hell do you mean—?"

His indignation was shortlived. Before the sheriff could even finish his sentence, the distant wail of a train whistle echoed from the north.

"I'd say that's the southbound for Memphis . . . right on schedule," said Roscoe. "It might be worth your while to move your car before it gets here."

North knew he was right. With a sigh, he left his spot on the root and stood up. "I'll be seeing you around, Ledbetter," he said. "And remember what I said."

"I will, Sheriff," said Roscoe, his grin a little less than sincere.

The black man sat on the nail keg and listened as Ed North hurriedly made his way back through the thicket. As the whistle grew nearer, Roscoe heard the police car roar into life. Soon, it had backed over the hump of the railroad bed and was heading back down Willow Drive for the middle of town.

Roscoe finished his beans and crackers just as the nine-thirty train roared into Pikesville, drowning out all other night sounds. The deafening rumble of the engine and the clack-clack-clack of the steel wheels against the joints of the rails provided a beat that the bluesman simply couldn't resist. As he picked up his guitar and slipped the tiny glass bottle on the end of his finger, Roscoe thought of his visit from Ed North. He really had nothing to fear from the lazy lawman, but there had been other sheriffs in other counties who had proven to be more of a threat. He thought of them as he cradled the Fender in his skinny arms and voiced a song he had been working on in his head.

"Mister Po-leeceman, won't you leave me alone? . . . Please try and believe me—I ain't done nothing wrong . . . Put away yo' handcuffs, yo' blackjack, and yo' hose . . . Mah po' ole head is achin' like nobody knows!"

Five minutes later, the southbound train had come and gone. As it rattled and roared on its way, heading toward the Cumberland River bridge and the far end of Mangrum County, Roscoe paused with his picking and singing long enough to swallow the last of the orange soda. Then he sat there and waited for the noise of crickets and cicadas to return. But, for some reason, the insects failed to resume their nocturnal singing.

The night was as quiet as a tomb.

Roscoe sat, still as a statue, atop his nail keg. He strained his ears for sound, his heart beating like a hammer in his shallow chest. It wasn't only his hearing that told him that something was amiss, but also his sense of smell. His dark nostrils flared at a dry, acrid stench that hung heavily in the track-side thicket. It was a smell Roscoe Ledbetter was familiar with. The distinctive odor of a snake.

And, from the godawful stink of it, a mighty *big* one. The first thing that came to mind was the time he'd played on the midway of a traveling carnival in his younger days. Roscoe had shared the stage with the fire-eater, a pair of Siamese twins, and Felona the Snake Charmer. Felona had been a real looker; a pretty blonde with tits the size of ripened cantaloupes. But no performer or roustabout would go near her. That was mainly due to her constant companion, a fifteen foot boa constrictor by the name of Cleopatra, which was always draped over the blonde's shapely shoulders. The two things that Roscoe recalled the most about Cleopatra was its shiny brownish-gray skin and its rancid, snaky odor.

The smell he now encountered was similar to that of the boa, but a dozen times worse. There was something else that mingled with it; the dead-carcass stench of decayed meat. The type of smell you catch downwind of a dog who has been sideswiped by a car and left to rot by the road for two or three days.

Then the horrible odor was joined by a sound. It was a puzzling one at first . . . a long, nerve-grating rasp. It took Roscoe a moment of hard listening to identify the sound as being that of something coarse and scaly rubbing against a hard object, more than likely the trunk of a tree.

It is a snake, thought Roscoe, his mouth as dry as Memphis cotton. *A damned big snake . . . and it's rubbing against that big pine over yonder.*

Roscoe didn't want to look, but he did anyway. He lifted his head and directed his eyes toward the darkness beyond the far side of the pine tree. At first the glare of the campfire hampered his vision and he couldn't make anything out. Then he saw them, peering just around the southern edge of the tree trunk. Two oval-shaped eyes that were a pale shade of sickly yellow-green.

Good God Almighty! thought Roscoe. *The thing's head is bigger than a cow's.* The black man felt his bladder grow heavy. He couldn't tell for sure, but he thought he saw a grin of long, yellowed teeth just below the reflecting eyes. A grin that looked downright ugly . . . and more than a little hungry.

Roscoe felt like pissing in his pants, but he didn't. He steeled his nerves and stared right back at the thing on the far side of the tree. The pair of eyes shifted a little more into the open, and their movement was accompanied by the snap of a fallen branch beneath stealthful weight. *It's got feet!* thought Roscoe, in growing panic. An image instantly flashed into his mind. When he was a child, his Grandmother Ledbetter had owned an old Bible depicting one memorable scene for each book. The book of Genesis had been graced with a painting of Adam and Eve standing next to the Forbidden Tree. But it was what clung to the branches of that tree, nearly hidden from view, that had impressed Roscoe the most at the tender age of five. It was the Serpent, long and green, bearing catlike eyes and sharply-clawed feet . . . the snake's natural state before God had cursed it to slither on its belly for the rest of eternity.

The Devil! thought Roscoe. *I'm looking him square in the eye!*

As the creature took another slow step from behind the tree, Roscoe's mind worked frantically. He had no weapons around him. The Swiss knife had been folded and stuck back into his trouser pocket. All he had in his hands was the Nehi bottle . . . and his guitar.

A grin split the Negro's dark face, but it was a grin full of fear and tension. He knew what he had to do and he had to do it quick. Roscoe could tell that the thing behind the tree was taking its good time. It was stalking him, just like a cat stalks a mouse. If it had a mind to, it could be across the clearing and upon him in the wink of an eye.

Roscoe gripped the guitar neck in one black hand and positioned the fingers of the other over the strings of the hourglass body. Then he began to strum and sing "Amazing Grace" as loudly and with as much depth of feeling as he could possibly muster.

He saw the hymn's effect on the thing immediately. The oval eyes narrowed slightly and it released a low hiss of utter contempt. Roscoe couldn't see anything other than the eyes and the grin, but he could sense the rest of the creature's body quivering, its muscles locked, yearning to spring forward, but held at bay by the holy chorus the black man sang at the top of his lungs.

When Roscoe reached the end of the hymn, he didn't stop there. He continued with "The Old Rugged Cross," "Rock Of Ages," and "In The Sweet By and By." It was when he was through the second chorus of "Trust And Obey," that Roscoe knew that he had won the battle of wills fought between him and the thing beyond the tree. A low cry that could only be described as a cross between a contemptuous snarl and a whimper of defeat came from the far side of the tree. Then the serpentine eyes withdrew into the darkness.

Roscoe didn't let up. He finished the gospel hymn as he heard the rustle of brush and the dry rasp of the thing's scaly body rubbing against the trunks of the close-grown pines. After a few minutes, the sounds of retreat faded into the distance.

The bluesman sang one more—"We're Marching To Zion"—just for good measure. When he finally stopped, he found that his hands ached and trembled from the sheer frenzy of his playing. Roscoe Ledbetter wasn't a particularly religious man, but he certainly had been during the last ten minutes. And, in his heart, he knew that the hymns he had sang had been the only thing that had saved him from the thing behind the tree.

The night drew on. Eventually, the crickets and cicadas grew bold and began to sing again. Roscoe unrolled his blankets and stretched out before the campfire, but he didn't sleep. He lay there until dawn, his ears primed for the least little sound and his flattop Fender comfortably close at hand.

Seven

The Prison

The rich smell of bacon sizzling in the pan woke Jeb up early that Tuesday morning. He drew the meaty aroma through his nostrils in one long, lingering breath, then opened his eyes. His bedroom was still dim. The pale glow of dawn's first light shone through the open window. He glanced over at Sam's bed. His father had already left the room. As usual, the man had quietly made his departure and was hard at work with his morning chores.

Jeb knew he had his own share of chores to do before he was free to do as he pleased that day. The ten-year-old yawned and stretched, then hopped off the bed and began to dress. He considered putting on the overalls he had worn the day before, but knew that Grandma would notice the dusty denim and the ugly grass stains on the knees of the legs, and would hustle him right back to his room to change again. Therefore, he saved himself the trouble and took a fresh pair from the closet in the corner. Soon, Jeb had stepped into the overalls and pulled them up over his lean frame, slipping the straps of the suspenders over his freckled shoulders.

"Jeb!" called Grandma from the kitchen. "You up yet?"

"Yes, ma'am," he replied as he entered the hallway. "I'm coming."

A moment later he was in the kitchen. The room was

bright and sunny, as it always was, causing the yard beyond the side window to look downright dark and dreary in comparison. The table was draped with a white and red checkered tablecloth and set with three Blue Willow plates, three forks, and three small mason jars, which the family used as drinking glasses. There was a pan of big cat-head biscuits already on the table, along with redeye gravy, scrambled eggs, and a glass pitcher of cold buttermilk.

Grandma stood at the woodstove, keeping a watchful eye over an iron skillet of bacon slices. The strips popped and sizzled, the heat underneath the pan turning fatty pork into dark, crispy slices of heaven. Jeb's mouth watered in anticipation. He couldn't wait to gobble down his customary five or six pieces.

His grandmother had plugged the radio in the wall socket over the kitchen counter and the morning farm report droned through the speaker in that dull, twangy monotone that made Jeb want to crawl back into bed and go to sleep all over again. He ignored the prices of corn and porkbellies, crossing the kitchen to the big iron stove.

"Morning, Grandma," he said cheerfully.

The elderly woman turned and regarded him with a big smile. "Good morning to you, too, baby," she said. Grandma gave Jeb a quick hug, then turned her attention and her wooden spatula back to the unruly skillet of bacon.

"Anything you want me to do before breakfast?" he asked.

Grandma thought for a second. "Can't rightly say that I can think of anything. Breakfast is about done, so why don't you go on out and call Sam?"

"Okay," said Jeb. He opened the screen door and stepped out onto the back porch. The colorful light of dawn crept across the eastern horizon in soft hues of orange and pink. It played on the dewy grass that stretched between the farmhouse and the big barn that stood thirty yards away. Jeb drummed his foot on the boards of the porch to see if Buckshot had already left his favorite sleeping spot. When the dog failed to reveal himself, Jeb knew that he had already been roused, probably by the heavy footfalls of Sam's boots. Sometimes Buckshot liked to accompany Sam during his round of pre-dawn chores, while other times he preferred to stay right where he was and sleep well past noon.

"Sam!" the boy called out. "Sam, breakfast is ready!"

Jeb stood there for a moment, expecting to see the barn door open and his father emerge, a big grin on his face and a famished look in his childlike eyes. But, strangely enough, that didn't happen. The barn door remained closed and Sam failed to appear.

The boy scratched his head. Maybe Sam hadn't heard him. He stepped off the porch and into the yard. The morning dew felt cool against his bare feet. "Sam!" he yelled out, cupping his hands around his mouth. "Did you hear me? Breakfast!"

Again, he received no response. At least not from Sam. Instead, Jeb heard the distant barking of a dog, muted by the walls of the barn. It was Buckshot.

As Jeb moved across the backyard, past the hog pen and the outhouse, he sensed that something was wrong. Jeb knew Buckshot's barking like he knew his own voice; the way he bayed when he treed a coon, as well as the dog's plain old just-for-the-hell-of-it yapping. But this had an edge to it. Buckshot was frantic about something, that was for sure.

By the time he reached the towering structure of weathered lumber and rusty tin roofing, Jeb was at a dead run. He opened the door and stepped inside. The musky interior of the barn was dark, except for the light of a kerosene lantern shining from the stall at the far end of the building. That was where their one and only Jersey cow, Mabel, was tethered. Right then and there, Jeb decided that, indeed, something wasn't right. Sam always milked Mabel first thing in the morning. He should have had that chore over and done with a good hour ago.

"Sam?" called Jeb as he passed the toolbench and the stable where their mule, Nellie, stood, head hanging over the half-door as she munched on a mouthful of stale hay. "Sam, are you back there?"

Again, there was the excited barking of Buckshot and, abruptly, the hound dog appeared, leaping out of the rear stall. The bluetick rushed to his master, jumping and yapping. "What's wrong, boy?" asked Jeb, his heart beginning to beat faster. "Is something wrong?" He looked back toward the end stall. "Sam?" he called out.

This time he received a reply, but it was a faint one. Jeb heard a low groan and Sam's voice, almost in a whisper, say "Here."

A second later, Jeb stood in the open doorway of Mabel's stall. The black and white cow stood against the far wall, her eyes big, looking a little scared. It took the boy a moment of searching before he found his father. Sam lay in the back corner of the stall, next to the watering trough. He was curled up into a tight ball, his legs drawn up to his chest and his muscular arms wrapped tightly around his knees.

Jeb took the lantern down from off its nail on the stall post and came closer. "Sam? Are you all right?"

The moment the lamplight hit Sam's face, Jeb knew that the big man was far from being all right. Sam's eyes were tightly clenched and his broad face looked horribly swollen, the skin bearing an alarming reddish-purple color. Jeb also noticed that Sam was bleeding heavily from the nose. Fresh blood dribbled from his nostrils, down his chin and throat, and dyed the front of his chambray shirt an almost black shade of crimson.

"Oh, God!" breathed Jeb. "What's happened?"

Sam opened his eyes a fraction and looked up at the boy. "Get Grandma," was all he could manage to say.

Jeb didn't waste any time. He left the stall and ran along the shadowy corridor of the barn. When he reached the open door, he yelled at the top of his lungs. "Grandma!"

An instant later, the screen door opened and Grandma stepped out onto the back porch, wiping her hands on her apron. "What's the matter, boy?"

"It's Sam!" he said. "Something's wrong with him!"

Grandma didn't bother to ask what was wrong. From the grim look that crossed her face, Jeb had a feeling that she knew. Without hesitation, she bounded off the back porch and ran across the yard.

By the time she reached the barn, Grandma was pale in the face and nearly out of breath. That in itself showed how much strength she had lost; a few months ago she could have likely walked the length and breadth of Mangrum County and it wouldn't have fazed her. She leaned against the frame of the big barn door for a moment, clutching her belly and drawing in gulps of air. "Where is he?" she finally asked.

"Back in Mabel's stall," Jeb told her. "He's awful sick . . . drawn up like a stillborn calf and his face is redder than a sugar beet."

"Is his nose bleeding?" asked Grandma.

Jeb was surprised. "Yes, ma'am."

Grandma straightened her spine, fighting against her own bout of weakness. "Listen to me, Jeb. Go to the pump and draw up a bucket full of cold water. Fetch that and some dishtowels out of the counter drawer and bring them to me as quick as you can."

The boy nodded and set off on his errand. He went to the iron pump that stood midway between the farmhouse and the barn and, taking the galvanized bucket that stood next to it, positioned the container beneath the mouth of the spigot. He took the long handle in both hands and worked it a couple of times to prime the pump. A moment later, he heard a wet gurgle and felt the pressure of the water being drawn from the underground well. It came spilling out in a crystal-clear stream, as cold as a January night. It wasn't long before the bucket was filled nearly to the brim.

After the water had been drawn, Jeb left it sitting there beneath the dripping spigot and ran toward the house. He jumped up on the back porch and pulled the screen door open so forcefully it was nearly torn from the hinges.

He entered the kitchen and was startled to find dark smoke hanging in the air. Jeb looked over to the stove and saw the iron skillet in flames. Grandma had forgotten the bacon. He thought about dousing the burning pan with the pitcher of buttermilk, but remembered what Grandma had told him about grease fires. Instead, he ran to the line of canisters that sat on the side counter. Jeb took the big can that read FLOUR, opened the lid, and, getting as close to the fire as he could, dumped its contents into the skillet. The flour smothered the flames immediately, leaving only lingering smoke and the cloying scent of burnt bacon hovering over the stove.

With the threat of the fire gone, Jeb turned his attention back to the emergency at hand. He opened the end drawer of the kitchen counter and grabbed a handful of threadbare dishtowels. Then he left the house and, stopping only long enough to retrieve the bucket of well water, headed, lickity-split, toward the barn.

It wasn't long before he was back at Mabel's stall. Grandma was sitting on the hay and manure floor of the stable, cradling Sam's swollen head in her lap. "Quick, boy!" she instructed. "Bring that pail over here and douse those towels with cold water."

Jeb did as he was told. Grandma ran her hands tenderly across Sam's dark forehead and Buckshot sat in the corner whimpering helplessly as Jeb set down the bucket and dunked the dishtowels in the icy water. He wrung the excess out before handing them to Grandma. The old woman took each and tenderly wrapped them around the crown of Sam's head.

"What is it, Grandma?" Jeb asked, nearly in tears. "What's wrong with him?"

"It's the injury he got in the war," she told him calmly. "They told me he was bound to have fits every now and then."

Jeb nodded in understanding. Sam had only had one other attack that he could remember; five months after he had returned home from Germany. Jeb had missed out on most of it, having arrived home from school an hour or so after Sam's seizure had taken place. The boy recalled walking into the parlor to find his father stretched out on the sofa, his shirt bloody and half a dozen wet towels wrapped around his head. Grandma had gotten up from where she sat next to Sam and quietly explained to Jeb that the nature of his head wound sometimes caused his brain to swell. Only cold compresses and patience would provide relief. What Grandma hadn't told him, but something that Jeb secretly suspected, was that Sam's condition was potentially dangerous. If the pressure in his head lasted long enough Jeb figured there might be some permanent damage to Sam's brain. Then he would be much worse off than he was right now.

Jeb watched as Grandma wrapped the towels around Sam's head like an Indian turban. "Is there anything I can do?" he asked.

"Just pray," said Grandma. "And hold his hand. Let him know we're here."

The farmboy sat down next to the big man and took his

huge hand in his own. He stared at Sam's purple face and saw the man's eyes open slightly. "Don't worry none, Sam," Jeb said, trying hard to keep the fear out of his voice. "You're gonna be fine."

Sitting there, Jeb watched as his father's trembling eased a little and the color in his face began to gradually return to normal. Then, for a split second, something odd happened. Sam's eyes opened wide and stared straight at Jeb's freckled face. The boy was confused at first, then, slowly, something began to dawn on him. The look in Sam's eyes was recognition.

Jeb leaned forward and searched the man's eyes. For a moment, he saw the familiar expression of his father in those blue eyes; an expression full of intelligence. *He's back!* thought Jeb in elation. *He knows who I am!*

The boy squeezed his father's hand and the man squeezed back, strongly. *Come on, Pa,* he urged. *You can do it! Come back to me!*

Then, right when Jeb thought Sam was on the verge of calling him "Son," the expression of awareness vanished. Like something sinking into a bottomless lake, Sam's recognition retreated into the far reaches of his injured brain. Jeb knew then that, in a way, his father's mind was like a prison. A prison of tissue and bone, rather than of stone walls and barbed wire, but still just as confining and impenetrable.

Five minutes later, Sam was sitting up, his back to the boarded wall of the stall. His face was still a little red, but he wore the old look of mild befuddlement that he normally wore. "What happened?" he asked. "I was fixin' to milk old Mabel there, and the awfulest hurt hit me . . ."

"You just had another one of your seizures," Grandma told him. "You're okay now, but keep those towels around your head a while longer, understand?"

Sam smiled lamely in reply, unable to nod without causing the pain to flare up again.

With some effort, Grandma got to her feet and brushed the hay and dried cow manure from the seat of her flower print dress. "Come on, Jeb. Help me get Sam back to the house."

Jeb gladly did as he was told. Soon, they had escorted the big man through the center of the barn to the open door. "I reckon breakfast is stone cold by now," Grandma said sourly.

"That ain't all," added Jeb. "You forgot the bacon. It burnt plumb to a crisp."

Sam moaned. "Oh, no! Not the bacon!"

Jeb and Grandma looked at each other and laughed. "Looks like he's back to normal," the elderly woman said, relief showing in her ancient eyes.

Jeb said nothing in reply. Sadly enough, Grandma was wrong. Sam wasn't back to normal . . . but he almost had been. For one fleeting second, Jeb's father had returned, as strong of mind and spirit as he ever was. Then, just as quickly, the door of his mental prison had slammed shut and he was gone again.

Eight

Pig Killer

On Thursday night of that week, Jeb found himself in the midst of a horrifying nightmare.

He was dressed in his Sunday go-to-meeting suit, patent leather shoes, and that bow tie Grandma had bought him last Easter, the one that tended to press too tightly against his windpipe every time he swallowed. For some strange reason, he was being led up the steps of the McHenry Funeral Home, the only such establishment in the town of Pikesville. Several people he knew accompanied him up the stairs, all dressed in somber suits and black dresses with veils. There was Howard Drewer, Miss Claudine Johnson, and Miss Winston, his teacher at the elementary school the year before. All wore sad looks on their faces, although Jeb couldn't rightly figure out why.

When they reached the inner lobby with its burgundy carpet and walls of dark wood paneling, Jeb and the others were met by the mortician and funeral home director himself. Leman McHenry stared down at young Jeb with that long, cheerless face of his, then respectfully shook the boy's hand. His grasp was tight and as cold as ice. "Come with me, young man," he requested.

Jeb didn't want to, but knew that he must. Silently, he watched as Mr. McHenry opened a sliding door to one of the funeral home's four private mourning rooms. Soon, he was ushered inside by the others. Rows of wooden folding chairs lined the room on both sides, with only a narrow aisle separating them in the center. As Jeb walked down that aisle, toward the front of the mourning room, he was surprised to find every seat occupied. It looked as if most everyone in town had shown up. Ed North, Cy Newman, Bill Brownwell, and Harvey Holt were there, their prim and proper wives sitting closely beside them, dabbing their eyes with the tips of lacy white handkerchiefs. The banker, John Rutherford, sat to the right, along with Jeb's secret sweetheart, Mandy. The girl sat quietly beside her father, staring straight ahead. Jeb was surprised to see that Troy Jenkins and the Boone brothers were even there. The trio of bullies were dressed in crisp white shirts and had their hair slicked down with Wildroot Creme Oil, but they failed to display the same amount of grief and gloom that everyone else did. Instead, they smiled from ear to freshly scrubbed ear with a sadistic glee that could only be generated by purely evil hearts, especially in a place such as this.

"What's happening?" Jeb demanded to know. "Why am I here?"

Mr. McHenry said nothing in reply. He simply beckoned with a gaunt finger, urging Jeb to follow.

Fearfully, the ten-year-old continued toward the front of the mourning room. In all his born days, Jeb had never seen so many flowers in one place. Lilies, carnations, roses of all colors; it was like his grandmother's flower garden gone wild. In fact, speaking of Grandma, Jeb couldn't figure out exactly where she was at that moment. He looked around at the rows of people, but could find neither her or his father in the crowd. That, in itself, only increased the dread that began to build in the pit of his stomach.

It was only when he reached the front of the room that

Jeb realized that there were two caskets sitting there, perched on pedestals draped in silk. In a daze, the boy went to the first one. Inside, laying on crisp white linen, was Grandma Sweeny. She didn't look much like the woman who had raised Jeb from an infant; in fact, she looked more like some ill-sculpted wax figure than his paternal grandmother. Grandma looked skinny and shriveled, scarcely more than eighty or ninety pounds, and her burial gown hung on her loosely. It was her face that struck him the most severely. No amount of rouge or powder could hide the ravages that the cancer had left behind. Her eyes and cheeks were sunken and dark with shadow. It was as if someone had taken a human skull and plastered an almost transparent layer of yellowish skin over the sharp bones.

Shaken, Jeb turned to the second coffin. Inside lay his father. Sam Sweeny was dressed in his Sunday clothes, his big, work-calloused hands protruding awkwardly from the cuffs of his shirt. Jeb gasped out loud when he saw Sam's face. The man's head seemed to be twice its normal size, straining above the starched collar like a balloon that had been filled too full of air and was nearly to the point of bursting. No attempt at clever cosmetology had been done in hopes of altering the man's appearance. Sam's face was an ugly shade of purplish-black. His tongue was swollen and protruding, there was a nasty crust of dried blood beneath his nostrils, and his eyes were bugged from their sockets.

Jeb felt Leman McHenry's skeletal hand on his shoulder, more of a weight than a comfort. "They're dead, Jeb."

Shock ran through the boy's body like a jolt of electricity. "Where's my dog . . . Buckshot?"

The undertaker indicated a casket that Jeb had overlooked; a simple pine box the size of an orange crate. "Sorry, but I had to keep the lid closed," apologized McHenry. "Makeup doesn't work on a dog and there were no clothes to cover the stitches."

Abruptly, Jeb felt a loss like none he had ever experienced before. Everyone he had ever loved in his life—and had loved him in return—was gone now. His grief was swiftly followed by a mixture of fear and panic. He glanced over at Mr. Rutherford. The banker smiled smugly and, rolling up the deed to the Sweeny farm, quickly stuck it in his coat pocket. He looked around, trying to find Claudine Johnson. Grandma's best friend since childhood was nowhere to be found.

Then, suddenly, a stern voice called to him from behind. "Jeb Sweeny . . . come with me."

The boy turned to find a stone-faced woman in her mid-fifties standing in the center aisle. She was dressed from head to toe in black, but Jeb somehow knew that she normally wore such somber attire and not only to funerals. He also knew where she was from. She had come to take him to the state orphanage.

"No!" he cried, backing away from her. "I won't go!"

There was a lack of emotion in the woman's face that was almost godless in nature. "You have no choice."

Jeb felt trapped and helpless. He gauged his chance at escape and tried to dart past the matronly woman. He wasn't quite quick enough. Her hand flashed with a quickness he didn't expect, snatching him by the wrist. He tried to break free, but her fingers were like iron.

The farmboy screamed and called for help, but everyone simply bowed their heads, unable to look him in the eyes. As the woman dragged him bodily back down the aisle, he craned his head around and looked back at the three caskets. Those who lay inside the boxes could do nothing to prevent his abduction. He had no one to turn to now. His fate, however dire it might seem, had been sealed by the deaths of those he loved most in the world.

Jeb sat up in bed, his cheeks bathed in tears. His heart pounded wildly and the back of his throat ached with his silent sobbing. He sat there for a moment, trembling, trying hard to chase away those terrible images of death and abandonment. It was a hard task, trying to put such horrid pictures out of his mind, but, eventually, he was able to do just that.

The boy quietly climbed out of bed and stood there in the warm darkness for a long moment, steadying himself with the post of the varnished footboard. He listened to his father in the opposite bed, snoring in his sleep, and derived some comfort from knowing that he was still there, alive and breathing. Then Jeb left the room and padded down the hallway toward the kitchen.

Once he reached the pantry, he found himself an empty mason jar and, opening the door of the icebox, took out a pitcher of cold ice water. The Sweeny household had been blessed with electricity several years ago, but the privileges of indoor plumbing and a working toilet still eluded them. They still used the double-seated outhouse next to the hog pen, and depended on the pump over the underground well and a cold pitcher in the icebox for their daily water supply. Baths were taken in a large galvanized tub on the back porch, after the water had been heated on top of the cookstove.

Jeb poured himself a glass of ice water and chugged it down. It helped take some of the dryness from his mouth, but did little to chase away the hurtful feeling at the back of his throat. The nightmare threatened to creep back into his head, but he closed his eyes hard and fought it off. He knew if it did come back, it would stay in his thoughts until the morning and he'd never be able to get back to sleep.

He had set the pitcher back in the icebox and was closing the door, when he heard something outside. It was a rattling, wooden sound . . . as if something was dragging something tremendously heavy over a pile of discarded lumber.

Jeb walked to the back door and peered through the screen. The night was cloudy and there was scarcely any moonlight at all, but there was enough to see the hog pen and its squat shelter of sheet tin and weathered boards from where he stood. Jeb squinted, trying to detect any sign of motion out there. He saw it a moment later; a dark shadow, jerking and struggling, on the southern side of the waist-high fence.

Alarmed, the farmboy simply stood there at first, uncertain about what to do. He thought of rousing Grandma or Sam, but then thought better of it. Grandma was much too ill to be up and about at that late hour and his father would probably be no help at all. If the intruder turned out to be a raccoon or a fox, Sam would end up wanting to catch it and keep it as a pet, rather than kill it or chase it away.

Jeb knew it was up to him, and him alone, to deal with what was going on down at the hog pen. There were only five pigs in the pen, Jeb's prize winner Old Jack among them, and he couldn't see where they would let a meddlesome coon or weasel get the best of them. But, the fact of the matter was, no matter how small the intruder was, it needed to be taken care of now, so it wouldn't come back again some other night.

The ten-year-old went back to the pantry. In the darkness, he rummaged through a corner near the back of the closet. There, among a broom, a mop, and one of Grandpa Sweeny's old walking canes, was what Jeb searched for. He took the shotgun and went back to the kitchen. Quietly, he eased the back door open and stepped out onto the porch.

There, with what little moonlight shone from the sky overhead, Jeb studied the firearm he held. It was an old twenty-gauge shotgun with a single barrel and a pitted stock of hard walnut. He thumbed the locking latch to the right and allowed the breech to fall open. Inside was a single load. The brass casing at the end of the shotgun shell was green and tarnished with age, but Jeb figured it would have to do. There was half a box of shells somewhere in the pantry, but he couldn't rightly say where.

Jeb closed the breech and cradled the shotgun in the crook of his right arm. He stood on the porch for a long moment peering out at the hog pen. He searched for that strange jerking shadow again, but this time he could find nothing. Also, something else struck him as strange. Where was Buckshot? Usually, if some critter strayed onto the Sweeny property, the bluetick got wind of it immediately. He'd be out of a deep sleep and baying at the top of his lungs, loud enough to shame a banshee. But, for some reason, that was not the case that night.

Jeb stepped off into the dewy grass and, turning, crouched and peered under the edge of the back porch. "Buckshot?" he whispered. "Boy, are you awake?"

He was answered by a low whimpering. Jeb looked hard and, in the gloom, saw Buckshot huddling in the shadow of the foundation, his eyes bright with fear. Something had spooked the dog and spooked him very badly.

Jeb tried to coax the hound from beneath the porch, but nothing he could say would do the trick. Buckshot simply whined and turned his head, as if ashamed of his cowardice but not willing to give it up for a medal of bravery just yet.

"Then I reckon I'll just have to go out there alone," scolded Jeb. He thought about bringing a lantern along, but knew it would be too much trouble to round up one, let alone the matches to light it with. He took the twenty-gauge in both hands and, clad only in his underwear, started across the wet grass of the backyard toward the hog pen.

Jeb was puzzling over Buckshot's uncustomary fearfulness, when he reached the pen and realized exactly what had spooked the dog. Buckshot cringed from one thing and one thing only, and that was snakes. For some reason, the hound hated reptiles, even to point of running from them if he had to. And that was what Jeb smelled now as he approached the gate of the sturdy wooden fence. The musky scent of a serpent hung strongly in the night air. In fact, Jeb had never smelled it quite so heavily in one spot before.

The thought of stepping on a snake unexpectedly caused a shudder to run through the boy. Jeb didn't mind handling an innocent garter or green snake that he came across during his romps along Mossy Creek, but the woods that bordered the acreage of the Sweeny farm also held its fair share of rattlers and copperheads. And Jeb wasn't eager to hear the tell-tale buzz of an angry diamondback or feel the slamming sting of a copperhead's bite that night, particularly not so far away from the house.

Jeb stood still and listened. He expected to hear the hogs moving around in the shelter at the rear of the pen, maybe their excited snorting and snuffling. But he could hear nothing. The shed and the fenced-in lot around it was completely silent.

He knew then that something was gravely wrong. Once, a scavenging possum had been walking along the top of the fence and fell into the pen. Old Jack and his harem of sows had made enough racket to wake up every farmer along the rural stretch of Mossy Creek Road. By the time Jeb and Sam reached the pen, Old Jack had attacked the frightened possum and ripped the poor critter apart with his teeth.

But something more threatening than a measly possum had apparently invaded the hog pen that night. As Jeb unlatched the gate and stepped inside, he turned and looked at the southern end of the pen. Something had come through the fence, leaving a good-sized hole in the wooden slats. Before going over to investigate, Jeb walked to the hog shed and listened. He could hear the nervous breathing of the sows as they huddled in the darkness. At first he wondered if Old Jack was in there, too. But he knew the China white wasn't among them. The blue-ribbon winner was an ornery cuss and didn't have an ounce of fear in him. Maybe he had chased the intruder through the hole in the fence and off into the woods.

Once Jeb reached the demolished fence, however, he knew that wasn't what happened. He stepped into a puddle at the edge of the pen; a puddle that was much too warm and sticky to be muddy water. And, out of the corner of his eye, Jeb spotted something pale laying next to the splintered boards on the ground. He bent down and picked it up.

It was one of Old Jack's ears, torn clean out by the root.

In disgust, Jeb flung the bristly hunk of flesh away. He looked at the darkness beyond that hole in the fence, wondering exactly what had been large and ferocious enough to take on a six hundred pound hog and slaughter it without allowing it to utter a single squeal.

Suddenly, the shotgun felt incredibly heavy in Jeb's hands. His heart began to pound again as he stepped through the ragged hole and into the dewy grass just beyond. The clouds moved momentarily, shedding more moonlight with which to see. Jeb crouched and found a definite trail of blood and broken blades of grass . . . heading down into the south hollow, toward the edge of the forest.

Jeb looked back toward the farmhouse. He wondered if he should play it safe and fetch help, but figured it was his business to find the thing that had dragged the hog away. After all, Old Jack was his responsibility. Jeb had raised him

from a runt, fed and watered him, and stood by his side each
year he had been judged first-place winner at the Mangrum
County Fair. It was only fitting that Jeb would go after the
hog's killer and make it pay for what it had done.

He turned toward the dark hollow that dipped down toward
a heavy stretch of woods. A particularly dense mat of clouds
passed before the moon, turning the hollow as dark as the
mouth of a bottomless well. Jeb's heart beat quickly as he
heard the rustle of something heavy being dragged through
the high grass of the hollow. The boy breathed in deeply,
clutched the shotgun tightly in his hands, and started toward
the sound.

Every step down the grassy slope was pure torture for the
ten-year-old. He prayed that the cloudbank would thin out
and allow a little light into the hollow, but the wind was
nearly nonexistent that night and it was slow in moving.
Every so often, Jeb stopped and, holding his breath, listened.
Little by little, he was closing the distance between himself
and the thing that had abducted his prized hog. He could
hear the swish of grass and a grunt of effort scarcely twenty
yards away.

He was halfway through the hollow, when the clouds finally passed. The moon shifted into the open and shed its
pale light upon the bowl-like expanse of the grassy slope.
In an eerie blue-white glow, it revealed everything there . . .
including the one that Jeb hunted.

At first, the boy couldn't believe his eyes. Something long
and lanky and oddly shiny struggled with the pale carcass
of Old Jack. Jeb thought it was a large black dog at first
glance, a big German Shepherd or a great dane. But, as he
took a couple of steps forward, he realized that the creature
was not a dog at all. Instead, it appeared to be some hellish
cross between canine and serpent. The moonlight reflected
off roll upon roll of glossy, black scales; scales that covered

the creature from the end of its snout to the tip of its long tail.

Jeb pried his attention from the snake-critter and studied the limp form of Old Jack for a moment. The hog was dead, that was plain enough to see, even in the limited light of the moon. His eyes were open, shining dully from his bloody head and the pig appeared to have been slashed open from throat to testicles. The gaping wound glistened in the moonlight and Jeb could faintly detect Old Jack's naked entrails tucked neatly inside, almost on the verge of falling out.

The boy felt a queasiness hit him, turning his throat and the inside of his mouth hot and sickly. He gagged once, but kept from puking. Jeb managed to drive away the nausea and concentrate on the task that lay before him. Shakily, he lifted the twenty-gauge, leaning into the buttplate of the stock and aiming down the long, blued barrel.

He walked several more yards down into the hollow, then stopped. He suddenly realized that the snake-critter had also come to a halt. It lingered near the leafy edge of the thicket and, opening its toothy jaws, released the hold it had on Old Jack's left rear haunch. It snapped its slavering jaws threateningly and hissed sharply, its fetid breath escaping between fangs that were matted with stringy tissue and blood. Its huge, serpentine eyes narrowed slightly, as if warning the boy to back off.

Jeb stared into those eyes for a long moment, feeling strangely light-headed and listless. The shotgun seemed to grow heavier and heavier in his young hands, and, for a moment, he nearly dropped the weapon. Then, in the nick of time, he realized what was happening. When he was seven, Jeb had once watched as a king snake hypnotized a baby bird, causing it to turn immobile while it crept up within striking range. That was what the creature before him seemed to be doing now. Jeb pulled his gaze away and lifted the shotgun back into line. He aimed down the barrel and hooked his index finger through the trigger guard, ready to put the single load of buckshot squarely between those horrible yellow-green eyes.

But before he could act, another cloudbank showed up at the wrong time. It drifted in front of the summer moon, obscuring it completely and, once again, plunging the hollow into darkness.

Jeb didn't move. He didn't breath. He simply stood there for a long moment, listening intently. At first, he heard nothing, not even the chirping melody of crickets and tree frogs. Then came the rustle of grass and the hiss of harsh breathing. But it was no longer heading toward the edge of the woods. Instead, it was moving slowly and stealthfully back up the slope of the hollow.

With a cry, Jeb turned and ran. Revenge for the death of Old Jack was the furthest thing from his mind; plain and simple survival now occupied his thoughts. He struggled back up the slope as fast as his legs would carry him, but the hollow was a steep one and climbing it was much tougher than simply walking down. He stumbled and fell once, bruising his knee badly, but he wasted no time in getting back up. He could hear the swish of the grass behind him, as well as the hissing breath of the creature as it drew ever nearer. It was clear that the snake-critter was having less trouble climbing the grade than he was.

As Jeb reached the crest of the hollow, he felt his legs grow rubbery and he knew that his strength had played out. He dropped the shotgun, but the loss of the gun's weight didn't seem to help any. The footfalls of the monster seemed to be only a few feet behind him now and he could even feel its hot breath against his bare back, prickling his naked skin with goosebumps.

Oh, God! thought Jeb, sobs of desperation and utter exhaustion heaving up from his youthful lungs. *It's gonna catch me! Then it'll kill me just like it did Old Jack!*

Then, just when the boy had just about given up, an unlikely savior appeared out of nowhere. As Jeb reached the top of the hollow and his feet touched level ground, he heard a deep-throated growl. Buckshot stood there, his feet planted solidly and his yellowed teeth bared menacingly.

Jeb staggered past Buckshot and, unable to run any further, fell to the ground, gasping for breath. He turned and looked back toward the lip of the hollow. The dog's back was arched threateningly and its growling turned into a fit of loud barking. Jeb waited for the creature to top the rise and launch itself at the bluetick hound, but, for some reason, it didn't. The darkness beyond the top of the hollow remained empty.

"Good boy, Buckshot!" said Jeb. He found the strength to get back to his feet and soon joined his protector. The ten-year-old peered down into the hollow and heard the swish of grass parting. But, thankfully, the noise came from a distance. Buckshot's show of bravado had done the trick. The snake-critter had been bluffed into retreating. It uttered one last hiss of serpentine contempt as it descended into the hollow and returned to the dead hog it had left near the edge of the woods.

"Come on, Buckshot," said Jeb, breathing a sigh of relief. "You spooked him good, but he might get up his nerve and come back." Jeb hoped that he was wrong about that point, but he didn't want to take any chances. A thing like that was certainly capable of doing the unexpected.

Shakily, Jeb reached down and grabbed the back of the coonhound's leather collar. Once Buckshot gathered his nerve, he was difficult to keep at bay. Jeb tugged at the dog's collar until, reluctantly, the hound loosened up and accompanied Jeb home. The boy left the twenty-gauge where he had dropped it a third of the way down the hollow. He knew that the evening dew would likely rust the gun, but he didn't care. No amount of scolding or whipping on Grandma's part was more frightening to him than the dark thing that lurked at the bottom of the hollow, just out of sight.

Nine

Doubting Thomas

Sheriff Ed North sucked on the end of his handrolled cigarette and shook his head. He crouched and examined the jagged hole in the fence of the pigpen, then looked down at the pool of blood at his feet. Old Jack's ear lay a few feet away, more blue than pink now, surrounded by a buzzing halo of green-tailed flies.

"Is this where you saw the critter that made away with your hog?" he asked once again.

"No," replied Jeb. "Like I said before, I followed its trail to the hollow down yonder. That's where I got the first glimpse of it . . . near the edge of the woods."

"Um-hmm," said the lawman. His knees popped as he stood back up and he looked back toward the board and tin shelter, seeming more than a little perplexed. In the shadows beyond the little doorway, he could see the sows huddled there, still afraid to come out.

"What do you think, Sheriff?" asked Sam. "Huh? What was it that Jeb saw?"

North glanced irritably at the big man who stood nearby. "Don't rightly know right now," he replied. He looked back at the boy. "What caused you to come out here last night, Jeb? Did you hear Old Jack squeal?"

Jeb shook his blond head. "No, sir. In fact, as far as I know, Old Jack didn't utter a sound."

The sheriff snorted in disbelief. "That ain't likely. A hog would scream its durn fool head off if its belly was being ripped open, don't you think?"

"You calling my grandson a liar, Sheriff?" asked Grandma Sweeny. The elderly woman was looking more pale and peaked than usual that morning.

"No, ma'am," said North apologetically. "I wasn't implying anything of the sort. Just seems strange that something could slaughter that hog without waking up half the county."

"But, obviously, something did," said Grandma smugly.

"Yes, ma'am," replied the lawman. He stepped through the gap in the fence and studied the grass on the other side. The blades were bent and coated with droplets of tacky blood. "Looks like it hauled it down into the hollow here."

"Didn't Jeb just say that?" asked Sam.

The sheriff ignored him and started toward the edge of the hollow. Jeb, Grandma, and Sam accompanied him. Soon, they were making their way down the grassy slope. Jeb looked around. The hollow looked a lot less spooky during the daytime, but the shadowy woods just beyond still held a degree of menace.

A third of the way down, Ed North squatted and picked up the shotgun. The twenty-gauge was still coated with dewdrops. He opened the breech and checked the chamber. "It's still loaded, Jeb. Why didn't you shoot the critter if you had it in your sights?"

Jeb thought for a moment, unable to find an answer at first. "I don't know. I was just plumb scared, I reckon. But, anyway, I don't think it would've killed it if I had shot."

North rolled his eyes slightly. "Yeah, 'cause it was covered with scales. I've heard that before."

"From John Haskel," Grandma reminded with some satisfaction. "And Curtis Jones, too, I believe. Did you ever find out what got into his chicken coop and ripped apart all sixty of his prime laying hens?"

"No, ma'am," admitted North. There was an edge of hostility in the constable's voice. "Not yet."

The sheriff handed the shotgun to Jeb, then they continued down the steep embankment. Soon, they reached the bottom. Jeb pointed at an impression in the high grass. "I think this is where he dropped Old Jack long enough to chase after me."

North poked at the grass with the toe of his shoe, pushing the blades of sawgrass aside. "Plenty of blood, that's for sure," he said.

Suddenly, Sam's excited voice called to them from the edge of the woods. "Hey! Come here! Look at what I found!"

A moment later, they were squatting next to the burly farmer. He pointed to a track in the earth. It was hard to make out, but several features were clear enough. Whatever had left the impression had possessed uncommonly long toes, nearly four inches in length. And the ends had been topped with sharp claws.

"What do you make of that, Sheriff?" asked Grandma, a little winded from her long walk across the hollow.

North shrugged. "I don't know. A bear, maybe."

Grandma laughed. "A bear, my foot! Don't look like no bear track I ever did see!"

The lawman seemed embarrassed by the woman's rebuff. "I reckon you can do better, Mrs. Sweeny?" he asked a little snidely.

Grandma bristled. "Don't you sass back at me, Edward North!" she warned. "I taught you in Sunday school when you wasn't nothing but an ill-mannered, lazy young'un. You'd do better to show a little respect to your elders, let alone a county taxpayer who pays your salary every month."

The sheriff's face grew even redder than before. "Sorry, ma'am. I reckon this whole mess with all these animals being slaughtered has got me frustrated. Didn't mean to snap out at you like that."

Grandma didn't seem to fully believe him, but she let the matter go anyway.

The Sweeny family stood at the edge of the forest, while the sheriff drew his revolver and poked through the underbrush. It wasn't long before he gave up his half-hearted search. "Didn't see much of anything," he said when he returned. "Some more blood and a few broken branches, but that's all. I still think it was a bear. That's the only critter that'd be strong enough to drag a six hundred pound hog so far a distance."

Jeb looked a little angry. "Like I said before, I saw what it was. And it wasn't no stupid ol' bear."

Sheriff North placed a hand on the boy's shoulder. "Well, we'll see about that, Jeb."

Fifteen minutes later, they were back up the hollow and at the rear porch of the Sweeny house. Jeb and Sam helped Grandma onto an old milking stool that sat against the back wall, while North drew himself a dipper of cold well water from a covered bucket near the screen door.

"Well, folks," he said as he returned the dipper to its rightful place on top of the wooden lid. "I'll surely look into this and let you know when I find out anything."

Although Grandma was winded by her long walk to the bottom of the hollow and back, that still failed to put a damper on her temper. "I suggest you find the critter that's doing this killing, Sheriff. Folks are beginning to get skittish and scared. They'll start shooting at anything that passes by in the night before long, and that might mean somebody innocent getting hurt for no good reason."

North took her advice with a grain of salt. "I'll do my best." He tipped his brown fedora. "Good day to you all."

The elected sheriff of Mangrum County climbed back into his patrol car and, cranking the engine, backed down the dusty drive of the Sweeny farm. When he reached the rutted stretch of red clay known as Mossy Creek Road, he swung the steering wheel around and headed northward, back toward town. Ed North hated driving south of the Cumberland River bridge. For one thing, he despised leaving the fan-cooled comfort of his office on the second floor of the county courthouse. And, secondly, he didn't particularly enjoy breaking a sweat trying to wash the powdery film of clay dust off his car after a trip down Mossy Creek Road. Plain old water only made a mess. It took soap and elbow grease to scrub it clean again, and Ed wasn't much for exerting himself, particularly in the sweltering heat of summer.

As he drove, North thought about the series of strange animal killings he had been obligated to investigate. First there had been the bloody slaughter and devourment of John Haskel's Holstein cow, Buttercup. Then, a couple days later, Curtis Jones had heard a godawful racket coming from his henhouse and gone out to find all sixty of his laying hens dead. Something he had only gotten a fleeting glimpse of had ripped open every last one of them and sucked them dry of blood. Now it was Jeb Sweeny's prized hog, Old Jack, who had been brutally slain and stolen.

Thinking on it, the sheriff came to the conclusion that it wasn't the wanton bloodletting of the killings themselves that bothered him the most. Rather, it was the general description of the elusive culprit that bugged him to no end. All three— John, Curtis, and Jeb—had claimed that the murderous critter was some sort of half-dog, half-snake with big yellow-green eyes, long fangs, and a shiny coat of black scales.

Ed North was a narrow-minded and unimaginative man.

Even with three eyewitnesses, the sheriff simply could not
believe that such a creature existed, let alone roamed the hills
and hollows of Mangrum County. He had examined every
site of carnage, as well as whatever was left of the slaughtered animals, and, from what he'd seen, he knew that the
animal responsible was powerful . . . much stronger than any
dog could be, even if it was an incredibly big one. No, he
was convinced that some other critter was attacking the farm
animals, maybe a mountain lion or a bear.

When the sheriff crossed the Pikesville city limits, he
drove down the hot and deserted stretch of Main Street, made
a U-turn in the middle, and parked the patrol car out front
of Hudson's Cafe. As he climbed out of the car and walked
around the front bumper, North ran his finger across the
slope of the navy blue hood. A powdery coating of light red
dust smudged his fingertip and he cussed beneath his breath.
Looked like the old Ford was in for another scrubbing.

He opened the door of Pikesville's one and only restaurant,
and stepped inside. The jangling of a copper cowbell over the
door heralded his entrance, drawing the attention of the few
patrons who sat at the tables and counter at the hour of eleven.
Little Joey Pickford sat atop a padded stool, digging into a
double-scoop hot fudge sundae with chopped nuts and
whipped cream. Laura Tate, the first-grade teacher at the elementary school, sat at the end of the counter, drinking a glass
of lemonade and nibbling on a chicken salad sandwich while
reading a *Life* magazine with Clark Gable on the cover. Cy
Newman and Bill Brownwell sat at a table near the front window, drinking black coffee and, naturally, playing checkers.
Both men glanced up when the sheriff walked in, traded a sour
look, then returned to their seventh game of the morning.

North heard someone clear their throat and he looked over
to where the cafe's owner, Gladys Hudson, stood behind the
counter, dressed in her pink and white uniform, her hands

planted firmly on her sizable hips. "You got a head cold, Sheriff?" she asked sharply.

The lawman knew what she was driving at. Remembering his manners, he removed his hat and hung it on the coat rack next to the door. The dusty fedora joined the ancient headgear of Cy and Bill. Ed smoothed down his rusty red hair and took a stool at the counter. "What's the specialty today, Gladys?" he asked.

The buxom, middle-aged woman in the too-tight uniform didn't bother to hand him a menu. "It's Wednesday, ain't it?" she said gruffly. "Chicken salad sandwich with your choice of tater chips or home fries."

North recalled the mess in Curtis Jones's henhouse. "Uh, no chicken for me. Just give me a big bowl of that fire-alarm chili of yours, heavy on the hot sauce and a bunch of packs of those little crackers." He glanced down at what the teacher was drinking. "Oh, and I'll have one of them lemonades, too."

"Dessert?" asked Gladys, knowing that the sheriff suffered from a notorious sweet tooth.

The sheriff looked over to the pastry shelf and saw a fresh pie sitting on the cooling rack. "Banana creme?" he asked hopefully.

Gladys nodded. "With plenty of meringue on top, just the way you like it."

North's mouth watered. "Then put me down for a slice of that, too."

As Gladys went about the task of preparing the sheriff's order, North looked around the interior of the cafe once again. Despite the four ceiling fans that spun lazily overhead, the place was too hot and humid. He glanced back at Cy and Bill, but they ignored him. He turned toward Joey. The six-year-old rewarded him with a smile wreathed by a gooey beard of fudge and whipped cream. He avoided looking at the pretty teacher altogether. Ed knew if it got back to his wife, Florence, that he'd even eyed Laura Tate, there would be hell to pay in the bedroom for at least a month.

Suddenly, he looked toward the row of booths that ran along the side of the wall and spotted someone he had missed before. "Gladys," he called. "When my food's ready, bring it to that back booth over yonder, will you?"

The sheriff knew that she'd heard him, although she didn't give any indication of having done so. He left the stool and walked around the dozen empty tables that awaited the lunchtime crowd. Soon, he was standing next to the back booth. "Howdy, Skyler," he said.

A tall, raw-boned man in his late fifties sat on one of the booth's bench seats. He wore a filthy V-neck shirt beneath even grungier overalls, and what little hair he had left stood up in jagged, unruly cowlicks. The man looked as if he'd tripped and fallen into an open cesspool, and nearly smelled just as bad. From where North stood, he could detect the sour stench of the man's body odor. It reminded him of sliced onions that had lain out in the open way too long.

Skyler Lee looked up from his meal, which consisted of a BLT, home fries, and a sweating glass of iced tea with several slices of lemon floating on the top. A mixture of irritation and suspicion shown in the man's eyes. "What'd I do now, Sheriff?"

North understood what the man meant. Skyler Lee was no stranger to the Mangrum County jail. Every other week, Ed picked the old hermit up for cussing old ladies or children, or just plain old public drunkenness. Once, last summer, Skyler had downed a whole quart of home-brewed moonshine and staggered down the center of Main Street, plumb buck naked. That, in itself, had cost Skyler ninety days in the hoosegow.

"Nothing, Skyler," assured the sheriff. "I just thought I'd join you for lunch, if you don't mind the company."

Skyler looked at the lawman as if he were a two-headed rooster. "Being right sociable today, ain't we, Sheriff? I reckon next you'll be inviting me over to your house for Sunday supper and homemade ice cream on the front porch afterwards."

North ignored the man's sarcasm. "So, Skyler, how've you been? Haven't seen you in town a while."

"Been busy," was all he said in reply.

"The jail hasn't been the same without you."

Skyler expelled a mule's bray of a laugh. "Yeah, sure!"

North waited until Gladys had brought his chili, pie, and lemonade. He peeled the saltines from their wrappers, ground them between his fingers, and mixed them in with the thick concoction of spicy beans and beef. When he had finally done that, he wet his whistle with a sip of lemonade—a little too tart for his taste—and decided it was time to come to the root of the matter. "Truth is, Skyler, there was something I wanted to talk to you about."

Again, that flare of hostile suspicion. "What?"

"It ain't nothing you've done," said the sheriff. "It's this damned rash of animal killings that's been going on lately."

For the first time since North's intrusion to his meal, Skyler seemed a tad interested in what the sheriff had to say. "I reckon you mean John Haskel's cow and Jones's flock of hens."

"Yes," admitted Ed. "That and Jeb Sweeny's China white hog."

A troubled look came to Skyler's eyes. "You mean Old Jack? Well, ain't that a bitch! When'd it happen?"

"Last night. Something broke into the Sweenys' pigpen and made away with the hog. Dragged it clear down into a hollow and off into the woods."

"All six hundred pounds of it?" asked Skyler. An expression of mild amusement suddenly gleamed in the hermit's eyes. "What do you think did it, Sheriff?"

"Had to be a mighty powerful critter," said Ed. "A bear, more than likely."

"A bear!" barked Skyler. "You know well as I do that's a load of bullshit! There ain't been a bear within two hundred miles of Mangrum County in the last sixty years!"

North was annoyed by the man's statement. "Then what the hell do *you* think it was?"

Skyler grinned, showing off a crooked picket fence of tobacco-stained teeth. "Well, way I've heard it, it was some sort of ornery, black snake-dog."

"But, dammit, that don't make any sense!"

"Take it from me, Sheriff," said Skyler. "There's things out there that God made, but would just soon forget about. Maybe this critter is one of 'em."

North didn't want to consider the impossible, but couldn't help but at least try. "I reckon it could be some kinda sideshow freak that got loose. That circus train did derail last May up near Watertown."

"Hell!" growled Skyler as he downed his last bite of bacon, lettuce, and tomato on toast. "Weren't no freak. That's what a lot of other folks in town are saying."

"Then I suppose you have the answer," retorted North, a little peeved.

"Maybe," said Skyler. "I've been studying on the matter a bit on my own time and I've just about figured that, whatever it was, didn't come from right here in Mangrum County."

The lawman shook his head. "Now, come on, Skyler, don't give me that crap about this critter coming from—"

"Fear County?" asked Skyler Lee. "And why not? Everybody knows that place is bad medicine. Hell, even the railroad and the state highway snakes around it instead of cutting plumb through. When I was a young'un, my pappy told me horror stories about that place. How nothing lives within its border but things evil and out of sync with the rest of nature. A cancer on the state of Tennessee, that's what it is!"

Ed North's broad face grew stubborn. "I ain't gonna listen to it, Skyler! Old wives' tales, that's all it is."

"Just trying to be helpful," said Skyler, slurping down a gulp of iced tea.

The sheriff picked at his chili for a while, then pushed it aside and went straight to the banana creme pie. "Skyler, do you still have those two redbones of yours?"

"Slim and Jim?" asked Skyler with a proud grin. "Why, sure I do. Finest damned pair of coonhounds in the state!"

"You think you could help me track down this critter if it comes down to it?"

For a moment, uncertainty clouded Skyler's eyes. Obviously, his belief about the creature originating from Fear County had not been a joke, but a genuine concern. "Well, I don't know about that, Sheriff . . ."

"Don't think those dogs can handle it, huh?" goaded North.

To Skyler Lee, questioning the ability of a man's hunting dogs was the same as making fun of the size of his pecker. "Damn straight they can handle it! If that bastard's out there, Slim and Jim'll track it down! I'd bet my bottom dollar on it!"

"Good," said North, satisfied with the trick he had just pulled on the ignorant hermit. "Then, if these killings continue, I can depend on you to help me out? Of course, I'm sure the county will be more than happy to pay you for the use of your dogs."

Skyler's eyes twinkled at the promise of drinking and gambling money. "Yes, sir, Sheriff. You just give me a call and we'll be ready."

"Fine," said Ed North. He dug into the heart of the pie, his fork poking through two inches of gooey meringue and hitting the creamy filling underneath. He shoveled a heaping bite into his mouth. He was determined to show the folks of Mangrum County that he wasn't the lazy-butt everyone thought he was. With the help of Skyler Lee and his hounds, he would track down the critter that had been terrorizing farms all over the county and prove that it was not some devilish monster, but something plain and unremarkable, just like he had claimed all along.

Ten

On the Corner of Willow and Main

It was the following Saturday when Jeb once again walked the sun-baked streets of Pikesville. The boy had accompanied Sam and Grandma to town, hoping that this trip to town would turn out to be much more agreeable—and much less painful—than the previous one. He and Sam had parked the wagon next to the courthouse lawn, then started walking toward the heart of Main Street. Grandma had gone into the courthouse to visit the county clerk on the ground floor and attend to some "legal business," as she had put it. That phrase alone was enough to bother Jeb and revive some of the fears the ten-year-old harbored about his grandmother's failing health and the questionable future that lay ahead for them all.

As he and Sam crossed Willow Drive, Jeb pushed such grim thoughts from his mind. The cold-blooded murder of Old Jack, as well as the thing that had made away with the hog afterwards, was more than enough to occupy his young mind. Obviously, Sheriff North hadn't believed his story about the half-dog, half-snake, and neither did a lot of other folks in Mangrum County. They thought he was just some motherless child starving for attention and making up stories. The same disbelievers might swallow similar tales told by

John Haskel or Curtis Jones, but that was only because they
were adults.

One of the reasons why Jeb had chosen to come to town
with Sam and Grandma that morning sat on an empty nail
keg on the corner of Willow and Main, just to the left of
the front entrance of the Mangrum County Bank. Roscoe
Ledbetter hunched over his time-worn Fender flattop, making
the guitar squeal and squall like a wooden box full of angry
piglets. Some folks might have considered the blues that
flowed from the instrument to be just a bunch of noise and
racket, but that was only the opinion of those who thought
there was no other music in the world but gospel and bluegrass. Jeb knew better. He knew there was something in Roscoe's unique rhythms and moaning lyrics that came from
some place other than his fingers and voice box. Jeb was
sure the sorrowful songs of chain-gangs, lost love, and whistling freight trains in the dead of night came from deep down
in the Negro's soul; a soul that had suffered many of the
same trials and injustices that Roscoe sang about with such
agonized abandon.

Roscoe was finishing up the last chorus about a man sinking to his death in a moonlit swamp, when Jeb and Sam
stepped upon the curb. A couple of men who worked at
Benny Saunders's sawmill waited until the black man finished his song, tossed a few spare cents into the hat at his
feet, then headed on down the sidewalk toward Hudson's
Cafe for a rootbeer float and some joking around with Gladys.

As Roscoe eyed the collection he had netted so far that
summer morning—a whopping take of eleven cents—he
lifted his bald head and grinned broadly. The sun hit his
dental work just right, nearly blinding the boy and his slow-
witted father with a burst of golden light. "Well, I'll be dog-
gone if it ain't Jeb Sweeny!"

"Howdy, Roscoe," said Jeb. The man's apparent happiness to see him helped cheer the boy up, if only a little bit.

The Negro shifted his gaze from Jeb to the husky man that stood next to him. His eyes narrowed a bit behind the thick lenses of his glasses. "And who is this here? Why, it's Sam Sweeny! Lordy mercy, man, I ain't seen you in a coon's age!"

Sam stood there for a moment, uncomfortably appraising the black man's outstretched hand. "Uh, who are you?" he finally said, looking more than a little dumbfounded.

Roscoe stared at the big farmer for a long moment. "Aw, now, come on, Sam! Quit your funning. It's me, your old picking and singing partner, Roscoe Ledbetter."

Sam studied the bluesman hard, trying to remember. "Sorry," he finally said with a shrug of his huge shoulders. "I just don't recollect you at all."

As Roscoe sat there on his nail keg, looking a little confused and hurt, Jeb tugged on the sleeve of Sam's chambray shirt. "Sam, why don't you go on down to the drugstore. Mr. Nipper's bound to have the new Superman in today. I know you can't read the words, but you can look at the pictures until I get there. How does that sound?"

"Swell!" said Sam with a grin. "But don't be too long, Jeb. Mr. Nipper don't much like it when I look at the funny books and don't buy nothing."

"I'll be along directly," promised the boy.

Jeb and Roscoe watched as the big man continued on down the sidewalk, careful not to step on a crack in fear of breaking a bone in Grandma Sweeny's back. When he had reached the entrance of Nipper's Rexall and stepped inside, Roscoe turned to the boy. "What's the matter with your papa, Jeb? He didn't no more know me from the man in the moon."

If there was one thing Jeb hated to do more than anything

else, it was trying to explain his father's condition. But he knew he owed it to Roscoe. After all, the rambling bluesman had saved him from the awful fate of having to swallow and digest a live shit beetle. "He got hurt in the War," Jeb told him. "He was crouched in a foxhole, fighting them dirty Nazis, when a cannon shell landed smack-dab in the center of the trench. Everyone else in his unit was killed, but the force of the explosion, it gave Papa what the doctors call a "concussion." It addled his brain and made him forget pert near everything. He's a lot better than he was when he first came home, but he still can't do a lot of things he could do before. Things like read or drive or cipher numbers in his head."

"Or play a guitar like he once did?" asked Roscoe.

"Yes, sir," admitted Jeb sorrowfully. "He wouldn't know one end of a guitar from the other."

A great sadness filled the Negro's eyes and, at first, Jeb was sure that he might start crying. "That's a shame, Jeb," he said. "A godawful shame, if I ever did hear one in my life."

"Yeah," agreed the boy. "It is that."

"It pains me, Jeb. Pains me deep down in my soul."

Jeb nodded silently. He knew how that felt.

Wanting to change the subject, Jeb peeked into the sweat-stained bowl of Roscoe's hat. "So, how are you doing out here this summer?" he asked. "Making any money with your playing?"

Roscoe shook his shiny head. "Afraid pickings have been thin last few days, but, then, folks are usually stingy when I first set up shop in a town. Takes a spell before they grow accustomed to me being here. After that, they loosen up their pursestrings a bit and I'll end up making up to a dollar or two a day."

"That ain't bad," said Jeb.

"In the meantime, I've had time to write a few songs of my own," Roscoe told him. "Matter of fact, I thought up a new one this very morning. It's called the "Cranky Woman Rag." Here, let me play you a little of it."

Jeb watched as the bluesman hugged his guitar closely and began to run the slide-bottle up and down the inlaid neck. The instrument moaned mournfully in Roscoe's black hands and he began to sing in that gravelly voice of his.

"My woman, she's skinny and she's lean . . . Ain't much to look at, but she can cook and she can clean . . . She can lay that loving on you, like an angel in a dream . . . But it's that time o' the month, Lawd . . . She's ornery and she's mean!"

Amazed, the boy watched as the Negro's hands fluttered along the hourglass body of polished wood, inlaid mother-of-pearl, and taut steel strings. It was a pure wonder, the way the man pulled so many conflicting sounds from a single musical instrument.

After a moment of picking and strumming, Roscoe sang the ending chorus. *"Why she be so doggoned cranky? . . . Lawd, please help me through the day . . . If she don't stop her bitching and moaning . . . Hooo, I might just run away!"*

When the song was done, Roscoe lifted his eyes to the boy. "Well, what do you think?"

Jeb shrugged. "I didn't rightly understand all of it, but the guitar picking was pretty good."

Roscoe could detect a shade of confusion in the boy's eyes. "I reckon you ain't quite old enough to fully appreciate such a song just yet. But you will one day. God help you, you will."

For a while, they discussed such dry topics as the hot weather and the big Fourth of July celebration that was scheduled for the following weekend on the front lawn of the Mangrum County courthouse. Then Roscoe regarded the tow-headed boy with the clear blue eyes and the spattering of dark freckles. "Seems that I heard you had a little excitement over at your place a few nights ago," he said. "Something killed your hog."

"Yes, sir," replied Jeb. He looked up and down the sidewalk, but nobody seemed to be within earshot. "Some critter broke through the fence and butchered Old Jack, my blue-ribbon winner. Then it dragged him off down the hollow and into the woods."

There seemed to be something other than interest in the black man's inquisitive gaze. "And this critter . . . exactly what did it look like?"

Jeb hesitated. "Aw, you'd probably not even believe me if I told you."

"Give me a try," urged Roscoe. "I might surprise you."

"Well, it was long and lanky, about seven feet from snout to tail. It had a long, triangle-shaped head like a snake's and greenish-yellow eyes and sharp teeth about as long as your middle finger. Oh, and it had scales. Pitch black ones, on every inch of its body."

Roscoe nodded sagely. "And I suppose nobody believes you, either. Most particularly the sheriff."

"Yeah," agreed Jeb, surprised by the man's understanding. "They all think I was seeing things or sleepwalking. Either that or flat out lying through my teeth."

"Well, Jeb Sweeny," said the old Negro. "If it'll make you feel any better, let me tell you right here and now that I believe you. I believe every last word of what you've just told me."

"You do?" asked Jeb. "Why's that?"

"Well, if you promise to keep it a secret, I'll be glad to tell you," said Roscoe.

Jeb crossed his heart and spit on the sidewalk. "Honest injun and hope to die!"

Ledbetter nodded, knowing that the boy's word was as good as gold. "The reason I believe you, Jeb, is because I saw the same critter myself just last Monday night. Kinda half dog and half black snake it was. The spawn of Old Scratch him ownself!"

"That's right!" said Jeb excitedly. "Did it attack you?"

"No, but it had a mind to at first," said Roscoe. "Had a hungry look in those big, ol' yeller eyes, like it was sizing me up for a meal. And it probably would've given me a try, if I hadn't chased it away."

"How'd you do that?"

"By singing to it," said Roscoe with a sly wink.

Jeb frowned. "Aw, you don't sing all that bad, Roscoe."

The Negro laughed loudly and slapped the threadbare knees of his trousers. "Naw, son, that ain't what I meant! I sang hymns at the critter; gospel tunes of Jesus dying on the cross, the pearly gates of heaven, and redemption. For a hellish creature such as it, those songs were like pure poison. Seized its muscles up and wouldn't let it take another step toward me. After a while, the critter grew tired of fighting and slithered off into the woods to find easier prey."

"But what is this thing?" Jeb wanted to know. "And where did it come from?"

"Well, I can't rightly say what the critter is, except that it ain't no normal member of the animal kingdom," said Roscoe. "As for where it hailed from, well, some folks in town have a definite opinion about that, particularly the superstitious kind."

Jeb nodded in understanding. "Fear County."

"Yep, that's what they say. And I ain't about to dispute it, either."

"Have you ever been there?" asked the boy. "Have you ever been to Fear County?"

A dark shadow seemed to veil the black man's normally cheerful eyes. "Yes, son, I have been there once in my life. But I sure as hell ain't ever going back again."

"Why?"

The seriousness in Roscoe's eyes was almost frightening in its intensity. "I'll tell you why. 'Cause it's an evil place, that's why. Ain't nothing within its boundaries but badness, cruelty, and hate. There are folks and critters there that ain't like any you ever came across in your life, and hopefully never will. It's like Hell opened up and belched up its worst, and the state of Tennessee put it on the map and called it Fear County."

"You mean there ain't no good at all there?" asked Jeb.

Roscoe's eyes softened a degree. "Now let me back up here a little. I was wrong. There *is* one point of decency and goodness in that dark land. And that's the one known as the Granny Woman."

"The Granny Woman," Jeb said softly. Speaking her name was like mentioning the great and powerful Wizard of Oz or Santa Claus, it held that much reverence.

"Yes," said Roscoe with a smile. "She's a witch, but a good one. They say she lives in the black heart of that sinful county and that she's like a burst of pure, clean sunshine in the dead of night. Folks even claim she can heal the sick and bring the dead back to life, if she has a mind to."

"You don't say," said Jeb, his young eyes wide with awe.

"Well, personally, I don't know one way or the other," admitted Roscoe honestly. "I've never had the honor of meeting the lady. But I've heard that she does have the power to do a lot of things ordinary folks could never dream of doing."

Before Jeb could find out more about Fear County or its inhabitants, the joyful voice of a thirty-eight-year-old man drew his attention from down the sidewalk. "Hey, Jeb!" called Sam, standing in the doorway of the drugstore. "You were right. Mr. Nipper got in the new Superman, just like you said!"

"I'll be there in a minute, Sam," promised Jeb. "Just hold your horses."

"Okay," said the slow-witted farmer. "But hurry, will you? It looks like a real humdinger!"

Roscoe shook his head sadly. "Ain't there nothing the doctors can do for him, Jeb?"

"Afraid not," Jeb told him. "They say operating on his brain is too risky. It could end up killing him for sure."

The boy looked over at the black man for a reply, but he said nothing. However the expression in his magnified eyes said it all. A man who doesn't remember his friends and family is better off dead, they seemed to say. Jeb knew the traveling bluesman had too much tact and compassion to say such a harsh thing out loud, but then, Jeb had thought the same thing himself more than once.

"Well, I reckon I'd best get on to the drugstore," said Jeb. "I promised Sam that I'd read him that funny book. Besides, I have to pick up some medicine for my grandmother."

Roscoe reached out and offered his coal black hand. When the ten-year-old took it and they exchanged a vigorous shake, the guitar-player grinned broadly. "It surely was nice visiting with you, Jeb," said Roscoe sincerely. "Whenever you're in town, stop on by and we'll chew the fat for a spell."

"I will," promised Jeb. "How long will you be staying in Pikesville?"

The old man shrugged his bony shoulders. "I came to see the fireworks, but I'll probably stick around till the end of July. When I find a place where folks tolerate me and don't burn a cross near my campsite, well, I tend to want to stay put for a while."

Jeb wasn't sure what the Negro was talking about. A cross was supposed to be a sacred thing. Who would be mean enough to set fire to one?

"I'll see you around," he said and started for Nipper's Pharmacy.

"You take care, Jeb," replied Roscoe with a golden grin. "And keep an eye on your Papa. Slow-minded people are a lot like niggers; some folks are scared plumb to death of them and, sometimes, that can turn into hatred, pure and simple."

Again, Jeb wasn't quite sure what Roscoe meant. He didn't let on, though. He simply nodded and headed down the sidewalk. He knew Mr. Nipper didn't like Sam hanging around the drugstore for too long. Some of the kids who came in to buy copies of their favorite comics shied away when they found a thirty-eight-year-old young'un standing by the magazine rack, grinning and giggling at the exploits of Batman and Little Lulu.

As he stepped inside the shop—which smelled of peppermint, pipe tobacco, and rubbing alcohol—Jeb thought again about his interrupted conversation with Roscoe Ledbetter. He thought of the snake-critter, the Granny Woman, and the providence of Fear County, which lay scarcely sixteen miles away, yet seemed as far from reach as Africa or Egypt.

He found himself wondering if the notorious county was similar to the dark dreamscape that had plagued his sleep for the past couple of weeks. He thought of the nightmares, full of black shadows, unfamiliar sounds, and things that crept through the underbrush, just out of sight. And Jeb wondered if the dreams had been only that . . . and not something more sinister and prophetic in nature.

Eleven

Damsel In Distress

"Come on, boy!" called Jeb as he waded, barefooted, through the center of Mossy Creek. That Sunday afternoon was oppressively hot and muggy, and it felt good to be out of his church clothes and back into his loose-fitting overalls. The water of the stream was deliciously cool around his feet. A couple of hours ago, he had been imprisoned in tight, patent-leather torture devices, but now they were gone, tucked away in the dusty shadows beneath his bed. Jeb could wiggle his toes again and, in his youthful mind, that meant freedom.

Jeb turned and regarded his dog. Buckshot was standing, knee deep, in the babbling brook, looking for crawdaddies. Jeb shook his head and laughed. He knew the bluetick's vigilance was due more out of fear than menace. Only a few days before, the hound had played a game of cat-and-mouse with a pink-shelled crayfish in the shallows of the very creek they were now in. His leisurely stalking had backfired however. The crawdaddy had grabbed hold of the dog's upper lip with its pincher and refused to let go until Jeb pried it apart. Buckshot had ended up with a swollen muzzle and a new respect for anything bearing tenacious claws.

"You'd best get a move on, Buckshot," Jeb said with a

grin. "I recall there's a nest full of crawdads somewhere here-abouts."

The boy knew his dog couldn't understand him, but he seemed to. Buckshot quickened his pace, his eyes studying the sandy bottom of the creek, alert for the first sign of a pesky crustacean with darting pinchers.

Somewhere in the distance, thunder rumbled, heralding the promise of a summer shower. Jeb ignored it and continued along the winding channel of Mossy Creek. A mile to the north, the creek connected with the Cumberland River, just a spit and a holler from the concrete supports of the bridge. Jeb really had no purpose to his roaming that day. He simply relished the coolness of the water around his feet, the dense shade of the trees that grew heavily along the creekbank, and the solitude of simply being alone.

That, however, was about to change.

He was approaching a bend in the stream, when he thought he heard something up ahead. The gurgle and trickle of water over smooth creekstones masked the sound at first and he had to strain to hear it a second time. Then it came to him. It was a voice; a clearly *female* voice.

"Here, puss! Here, puss, puss!"

Jeb scratched his blond head and turned to Buckshot. "Who in tarnation could that be?" he asked.

The bluetick hound simply stared back at him silently, twitching an ear at a gnat that was too stubborn to leave him alone.

"Come on, boy," said Jeb. "Let's take a look."

The farmboy rounded the bend in Mossy Creek and knew immediately where he was. It was a beautiful spot where the creekbanks were covered with soft moss and tall green ferns. The stream split in half at one point, snaking around a long sandbar that stuck up out of the water like the barnacled back of some prehistoric sea monster.

What surprised Jeb the most when be reached the spot was the one who stood atop that pebbly sandbar, yelling to the top of her lungs. In fact, it was probably the last person on earth Jeb expected to find there, out in the middle of the backwoods.

Mandy Rutherford stood there, dressed in a frilly Sunday dress of pastel pink, puffed sleeves, and white lace. The dark-haired girl wore an expression of desperation as she cupped her hands around her mouth and called out once again. "Here, puss, puss! For goodness sakes, Queenie, where are you?"

Jeb could only stand there in the middle of the creek, his mouth hanging open clear to his Adam's apple. It was his secret love, Mandy, out in the middle of the boondocks, looking for her mangy old cat.

The boy looked over his shoulder, but Buckshot was no longer behind him. Buckshot had scrambled up the mossy bank and was heading eastward, his nose glued to the ground. Whatever the dog smelled, it wasn't a possum or a coon. If it had been, the hound would be howling loud enough to split eardrums. Instead, he was quietly taking his time, following the odd scent away from the vicinity of Mossy Creek.

Jeb turned his eyes back to Mandy. The girl had her back to him, so she wasn't yet aware of his presence. Jeb wondered if it would be better to leave it that way. He could backtrack the way he came and the noise of the creek would mask his footsteps. But, upon further thought, he really didn't want to run from Mandy. His heart began to pound rapidly like it always did when Mandy was nearby and his palms grew hot and sweaty. He felt a little scared, but, then again, there was some sort of inexplicable attraction, too.

The farmboy finally decided to make his presence known. He swallowed deeply, then tried on five different smiles before he found one that wasn't too goofy. When he'd gathered his nerve, Jeb cleared his throat and spoke up. "Hi, Mandy!"

Her reaction wasn't exactly what he had hoped for. The girl gave out a startled cry and whirled around, her eyes wide and frightened. At first, she didn't seem to recognize him. Then came dawning recognition, as well as a look of utter disdain. "Oh," Mandy said, wrinkling her pug nose. "It's only *you.*"

Jeb's nerve faltered a little at her remark, but he managed to keep his spine straight and that silly grin plastered across his face. "Yep, just me. Uh, what are you doing way out here, Mandy?"

The banker's daughter looked annoyed. "I'm searching for my cat, stupid."

The insult slid off Jeb like water off the back of a duck. "Queenie? What happened? Did she run away?"

"Yes," said Mandy, refusing to look his way. "She always strays away from the house when she's in heat." Suddenly, she turned her eyes toward her classmate, a glint of mischief in her lovely eyes. "You do know what that means, don't you?"

Jeb's smile slipped a degree. "I was raised on a farm, you know. I ain't ignorant. Anyway, she couldn't have gone this far. It's two and a half miles from town."

Mandy turned back toward the woods that surrounded Mossy Creek. "She's out here," she said firmly. "I've been following her since just after dinner." The girl cupped her hands to her mouth again. "Queenie! Where are you, precious?"

Jeb took a couple of steps forward. "Uh, I'll be glad to help you look for her, Mandy."

The girl looked back at Jeb. "What makes you think that *you* could find her?"

"I know these woods like the back of my hand," Jeb

boasted. "And I've got Ol' Buckshot to help me. He can track a coon for miles on end. Wouldn't be nothing for him to find some dumb old cat."

"She *isn't* dumb!" snapped Mandy. "Besides, I can do without your help."

"Why?" asked Jeb, unable to understand.

"I'll tell you why," said Mandy. "My daddy is the most important man in Pikesville and he says anybody who lives south of the river is nothing but poor white trash."

Jeb bristled at that statement, but fought to hold his temper. After all, she was his beloved. "That ain't a nice thing to say. There's a lot of good folks on this side of the river."

"Maybe, but you're not one of them," said the girl hatefully. "Tell me something . . . why do you look at me so funny all the time? Whenever I see you at school or in town, you have this silly look on your face . . . just like right now."

Jeb's heart began to beat faster and his face grew bright red in embarrassment. His mind raced for a moment, trying to find a suitable answer for her question. Jeb's brain wanted to tell the truth. It wanted to say "Because I love you, Mandy." But that wasn't what came out. Instead, Jeb grew flustered and tongue-tied. "Uh . . . I dunno!" was all he could manage.

"Then why don't you just leave me alone, Jeb Sweeny?" said Mandy. "I can find Queenie myself."

Dejected, Jeb hung his head and turned back the way he had come. He had taken only a few steps, when a familiar voice rang from behind him. It wasn't Mandy's voice, though. It was a boy's voice, brimming with cruelty and pure meanness.

Jeb recognized it immediately. It belonged to the person he feared most in the world . . . Troy Jenkins.

"Well, what've we got here?" asked the bully. Jeb looked to the eastern bank of the creek. Troy stood on the mossy rise, his arms crossed menacingly and a big, hateful grin splitting his ugly face.

"Yeah," echoed a voice from the opposite bank. "What the hell is *she* doing out here in our neck of the woods?"

Jeb felt his stomach clench. He turned his head and saw both of the Boone brothers standing on the western bank. *We're surrounded!* he thought miserably. He looked around for Buckshot, but the dog was nowhere to be seen. Jeb would have to face the three alone, with no reinforcements.

"Maybe she came out here looking for us," laughed Troy. "Maybe she's been dreaming of us in school and came out here to give us a big wet kiss!"

Mandy looked repulsed. "Shut up, Troy Jenkins! I'm looking for my pet cat . . . and that's all there is to it."

Troy's sickly green eyes narrowed mischievously. "Was it a big, fluffy white cat with a rhinestone collar?"

The girl's face suddenly filled with hope. "Yes, that's her."

The bully looked across the creek toward his cronies. "Wasn't that the cat we came across an hour or so ago?" he asked them. "The one whose eyes we poked out with a stick?"

Danny Boone cackled. "Yeah, I do believe so!"

Troy's grin grew wider as Mandy Rutherford's face grew pale. "You should've heard that cat scream when that stick went in. Those eyes popped just like blisters, squirting jelly all over the place."

"No!" yelled the girl, her eyes brimming with tears. "I don't believe you!"

"That ain't all!" put in Donnie Boone. "After we blinded the kitty, we took a tree branch and hit it across the back. Snapped its spine clean in half. It couldn't do a thing but lay there and meow. Pitful sight, I must admit."

"You're lying!" shrieked Mandy. Tears rolled freely down her rosy cheeks now and her eyes were full of terror.

As the three boys laughed at her reaction, Jeb felt a great anger well up inside him. He couldn't stand to see a girl cry and especially not one he had a huge crush on. He took a step forward, his fists clenched into hard knots. "You guys cut that out!" he demanded. "Can't you see you're scaring her?"

Troy Jenkins glanced at him like he was some sort of bothersome bug. "This ain't no business of yours, Sweeny. If you know what's good for you, you'll high-tail it back home while you still can."

Jeb stood there in the middle of Mossy Creek for a moment, uncertain of what to do next. His mind told him to make a run for it, while his heart told him to stand his ground and fight for the honor of Mandy Rutherford. He was about to speak up again, when he noticed a subtle change in Troy Jenkins's algae-colored eyes. Jeb had seen that shifting of emotional gears once before, when he had intended to force the doo-doo bug on Roscoe Ledbetter. Troy's expression of boyish mischief had changed. It had darkened, grown more unsavory, until only pure, lowdown meanness shone beneath those arched brows. It was clear to see that his bout of cruel horseplay was over with. He had obviously come to the realization that he had been presented a rare opportunity. He had a girl, alone and isolated from the world of adults, and that set his slimy little mind into motion.

"Hey, boys!" he called across the creek to the far bank. "What do you know about the female anatomy?"

"Just what Miss Winston taught us in science," said Donnie, not sure what Troy was up to. "You know, skin and bones and organs and such."

"No, you numbskull!" snickered Troy. "I mean, what the teacher *didn't* tell us. What she was afraid to tell us."

Danny Boone grinned. "Oh, you mean about their *private* parts!"

"Yeah, that's what I'm talking about," said Troy. "Do either one of you know what a girl's got . . . down *there?*"

The Boones looked bumfuzzled. Apparently, their folks had neglected to sit them down and tell them the facts of life. "I don't know," said Donnie, his cheeks growing red. "A pecker?"

Troy laughed. It wasn't a nice one to hear. "You imbecile! Girls don't have peckers!"

Danny looked just as uncomfortable as his brother. "Then what do they have?"

"A hole."

"What?" blurted Donnie. "You're crazy!"

"No, it's true," claimed Troy. "My uncle showed me a pack of French postcards he brought back from the War. Nary one of them ladies had a sign of a Swinging Johnson. Just an ugly ol' hole where one oughta be."

"Aw, come on, Troy!" scoffed Danny.

"Don't believe me, huh?" asked Troy, his grin growing more sinister with each passing moment. "Well, I'll be happy to prove it to you."

"How?"

"We'll just pull down Mandy's panties and take a look," said Troy. "That oughta settle it, once and for all."

Danny and Donnie looked at one another. Their uncertainty was conquered by plain, old adolescent curiosity. With dirty grins of their own, they eyed the girl standing on the sandbar, yearning to see what lay underneath her frilly skirt.

As Troy and the Boones hopped off the creek banks and landed with a splash in the stream, Jeb looked toward Mandy. The girl was frozen, like a deer in the headlights of a car. Fear and panic shown in her eyes, but she had nowhere to run. The three bullies were already advancing on her, eager to wrestle her to the sandy earth and take a look at something none of them had ever seen before.

"Stop it!" she cried. "Stay away from me!"

Troy Jenkins ignored her plea. "Come on, Mandy. I'll help you find your pussy . . . if you show me yours first."

That was when something strange happened inside Jeb's head. All fear vanished, replaced instead by a flood of cold fury. His jumpy nerves and the excited pace of his heart grew calm. "Git away from her," he told them.

"I thought I told you to skedaddle, bastard," growled Troy. "If you don't, I'll finish that ass-whupping you weaseled out of the other day."

The threat didn't faze the boy. Purposely, he reached to the back pocket of his overalls and withdrew the slingshot he had made himself. Then he dipped his other hand into his side pocket and withdrew a handful of ammunition; marbles, wheat pennies, and smooth creek pebbles. "I said for ya'll to git away," he repeated.

The boys ignored Jeb. They waded through the shallow creek, making their way slowly toward the sandbar and the cringing form of Mandy Rutherford.

Jeb gave no further warning. He unfurled the length of cut innertube that was tied to each end of the forked stick, then chose his first projectile. He deposited a large cats-eye marble in the center of the slingshot's cradle, pulled back with all his might until the rubber strap was as taut as a fiddle string, then took aim.

He unleashed the missile just as Troy took his first step onto the sandbar. The cats-eye hit him square in the left elbow with a brittle crack.

"Yeeeoww!" yelped Troy, grabbing for the reddened knob of his elbow and stepping back into the stream so quickly he nearly lost his footing and fell down.

Jeb didn't let up. He took a pebble and sent it flying toward Danny Boone. The rock struck the boy across the knee-cap, causing him to cuss and hop around on one foot. Donnie turned to retreat, but that was his biggest mistake. Jeb loaded the sling again and aimed it squarely at Donnie's butt. The wheat penny hit the boy smack dab on the right buttock, hard enough to raise a painful welt.

Clutching his elbow, Troy Jenkins bared his teeth and started toward Jeb. "You've done it now, Sweeny!" he growled, his green eyes flashing with raw hatred. "I'm gonna beat the living shit outta you and, when I'm finished, I'm gonna do the same to your sweetheart here, just for good measure."

Jeb could tell by the rage in Troy's eyes that he was telling the truth. If Jeb didn't do something, and do it fast, both he and Mandy were in for a whale of a beating. The farmboy picked the most lethal missile from the handful of marbles and rocks. It was a metal jack from a set of ball and jacks he had won at the ring toss booth at the county fair last fall.

A cold emotion gripped Jeb as he cradled the spiky jack in the sling and pulled the innertube taut. He closed one eye and aimed the slingshot unerringly at Troy's head. The bully was scarcely twelve feet away and closing the space between them swiftly. "Stop right where you are, Troy Jenkins," he warned, his voice composed and steady. "Come any closer and I'll put this jack through your right eye and into your brain."

The deadly threat caused Troy to slow down a little. Uncertainty replaced the fiery rage in his eyes and he moved cautiously toward the boy with the slingshot, his fists balled into dangerous knots of bone and gristle.

The calm deliberation in Jeb's face didn't falter for a moment. He pulled the sling back a fraction of an inch, increasing the tension. "I ain't kidding, Jenkins," said Jeb. "I swear, I'll kill you for sure."

Troy stopped dead in his tracks. He stared at Jeb for a long moment and, despite his bravado, a chill went through him. He knew that he had pushed the farmboy too far this time.

With disgust, Troy spat into the creek and sneered. "Aw, I'm tired of fooling with you, Sweeny. You ain't even worth the trouble." He whirled on his heels and started back toward the eastern bank of the creekbed. "Come on, fellas. Let's head into town and see if there's anything to do there. I'm sick of messing around this damned ol' creek."

"But ain't we gonna—?" started Danny, pointing in the general direction of Mandy's skirt.

"Just shut up and come on!" ordered Troy. His voice was angry, but there was something else there, too. Frustration and a hint of fear.

Silently, the Boones followed. A moment later, the three boys were up the mossy embankment and marching along the crest, heading north toward the Cumberland River.

For a while, Jeb and Mandy could only stand there silently. Then the farmboy put his slingshot back into his pocket and walked toward the sandbar. "Are you all right, Mandy?" he asked.

The girl wiped away her tears and nodded. "Yeah, I'm okay. They just scared me, that's all."

Jeb wanted to brag and boast, but he knew it'd be a lie to do so. "Me, too," he finally confided.

Mandy seemed surprised. "Really? You didn't look it." She regarded him curiously. "Tell me something. Would've you really shot out his eye with that slingshot?"

Jeb thought for a moment. "Yeah, I think I would've."

"Just to keep them away from me?"

The boy nodded. A red blush rose in his freckled cheeks. "I . . . well, I really think you're swell, Mandy," he blurted before he could chicken out at the last moment.

Suddenly, the banker's daughter seemed to see the tow-headed boy in a new light. She now saw him more like a knight in shining armor than a poor farmboy who sat at the desk behind her in school. "You know something? I kind of think you're swell, too."

Jeb swallowed dryly. His pounding heart slowed a few beats and he smiled. He was even more pleased when the dark-haired girl in the pretty pink dress smiled back at him.

Before he could take another step toward her, a distant baying sounded a quarter mile to the south. "That's Buckshot," said Jeb. "I think he's found your cat."

"How can you tell?" asked Mandy.

"'Cause I know how he barks when he's treed a possum or coon," he told her. "He sounds kinda peeved and frightened right now, so it's gotta be some critter he ain't too familiar with."

He crossed the creek to the eastern bank. "Come on," he called, offering his hand. "Let's go take a look."

Mandy seemed reluctant at first. Then she decided that her precious Queenie was more important than her pride. Mandy stepped off the sandbar, walked primly through the ankle-deep water, and, taking Jeb's hand, allowed him to help her up the bank of moss and ferns.

Together, they ran through the dense backwoods along Mossy Creek until they finally reached their destination. Buckshot had his forepaws planted on the base of an old maple tree, yelping and yowling to the top of his lungs. His nose was pointed squarely at a long limb halfway up the tree.

Mandy followed the dog's gaze and was overjoyed to see a bundle of white fur perched there. "You were right, Jeb!" she said. "It is Queenie!" Apruptly, her elation turned into dejection. "But how are we going to get her down?"

"Leave that to me," said Jeb, taking his new role as chivalrous gentleman a step further. He yanked on the back of

Buckshot's collar until the dog finally stopped his barking. "You go on over there and sit yourself down," he ordered. "Ain't you ashamed, making such a fuss over one little ol' cat?"

Buckshot whined pitifully, then walked away from the tree and laid down, floppy-eared head resting on his paws.

Jeb jumped up and, grabbing the lowest limb, hauled himself up. He reached the limb, sat down for a moment, then gauged the distance between himself and the white cat. There was a good ten feet of climbing to accomplish.

"Be careful," called Mandy.

Jeb was pleased by the concern in her voice. "Don't worry," he told her. "It'll be a piece of cake."

Carefully, he made his way up the tree, limb by limb. He pulled his attention from the girl below and concentrated on his climbing. Jeb knew it would be terribly embarrassing if he showed off and accidently fell, breaking his leg. Then the impression he had made on his secret love would be shattered, along with his bones.

Finally, after ten minutes, Jeb had reached the limb where Queenie sat. At first, he was afraid she would either run from him or try to claw his eyes out, but, luckily she was thoroughly domesticated and, therefore, lazy. Jeb picked her up with no trouble at all. A short while later, both he and the cat were back on the ground again.

Mandy bundled the white cat in her arms and hugged her tightly. "Queenie! Whatever got into you, running away like that!" Then the dark-haired girl turned to Jeb. "Thanks for getting Queenie down for me. And for chasing those bullies away, too."

Jeb couldn't rightly say when he'd seen eyes quite that beautiful before. "Aw, shucks, it wasn't nothing."

"Yes, it was," Mandy assured him. "Will you be coming to the big picnic on the Fourth of July?"

"Sure will. Wouldn't miss it for the world."

"Then I'll probably see you there," said Mandy almost shyly.

"I hope so," said Jeb with a croak. All the spit in his mouth seemed to have suddenly dried up.

"Well, I'd best get back home," said the girl. "I'm sure Daddy and Mommy are worrying their heads silly over me."

"Your best bet would be to walk that way," suggested Jeb, pointing eastward. "You'll meet up with the main road and you'll likely avoid crossing paths with Jenkins and the Boones."

A touch of fear showed in Mandy's eyes. "I wouldn't want to do that. Well, goodbye, Jeb Sweeny. I'll be seeing you next weekend."

"Yeah," said Jeb with a grin. "I reckon so."

He watched as the girl began to pick her way carefully through the woods, holding the white cat in her arms. He thought about warning her about snakes, but figured it would only frighten her. Anyway, if there were any around, the scent of the cat would likely scare them out of her path.

Jeb stood there for a moment, breathing in the rich aroma of honeysuckle and fresh, green leaves. As he turned and beckoned Buckshot to follow, he decided today had been a rather nice one. After all, he had broken down the wall between Mandy Rutherford and himself, and faced down Troy Jenkins and the Boones all at one time.

By his estimation, he was pretty much on top of the world.

Twelve

The Cave

Around three o'clock, the sky opened up and it began to rain.

It was not a gentle shower, like those common in the spring. No, this was a heavy downpour of torrential proportion. The rainfall seemed to carry a little extra weight to it, hitting whoever was unfortunate to be caught out in the open like a hail of tiny stones.

One person who fell victim to the storm was Troy Jenkins. He had parted company with the Boones a half hour before, going his way while they went theirs. It was when he reached the southern bank of the Cumberland River that the bottom dropped out of the barrel and he was caught in the middle of the downpour.

"Shitfire!" Troy cussed as the woods behind him and the river before him turned into a watery blur. Scarcely a moment had passed before his hair and clothing were completely drenched. Soon, they were plastered to his head and body like a second skin.

Desperately, the twelve-year-old cupped his hand over his eyes and peered toward the east. He could barely make out the steel and concrete structure of the bridge, standing a couple hundred yards away. He knew it would take him five minutes or more to cover the distance and, in the meantime, the clay bank of the river would grow muddy and treacherous. Troy had heard of hoboes and deer hunters losing their footing while walking the bank and falling into the roaring rush of the Cumberland River, never to be found again. If he wasn't careful, he might just suffer a similar fate.

"Damn it to hell!" grumbled the boy. He stood there in indecision for a moment, then an idea came to him. There was a cave no more than thirty yards from where he was. It was set in the side of a limestone cliff, just below a heavy growth of scrubby sycamores. Troy had spent many a day there, smoking cigarettes he'd stolen from his father and reading the dirty magazines he'd found in the trash bin out back of Holt's feedstore from time to time. It would be a perfect place to wait out the duration of the storm.

Cautiously, he made his way along the edge of the riverbank. The earth beneath his feet was already turning into slippery mud. Finally, after a couple minutes of enduring the pounding downpour, he reached the clump of sycamores. Troy crept to one that hung over the lip of the riverbank and, taking hold of its gnarled roots, lowered himself over the side. His feet touched a ledge of rock that jutted from the side of the limestone cliff and he let go. It was not a very large platform— scarcely six feet wide and twelve long—but it was sturdy enough to hold a wagonload of fat men.

Troy looked out over the river. The clouds overhead were dark and full of turmoil. The rainfall would more than likely continue for a while. He then turned toward the cliff wall just beneath the growth of sycamores. A large crevice the size of a barn door split the limestone, giving access to Troy's secret hiding place.

Quickly, Troy ducked through the opening. Dry darkness met him and he was thankful to be out of the rain. Carefully, he made his way along one wall, which was cool and dank to the touch. He lowered his head as he made his way further into the cave, knowing there was a treacherous overhang of rock directly ahead. Soon, the cavern began to widen a bit and he found the spot where he spent the days he played hooky or the times he just wanted to get away from the Boone brothers for a while.

Troy sat down, his back to the wall, and felt around in the darkness. He grunted in satisfaction when he found the stack of nudie magazines and a Tampa Nugget cigar box right where he last left them.

The bully of Pikesville Elementary was a little angry that stormy afternoon. No, angry was too tame a term for what he felt. Pissed-off was more like it. Most of his ill-feelings was due to what had happened at Mossy Creek an hour before. When he had seen Mandy Rutherford standing there, helplessly, in the middle of the sandbar, Troy knew he had been presented with a rare opportunity. If things had gone his way, he could have satisfied a curiosity that had nagged at him since he had first come upon those skin mags behind Holt's. He could have seen a real-live girl naked in the place that counted the most, at least to Troy. He might have even ended up *touching* her down there. But someone had stood in the way of his sleazy wishes. And that someone had been Jeb Sweeny.

Troy's rage flamed anew with the very thought of the blond-headed farmboy with the freckles and the faded overalls. He had always considered Sweeny to be at the top of his list of victims, both on the schoolyard and off. But Sweeny's show of bravado that afternoon had changed all that. Troy rubbed his sore elbow and recalled how Jeb had brandished that homemade slingshot of his. He also thought back to that tense moment when Sweeny had almost unleashed the steel jack. Troy's right eye twitched at the very thought of the injury that might have been sustained. Troy's cousin, Lou, had accidentally shot himself in the eye with a

BB rifle the summer before and, while the tiny projectile hadn't reached Lou's brain, it had blinded him for life.

The twelve-year-old fumed in the darkness for a while, then took the cigar box and fumbled through its contents. Troy had been forced to back down and retreat in front of the Boones. And, in his mind, that was a humiliation he could never forgive or forget. Troy wasn't one to abandon a grudge . . . and he had formed a king-sized one against Jeb Sweeny during his angry walk to the river. He intended to sit there and wait out the thunderstorm and, in the meantime, devise some suitable retribution toward the farmboy and his prissy girlfriend.

Troy's fingers rummaged through the clutter of the cigar box; a bag of Bull Durham with rolling papers, marbles and Cracker Jack toys, and a couple dollars worth of lunch money he had extorted from some of the wealthier kids at school. Eventually, he found what he was looking for. He took out a stub of a wax candle and a box of sulfur matches.

As he prepared to light the candle, Troy was suddenly aware of something he hadn't noticed before. There was a smell inside the cave; a smell that was very strong and musky. At first, he couldn't place it. Then, it came to him. It was the sharp odor of a snake. Troy had killed his share of the reptiles—both harmless and poisonous—to know that smell intimately.

As the match was struck and the flame lit the wick of the candle, a glint of cruelty sparkled in Troy Jenkins's eyes. The bully was no stranger to death, albeit on a limited scale. Since he was six years old, Troy had tortured and killed small animals in the privacy of alleyways and backwoods. Puppies, kittens, mice, frogs, and snakes; all had been mutilated or set afire with sadistic pleasure. Now that familiar urge to reek physical havoc was rekindled, stoked by the rage that lingered toward Jeb Sweeny.

Troy found a good-sized rock, about five pounds in weight. Taking the candle in one hand and the stone in the other, he started toward the back of the cave. The underground cavern was divided into two chambers; the one that was linked to the entrance and another that lay beyond two large boulders. That second chamber was twice as large as the other and a good foot or so taller in height.

He squeezed through the space between the two boulders, a big grin splitting his face. It was much cooler in the rear chamber, but drier than the one he had just left. Troy listened for the brittle buzz of a diamondback's rattlers, but he heard nothing. "Come on, snake," he said beneath his breath. "Where the hell are you?"

The further Troy ventured into the cave, the stronger the scent of snake became. *Damn!* he thought to himself. *Smells like a whole nest of 'em!* The idea of coming upon a bundle of deadly snakes both frightened and exhilarated the youngster. He clutched the rock in his hand more tightly and held the candle low to the ground, shedding a swath of flickering light upon the stone floor.

As he approached the rear wall of the big chamber, Troy's anticipation began to flag. In its place, confusion began to dawn. In a far corner, lay a pool of dark shadow . . . or what he thought was shadow. Upon further inspection, he found it to be something much more solid. It was jet black, but the glow of the candle seemed to glisten off it, giving it a slick and shiny appearance.

"What the hell is this?" he whispered and took a step closer. He could hear the thing breathing now; low and husky. The smell of a serpent was so cloying that it was nearly overpowering.

Abruptly, Troy stopped. From where he stood, he could see the thing's features more clearly. The long-snouted, triangular head, the long reptilian tail, the coat of scaly black skin that seemed to be peeling away in places—all painted a picture so horrible and grotesque that Troy could scarcely believe that it was for real. He began to recall the stories that had circulated around the county during the past week; stories of farm animals being ripped apart and devoured by some strange creature. A creature that, some folks claimed, was an unholy cross between a large dog and a black snake.

Suddenly, the rock in Troy's hand seemed totally useless. Fearfully, he watched as the critter stirred and awoke with a snort. Troy held his breath as it lifted its ugly head and began to sniff. Obviously, it had caught a whiff of him.

The boy began to back away, heading toward the narrow space between the two boulders. But he knew he would never reach it in time. Already, the creature's eyes were opening. They were narrow slits at first. Then they widened into horrible, oval orbs of yellowish-green. The pupils were not round, but thin black slits, like those of a snake, only twenty times larger in size.

Troy caught a glimpse of something at the opposite side of the cave. He pulled his eyes from the monster long enough to see what it was. He was shocked to see a pile of blood-stained bones stacked in the far corner. On top of the heap was a single skull. It took him a moment to realize that it was the skull of a full-grown hog. More than likely, it belonged to Jeb Sweeny's prize-winning boar, Old Jack.

A dry rustling sounded in Troy's ears and he shifted his gaze back to the thing in the cave. It was rising slowly to its feet, the sly and stealthful way a cat rises when it catches a glimpse of a mouse out of the corner of its eye. Troy began to back away, then stopped in his tracks again. This time it was not by his own choice. Those eerie eyes locked with his own and he felt oddly light-headed. He had the strangest compulsion to walk *toward* the critter, instead of fleeing from it.

Helplessly, Troy watched as the huge head rose on the end

of its slender neck. The creature's jaws opened, exposing rows of slaver-coated teeth as long and sharp as a shoemaker's awl. The head drifted back a few inches; lazily, hypnotically, like a king cobra Troy had once seen in a Tarzan movie.

It wasn't until a moment later, that he realized what the critter was about to do. It drew its lungs full of cool cave air, held it for a second, then exhaled powerfully.

Troy felt the gust of the creature's breath, even from where he stood ten feet away. As it engulfed him, it hit the flame of the candle. *God help me . . . no!* thought Troy as the fire flickered precariously upon its wick, then went out.

An instant later, the cave was plunged into pitch blackness.

The boy screamed, but no one heard his cry.

He could do nothing but stand there, rooted to the spot, as he listened to the sound of clawed feet scampering through the darkness toward him.

Part Two
The Decision

Thirteen

The Shadow Deepens

A loud splash of water and a low groan startled Jeb from a light sleep. Dazed, he sat up in bed, peering into the darkness of his and Sam's bedroom.

He shook the sluggishness from his mind and tried to recall the last thing that he remembered before falling to sleep. After a moment, it came to him. It was Wednesday night, which was one of the nights, along with Saturday and Monday, that Grandma Sweeny took a bath after he and Sam had retired for the evening. Jeb had laid there in bed, listening to the rusty squeak of the pump handle as she drew several buckets of water and carried them inside to the woodstove in the kitchen. After heating them, she had dumped the warm water into the big tub of galvanized steel that sat out on the back porch. That had been the last thing Jeb remembered before slumber had claimed him; the sound of water being poured into the bathtub.

Now something had awakened him and he wasn't quite sure what it was. He held his breath and blocked out the monotonous singing of the crickets outside the open window. A second later, the groaning came again. He could tell immediately that it came from his grandmother.

Jeb hopped out of bed. He looked over to where his father slept. Sam was laying on his back, his head cocked back on his pillow and his mouth wide open, emitting a steady melody of coarse snoring. Jeb knew that Sam was exhausted from cleaning out the fencerow and repairing the roof of the henhouse that day. When he was in such a state, it took several minutes to rouse him from his sleep.

The boy decided there was no time to waste. He opened the bedroom door and ran down the hallway to the kitchen. The light was on, but no one was there. He was halfway across the room, when he heard Grandma moan again. As he approached the back door, he called out. "Grandma? Where are you?"

Another groan and then his grandmother's feeble voice. "I'm out here, child. On the porch."

Jeb opened the screen door and stepped out onto the back porch. The single bulb overhead was on, attracting moths and candleflies, and shedding an island of pale light on the boards of the porch. Immediately, Jeb saw what had happened. Grandma had been trying to get up out of the tub when she had slipped and fallen. The tub had overturned, spilling both soapy water and Grandma onto the rough boards of the back porch. Jeb's heart leapt into his throat when he saw his grandmother laying there, completely naked, and he quickly turned his eyes away from her.

"Are you okay, Grandma?" he asked. "Are you hurt?"

"I'm not sure," she said, her breathing labored. "The awfulest pain hit me and I lost my footing. Lost my balance and I fell plumb out of the tub."

"Can you get up?"

"No, son, I've tried," Grandma told him. "I can't seem to summon the strength."

Jeb turned back toward the kitchen. "I'll go fetch Sam."

"Don't, Jeb," said Grandma. "Your papa's never seen me naked once in his life. I'd just as soon he not see me now."

Jeb knew the true reason why Grandma didn't want him

to wake up Sam. She hadn't yet told her son about her illness and she wanted to keep him in the dark about it as long as she possibly could.

"Jeb, do you think you could help me up?" asked the elderly woman.

"I could give it a try," said Jeb. His cheeks flushed red-hot with embarrassment. "But you're—"

"There's a towel draped over that porch railing yonder," Grandma told him. "Fetch it and I'll cover myself up the best I can."

"Yes, ma'am." Keeping his eyes turned away, Jeb made his way across the porch to the railing. He found the towel and tossed it to his grandmother. He stood there patiently as the woman arranged the towel around her sagging breasts and hips.

"All right, I'm ready," she said. "Now let's see what we can do."

Jeb turned and regarded his grandmother. He was shocked at how pale she was and how loosely the skin hung from her arms and legs. It looked as if the cancer she was suffering from was devouring her from the inside out.

The boy put the disturbing observation out of his mind and went to his grandmother. He looped her left arm around his shoulders and tried to lift her to her feet. But, despite the considerable weight she had lost, she still weighed a good hundred and seventy or eighty pounds. He could only budge her a couple of inches, before she sank back to the damp floor of the porch.

"You're gonna have to help me, Grandma," he said. "I can't do it all on my own."

"I'm trying, Jeb," she said, her face creased in effort. "But these old legs . . . they just don't have no strength to 'em at all."

After several attempts, Jeb shook his head. "I'm sorry, bu
I just can't do it, Grandma."

"I know, darling," she said softly. "Thanks for trying a
the same."

"I'll go wake up Sam," he suggested once again.

"No," Grandma said firmly. "He wouldn't understand. It'
just upset him."

Jeb knew she was right. "But how're we gonna get yo
up?"

Grandma thought for a moment. "Run and get Mis
Claudine. Cut across the north pasture and climb over tha
bobwire fence between our property and hers. But be careful
It's dark out tonight."

"I'll be back directly," promised Jeb. Then he jumped of
the back porch and headed through the dewy grass towar
the pasture. As he went, Buckshot crept out from under th
porch and, finding Grandma laying on the boards above hi
sleeping place, settled down beside the old woman to kee
her company.

Across the open pasture, Jeb ran, dodging old cowpies an
puddles left over from last Sunday's rainstorm. He was nearl
out of wind when he reached the fence that separated th
Sweenys' property from that of Claudine Johnson. He heede
Grandma's warning and carefully climbed over the fence wit
its strands of wicked barbs. With that obstacle out of th
way, he ran toward the dark, two-story structure of Mis
Claudine's farmhouse an acre or so away. Only once durin
his mad dash through the darkness did Jeb think of th
snake-critter he had encountered in the hollow. Even then
the fear of running into the creature passed almost as swiftl
as it had surfaced. The well-being of his grandmother wa
much more important to him at that moment.

When Jeb reached the front porch of the farmhouse, h
found all of the windows dark. That was not uncommon a

that hour of ten o'clock. Most of the farm folks in that part of the country preferred to live according to Ben Franklin's old adage of "Early to bed, early to rise." Most families were asleep by nine o'clock and up to tackle their morning chores at the first crow of the rooster.

Exhausted by his run, the ten-year-old stumbled up the steps and across the porch. He jerked open the screen door and pounded on the heavy oak door. "Miss Claudine!" he called. "Wake up!"

A few moments passed before a light winked on upstairs and he heard footsteps making their way down the staircase. Then the lock was disengaged with a loud snap and the door opened. Standing on the other side of the doorway was Claudine Johnson, Grandma's best friend since childhood. Miss Claudine was a tall, skinny woman with sharp blue eyes and a wrinkled face as tough and tanned as old leather. The elderly woman was a self-proclaimed spinster, full of vim and vinegar, and beholden to no man. For most of her sixty-seven years, Miss Claudine had toiled a living from the farm she had inherited from her father and done it alone, with no help whatsoever. She was also the subject of some lively conversation in town from time to time. She wore flowery hats and gingham dresses while in town, but when she tended to her garden or did repairs around her barn, Miss Claudine sometimes wore denim overalls, something that most men in Mangrum County weren't rightly accustomed to.

That night, the elderly woman wore a simple flannel nightgown and a black net over her iron gray hair. Jeb was a little surprised to see her holding a gun in her right hand: a long-barreled Colt .45 revolver, just like John Wayne brandished in the movies. Miss Claudine's eyes were full of caution at first, but when she saw Jeb standing there, clad only in his drawers, she lowered her pistol and shook her head. "Land sakes alive, Jeb Sweeny!" she said, exasperated. "You plumb near gave me a heart attack!"

"I'm sorry, ma'am," apologized the boy. "But it's Grandma."

Miss Claudine's eyes softened. "What's happened, Jeb? What's the matter with her?"

"She was taking a bath on the back porch, but when she tried to get out, her legs gave on her and she fell," he explained. "I tried my best to help her up, but she's a mite too heavy."

The woman nodded to herself. "And of course she's too blamed proud to let you get Sam to help you, I suppose?"

"Yes, ma'am."

Miss Claudine wasted no time. "Let me fetch a light. Wouldn't want to go stumbling through the dark and break one of these old bones."

She went to a closet just off the foyer and took a big four-battery flashlight from the top shelf. As they left, Jeb was surprised to see that the old woman carried the hogleg Colt with her, instead of leaving it behind.

Jeb thought at first that they would take the long way around and travel back to the Sweeny house by road. But Miss Claudine was a tough old bird. She climbed the bob-wire fence as gingerly as any tomboy would.

Five minutes later, they arrived at the back porch. Grandma was still where she had been when Jeb left. Buckshot lay next to her, so sleepy that he could hardly keep his eyes open.

"Praise the Lord, you're here," she said in relief.

"If you weren't so dadblamed stubborn, you'd have woke up Sam and given this old lady her well-earned sleep," said Miss Claudine. Despite her scolding, there was a deep concern in the spinster's voice. "Are you hurt, Lucille? Didn't break your hip, did you?"

"No, nothing's broken," said Grandma. "I was just getting out of the tub and lost my balance, that's all."

"Tuckered yourself out toting those buckets of bathwater, I'd say," replied Miss Claudine. "Why didn't you have Jeb or Sam fetch 'em for you?"

"Never needed 'em to do it for me before."

"Well, things have changed," her friend said firmly. "The sooner you face up to that fact, the better."

Grandma didn't answer. Her friend's good-natured reprimand was true and she knew it.

"Enough chit-chat," said Miss Claudine. She set her gun and flashlight on the porch railing, and rubbed her hands together. "Let's see about getting you into the house."

It took Claudine Johnson and Jeb several tries before they finally lifted Grandma from the porch and back on her feet again. The time it had taken the boy to travel to the neighboring farm and back had done her some good. She had caught her wind and gathered enough strength to walk, with the help of Jeb and Claudine.

Carefully, they escorted Grandma to her bedroom. Jeb stood outside in the hallway, while Miss Claudine helped his grandmother into her nightgown. He heard them talk quietly for a few minutes, although he couldn't make out exactly what they discussed. Then Miss Claudine cut off the light and joined him.

The elderly woman laid a bony, but strong, hand on his bare shoulder. "Let's go to the kitchen and talk, Jeb."

Without protest, Jeb did as she requested. He knew in his heart that what she had to say would not be pleasant to hear. But he also knew he had no choice except to be brave and take it like a dose of bad medicine.

Once they reached the kitchen, the two sat down at the table. Miss Claudine's long face grew even longer and she reached out and took hold of Jeb's hand. "Your grandma told me the other day that you already knew about her illness," she said softly.

"Yes, ma'am," admitted Jeb. "And that ain't all. I know that she's dying, too."

Miss Claudine squeezed his hand. "Well, that's good. It's good that you know. But it don't make it any easier to accept, does it, son?"

"No, ma'am . . . it don't."

"I know that it's bound to hurt you, Jeb," she told him. "Blood kin always hurt more at such dire news. But I hurt, too. Probably more'n you could imagine."

Jeb simply nodded.

"Me and your grandma, we've been friends for over sixty years," said Miss Claudine. "Not mere acquaintances, but deep-down, soul-to-soul friends. I love that woman in there like she was my own sister. And it tears me plumb apart knowing she won't be around much longer."

Jeb swallowed dryly. "Exactly how long does she have?" he asked. "She kinda neglected to tell me that."

"Not much longer, I'm afraid," Miss Claudine told him, knowing that to lie needlessly would be more cruel than compassionate. "She'd been having pains for quite a spell, but you know your grandma. She'd just as soon be beaten with a hog cane than go to a doctor. When I finally pestered her enough, it was too late. The cancer had spread too far."

Jeb felt that painful hurt of emotion in the back of his throat, but swore that he wouldn't cry. "Can't they cut it out?"

"No, son," replied the old woman. "They'd have to gut her like a fish."

It was then that the fact of the matter finally set in, hitting him like a ton of bricks. His grandmother was going to die and there was absolutely nothing that he could do about it. And, no matter how hard he prayed when he went to bed at night, there was nothing God could do about it, either.

The two sat there in silence for an awkward moment, then Claudine spoke up again. "Jeb . . . what happened with your grandma tonight . . . well, it ain't gonna get no easier. She's gonna grow weaker and more frail, and she won't be able to get around like she once did. And the pain—that damned pain—it'll just grow stronger and stronger."

"But what about that stuff she drinks?" Jeb asked.

"The laudanum? Well, sooner or later, it just won't be enough. Likely, the doctor will have to ease her pain with morphine."

Jeb didn't rightly know what morphine was, but the very mention of the word sounded wicked. "What'll happen when she can't get around anymore?" he wanted to know.

Miss Claudine took in a deep breath and sat up straight in her chair. "That's when you come calling on me. When things reach that point, I want to move Lucille to my house and take care of her . . . right up to the end."

"But we couldn't ask you to do that, Miss Claudine," Jeb said.

"Wouldn't have to ask me at all," declared the elderly woman. "I'd see it as a duty to a good friend. Besides, the condition your grandma'll be in, well, there won't be much you or Sam will be able to do for her."

"She'll be that bad off?"

Another squeeze of the hand from Miss Claudine. "Yes, Jeb, she will."

Again, silence stretched between them. Both Jeb and Claudine Johnson sat there quietly, fighting against the tears that threatened to break through. Then the old woman started the conversation in a new, yet frightening, direction. "Jeb . . . have you given any thought to how things'll be *after* your grandma's gone?"

Dread filled the boy. "Yes, ma'am. I have."

"I don't know if you're aware of this, Jeb, but your

grandma mortgaged this farm when your Grandpappy Sweeny was sick with the stroke," Miss Claudine told him, gently yet bluntly. "She had to just to pay the hospital bills. Well, after your papa came home from the War and couldn't keep the place up, Lucille couldn't pay the bank the way they wanted her to. That Charles Rutherford is a hard man, but he gave her some extra time here and there. The thing is, Jeb, when your grandma passes away, I don't think his patience or his generosity is gonna last much longer."

"What do you mean?"

"What I'm saying," said Miss Claudine, "is that he'll more than likely collect on that mortgage and take the farm away from you and Sam."

Jeb was shocked. "But we can keep it up. We can make it work again."

"Maybe if your papa was still in his right mind," she told him. "But you know as well as I do that he can't handle it. And they sure ain't gonna put their faith in a boy as young as you, although I know you'd do your level best."

"But if they take the farm away, me and Sam won't have no place to live," said Jeb, his worse suspicions again rising to the surface. "And then they'll haul Sam off to the state asylum . . . and me to the orphanage."

The pained look in Miss Claudine's face was difficult to even look at. "More'n likely, yes." She squeezed Jeb's hand until he was sure she would crack his knuckles. "Jeb, if there was any way in the world I could let you and your papa come live with me, I'd do it in a heartbeat. But, the truth is, I'm an old woman and I ain't getting any younger. I may look tougher than nails and seasoned hickory, but my heart's been giving me fits lately. I've got a niece down in Chattanooga that's been wanting me to sell my place and move down there to live with her. God knows I love my farm, but it's harder and harder to keep up everyday."

"I understand," Jeb said. His last hope had been dashed into a million tiny pieces. Finally, he could play the brave little man no more and he began to cry.

Miss Claudine left her chair and, drawing the boy to her, embraced him tenderly. "I'm sorry, Jeb," she said, her own eyes brimming with tears. "I'm so very sorry. But there's nothing much more I can do."

"I ain't blaming you, Miss Claudine," he told her. "It's just that I don't know what to do about it all."

Again, the old woman's spine straightened in that spit-the-devil-in-the-eye way of hers. "Well, we've still got some time left. We'll put our heads together and think of something. I promise you that."

Jeb simply nodded. He knew that Miss Claudine's intentions were good, but felt that there was absolutely nothing that could be done. It was almost as if his and Sam's fates had already been decided upon by a higher power and no amount of brainwork was going to change things.

After a few moments, Miss Claudine pulled away and wiped her eyes. "Well, Jeb, I reckon I'd better get home. Gotta get up with the first light and attend to my chores."

Jeb accompanied the elderly woman to the back porch. The night was dark and thick with the sound of crickets in the wet grass. Buckshot lay on his side on the porch floor, his legs twitching in some fitful dream he was having, more than likely about eating or hunting.

Miss Claudine picked up the flashlight, then turned to the ten-year-old. "Have you got one of these hand-held lights, Jeb?"

"No, ma'am," he replied. "Just a lantern, that's all."

She handed the long-handled flashlight to him. "Well, here. You take that. I've got another one at the house. Might help you find your way better the next time you have to fetch me in the middle of the night."

Jeb took the flashlight, which seemed heavier than lead. "Much obliged," he said. "But can you make it back to your house without it?"

"I'll be careful and watch my step," she promised. Before she left, she retrieved the Colt .45 from off the porch railing.

Despite all that had happened that night, Jeb's boyish curiosity still broke through. "Uh, where'd you get such a gun, Miss Claudine?"

The old woman smiled. "Looks like something out of a Saturday matinee, don't it? It was my papa's gun. You might not know it, but he was sheriff of Mangrum County some fifty or sixty years ago."

Jeb was surprised. "I didn't know that."

"That's right," said Miss Claudine. "He was an honest man, my papa, and one who took his duties seriously. If there'd been a snake-critter on the loose whilst he was in office, he'd have hunted it down and nailed its hide to the barn door by now."

At the mention of the snake-critter, Jeb was sure that the elderly woman was poking fun at him. But the seriousness in her aged eyes told him otherwise. It was plain to see that Miss Claudine believed that what he told Sheriff North was the gospel truth.

"If you need any more help with your grandma, you come and fetch me, you hear?" she called as she started across the shadows of the backyard, six-shooter in hand.

"Yes, ma'am," he promised. "I surely will."

Jeb waited until she vanished into the darkness. Then he cut off the porch light and went back inside. As he passed through the kitchen and into the hallway, Jeb could hear his grandmother's coarse breathing from the other side of her bedroom door. It was not a sound that comforted him. In his youthful ears, it was like listening to the ticking of a clock that hadn't been wound in a very long time . . . one that was slowly bound to give out and grow forever silent.

Fourteen

The Discovery

The next morning found Jeb Sweeny roaming along the shaded channel of Mossy Creek once again. This time his journey wasn't out of curious exploration or idle boredom, but centered more around reflection and escape from those problems that worried him so much that summer.

As he reached the end of the creekbed and approached the lofty south bank of the mighty Cumberland, Jeb thought about the night before and the things Claudine Johnson had said to him over the kitchen table. The foreclosure of the Sweeny farm preyed the most on his mind and he recalled his dream of a few nights before; the one that had taken place in the mourning room of the McHenry funeral home. He remembered Charles Rutherford smiling smugly and slipping the deed into his coat pocket. Sometimes Jeb wondered if he possessed the gift of second sight, if only every now and then. He'd heard of children being blessed with such a gift before and remembered a story Grandma had told him once about a girl who had helped solve a mass murder over at Coleman in nearby Bedloe County.

But, on second thought, Jeb knew he possessed no such powers. He had just picked up on things during the course of time that he hadn't understood at the time. In any case, Miss Claudine's talk with him had cleared up some questions he'd had and revealed some things that made the whole tragedy of Grandma and her cancer seem less mysterious. But their discussion hadn't, however, made things any easier to deal with.

That was one of the reasons why Jeb was heading for the riverbank that morning. The more he stayed around the farm, the more his problems seemed to gang up on him and flood his mind with despair. He needed a little time alone to himself. Maybe then he would be able to find some sort of middle ground where he could stop feeling so blasted lousy and try to find some kind of solution, at least to some of the problems that he and Sam would be forced to face after Grandma's death.

The only cheerful news he had heard in the last few days had concerned the disappearance of Troy Jenkins. Strangely enough, the bully had never returned to Pikesville following his walk along Mossy Creek. Jeb always felt a little sad when he heard news of a fellow kid being hurt or lost, but this time he really didn't feel that sorry at all. In fact, "good riddance" kept coming to mind over and over again for some reason.

He reached the river bank a little after the hour of eleven. It was a bright, sunny day, but, already, the temperature had topped ninety-five and the air was hot and muggy. Jeb wiped sweat from his forehead and glanced behind him. Buckshot wasn't far behind. The dog paused to pant and lap water from the creekbed, an act the hound had performed at least a couple dozen times since leaving home.

Jeb left the end of Mossy Creek and headed along the riverbank, which rose steadily upward. To the east he could see the steel and concrete expanse of the bridge. Even as he watched, Jeb saw a bright red Coca Cola delivery truck crossing the bridge, heading north for town. He thought of the cold bottles of soda it carried within its refrigerated cooler and would have given his eye-teeth for one at that moment.

Knowing that his hankering was pointless, Jeb continued along the bank. Eventually, he reached his destination; a scrubby grove of sycamores that grew along the very edge of the high bank. He reached the trees and, hanging onto one that grew a little further out than the others, looked down. The ledge of rock awaited him, as well as the opening in the wall of gray limestone.

Jeb hefted the tow sack he had brought along over his left shoulder, then looked over at Buckshot regretfully. "Sorry, boy, but this is as far as you go," he said. "I'd tote you down across my back, but I'd likely slip and dump both of us into the river."

The dog peeked over the edge of the bank and seemed to understand. He walked over to a gooseberry bush and collapsed underneath it. Almost immediately, the hound was fast asleep. Jeb grinned and shook his head. He'd known the dog to take a nap in the middle of Main Street on a busy Saturday morning, with cars and trucks zooming around, and be none the wiser.

Jeb turned back to the ledge in the side of the cliff. He took hold of the exposed roots of a sycamore and carefully lowered himself over the side. He let go and landed on the stone shelf, nearly losing his balance when his feet hit. He steadied himself, then stepped into the dark portal of the cliffside cave.

After a few steps inside, he found it too dark to see where he was going. Jeb opened the tow sack and withdrew the flashlight Miss Claudine had given him the night before. He snapped on the switch and was pleased at the circle of yellowish-white light that illuminated the tunnel before him. As he moved onward, the passageway began to widen into a funnel-shaped chamber. He ducked an outcropping of rock that hung overhead and played his light toward the left wall of the cavern. There, on the stone floor, was a cigar box and a stack of discarded girlie magazines.

Jeb had first discovered the cave when he was seven years old, but even then, he had the feeling that he wasn't the only one who borrowed its solitude from time to time. Occasionally, he discovered cigarette butts or candy bar wrappers in the cave. And earlier that spring, he'd found the cigar box and dirty magazines there on the floor. He hadn't bothered the stuff, though. Part of his abstinence from curiosity had been out of respect for someone else's belongings, while part had been out of fear. He didn't want to get on the wrong side of some smelly hobo or some gun-toting hunter who made the cave their lodge every now and then.

The boy was about to sit down and unload his sack—which held a baloney and cheese sandwich, a green apple, and a big piece of Grandma's chocolate cake wrapped in tinfoil—when something drew his attention. It was a smell; one that conjured a sense of uneasiness in him. He breathed in a couple of gulps of cool cave air and instantly recognized the stench, as well as the last place he had smelled it.

It was the musky odor of snake, just like he had experienced in the yard of the invaded hog pen the night Old Jack was killed.

It's in here, he thought, his heart thundering in his chest. *I've found where it hides out!*

Jeb was about to turn and leave before he alerted the creature of his presence, but he only got a few steps. Something stopped him before he could reach the tunnel that led to the outside. It was a low sound that his ears almost missed at first. He paused and listened again. This time he knew what it was. It was a low moan. The moaning of a child.

He knew it would be best to run and fetch a grown-up but the unspoken code common to young boys had him by the shirt-tail. If one of his own kind was back in the chamber beyond the two boulders and the snake-critter had hurt him somehow, Jeb knew it was his duty to see if he could do anything to help. He knew that was a stupid chance to take, considering the creature that was terrorizing the countryside, but he simply couldn't back down. If he had been in a similar predicament, he would've hoped that a fellow kid would've done the same for him.

Jeb drew his slingshot from his back pocket, then dug around in his overalls for ammunition. He found what he was looking for; a big steel bolt that had come off an old tractor engine. The bolt was heavy—nearly three ounces in weight—and, even if it didn't kill the thing in the cave, it was sure to give it a colossal headache if the correct English was put into the tension of the sling.

The boy tucked the big flashlight beneath one armpit. Then, holding the haft of the slingshot in one hand and the cradle of the innertube in the other, he squeezed through the space between the two boulders.

At first, Jeb was sure that his mind was playing tricks on him and that the back chamber of the cave was empty. Then the moan came again and he turned toward the right wall. The beam of the flashlight was askew due to its position beneath his armpit, but it illuminated the sloping wall of water-stained stone clearly enough. When the light shone on the source of the moaning, Jeb could scarcely believe his eyes.

There, above a pile of stripped hog bones, lashed to the wall by something that looked like strips of transparent snakeskin, was a boy. The kid was as pale as baking flour and had eyes as big around as a Liberty half dollar. As Jeb grew closer, he was shocked to discover that he knew the boy. In fact, he knew him extremely well. It was Troy Jenkins, the major nemesis of his young life.

Except that, imprisoned in the cocoon of tattered snakehide the way he was, Jenkins no longer resembled the threatening bully. Now he simply looked like a frightened boy who wanted in the worst way possible to break his bonds and run home.

At first, a nasty thought crept into Jeb's brain. For one fleeting second, the farmboy almost turned around and left. All the pains and injustices that Jenkins had inflicted on him during the past few years came flashing back, along with all the resentment Jeb had generated toward the bully. The only thing that kept Jeb from exacting a fitting revenge on the twelve-year-old and leaving him to face whatever horror the creature had in store for him, was the decency that Grandma Sweeny had instilled in him during his upbringing. No matter how much he hated Troy Jenkins, he knew in his heart that he simply couldn't run off and leave him hanging there on that cave wall. He just didn't have enough cruelty in himself to do such a despicable thing.

"Troy?" he whispered. "Troy, it's me."

At first, the boy's eyes seemed to look right through Jeb. Then they lost their glazed look and sharpened a bit. "Who is it?" he asked, a little louder than Jeb would've liked.

"Pipe down," he said softly. "It's me . . . Jeb Sweeny."

Troy's eyes widened both in recognition and desperation. "Sweeny? What're you doing here?"

"I was just gonna ask you the same thing," replied Jeb.

The bully's eyes darted nervously from side to side. "I got caught in the downpour Sunday and I came in here to get out of the rain. I smelled a snake back here and I went looking for it." Troy shuddered in the straight-jacket cocoon of snakeskin. "That's when I found *it.*"

"The snake-critter," breathed Jeb.

"Yeah," said Troy with a nod. "I tried to run, but it caught me. It bit me right here on the side of the neck and, a minute later, I couldn't move a damned muscle. I just laid there and watched it wrap me up in this snakehide. Then it hung me on the wall here."

Jeb couldn't comprehend why the creature would keep Troy prisoner for four days without having some motive for doing so. "Uh, why does it have you trussed up here like this?" he asked.

Troy's face grew even whiter than before and Jeb was sure he was about to puke. "It's . . . it's *feeding* off me, Jeb. God help me, it's drinking my *blood* . . . just like Bela Lugosi in that vampire movie."

Jeb knew the film Troy was talking about. He had seen *Dracula* at a theatre in Nashville, along with *Bride of Frankenstein* and *The Wolfman*. He recalled the cloaked count with the spidery hands and hypnotic eyes, and the mere image of the vampire conjured memories of Jeb's encounter with the snake-critter. Both held the same unholy menace; an evil that shown more through sinister eyes than anything else.

Tears began to form in the bully's eyes. "It's bitten me on the side of the neck," he moaned. "Take a look at it, Jeb. It hurts like hell."

Although he didn't exactly want to, Jeb directed his flashlight at the right side of Troy's neck. What he saw there horrified him. Two scabbed-over wounds the size of dimes marred his blood-stained skin. The fang holes were set three or four inches from one another, and they were purplish-blue and puckered, as if something had been sucking on them every so often.

"How does it look?" asked the bully. "Is it bad?"

Jeb knew he would only have trouble on his hands if he told Troy the truth. "Naw," he lied. "It ain't that bad a'tall."

"Jeb?" whispered Troy, breaking the farmboy's train of thought.

"Yeah?"

Troy's eyes were pleading. "I know I've done you wrong in the past. Done some godawful things to you . . . but you gotta help me. Get me outta here and, I swear to God, I'll be your pal for life."

Jeb wasn't sure he wanted that much of a reward for saving the bully's life, but he knew that he really had no choice. "Just hang on," he said. He stuck his slingshot back into his pocket and took out his Case knife. "I'll see what I can do."

"Hurry, will you?" asked Troy. "I wanna get the hell outta this place!"

The bully's words matched Jeb's thoughts down to the letter. He didn't want to spend any more time in the cliffside cave than was necessary. Jeb unfolded the pocketknife's longest blade and began to tackle the strands of thick snakeskin.

After a minute of slashing and sawing, Jeb shook his head. "I'm sorry, Jenkins, but it's just too tough to cut. The blade just slides right off it."

Hysteria bloomed in Troy's eyes. "What do you *mean* you can't cut it! You've gotta cut it! You've gotta get me outta here!"

"Lower your voice," Jeb hissed in irritation.

"The hell I will!" raved the bully, his face livid. "Now you cut me outta this damned stuff, or I'll give you an ass-kicking you ain't never gonna forget!"

Jeb was about to try again, when he looked up at Troy's face. In the glow of the flashlight, he watched as Jenkins's expression changed from anger to complete terror. Jeb didn't know exactly why . . . until he noticed that Troy wasn't looking directly at him, but past him, over his left shoulder.

That was when Jeb heard something in the darkness behind him. It was a low, hissing sigh. That and the dry rasp of scales rubbing against coarse stone.

Jeb forgot all about trying to release the imprisoned bully.

Instead, he stuck the knife back into the side pocket of his overalls and grabbed for the slingshot. He whirled and the flashlight stuck in his armpit shifted its beam to the far side of the cave.

In the circular light, stood the snake-critter, rising from where it had been napping next to the opposite wall. The creature yawned, displaying a wicked collection of jagged teeth jutting from milky black gums. Jeb watched as the thing stretched, shrugging the lingering stiffness of slumber from its muscles and bones. Looking at it from where he stood, Jeb was certain that the creature was *larger* than when he had encountered it in the hollow near the woods. Perhaps only a few inches taller and a foot longer, but larger, nonetheless.

Jeb fumbled in his pocket for the tractor bolt, found it, and placed it in the cradle of the sling. He felt the flashlight begin to slip as the sweat of panic slickened his armpit. Jeb knew he would drop the light if he didn't do something, so he released it from beneath his arm and stuck it, head up, in the side pocket of his overalls. The beam was now aimed directly at the craggy ceiling of the cave, casting an eerie gloom throughout the chamber. He had a hard time seeing the creature now. It was only a dark shape against an even darker background, but its eyes stood out in the sparse light. They sparkled greenish-yellow, narrowing to thin slits as they caught a glimpse of Jeb at the far side of the cave.

The farmboy hated to leave Troy where he was, but he knew he had to get out of there before he suffered the same fate. Jeb began to back away, again gripping the slingshot in both hands, ready to put it to use if necessary.

"Jeb!" screamed Troy as the light followed the farmboy and left him in darkness. "For God's sake, don't leave me here, Jeb! Come back! Please, come back!"

Jeb said nothing. He backed a few steps more, then felt the coolness of one of the boulders against his shoulder blade. He stepped to the side and sensed that the opening between the stones was directly behind him. He also sensed that the snake-critter was coming for him. He could see its long, dark form moving through the gloom and hear the sharp claws of its reptilian feet clicking upon the stone floor. Soon, its muscles had warmed up from its nap and it was across the rear chamber in a flash.

Jeb wasted no time. He squeezed between the two boulders and found himself in the outer tunnel. As he made his way back through the passageway, Jeb heard a loud growl behind him. He turned and was stunned to see the critter straining to squeeze through the space between the boulders. It was working its way, slowly but surely, through the opening. Its scaly muscles rubbed against the flats of the stones, emitting an ear-piercing noise not unlike the sound of untrimmed fingernails on a school blackboard.

In horror, Jeb watched as the snake-critter squeezed through the opening, inch by inch. He knew that it would be past the barrier in a matter of seconds and then he would be in a mess of trouble. Jeb glanced back down the tunnel. The entrance to the cave was a good twenty feet away. There was no way Jeb could possibly make it out of the cave and back to the top of the riverbank before the thing caught up with him. He would scarcely have his hands on the roots of the sycamore, ready to pull himself up, when the monster grabbed hold of him and dragged him back into the cave.

He knew then that he would have to stand his ground. His hands shaking, Jeb lifted the slingshot at arms length and pulled back on the sling. The bowed length of innertube thrummed with tension as he drew it back nearly to his opposite shoulder. Jeb gripped the cradle and its projectile tightly, waiting for just the right moment. It came an instant later. He saw the long black fingers of the creature's right front paw snake through the opening and knew that the rest of it wasn't far behind.

Jeb closed his eyes and, loosening his grip, let the missile fly.

The boy's aim proved to be true. The tractor bolt spun through the widening tunnel and slammed into the end of the creature's snout. With a yelp of surprise and pain, the thing jerked back, retreating through the opening. A moment later, it was back inside the rear chamber, dazed by the three ounce projectile that had bloodied its nose.

Jeb didn't wait to see if it would show itself again. He turned and ran for the entrance of the cave. When he burst into the sunlight, Jeb stuck the slingshot in his back pocket, then leapt for the tangle of roots that jutted from the upper edge of the cliff. He missed the first try, but succeeded at the second. Soon, he had hauled himself back up to the top of the riverbank.

"Jeb!" Troy Jenkins's frantic voice echoed faintly from the cave beneath his feet. "Oh, please, Jeb . . . don't leave me here!"

The farmboy cupped his hands around his mouth and yelled as loudly as he could. "I'll go fetch somebody, Troy. We'll get you out! Don't worry!"

With that said, Jeb knew he had to put some distance between himself and the cave, in case the snake-critter decided to venture out of its lair. "Come on, Buckshot!" he called. "We gotta get away from here, boy!"

The bluetick's ears perked up and he seemed to sense the urgency in his master's voice. Soon, he was on Jeb's heels as the boy ran eastward along the riverbank, heading for the Cumberland River bridge and the road leading toward town.

Fifteen

Deaf Ears

Forty-five minutes after Jeb Sweeny had left the cave in the limestone cliff, he arrived at the outskirts of Pikesville. Both he and Buckshot were tuckered out by the time they reached the Baptist church, but, fortunately, they didn't have to travel all the way to the courthouse to find the person they were looking for. Ed North's navy blue patrol car was parked out front of the steepled structure, where Alfred Harris was on a fifteen-foot ladder, giving the slats of the building a good coat of snow white paint.

"Sheriff!" called Jeb as he stumbled across the gravel parking lot. "You gotta come quick!"

North was sitting on the front bumper of his car, watching Alfred work and drinking a 7-Up. When he heard the commotion behind him, he turned and regarded Jeb with surprise. "Whatever is the matter, Jeb Sweeny? Boy, you look like you've done seen a ghost."

"A lot worse than that," said Jeb, catching his breath. "It was that snake-critter, Sheriff. I saw it again!"

Annoyance flared in the constable's eyes and he glanced up at the painter. Alfred Harris was only fifty, but had spent nearly thirty years working in a tool and die shop in Nashville. The stamping presses he had operated had pretty much shot his hearing to hell, so there was no danger of him overhearing the boy's statement. He knew Alfred had picked up a little lip-reading, though, and if he turned around on his ladder, he would find out right quick what Jeb was so excited about.

North hopped off the chrome bumper and grabbed Jeb by the arm. "Come on, boy. Let's go for a drive and you can tell me your story."

Jeb rarely got the chance to ride in an automobile, so he didn't mind the sheriff's suggestion at all. After North had opened the driver's door and Jeb had scooted across the bench seat, he glanced out the door at Buckshot, who sat next to the car, looking a little perplexed. "What about my dog?" he asked. "You can't just leave him here."

The sheriff frowned distastefully. "Well, hell, where am I gonna put him?"

"The backseat, I reckon."

North looked uncertain. "He ain't gonna piss all over the place, is he?"

"Shoot no, Sheriff!" assured Jeb, rolling his eyes. "Ol' Buckshot is a good dog. He wouldn't do such a thing."

North opened the back door of the sedan. "Oh, all right. I reckon it can't hurt." A moment later, the dog was jumping onto the backseat and making himself comfortable.

The slamming of the rear door, alerted Alfred Harris on the ladder. He turned and stared down at the sheriff. "Where're you going, Ed?"

"Got some law business to attend to," said North.

Alfred cupped a hand to his left ear. "Say again?"

"I said I gotta attend to something," he yelled louder.

The painter simply nodded and turned back to his painting, totally unaware of what had gone on behind his back a moment before.

Soon, the patrol car had made a U-turn in the church parking lot and was pulling out onto the main road. Jeb pointed south, so North turned in that direction. "So, what's this all about?" asked the sheriff.

"Like I said before, I came across the snake-critter again!" said the boy. "The one that killed Old Jack."

That familiar shadow of disbelief settled in North's droopy eyes. "Oh, yeah? And where did you see it this time?"

"You know that cave in the south bank of the Cumberland?"

North thought for a moment. "The one that's a stone's throw from the bridge?"

"Yes, sir," replied Jeb. "Well, it's been hiding out in there. And that ain't all."

The sheriff sensed that the farmboy was about to tell him something he really didn't want to hear. "What do you mean?"

"It's got Troy Jenkins in there, trussed up in a cocoon of snake hide," Jeb said frantically. "And its feeding off him! Drinking his blood like a tick!"

Sheriff North's reaction to the news was the complete opposite of what Jeb expected it to be. The lawman slammed on his brakes, squealing the tires against the pavement of the highway and steering the sedan toward the shoulder. The patrol car stopped with a jerk so abrupt that Jeb nearly butted his head against the dashboard.

Startled, the boy looked over at the man in the driver's seat. North simply sat there, staring out the bug-speckled windshield. His face was fire engine red and his hands gripped the steering wheel so tightly that his knuckles were white with strain.

"Stop it," the lawman said between clenched teeth. "You stop this nonsense right here and now!"

"But it ain't—" stammered the boy.

"Just sit there and listen to me," said North. He turned toward Jeb so suddenly that, at first, the farmboy was sure he was about to be struck. "I want you to stop all this damned-fool talk about snake-dogs and such! All it does is make my job a helluva lot harder than it oughta be."

"But it's true!" protested Jeb. "I swear it is!"

North's temper flared. "You just shut your yap, boy, and keep it shut! All this talk about a damned monster has made me the laughingstock of the county! Half of Pikesville believes in this critter, while the other thinks it's a dadblamed joke. I've got folks tugging at me from both sides, expecting me to do something. But I can't until I find out exactly what it is, and you sure as hell ain't helping any."

Jeb knew he should have expected such a reaction, given the way North had acted toward him the morning after the hog killing. "So you don't believe me at all?"

"No, boy, I don't!" declared the sheriff. "And I'm sick and tired of hearing your tall-tales. If your grandma was raising you right, she'd lay a switch to your butt and put a stop to all this lying and storytelling!"

Jeb's heart sank. "But ain't we gonna get Troy out of that cave?"

"I thought I told you to stop it!" said North, leveling a pudgy finger at the boy. Jeb couldn't remember seeing the man quite so angry before. "Let me tell you something about Troy Jenkins. The kid's got a record of making trouble as long as the flagpole out front of the courthouse. And, as for running away, he's done it a dozen times in the past couple years. Last time he was gone for ten days. Hopped a freight train and ended up clear down in Memphis. Well, he's been gone for little over four days this time, and I ain't wasting my time looking for the little turd. I'd just soon he stay gone and save the town the bother of having to put up with him."

Although Jeb had no great love for the twelve-year-old bully, he simply couldn't allow him to remain in the cave, at the mercy of the snake-critter. "But if we leave him there, that thing'll kill him for sure! It'll bleed him dry as a bone!"

Ed North's anger exploded into full-fledged rage. Before Jeb knew what was happening, the sheriff reached over and, grabbing one of the straps of Jeb's overalls, hauled the boy across the seat. "Now you listen to me, Jeb Sweeny!" he growled. "I don't wanna hear another word from you concerning this critter. I don't wanna hear you mentioning it to anyone else, either. If I do learn that you've been running your mouth, I'm gonna stripe your ass with the buckle-end of my gunbelt, then drive you straight to the state reformatory. And you know what those white trash boys'll do to you up there? They'll eat you for breakfast with a side order of grits, that's what!"

The sheriff's threat of sending him to the reform school made Jeb clam up. He still feared for Troy Jenkins, but he also was concerned for his own hide. The orphanage was bad, but the state reformatory was ten times worse, and Jeb intended to stay as far away from it as possible.

"Do you understand me now, boy?" asked North gruffly. "Are you gonna keep on being a troublemaker and make me pack you off to that school? Or are you gonna be good and keep your damned mouth shut?"

Jeb was quiet for a moment, then he sighed. "I ain't gonna say nothing else," he replied.

"Well, that's good to hear," said the lawman, grinning cruelly. "'Cause if I did have to send you away, the state wouldn't have no choice but to put your brain-dead daddy in the asylum. There wouldn't be nothing else to do, what with your grandma nearly in her grave."

Jeb suddenly realized that underneath Ed North's lazy demeanor, there was a hidden streak of downright meanness. His general dislike for the man suddenly increased threefold.

The sheriff pointed to the handle on the inside of the passenger door. "I'm through talking to you, boy. You go on and git now. Go home and keep your trap shut, or I'll be picking you up for that ride to the reform school. Understand?"

Jeb nodded solemnly. "Yes, sir. I understand." Then he climbed out of the car and, opening the rear door, let Buckshot out, too.

When the boy had closed the door, Sheriff North gave him one last, warning look. Then the lawman made a U-turn in the road and headed back for town.

Angrily, Jeb kicked at the dirt at the side of the road. He thought about telling Sam and Grandma about Troy and the critter in the cave, but knew if word got back to the sheriff, North would keep his promise and send him off to the reformatory for two or three months. By the time he got out, Grandma would already be dead and Sam would be locked up in the state asylum indefinitely. So he had no other choice but to keep his mouth shut, whether he liked it or not.

Jeb glanced over at his dog. Buckshot was sitting in the crabgrass at the side of the road, rubbing his haunches back and forth. Jeb recognized the hound's motion for what it truly was and a grin began to form on his lips. "Buckshot . . . did you take a dump in the sheriff's car?"

The dog simply grunted and, finishing, stood up. Jeb noticed that the blades of grass the bluetick had sat upon were a little less green than they had been a moment before.

Jeb wanted to laugh at the present Ed North would find on his backseat when he reached town, but he simply couldn't. He walked for a while and, when he crossed the Cumberland River bridge, he looked over the side and saw the opening in the limestone bank several hundred yards away. He had the urge to go down there and try to release Troy on his own, but knew it would be stupid to try such a thing. If he did, the snake-critter would catch him this time and subject him to the same horrors that Jenkins had suffered for the past four days.

Feeling worse than he had that morning, Jeb left the bridge and started home.

Sixteen

Fourth of July

That Saturday, Jeb, Grandma Sweeny, Sam, and Buckshot climbed into the one-mule wagon and headed down the dusty stretch of Mossy Creek Road for the main highway. Once upon the rural stretch of two-laned pavement, they crossed the Cumberland River bridge and drove straight into town. Jeb and Sam were smiling from ear to ear in anticipation of the festivities to come, while Grandma and Buckshot were slightly calmer, the latter sleeping on the tailgate of the buckboard most of the way.

Once they reached the outskirts of Pikesville, the serenity of the country gave way to hectic excitement. Cars and trucks were parked, bumper to bumper, on both sides of Main Street and folks crowded the sidewalks, standing three deep in spots. The canvas banner that stretched above the avenue, from Sherman's Grocery across to Drewer's Barber Shop, told it all. "PIKESVILLE 4TH OF JULY CELEBRATION," it read."PARADE, FOOD, SPORTS, MUSIC, & FIRE-WORKS!"

"Look, ya'll!" pointed Sam as they passed the fire station next to the grocery store. It was a little past eleven-thirty and the participants for the noon parade were already assembled in front of the red-brick building. "This is gonna be swell!"

As they passed beneath the banner and headed along Main

Street toward the courthouse, Grandma eyed the people that lined the sidewalks on both sides. "Sure is crowded," she said. "Everybody in Mangrum County must be here."

"Looks like it!" said Jeb with a big grin. He leaned over from where he sat in the bed of the wagon and shook his dog. "Wake up, Buckshot! You're gonna miss it all!"

With some effort, the hound opened his good eye and peered at the crowd they passed as they went by. The twin rows of men, women, and children—most holding small American flags in their hands—held absolutely no interest for him. Buckshot was about to go back to sleep, when the wagon reached the front lawn of the county courthouse and his nose began to twitch. The delicious scents of home cooking snaked up the coonhound's nostrils and, abruptly, he perked up. Soon, Jeb had to keep a firm grip on the back of Buckshot's collar just to keep him from jumping out of the wagon.

They found a place to park in the gravel lot next to the elementary school, then the Sweeny family climbed out of the wagon and headed for the courthouse lawn. When they reached the shady expanse of green grass and clover, Grandma headed straight for a long line of tables constructed of plywood and sawhorses, set end to end. Arranged on the tables was every type of Southern delicacy imaginable: fried chicken, deviled eggs, green beans with bacon, fried cornbread, creamed corn, macaroni and cheese, buttermilk biscuits, breaded catfish with hushpuppies, fried apples flavored with cinnamon, fruit salad, pickle relish, sweet potato casserole, pork barbecue, baked beans, corn muffins, yellow squash, fried okra, big slabs of country ham, mashed potatoes, stewed potatoes, fried potatoes, boiled cabbage, roast beef, glazed carrots, corn on the cob, turkey and dressing, chocolate cake, angelfood cake, coconut cake, pineapple upside-down cake, prune cake, walnut brownies, potato candy, pecan pie, fudge pie, chess pie, apple pie, lemon meringue pie, molded Jello, peach cobbler, banana pudding, and, of course, gallons of sweet iced tea and cold lemonade.

Grandma added her own additions of turnip casserole, blackeyed peas, and blackberry cobbler to the spread. Jeb tugged on the sleeve of the old woman's dress and found it to be much looser than it had been a couple of weeks ago. "Grandma, we're going over to watch the parade. Want to come?"

Lucille Sweeny smiled down at her only grandson. "No, you and Sam go on. I'm gonna stay here and help the ladies get everything set up."

"Are you sure?" asked Jeb.

"I'm sure," said the elderly woman, running her hand through his honey blond hair. "Just go on and have fun."

Jeb and Sam set off across the lawn toward the junction of Willow and Main. Finding the entire length of Main Street to be too congested, they settled for a spot on the corner next to a streetlamp. An old man in a straw hat and sleeve garters walked by, selling flags for a nickel each, and Jeb bought one for him and Sam to wave. The Fourth of July was a time of intense patriotism in the town of Pikesville and anyone who didn't make an effort to fit in with the rest of the crowd was sometimes looked upon as a malcontent or even a red communist, even though Jeb wasn't exactly sure what that was.

As the big clock in the courthouse tower struck the hour of twelve, a whistle sounded shrilly in the hot July air, followed by the staccato rhythm of a drum. Instantly, a cheer went up in the crowd and necks strained as folks tried to get the first glimpse of the Mangrum County High School band. Two majorettes headed the parade, wearing skimpy red, white, and blue uniforms and twirling batons. They were followed by four color guards holding a green and gold banner that bore the snarling face of the king of beasts and the words "GO MANGRUM COUNTY LIONS!" After that, came the two dozen pimply-faced teenagers that made up the high school band. They wore uniforms that had been passed down from one class to the next and were held together by sewing thread, safety pins, and lots of prayer. Their instruments were polished to a high gleam, but the version of "The Battle Hymn of the Republic" they played was a little slow and off-key. No one in the crowd minded, though. They cheered their youth on with pride and exuberance, waving their flags and whistling through their teeth.

As the band launched into a rousing rendition of "Dixie" the next feature of the parade showed up. It was four men of varying age, all dressed in military uniforms. Jake Jefferson, a strapping young man of twenty-four was the most decorated soldier of Mangrum County and had fought the Yellow Peril at Iwo Jima. He was followed by forty-five-year-old Hank Pugh, who had fought in World War I and won three Purple Hearts and the Bronze Star, and Elmer Thompson, a spry seventy-three-year-old who had accompanied Teddie Roosevelt up San Juan Hill during the Spanish-American War. The last one in the procession, pushed in an old-fashioned wooden wheelchair by one of his great-grandsons, was John Henry McGowen, dressed in the baggy, moth-eaten uniform of a Confederate soldier. John Henry was ninety-nine years old and had fought under General Hood when he was barely fifteen years old. Jeb had heard that the old man still had a mini-ball lodged a few inches from his lower spine where he had been shot during the bloody Battle of Franklin over in Williamson County.

Following the veterans, was the choir of the Pikesville Methodist Church, holding hymn books and wearing immaculate white robes trimmed in violet. After they had passed, singing "Nearer My God to Thee," came Mangrum's one and only fire engine. It was a long, red, 1925 Ford hook-and-ladder truck driven by the fire chief, Will Foster. Millie, the department dalmatian, sat obediently on the seat next to him and, next to the speckled dog, sat the mayor of Pikesville, Andrew Thorne II. Mayor Thorne was a rotund fellow who topped three hundred pounds and was dressed in his customary white suit and light tan fedora. The heat seemed to be a little too much for the fat man. Jeb noticed that his face was redder than usual and that dark circles the size of cake pans had formed beneath the armpits of the Mayor's bleached suitcoat.

The last one in the parade procession was Sheriff Ed North. He was dressed in the navy blue uniform and badged cap that he never wore during his daily duties, and waved from the window of his patrol car, which had been scrubbed to a glossy finish. The red light was spinning and the siren was on full-blast, but no one seemed to be particularly impressed. By the time he was halfway down Main Street, the crowd was already disbanding and heading north toward the courthouse and the bounty of food that awaited them.

Jeb and Sam were the seventh and eighth in line. They picked up paper plates and silverware, then ran the gambit of casseroles, meat platters, vegetable bowls, and desserts, piling on a little of each as they went. By the time they reached the end and had picked up cups of iced tea, their plates were nearly sagging in the middle.

As they went to find a place to eat, Jeb noticed that there was a separate table set up several yards away. The black folks of Mangrum County congregated there. Among them was Roscoe Ledbetter, holding a plate full of fatback and collard greens in one hand. Jeb waved to the old bluesman and he waved back, flashing a gold and ivory grin. It was only in the last couple of years that Jeb had begun to wonder exactly why the colored folks had a table separate from that of the white folks. He supposed it was for the same reason that Negroes weren't allowed to drink from public water fountains or use white rest rooms, although Jeb couldn't understand exactly what that reason was.

Jeb and Sam found a cool spot beneath the tallest oak tree on the lawn, then began to dig in. Jeb's plate was modestly garnished in comparison to the mound of food and cornbread that Sam had loaded on, which was nearly as high as a good-sized mole hill. The man wasn't allowed to indulge in it alone, however. Before Sam could shovel the first bite of food into his mouth, Buckshot was sitting down next to him, whimpering pitifully. Sam smiled benevolently at the hungry hound and began to toss him bits and pieces from his plate.

After everyone had eaten, folks stood around in groups, talking and letting their food digest properly. Jeb and Buckshot walked through the crowd, looking for something interesting to do. As they passed through the pockets of people, Jeb overheard snippets of conversation, all of which seemed to be uttered in excited whispers and centered on the same subject.

"Did you hear about the Huff baby?"

"Crying shame, wasn't it? Have they found the poor darling yet?"

"Nary a trace."

"The mother claims a dog came through the window and took it."

"Hogwash! Everyone knows Saundra Huff and that boozing husband of hers ain't nothing but pure white trash!"

"Surely, she couldn't have had nothing to do with it."

"Well, who knows? She's got eight youngsters already. Maybe she just got tired of caring for that baby."

"That's an awful thing to say! Did they find any blood in the cradle?"

"Yep. No more than a few drops, but there was blood on the poor thing's blanket, just as sure as I'm standing here."

Jeb tried to find out exactly what everyone was gossiping about, but the talk was interrupted when Mayor Thorne called for everyone's attention from the courthouse steps. As the politician proceeded to make one of his long-winded speeches, Jeb looked around and tried to catch a glimpse of Mandy Rutherford in the crowd. So far that day, he hadn't seen hide nor hair of the pretty, dark-haired girl. Disappointment began to set in. He recalled their encounter at Mossy Creek and the way her attitude had changed toward him after he had saved her from the threat of Troy Jenkins. He hoped she hadn't forgotten it all and was deliberately trying to steer clear of him. If it turned out that way, Jeb knew the rest of that day's festivities would seem lackluster due to his broken heart.

After Mayor Thorne finished his speech, he instructed everyone to assemble in the football field next to the high school. Fifteen minutes later, everyone was there. A number of sporting events were squared off with wooden pegs and twine, and folks began to line up to take their turn at footraces and horseshoe pitching.

When Jeb suggested that he and Sam try the three-legged race, Sam scratched his head. "But that's mostly for kids and their daddies, ain't it?" he asked.

Jeb felt that familiar pang of irretrievable loss nag at him once again. "Yeah, that's right," he said. "But you could pretend that you're my daddy, couldn't you? Just this once."

The suggestion seemed to strike Sam as being funny and he laughed. "Yep, I reckon I could, even if it is a little silly."

Jeb struggled to keep a smile on his face. "Come on. Let's give it a try."

When they reached the starting line and began to tie their legs together, Jeb was surprised to find that his beloved was already there. Mandy and her father, a tall dour man in a shirt and tie, had already tied their legs together with twine and were waiting for the shot of Ed North's blank pistol. Jeb was relieved when he looked over and found the girl smiling at him. The farmboy blushed bright red, but was bold enough to give her a quick wink. Then the crack of the gun went off and there was a mad rush across the field.

Jeb pulled his eyes from Mandy and concentrated on reaching the finish line. Somehow, both he and Sam worked together and kept from tripping up and falling like many others, Mandy and her father included. Surprisingly, Jeb and Sam were the first to cross the line. Amid cheers and pats on the back, Mayor Thorne held up their hands in victory and presented them with a blue ribbon.

Sam was ecstatic. "We won, Jeb! We won it!" he howled. After they had untied their legs, Sam gathered the boy up in a bearhug that threatened to crush all the air from his lungs. But Jeb didn't care. He simply hugged back and, for a brief moment, pretended that it was his true father embracing him and not a stranger with the mind of a five-year-old.

Around four o'clock, everyone tired of playing games. They met back at the porch of the courthouse for wedges of watermelon and bowls of homemade ice cream. By the time everyone had finished their snack, a bluegrass band called Joe Tucker and the Log Cabin Gang made a stage of the porch. They tuned up guitar, banjo, standing bass, and mandolin, while Joe Tucker himself rosined up the bow of his fiddle. Then as the sun began to set, they began to play and folks began to clap and stomp their feet. Soon, there was a full-blown square dance in progress. Men and women, boys and girls began to pair off and shake a leg to "Turkey in the Straw," "Cotton-Eyed Joe," and "Buffalo Gals."

Jeb wasn't much for dancing, so he went to the edge of the lawn and watched as the fire department began setting up the fireworks. He wasn't there but a moment or two, when he felt someone take his hand. Instantly a jolt like raw electricity shot up his arm to the base of his brain. He looked over to see Mandy standing next to him.

"Hi, Jeb," she said, flashing those pretty blue eyes at him.

Jeb's Adam's apple bobbed like a yoyo on a string. "Oh, howdy."

"Congratulations on the race," said Mandy. "Me and Daddy would've probably come in second, but he got all tangled up. Where's your ribbon?"

Jeb's hand began to sweat and he wondered if the girl noticed. "Sam's got it pinned to his shirt like it's some kind of war medal. He's right proud of it."

Mandy looked puzzled. "How come you call your papa by his first name?"

Embarrassment turned Jeb's cheeks red hot. "It's kinda hard to explain."

"My daddy says he got hurt in the War," said Mandy. Her hand tightened a bit. "That there was some kind of explosion and it made him simple-minded."

"He ain't simple-minded!" snapped Jeb. "It's just that he don't remember a lot of what he used to. It's like it erased the person he was before."

"Oh, I see," said Mandy, although Jeb knew she really didn't understand.

The farmboy looked down to see that the girl held something in her other hand. "Whatcha got there?"

The girl held up the brightly colored box. "Sparklers. Mommy would have a fit if she knew I had them, but Daddy said it was okay, if I was careful."

"You got matches, too?"

"Of course, silly!" laughed Mandy. "They wouldn't be worth anything without matches, would they?"

"Let's light a couple," urged Jeb.

"Not until dark," she said. "Not until the fireworks, okay?"

Jeb shrugged. "Okay."

They watched Chief Foster and his men set up the rockets and Roman candles until it was almost time for the fireworks to begin. The twilight had deepened and the only lights that shown across the courthouse lawn were those around the makeshift bandstand and the winking pinpoints of fireflies hovering in the darkness.

"This ought to be the best place in the world to see the fireworks," said Mandy.

"Naw, I know a better place," said Jeb. He tugged at her hand. "Come on. I'll show you."

Together, they ran across the courthouse lawn, past the crowd of dancing folks and those who simply stood and clapped along. Mandy was surprised when they stopped at the base of the towering oak tree. "Here?" she said, disappointed. "But you can't see a thing for all the leaves."

Jeb rolled his eyes. "Not here at the bottom. At the top!"

Fear shown in the girl's pretty face. "But . . . I can't."

"Aw, heck, you've climbed trees before, ain't you?" asked Jeb.

The look of apprehension in her eyes instantly told him that she hadn't.

He tightened his grip on her hand. "Well, there ain't nothing to be scared of. I'll help you up every step of the way."

"But, I'll fall," she said, her voice tiny.

"No, you won't," Jeb assured her. "I won't let you."

Carefully, they began to shimmy up the trunk of the tree, hugging its rough column with their arms and legs. When they reached the lowest limb, they swung over and pulled themselves up. Jeb and Mandy sat there for a moment, catching their breaths.

"Are you okay?" he asked.

"Sure," she replied, although her face was a little pale.

"Then come on," he said, standing and reaching for the branch above them.

Slowly, limb by limb, the two made their way up the oak. Finally, they reached the uppermost branches. Finding a broad crook between two limbs, the boy and girl parked themselves there. The foliage was open above them, giving the two an unobscured view of the vast, night sky.

For a while, they sat there and talked about how the summer was going so far and what the coming school year would bring. Finally, the subject that had nagged Jeb the most during the day came to mind. "I've been hearing folks talking about some baby disappearing. You heard about it yet?"

"Goodness gracious yes!" piped Mandy. "I heard Daddy and Mommy talking about it over breakfast this morning. Saundra Huff's new baby boy vanished out of its crib in the middle of the night. The window next to its bed was open and when its mother came to feed it early this morning, the cradle was empty, except for a few drops of blood. Daddy knows those Huffs and he thinks something odd might be going on. He don't believe that a dog snatched it, like Mrs. Huff thinks happened."

"He thinks she did something to it, don't he?" asked Jeb.

"Well, a lot of folks do," said Mandy. "After all, she is white trash."

"Just like he thought I was?"

Mandy Rutherford grew quiet at Jeb's question, knowing now that her father had been wrong, if only that once in his life.

"I don't think it was Mrs. Huff," Jeb told her. "And I don't think it was no dog, either."

"What then?" Mandy wanted to know.

Jeb swallowed dryly, then went ahead and said it. "The snake-critter, that's what."

Mandy giggled. "Aw, come on! That's just a made-up story that's been going around town."

"No it ain't!" declared Jeb. "And I'll tell you why! 'Cause I saw it with my own eyes!"

Mandy was about to ask him more, when their discussion was interrupted by a loud *whoosh*. A dark column of smoke rose into the starry summer sky, followed by an eruption of dazzling light the color of polished silver.

"Wow!" said Jeb in awe. "Will you look at that!"

Another rocket rose into the sky. A spreading bloom of bright red sparks blossomed with a brittle crack. "You were right, Jeb!" cried Mandy, her eyes wide. "This is the best place to watch!"

For the next twenty minutes, the sky over Pikesville was filled with sparkling light and the smell of burnt gunpowder. The crowd on the lawn below ooohed and ahhhed with each firework that lit the sky. Jeb and Mandy, however, were struck speechless. Finally, Chief Foster unleashed the big finale. Rockets and Roman candles went off in one gigantic burst, cloaking the sky in a cascading umbrella of spinning lights. For a moment, it was almost as if the dark blanket of the night had been opened up and it was daylight again.

"It's beautiful!" said Mandy.

"Yeah, it is," said Jeb. "Just like you."

The farmboy groaned inwardly at the corny statement he had just uttered. He was afraid it might draw a laugh or a slap in the face from the girl next to him. But, pleasantly enough, it had the opposite effect. He felt her grip on his hand tighten a little. When he turned his head, he found her staring straight at him.

"Have you ever kissed a girl before?" she asked.

Jeb swallowed dryly. "Can't say that I have."

"Would you like to?"

Although he was scared half out of his wits, he couldn't pass up the invitation. "Yes."

As the last burst of fireworks erupted in the night sky and the crowd below them began to clap and cheer, the two children leaned in close to one another. There was a moment of hesitation, then they closed their eyes and allowed their lips to meet. The kiss was a short one, lasting barely three seconds. But it was enough for Jeb Sweeny. A sensation of warmth and lightheadedness engulfed him and, for a second, he felt as if he might sprout wings and soar into the smoky black sky. When he finally pulled away, he felt a little disoriented and almost lost his seat on the limb beneath him.

An instant of panic gripped Jeb and he was certain that the girl would either gag or start giggling. But, mercifully, she did neither. Instead, she seemed to be just as giddy as Jeb. "Wow," she said softly.

"Yeah," was all that Jeb could say in reply. They had forgotten all about the girl's sparklers, but he didn't care. The kiss he'd shared with Mandy was better than a whole crate of dumb old sparklers.

As the crowd dispersed and folks began to drift toward their trucks and cars, a familiar voice called from below. "Jeb! Jeb Sweeny . . . where in tarnation are you, boy?"

Jeb shook his head in annoyance. "Aw, that's my grandmother," he told the girl sitting next to him. "I'd better go or she'll tan my hide."

"I've got to go, too," said Mandy. "Daddy and Mommy are still mad at me about wandering off Sunday like I did."

Jeb tightened his grip on her hand. "Come on, but be careful. It's a little trickier going down than it is going up."

Five minutes later, they were back on solid ground. "Well, I'll see you around, Mandy," said Jeb, a little reluctantly.

"Sure," said the girl. She released the boy's hand, since it would have been sheer disaster for one of their peers to see them acting so affectionately toward each other. Suddenly, she remembered the box of sparklers. She opened the flap, withdrew six or seven of the silvery sticks, and handed them to Jeb. "Here, you can take these home with you."

"Thanks," said Jeb with a smile. "Well, I gotta go."

Mandy nodded shyly. "Me, too. I'll be looking for you next weekend."

"We'll be coming to town next Saturday," Jeb assured her. "So I'll see you then."

The girl leaned forward and gave him one last peck on the cheek. Then she scurried off into the milling crowd of weary people.

Jeb savored the kiss, vowing not to wash that particular cheek for at least two or three days. He turned and saw Grandma and Sam looking for him. He slipped the sparklers into the side pocket of his overalls, then went to join them.

A half hour later, they were well out of the Pikesville city limits and back on the main road again. As the wagon crossed the bridge, Jeb looked out over the dark channel of the Cumberland River. He thought of Troy Jenkins down in the cliffside cave and wondered if he was still alive. He also wondered if the bully had any company in the cavernous prison. Perhaps a tiny, squalling bundle stuck to the cave wall in a cocoon of snakehide.

Jeb rose to his feet in the bed of the wagon and listened. Far away, toward the south, he was certain that he heard something, if only for a moment.

It almost sounded like the shrill cry of an infant.

Jeb lurched to the front of the wagon and tapped Sam on the shoulder. "Stop the wagon for a minute!"

"Why?" asked Sam.

"Just do it!" said Jeb.

Sam pulled back on the reins and hollered "Whoa!" Nellie the mule snorted and stopped in the center of the bridge.

They sat there for a long moment, while Jeb jumped out and ran to the side railing.

"Whatever is the matter, Jeb?" asked Grandma.

Jeb stuck his head over the side of the bridge and listened. "I thought I heard something."

"Well, what did you hear?"

After a few moments of straining his ears, Jeb heard absolutely nothing out of the ordinary. "Nothing, I reckon," he finally said.

"Then hop back in this wagon and let's get on home," Grandma said. It was plain to see that the day's festivities had taken a lot out of her. "It's getting late."

Jeb stared toward the southern bank of the river one last time, then went back to the wagon. As he settled down in the bed, the wagon lurched back into motion once again.

Even when they were a mile or so beyond the Cumberland River bridge, Jeb still couldn't get the incident out of his mind. He sat and stroked Buckshot's head, wondering if the cry in the night had been for real or was simply a product of his youthful imagination.

It could have very well been an illusion conjured by the roar of the river and the squeak of one of the wagon's ungreased axles.

But, in his heart, he was sure that it was something more.

Seventeen

The Dreaded Moment

The following Monday, Jeb set off for the woods following the completion of what little chores he had to do that morning. Since there were no crops to tend to in the fields and Sam was capable of feeding the animals, Jeb found that he had a lot of time on his hands that summer. He also had a lot of time to think as well, and he found himself roaming the backwoods, racking his brain for solutions to the many problems he and Sam would face following Grandma's death. But, for the most part, those solutions seemed to elude him, which led him to feeling more frustrated and depressed than ever.

That day, Jeb packed a sack of cheese and crackers, a canteen of water, and a green apple, and set off for the wilderness of the forest. He purposely avoided the northern end of Mossy Creek, aware that the snake-critter might roam there, in search of fresh victims. Jeb found himself thinking more and more about the creature and exactly why it had come to Mangrum County. One fact was clear in his mind; following the abduction of Troy Jenkins, the string of animal killings had abruptly ended. But why? Before, the creature had glutted itself with fresh meat, but now it seemed content to sleep and feed off the blood of Troy. Jeb could only come up with one reason for that. Maybe the snake-critter was unaccustomed to devouring human flesh. Maybe it had to allow its system time to tolerate the new diet before it began to feed again. The very thought made Jeb shudder. When it did develop a craving for human flesh, then what? He could imagine the creature stalking Mangrum County, snatching children from their beds at night, and maybe even full-grown folks, if it grew bold enough.

Jeb again thought of telling someone about the whereabouts of Troy Jenkins. But who? He'd considered going to Mayor Thorne. After all, he was Ed North's boss, in a sense. But Jeb abandoned that idea. The Mayor was a no-nonsense man and was notorious for being intolerant of children. If Jeb did tell him his story, the obese politician wouldn't believe him. And when Sheriff North got wind of Jeb spilling the beans, he wouldn't hesitate to make good on his promise and send the farmboy off to the state reformatory.

All that day, he roamed the woods with Buckshot, running that problem and others over and over in his head. When he finally grew tired of thinking, Jeb headed for a hidden waterhole that lay a good two miles back in the dense woods. He crossed the railroad tracks that headed north to south, then made his way down a shadowy hollow. When he reached the bottom, he found the broad pond unoccupied. There had been times when he had gone there and found other kids swimming there, or a herd of white-tailed deer drinking at its edge. But, that day, it appeared as though Jeb had it all to himself.

Quickly, Jeb shed his overalls. Naked, he let out a whoop and plunged into the swimming hole. The water was deliciously cool in comparison to the sweltering humidity that Jeb had been forced to endure during his wandering. Once, during one of Jeb's previous swims there, the boy had held his breath and tried to dive to the bottom of the pond. But he had never found it. Jeb had surfaced for air, certain that the pool was either incredibly deep or bottomless. He preferred to believe the latter. It made it much more fun to swim there thinking that the hole reached clear to the center of the earth.

Jeb swam in the pond for several hours. When he finally climbed out and began to tug on his overalls, he looked at the position of the sun overhead. From where it hung, he could tell that it was well past four o'clock in the afternoon. Jeb knew that he had a good hour of walking before he made it back home again and Grandma always had supper on the table at five o'clock sharp, with no exceptions.

"Come on, Buckshot!" called Jeb. "We gotta hightail it on home. If we're late, Grandma'll take a willow switch to our backsides!"

Lazily, the bluetick hound yawned and pried himself from a bed of soft ferns that grew at the pond's edge. A dragonfly hovered above the still water, then flew at the dog, dive-bombing his head. Buckshot snarled and snapped at the winged insect, then followed his master up the kudzu-covered slope of the backwoods hollow.

By the time they reached the Sweeny farm, the sun was already setting in the west. "Come on, boy!" Jeb urged, nearly out of breath. "We gotta hurry." He didn't know exactly what time it was, but he knew it was five-thirty or even later.

However, the moment he stepped upon the back porch, Jeb knew that something was wrong. The kitchen light was on, but there were two very important things missing when he opened the screen door; the heat of the iron cookstove and the delicious smell of freshly-cooked food.

A sensation of cold dread filled him and he turned toward the kitchen table. It wasn't even set, not even the plates and silverware. And that wasn't all. Sam sat in his chair at the far end of the table, his hands fidgeting with one another and his eyes moist and red. It was plain to see that he had been crying . . . and for a while now.

"What's wrong, Sam?" asked Jeb. "Why hasn't Grandma got supper on the table?"

Fresh tears rolled down the big man's cheeks. "Something's wrong with Grandma," he said, his eyes full of confusion. "She's sick or something. Awful sick. She's in bed and she won't get up. I tried to help her up, but all she does is groan and draw up into a ball."

Jeb swallowed nervously. As he walked past Sam, he patted his father on the shoulder. "You stay here, Sam. I'll go see to her."

As the boy started down the hallway toward the door of Grandma's bedroom, he felt fear grip him. What if she was dead when he got there? What would he do then? He felt the wet heat of tears threaten to surface, but he choked back the crippling emotion. He knew he had to be strong, both for Grandma and for Sam.

Jeb reached the door and slowly pushed it inward. The shades on the windows were down and Grandma's room was gloomy. "Grandma?" he asked, his voice shaky. "Are you all right?"

At first, he was sure that she was dead. She neglected to answer him and he was certain when he touched her, she would be as cold as a ham in a winter smokehouse. But when he reached Grandma, he found her to still be as warm as ever. In fact, she seemed to be *too* warm. He placed the palm of his hand against her clammy forehead and discovered that she was in the throes of a high fever.

Grandma groaned. Feebly, her hand reached up and took his. It was like holding hands with a skeleton. "Jeb. Praise the Lord you're here, son."

Jeb saw the pain in the old woman's eyes. "Are you hurting, Grandma?"

"Yes," she replied. "Badly. Have been since around one or two o'clock."

The thought of his grandmother hurting for so long a period of time was nearly unbearable for him. "I'll go fetch your medicine," he said.

"No need," she whispered, her breathing shallow. "It's all gone."

Jeb glanced at the nightstand next to her bed. The laudanum bottle stood there with the cap beside it. The container was completely empty.

"Go get Claudine," Grandma told him. "Hurry, boy. I don't know how much longer I can stand this pain."

Jeb kissed his grandmother's sweaty forehead. "I'll be back as quick as I can," he promised. Then he ran through the house, toward the back door.

By the time his feet hit the grass of the backyard, Jeb heard a scream echo from behind him. He knew it was the agonized cry of his grandmother and, for a moment, he considered going back to her. But he knew that he couldn't help her that way. He headed north for Claudine Johnson's house, the horrible screams of raw pain driving him faster and faster.

An hour later, Jeb, Sam, and Claudine Johnson sat at the kitchen table, waiting patiently. After Miss Claudine had called Doc Griffith on her telephone—she owned one of the few south of Pikesville—she and Jeb had returned to the Sweeny house. Once the doctor arrived and was tending to Grandma's misery, Miss Claudine put on a pot of vegetable soup. They now sat and ate their late supper, although no one at the table was particular hungry.

Eventually, they heard the door to Grandma's bedroom close and the sound of footsteps in the hallway. Pikesville's only medical practitioner, Dean Griffith, stood in the kitchen doorway a moment later. He looked tired and not at all optimistic.

"How is she, Doc?" asked Miss Claudine.

"Resting comfortably now," he said. "I had to give her a shot to help ease the pain."

Jeb tried hard to remember the name of the pain-killer Miss Claudine had mentioned before. "Morphine?" he asked.

Doc Griffith's eyes softened. "Yes, son. I'm afraid so." He turned toward the elderly woman. "Can I talk to you for a moment in private, Claudine?"

"Of course," she said, getting up. "You boys finish your soup and I'll be back in a jiffy."

Miss Claudine accompanied Doc Griffith to the front door, leaving Jeb and Sam alone. "Is Grandma gonna be all right?" asked Sam glumly, staring down at the hunks of carrots and celery that floated in his soup.

Jeb knew the time for lying was over with. "I don't know, Sam," said the boy. "I honestly don't know."

They sat in the kitchen for a while. Jeb heard the low voices of Miss Claudine and the doctor as they discussed something. Then he heard the old woman enter the house and the roar of Doc Griffith's '45 Packard starting up. When Miss Claudine entered the kitchen, Jeb was shocked at how very pale and scared she looked. She walked over, sat down in her chair, and placed something on the table beside her plate. It was a long, thin bundle wrapped in butcher paper and secured with string.

"What's that?" asked Jeb, although he had a good idea already.

"It's medicine for your grandma," she simply said.

An awkward silence hung around the kitchen table for a long moment. Then Sam spoke up. "What'd the doctor say, Miss Claudine?" he asked. "Is Grandma gonna be okay?"

Claudine Johnson stared at the innocent face of Sam

Sweeny and, at first, Jeb was sure she was going to burst out crying. But she straightened her spine and contained herself. "I ain't gonna lie to you, Sam. No, she ain't gonna be okay. Grandma's sick . . . and she ain't ever gonna be well again."

"What do you mean?" asked Sam, confused. "The doctor was just here. Didn't he make her well again?"

Miss Claudine struggled to find the right way to tell him. "The sickness that Grandma's got, well, it's the kind that Doc Griffith doesn't have a cure for. He's given her some strong medicine to keep her from hurting, but that's all it's good for."

"I don't understand," said Sam. Tears began to bloom in his eyes again.

Miss Claudine reached over and took Sam's big hand in her own. "Grandma's gonna get worse and worse, until, some day, she just won't wake up again. Then she'll go to heaven to live with Jesus and God."

Sam recalled the things he'd learned in church following his return from the War. "She'll be an angel then and she won't hurt no more?"

"That's right," said Miss Claudine. She looked over at Jeb. "Remember what we talked about the other night?"

"About Grandma being too sick for us to take care of?" replied the boy.

"Yes," said the old woman. "Well, I think the time has come. I'd like to move her over to my house in the morning, if you two would be willing to help me."

Jeb nodded solemnly. Like it or not, the dreaded moment was at hand, even sooner than he had expected. The severity of Grandma's cancer had reached its crucial point. From then on, the woman he loved most in the world would gradually drift away from him. Her health would decline, day by day, until her bodily systems would shut down completely. When that eventually happened, Jeb knew it would be the darkest day of his young life.

"But how're we gonna eat?" asked Sam. "How're we gonna wash our clothes? Grandma did all that."

"Ya'll can come next door for all your meals," said Miss Claudine. "As for your washing and such, I reckon you'll just have to make do by yourselves."

"We can do it," assured Jeb. "Don't worry."

Miss Claudine left her chair and started for the hallway. "I'm gonna see to Lucille and see that she's resting comfortably. Then I'll go home and get some sleep and I'll be back over bright and early tomorrow morning."

"We're much obliged for your help, Miss Claudine," Jeb said sincerely.

The elderly woman smiled. "Like I said . . . she's the best friend I have in this world. It wouldn't be fitting for me to do any less for her."

After Miss Claudine had left the kitchen, Sam turned his bloodshot eyes toward the blond-haired boy in the Duckhead overalls. "Jeb," he said, his broad face full of unanswered questions. "What'll become of us after Grandma goes to heaven?"

Jeb shook his head glumly. "I can't rightly say," was all he said in reply. But, even as he uttered those words, his mind had already conjured vivid pictures of foreclosure signs, tearful goodbyes, and state institutions with dull gray walls and dozens of unwanted souls locked inside. He hoped that the images in his head were false; that they wouldn't be quite as grim and foreboding as his imagination painted them.

But sitting at the kitchen table with his grandmother slowly dying in the next room, Jeb couldn't help but believe that, in reality, they would turn out to be much, much worse.

Eighteen

Abduction

About the time that Jeb and Sam were sitting around the kitchen table, Mandy Rutherford had already been in bed for nearly an hour.

She was sleepy, but not yet asleep. The night was muggy and hot. Her bedroom window was open and an electric fan sitting atop her chest-of-drawers was aimed directly at her, but she still had the covers bunched down around her feet and the top buttons of her nightgown unfastened. She found it difficult to sleep comfortably during the summer months. Mandy's favorite seasons were fall and winter, mainly because she could burrow beneath her blankets and quilts and drift off to sleep immediately. The heat that hung in the air that July night, as well as the monotonous singing of crickets, made it difficult to relax.

From the downstairs parlor of the Rutherford's two-story Victorian home drifted music from the radio. Even though it was almost too low to make out, Mandy recognized it as a Big Band song, perhaps from Benny Goodman or Glenn Miller. She couldn't say for sure exactly which it was; they all sounded about the same to her.

Mandy pictured the parlor with its marble fireplace, silk draperies, and the antique chairs and sofa that been passed down to her mother from her now-deceased grandmother. Her father would be sitting next to the radio, his nose stuck in the Nashville newspaper, reading the political and financial sections. Her mother, a thin, birdlike woman with dark hair, would be sitting on the far end of the sofa, reading a copy of *Good Housekeeping* or *Gone With The Wind* for the twelfth time. There was one thing for certain; they probably wouldn't be engaged in conversation. For some reason Mandy couldn't understand, her parents didn't talk to one another very much any more.

She lay there in bed and closed her eyes once again. She thought of the sky full of sparkling fireworks, Jeb Sweeny, and the kiss they had shared. Mandy smiled to herself. Her father would wear her out with his shaving strop if he ever found out that she'd actually kissed a boy from the "wrong side of the tracks" smack-dab on the lips. But, unless someone else had seen them at the top of the oak tree, it was doubtful that he would ever find out. Her father was a stern man who had a head full of business and very little time for anything beyond the doors of the Mangrum County Bank, his family included. The only reason he had consented to joining Mandy in the three-legged race was because she had pouted around until he couldn't stand it any longer. Mandy was a master at the art of pouting. The simple tearing of an eye or protrusion of a lower lip had netted her most of the toys that decorated her bedroom; the three-story dollhouse, the zoo of stuffed animals, even her precious Queenie when the fluffy cat had been a mere kitten.

Speaking of Queenie, the cat was stretched out on the bedsheet that covered the girl's ankles. Mandy enjoyed the added warmth during the cooler months, but that night it only made her feet sweat. But she didn't push Queenie away. Except for the times the feline was sick or in heat, she was constantly at her mistress's side. In fact, sometimes, Mandy thought that Queenie was her only true friend. Most of the kids at school saw only her father's prominent position in the community or the big fine house she lived in, and not Mandy for herself. But she supposed that was how kids who had little or no money at all acted toward one who had way too much.

The sound of jazzy brass ended and an advertisement for Arm & Hammer Baking Soda followed. It was during that break in the radio show that Mandy noticed something peculiar. The constant creaking of the crickets had abruptly ceased. All that she heard from beyond the window was the rustling of a breeze through the leaves of the sugar maple tree that grew directly beside the house. But, no, it couldn't be the wind. There was none that muggy July night. The summer air simply hung there and failed to stir.

Queenie seemed to sense that something was amiss the same time that Mandy did. The white cat left her prone position and jumped to her feet. The girl watched as the pet arched her back and hissed with an uncharacteristic display of tiny white teeth.

Mandy looked toward the open window. "What is it, Queenie?" she asked almost breathlessly. "What's out there?"

The rustling of leaves grew closer and, suddenly, Queenie was leaping off the bed and onto the hardwood floor. Before Mandy could kick the cover off her feet and go after her, the cat had jumped up on the window ledge, then hopped out into the night.

"Queenie, come back here!" called Mandy. "Don't go out there!"

Only silence followed Queenie's disappearance as the girl approached the open window on barefeet. Then came a low-throated growl, followed by a shrill yowl. Horrified, Mandy recognized the latter sound as belonging to her cat. She had heard Queenie utter a similar cry before, when Grandmother Rutherford accidently mashed the cat's tail beneath the runners of her rocking chair. But upon further thought, Mandy decided it had sounded different this time. It was more a scream of intense agony than one of mild pain and surprise.

"Queenie? she whispered. "Are you all right, girl?"

The cat uttered no other sound. The darkness beyond the window was deathly quiet.

Although she knew it was foolish to do so, Mandy crept to the window and, leaning forward, looked out. Beyond the leafy branches of the maple tree, she could see the distant streetlights that lined Main Street. For all outward appearances, the night seemed like any other summer night in Pikesville. Except, of course, for the absence of crickets singing in the darkness.

When Mandy looked downward toward the freshly mowed lawn below, hoping to catch a glimpse of a white cat against black shadows, the rustle of maple leaves came again . . . directly beneath her bedroom window. Startled, she stared at a long limb that stretched from the column of the maple's trunk and nearly touched the clapboard wall of the house.

Something clung to that limb. Something long and as shiny and black as wet tar. And, although she found out too late, something that was patiently waiting for Mandy Rutherford to show herself.

The girl froze, unable to move back into the safety of her bedroom. In horror, she watched as two eyes peered at her through the dense foliage; huge, oval eyes that blazed up at her like raw foxfire.

Mandy tried to pry her gaze away, but she seemed to be drawn by those awful, almost hypnotic eyes. Before she knew what was happening, she found herself leaning forward, over the edge of the sash. At the same instant, the creature on the tree limb seemed to lengthen and uncoil. Mandy tried to scream, but only a low whistle of air would exit her throat, so powerful was the influence of those serpentine eyes.

Then, a moment later, it had her. Mandy felt talons latch

onto her around the waist, their hooked claws ripping through her nightgown and anchoring into the flesh of her belly and back. As it pulled her completely from the window and brought her closer to those terrible eyes, Mandy began to struggle. She shifted her gaze away and felt her senses dizzily returning. Mandy was about to unleash a blood-curdling scream, when the dark face beneath the monstrous eyes split into a toothy grin. She watched, terrified, as two of the fangs seemed to push out from the slimy black gums and grow longer than the others. Something vile and green seeped from the ends of those fangs, coating the needle-fine points like a thick syrup.

Without warning, the creature's head lurched forward with incredible speed. Mandy felt the fangs strike her in the side of the neck with a dull, stinging sensation. Dazed, she waited for pain to come, but it never did. Instead, a soft feeling of numbness spread through her neck and down her spine. It was not unlike the shot of novocaine that Dr. Hayes had given her when he had pulled that tooth she had shattered on a stubborn jawbreaker last spring.

Mandy tried to pull free from the monster's grip, but the bite was affecting her strangely. The numbness quickly spread to her arms and legs, making them seem rubbery and boneless. It wasn't long before she could do nothing but dangle there limply, able to see and breathe, but that was all.

Below, toward the front of the house, came the slam of a screen door. Mandy recognized the authoritative footsteps of her father on the floor of the porch.

"What is it, dear?" asked her mother's voice from the open window of the parlor.

"It was that damned cat of Amanda's," said Charles Rutherford. "I'm sure of it!"

Daddy! the girl wanted to scream out. *Help me, Daddy! Something's got a hold of me! Something horrible!* She wanted to say that, but her vocal cords were just as impotent as the rest of her body.

"Well, do you see it out there?" her mother asked again.

"No," admitted her father. "I can't see a thing."

"Then come back in and finish your paper."

At first, Mandy thought her father would step out into the yard to investigate. Instead, he followed his wife's advice. His footsteps moved back across the porch, then the front door closed behind him. Mandy knew then that her father would not come to her rescue. She was at the mercy of the beast that had her in its grasp.

Mandy felt her head swim and the darkness of the night around her deepened even more. She fainted soon thereafter. The last sensation Mandy was aware of was the slow descent of the creature as it made its way downward, one limb at a time, to the ground below.

Nineteen

Helpless Knight

The following afternoon, Jeb was sitting on the front porch of the Sweeny house, thinking of what had taken place last night, as well as the grim transfer of Grandma to Miss Claudine's house earlier that morning.

Claudine Johnson had cooked him and Sam a breakfast of flapjacks and sausage, then told them that it was time. Quietly, scarcely uttering a single word between them, Sam, Jeb, and Miss Claudine had carried Grandma from her bedroom and loaded her onto the bed of the mule wagon. Jeb had been stunned by how Grandma had looked in the bright sunlight of early morning. Her face was as yellow as the pages of an old book and the spaces beneath her cheekbones and around her closed eyes seemed dark and sunken. As they laid her in the wagon, she had been jolted out of her drug-induced sleep, but her eyes were glazed and beyond comprehension. She had stared at her son and grandson as if they were total strangers, then drifted back to sleep again.

After they had made the short trip to the Johnson farm and made Grandma comfortable in the guest room, Miss Claudine had assured them that she would attend to her friend's every need and told them to come back at noon for dinner. When they had showed up at twelve o'clock and feasted on a meal of chicken and dumplings, Jeb had gone to the second-floor bedroom to check on Grandma. She was still asleep, although fitfully so. Before he left the room, the boy noticed the contents of the package Doc Griffith had given Miss Claudine lying on the nightstand next to the bed. It was a hypodermic syringe, a pack of spare needles, and a small bottle of crystal-clear liquid. Morphine, thought Jeb and he had to leave the room fast, for fear that he might start crying.

Having finished most of his chores for the day, Sam had asked if he could do anything around the farm for Miss Claudine. Jeb knew he only wanted to be close to Grandma, in case she "hauled off and went to heaven," as he put it. Jeb, on the other hand, couldn't stand to stick around. He walked back home and spent the remainder of that afternoon doing nothing but sitting on the front porch and brooding. Not that it had done him any good. Thinking about Grandma's illness and what it would eventually lead to only seemed to plunge him deeper and deeper into despair.

His dark thoughts were interrupted by the sound of an engine grinding its way along Mossy Creek Road from the direction of town. Jeb knew that sound immediately. It was Reece Tilton's mail jeep making its daily rounds. Reece was one of Mangrum County's three mailmen, and Jeb's favorite among the trio. Reece Tilton was a portly, gray-haired gentleman who always had a smile on his face and a joke on his lips, even on rainy days. Whenever Jeb received one of the many cereal box premiums he sent off for—like a Green Hornet decoder ring or an autographed photo of the Lone Ranger and Tonto—it was Reece who cheerfully delivered it to the Sweeny mailbox.

Thinking that a visit with Reece might brighten his day, Jeb left the front porch and walked out to his mailbox. The postman was pulling up in his army jeep—which was painted primer gray—by the time the farmboy reached the road.

"Howdy, Jeb!" called the mailman, throwing up a pudgy hand.

"Howdy, Mr. Tilton," replied Jeb. "Got anything for us today?"

The man handed Jeb a couple of envelopes and a folded paper. "Not much. Just letters from the power company and the bank. Oh, and an advertisement from that new beauty shop that's opening up on Main Street." Reece laughed to himself. "It's only for women, but it's still got Howard Drewer in a foul mood."

Jeb looked down at the letter from the Mangrum County Bank. He could imagine what it said inside. "Thanks," he muttered, not really meaning it.

When he glanced back at the mailman, he saw a somber look on his ruddy face. It was an expression that didn't suit the good-natured postman. Jeb knew then that Reece Tilton wouldn't be telling any jokes that day.

"Jeb," began the man, looking a little uncomfortable. "Son, I heard about your Grandma. Doc Griffith told me this morning."

The boy said nothing, he simply nodded.

"A blasted shame is what it is," said Reece. "No finer woman's walked the earth than your grandma and here something like this happens to her. Makes you wonder if there's any fairness left in the world."

"I know what you mean," said Jeb.

A nostalgic look came into the mailman's soft brown eyes. "You might not know it, Jeb, but I courted your grandmother once."

Jeb was surprised. "Really?"

"Yep, but then your grandpa came along and she took a shine to him instead. I reckon it was for the best, 'cause I met my Charlotte right after that and we've been married for pert near fifty years now."

Jeb forced a smile, then decided to head on back to the house. "Well, thanks for thinking of Grandma, Mr. Reece. I'll sure tell her you stopped by."

Before Jeb could turn and leave, though, the mailman said something that stopped him in his tracks. "I ran into Ed North this morning, too. He said one of your little classmates has turned up missing."

"Yeah," said Jeb. "Troy Jenkins."

"Naw, that's old news, boy," said Reece. "This one was a girl."

Jeb felt his heart sink. "Who?" he asked. The names of his classmates ran through his mind. Shirley Brown, Linda Hackett, Tammy Lou Daniels. . . .

"Amanda Rutherford," said the mailman. "You know, the banker's daughter."

"Yeah," uttered Jeb dully. "I know her."

Reece Tilton shook his gray head. "Whole town's up in arms about it. Seems that someone climbed through her bedroom window last night and made off with her. The sheriff and her father seem to think it was a kidnapper, but I ain't at all sure."

Stunned, Jeb looked at the old man. "Why's that?"

"They found the girl's cat underneath that maple tree next to the Rutherford's house. The poor thing had been torn completely in half."

In a flash, it all became clear to Jeb. He knew at that moment who—or more precisely *what*—had abducted his beloved Mandy.

Reece reached out and patted Jeb on the shoulder. "Boy, you're whiter than lard. Didn't mean to scare you none."

"I'm okay, Mr. Tilton," he said. "Really, I am."

"Well, I reckon I'd best be going," said the mailman. "You

take care, young man. And remember . . . me and the Mrs., we'll be praying for your grandma."

"I appreciate that," was all that Jeb could find to say.

He watched as the jeep continued its way southward along Mossy Creek Road. For a long moment, he simply stood there, his mind addled by the news that Reece Tilton had brought, along with a handful of overdue bills. Then, abruptly, a sense of urgency struck him like a bolt out of the blue. He turned and ran back to the farmhouse as fast his legs could carry him.

Jeb wrenched open the front door and sprinted down the hallway to the kitchen. Once he reached the pantry, he reached for the chain of the overhead light and snapped it on. He quickly gathered up the things he would need; the long-handled flashlight Miss Claudine had given him, as well as the twenty-gauge shotgun.

Then, with a mixture of fear and determination on his freckled face, he left through the back door and headed for the river.

An hour later, he reached the southern bank of the Cumberland. Winded by his mad dash, Jeb paused near the scraggly clump of stunted sycamore trees. Setting the shotgun aside, he placed his hands on his knees and breathed in deeply, trying to catch his breath. It was then that he spotted several tracks in the powdery clay dirt at his feet. The splayed paw prints were identical to those they had found in the hollow following the murder of Old Jack.

Identical, that was, except for one important factor. These were much larger. On the previous tracks, the length of each toe had been four inches. These were clearly *six* inches long, maybe more.

It's growing! thought Jeb in horror. *It's getting bigger!*

Although his heart pounded and he felt as if he were about to pee in his britches, Jeb knew that he had a job to do. No matter how scared he was, he had to climb down to that ledge and find out whether or not Mandy was in the cave.

He picked up the twenty-gauge and cracked open the breech. A single load of duck and goose shot was in the portal, and there were six more shells in the pocket of his overalls. He closed the breech with a snap and hefted its weight in his hands. The birdshot wouldn't kill the critter, but it might scare it away if it took a lunge at him.

Jeb made his way to the edge of the bluff and, carefully, lowered himself down to the ledge below, which was a tricky feat considering that he was toting a nine pound shotgun. When his feet touched rock, he steadied himself and let go of the sycamore roots. The dark doorway of the cave yawned before him, looking much more foreboding than it ever had before.

He knew if he yelled out loud, he would probably alert the beast of his presence, but he knew he had no choice. He cupped his hands around his mouth and called out. "Mandy? Are you in there?"

At first there was only the hollow ring of his own voice echoing through the inner cavern, followed by a stretch of silence. Then he heard it. The voice of a girl coming faintly from the far reaches of the cave.

"Jeb?" asked Mandy, her voice disoriented. "Jeb, is that you?"

"It's me," he replied, relieved to hear her voice. "Are you hurt?"

"I don't know," she said dully. "My neck kind of smarts, but the rest of me is numb. And I'm tied up in something or other."

Jeb recalled the cocoon of tough snakehide that had encased Troy and he shuddered. "Mandy . . . is Troy Jenkins still in there, too?"

"Yes, he's here," confirmed the girl. "But he isn't saying much. He sounds so weak, Jeb. I think he might be dying."

Once again, that familiar pang of guilt nagged at Jeb. He knew that it wasn't his fault, that it was Sheriff North's fault that Troy was wasting away more than anyone else's. He had tried to fetch help, but the constable had put a stop to it with the threat of the state reform school.

Jeb thought of the talk that had circulated among the Fourth of July crowd. "Mandy . . . is the Huff baby in there with you?"

There was silence for a moment, then the girl replied. "No, not that I know of. If it was, I think I would've heard it by now. It's so dark in here, Jeb. So very dark."

The boy's heart ached at the terror in his girlfriend's voice. "I know, Mandy."

Then, abruptly, a low growl echoed from deep within the cave, followed by Mandy's shrill screaming. "Jeb! Get away, quick! It's woke up . . . and it's coming for you!"

Jeb felt his legs shake, as if they wanted to take off running under their own power. But he wouldn't allow it. Jeb stood his ground firmly and raised the butt of the shotgun to his shoulder. The long, blued barrel wavered in his trembling hands, the muzzle moving involuntarily to one side of the cave entrance to another. He breathed deeply and tried to settle his nerves. From the darkness within, he could hear the chalkboard shriek of scales against stone as the thing squeezed between the boulders. Then came the sound of clawed feet scurrying across the rock floor.

The farmboy steadied the scattergun, aiming it directly at the center of the cave's mouth. He expected it to emerge from the shadows at any moment, snapping and snarling, its toothy jaws yearning to take a big bite out of him.

But that didn't happen. Instead, the sound of the creature's approach slowed, then came to an abrupt halt. It was there, however. Jeb could hear its harsh breathing no more than ten feet from the entrance and he could barely see the twin orbs of its monstrous eyes leering at him from out of the darkness.

"Stay back!" he warned. "Stay back or I swear I'll shoot you, you dadblamed son-of-a-biscuit-eater!"

Jeb waited for the creature to continue its advance, but it didn't. It simply stood there, watching him.

At that moment, Jeb felt like a knight facing the lair of a dragon. But it was not a heroic feeling. Rather, he felt like a knight without a sword or a shield. He knew in his heart that the shotgun would do nothing but irritate the beast. If he pulled the trigger, the creature would react and both he and Mandy would likely suffer with their lives.

"Mandy!" he called out, his voice full of regret. "I'm sorry, but I'm going to have to go."

"No!" shrieked the girl. "Please, Jeb! Don't leave me here!"

It was at that moment, that Jeb heard a brittle clacking sound from within the cave. It took a few seconds before he realized that it was something hard and hollow rolling across the stone floor of the cavern. Puzzled, he watched as the object left the shadows and rolled across the narrow ledge toward him.

At first, he thought it was a baseball. It was white and about the size of one. Then he saw two small holes in the object, along with a smaller one just beneath them. In shock, he realized exactly what it was that the creature had pitched his way.

It was a skull.

A tiny skull.

The skull of a baby.

With a yelp, Jeb stepped out of the way, almost losing his balance in the process. The skull of the Huff baby rolled past him and careened off the edge of the rock ledge. Jeb looked down in time to see it land, with a splash, in the churning waters of the Cumberland.

Shaken, Jeb turned back toward the cave. Inside, the eyes of the snake-critter narrowed to sinister slits and he heard a strange snuffling sound. It took him a moment before he recognized the noise for what it truly was. The creature was laughing at him.

"I'll find a way to get you out, Mandy, I swear I will!" he yelled. "And, when I do, I'll be back!"

The girl didn't answer. All he heard was the faint sound of her sobbing echoing from the rear of the cave. The sound wrenched at his heart and made him feel more like a coward than he ever had before.

He stared angrily at the pair of glowing eyes. "I'll be back for you, too," he said, then he made his way cautiously toward the wall of the bluff and the exposed roots of the sycamore that dangled overhead.

The monster made no move to apprehend him. It simply sat there in the darkness, laughing its sinister laugh.

A moment later, Jeb was back on top of the bank again. He stood there in indecision for a while, then it came to him. For the past week, he had turned a single idea over and over in his mind, abandoning it as foolishness every time it popped into his head. But, this time, it didn't seem quite as foolish as it had before. In fact, the more he considered it, the more it dawned on him that it was his only chance to defeat the snake-critter, and heal his dying family at the same time.

Jeb hid the shotgun amid the clump of sycamores, then began making his way along the riverbank for the bridge. Like last time, his goal was to make it to Pikesville as fast as he possibly could. But, this time, he would not be going to see Sheriff North.

No, he had someone else in mind. Perhaps the only person in town who could help him with what he had to do.

Twenty

Reluctant Guide

"You want to *what?*" asked Roscoe Ledbetter. The black man's eyes bugged behind the thick lenses of his spectacles. "Are you plumb crazy, boy?"

"No, sir," said Jeb. "I'm serious, that's all."

The bluesman looked up one sidewalk, then down the other. The town of Pikesville was practically deserted at that hour in the afternoon. Folks were still hard at work at their jobs, but it wouldn't be long before quitting time rolled around and then the walkways would be bustling. The only ones he saw on Main Street at that moment were Tom Nipper washing the windows of the drugstore and Howard Drewer on the far side, sweeping hair trimmings off the curb with a broom.

"This ain't no fitting place to be talking of such foolishness," said Roscoe. He retrieved his guitar, hat, and gear, then grabbed Jeb by the arm. "Come on and we'll talk about it in the alley out back."

Soon, the boy and the old Negro were in the narrow alleyway that stretched at the rear of the bank. Roscoe found a couple of packing crates at the back door of the Rexall and they sat down.

Roscoe wiped his dark face with a red bandanna, then

eyed the boy uncomfortably. "Now, let me get this straight. *Where* do you have a mind to go to?"

Jeb sat up straight on his crate, his expression steady. "I told you before. I aim to go to Fear County."

The bluesman shook his head vigorously. "No, sir, Jeb Sweeny! You'd best strike that notion plumb outta your mind!"

"I'm a-going and that's all there is to it," said Jeb firmly.

"And why would you wanna do a damned fool thing like that?" asked the guitar-picker.

"I'm going to see that witch you told me about before," said Jeb. "That Granny Woman."

Roscoe laughed, but it was a nervous laugh. "Boy, I don't even know if there is such a person. I was just telling you that before 'cause you wanted to know about Fear County. I surely didn't think you'd take it to heart."

"Well, I did . . . and I want to go see her."

"But why?" asked Roscoe.

The determination in Jeb's eyes faltered a little and misery showed there for a moment. "I'm going to see if she'll help me out with a few things. Maybe she can do some conjuring or some such magic."

"For what reason?" the Negro wanted to know.

Jeb grew annoyed by Roscoe's constant barrage of questions. "My folks for one thing. Maybe she can do something for Sam. Maybe make him right in the head again. And then there's my Grandma Sweeny."

Roscoe's eyes softened a bit. "But I heard tell that she's dying of a cancer."

"She is," said Jeb. "I thought maybe she had a cure for it. Then I could heal Grandma up and things would be back the way they were before."

The bluesman laid a dark hand on the boy's shoulder. "I wouldn't be getting my hopes up like that, Jeb. If there is a

Granny Woman and she can work the magic folks claim she can, there's a good chance that she won't be able to do nothing a'tall for your grandmother."

"Then that's just a chance I'll have to take," declared the ten-year-old.

Roscoe scowled. "You just ain't gonna listen to a word I say, are you, boy?" His eyes suddenly narrowed in suspicion. "Exactly why did you run to town and tell me all this, anyway?"

"'Cause I don't know anything about Fear County," Jeb told him. "But you do."

"What do you mean?"

"What I'm saying is that I'd like you to take me there," said the boy. "Kinda be my guide . . . you know, like them Indian scouts in the western movies."

Roscoe Ledbetter sat there with his mouth open clear down to the top button of his shirt. "You gotta be joking."

"No, sir," replied Jeb. "I ain't."

"Well, you might as well be, 'cause I sure ain't gonna take you there." The Negro shook his head and snorted in disbelief. "Of all the damn fool things to ask a man! I told you before, I've only walked through Fear County once in my life and I don't aim to do it again. So you'd best just get that through your head, right here and now."

Jeb frowned. "I thought I could count on you. I thought you were my friend."

"I am, boy," said Roscoe. "That's why I ain't gonna take you there. Ain't a fitting place for nobody to set foot in, especially an innocent such as yourself."

"I ain't as innocent as you think," snapped Jeb. "I've smoked my share of rabbit tobacco and I kissed a girl smack on the mouth only a couple days ago."

"Hoo-weee!" exclaimed Roscoe, rolling his eyes. "Then I

reckon you're ready to get yourself a tattoo and join up with the Merchant Marines!"

The boy seemed hurt by the man's sarcasm. "I don't care if you do poke fun at me. I'll go . . . with or without your help."

Roscoe reached out and stopped the boy before he could walk away. "Just hold up there, Jeb." He stared in the ten-year-old's eyes and saw the determination there, like something chiseled into stone. "You're dead set on doing this, ain't you?"

"Yes, sir, I surely am."

Roscoe studied the boy for a moment longer. "Does it just have to do with wanting to help your papa and grandma . . . or is there something else you want the Granny Woman to do for you?"

Jeb nodded grimly. "You know the Rutherford girl that disappeared late last night? The one they think was kidnapped?"

"Yeah, I heard about it."

"Well, I know where she is," Jeb told him. "Along with Troy Jenkins."

"And where's that?" Roscoe wanted to know.

"There's a cave on the south side of the river. They're being kept there."

Before the boy could say anything else, the old Negro nodded his head. Behind the thick glasses, understanding suddenly emerged. "It's that snake-critter, ain't it?" he asked. "It's made its home there and it's got them young'uns in there with it."

"Right," replied the farmboy.

"And that baby that was snatched from its cradle? Is it there, too?"

Jeb's freckled face paled a little. "It's dead. The critter must've eaten it right off."

A question came to mind, but Roscoe was hesitant about asking it. "Jeb . . . exactly what is that son-of-a-bitch doing to them kids? Why does it have 'em in that cave?"

"It's feeding off them, Roscoe," Jeb told him. "From holes it's bitten in the sides of their necks."

Again, the bandanna made its way around the Negro's sweating face. "Good Lord Almighty! I figured it was gonna get worse . . . but not this bad."

"That ain't all," said the boy. "It's growing bigger. The tracks I saw were nearly twice the size of the ones I saw when Old Jack was killed."

"That ain't a good sign, is it?" said Roscoe.

"No, it ain't," said Jeb. "If we don't do something to stop it, that critter will just get more and more cocky."

Roscoe recalled the night when the creature had approached his campsite. If he hadn't had his guitar and a head full of hymns, he might be trapped in that cave right along Mandy Rutherford and Troy Jenkins. "Have you told the sheriff about this yet?"

"I tried my best to several days ago," said Jeb. "But he wouldn't listen to none of it. Threatened to stick me in the state reform school if I breathed a word of it to anyone."

Roscoe spat on the ground in disgust. "Sounds like Ed North. Just trying to cover his own hide, that's all he's doing."

"Was I wrong to take him at his word and not tell someone else?" the boy wanted to know.

"No, son, you did the right thing," assured the black man. "North's shiftless and lazy, but he pretty much sticks to his guns whenever he makes a threat. He warned me to steer clear of Jenkins and his bunch after I scared 'em off a while back. He threatened to kick me clean outta Pikesville and he would've done it, too, if I'd given him reason."

Jeb stared at the bluesman for a moment. "Can't you see, Roscoe? I don't wanna go just on account of my family. If we don't do something to stop this critter, the whole town'll suffer. It'll just grow bigger and bigger, till nothing'll be able to kill it at all. Some folks think it came from Fear County, so I reckon that's the best place to look for a way to do it in."

Roscoe knew the boy was right. "I reckon there ain't nothing else to do then. I've gotta be crazy in the head . . . but I'll do it. I'll take you there."

The ten-year-old breathed a sigh of relief. "Thanks, Roscoe," he said. "I'm much obliged to you."

"Well, I'll tell you one thing," Roscoe warned him. "If we do go, you'll do as I tell you and not go gallivanting around by yourself. What about your daddy? Is he going with us?"

"Haven't given much thought to that," said Jeb. "I reckon he'll have to. He sure can't take care of himself and Miss Claudine's too busy tending to Grandma."

"If he does go, the same goes for him, too," said Roscoe. "If I'm gonna guide you, you're gonna have to listen to me and take my advice. 'Cause the place we're going ain't no Sunday stroll through the park. It ain't like no place you've ever gone before . . . and, God willing, we'll make it there and back home again in one piece."

"It ain't all that bad, is it?" asked the boy.

"Yes, it is," said Roscoe. "And even worse."

"Then you'll do it for sure? You'll take me to the Granny Woman?"

The black man extended his hand and the two shook on it. "I'll take you to her home in Paradise Hollow, but that's as far as we go. If the Granny Woman ain't there, we're gonna hightail it straight back, understand?"

"You've got a deal!" agreed Jeb.

As he gathered up his guitar and belongings, and followed the boy from the alleyway, Roscoe wondered exactly what he had gotten himself into. It had been thirty years since he had last stepped foot in the dark land known as Fear County, and, even then, it had presented enough hazards and odd occurrences to last a man an entire lifetime. Now, nearly three decades later, he was going back. And he was certain that, in all that time, nothing had improved within those sinister boundaries. In fact, according to the tales he had heard on street corners and around shared campfires, the region's degree of darkness and depravity had only grown more potent and poisonous with the passage of time.

Twenty-one

The Blessing

Twilight was descending upon the Johnson farm when Jeb and Roscoe walked up the drive to the two-story house. When they reached the front porch, they found Miss Claudine sitting in her rocking chair, while Sam sat on the steps, scratching Buckshot behind his left ear, or what little that angry she-coon had left of it.

"Howdy, Jeb!" called the big farmer, throwing up a hand. "Where in tarnation have you been?"

"Yes, Jeb," asked Miss Claudine. The boy could see the worry leave her stern eyes. "Supper was an hour ago. Ain't like you to run off without telling someone where you're going first."

"I went to town," he told her. "Had to go fetch Mr. Ledbetter here."

Miss Claudine eyed the Negro with a puzzled look. "Oh? And how come?"

Jeb knew there was no need to beat around the bush. "Can I talk to you in private, Miss Claudine?" he asked. "I have something important to tell you."

The elderly woman sensed the seriousness in the boy's request. "Very well. We'll go sit in the parlor." As she left her rocker, Miss Claudine regarded the bespectacled black man. "Make yourself to home, Mr. Ledbetter."

"Much obliged, ma'am," said Roscoe, removing his hat. As Jeb and the woman went inside the house, the Negro sat down next to Sam on the porch steps.

As they stepped into Claudine Johnson's front parlor, Jeb glanced up the stairway toward the upper floor. "How's Grandma been today?"

"Not so good," said Miss Claudine. "She woke up around three o'clock and had another fit of pain. It wasn't fifteen minutes before I had to give her another shot of that nasty stuff. It does the job, I'll grant it that, but it clouds her mind and she don't rightly know what's going on from one minute to the next."

"But that's better than her hurting all the time, ain't it?" asked Jeb.

Miss Claudine looked doubtful. "I ain't so sure." When they had sat down on a threadbare couch, the old woman turned to the boy next to her. "So, what's this all about, Jeb? What have you got to tell me that's so important?"

Jeb hesitated for a moment, then, taking a deep breath, proceeded. "Miss Claudine, I have something I have to do and I wanted to tell you about it first, before I go on and do it. But, before I do, I want to let you know that I've made up my mind. No matter how much you're against it, I'm going to do it anyway."

Miss Claudine looked a little confused. "Lordy mercy, boy, what're you talking about? What is this thing you're so all-fired determined to do?"

Jeb braced himself for the protest that was sure to come. "I'm going to Fear County," he said. "That's why I fetched Mr. Ledbetter. He's agreed to show me the way."

The old woman stared at Jeb, her face as still and emotionless as stone. "And why are you going there? Can you tell me that?"

Jeb searched in his mind for the best way to explain. "Uh, have you ever heard of the Granny Woman, Miss Claudine?"

The boy might have been mistaken, but he thought he saw the least glimmer of understanding spark in those ancient eyes. "Yes, Jeb. I have."

"Well, that's why I'm going," he told her. "I'm going to find the Granny Woman and see if she has a cure for Sam and Grandma."

Surprisingly enough, Miss Claudine remained calm. "I see."

Jeb was puzzled by the woman's lackluster response. "You do understand what I'm saying, don't you?"

"I ain't senile, child," said Miss Claudine. "Of course I understand"

"Then how come you ain't yelling and hollering at me?" he asked. "I figured you'd be upset about me going there."

"Well, I ain't," she said, "And I'll tell you why. The same idea's come to me time and time again, ever since that test of your grandma's came back from the doctor."

"So, you believe in the Granny Woman?" he asked.

"I surely do, Jeb," she replied. She smiled slightly at the stunned look on his face. "Boy, you'd be surprised in a lot of the things this old lady believes in."

"So you're not against me going?"

"Not if you promise to be careful and stick with Mr. Ledbetter," she said. "Truth of the matter is, I gave some thought of going to Fear County myself, more than once. But I'm an old woman and not up to traveling so far. And I couldn't very well ask any of the men in Pikesville to go for me. Hell, most of 'em are plumb chickenshit yellow when it comes to the subject of Fear County."

Jeb was surprised by the woman's cussing, but understood what she meant. "Do you mind if I take Sam with me?"

Miss Claudine frowned. "No, I reckon not. But keep a

close eye on him. Taking him into a place like that would be like letting a toddler loose in a brawling, boozing honky-tonk. He'll end up getting hurt if you don't watch him like a hawk."

Jeb couldn't fully comprehend what the woman meant, but he made out like he did. "He'll be okay. I promise he will."

"Just promising might not be enough," said Miss Claudine. She left the couch and walked to a lamp table next to the front window. She opened a shallow drawer and withdrew something. When she turned around, Jeb was surprised to see her holding the Colt .45 revolver. "Here, I want you to take this," she said, handing the firearm to him.

Jeb cradled the six-shooter almost reverently in his hands. "But, I can't take your gun, Miss Claudine."

"You'd better or you might not make it back home," she said grimly. "I don't mean to scare you, Jeb, but Fear County ain't nothing like Mangrum. I've known grown men who've wandered over there while hunting deer and such, and hide nor hair was ever seen of 'em again. Has Mr. Ledbetter told you how bad things are in that place?"

"He tried to talk me outta going, if that's what you mean," said Jeb.

"Well, whatever he's told you is true," the old woman assured him. "I'd forbid you from going, too, if your grandma wasn't in such dire straits. I'm only giving you my blessing because you're the only chance she's got left, Jeb. Find that Granny Woman, if she exists, and see what you can do. That's all I ask. Maybe our instincts will prove true and she'll have something that can make Lucille well again."

"That'd be good, wouldn't it?" he asked, hope gleaming in his young eyes.

"Yes," replied Claudine Johnson. "It would be wonderful."

After she had given Jeb a box of cartridges to go with the peacemaker, Miss Claudine studied the boy for a moment.

"Jeb, do you have some other reason for going to Fear County? Besides the sake of your father and grandmother?"

Jeb thought of Mandy Rutherford in the cliffside cave and he squared his shoulders. "Yes, ma'am," he admitted. "It has to do with that snake-critter I saw in the hollow a while back."

"What about it?" she asked with interest.

"Well, it's behind all the kids who've been turning up missing," he told her. "It's taken 'em and put 'em in a cave."

Miss Claudine seem to pale a shade or two. "I suspected as much. Jeb, how do you know about this?"

"I've seen 'em, that's how," he said. Jeb explained to Miss Claudine about how he had approached Ed North concerning the matter and the threats he had made in return.

"I always knew he was a spineless worm underneath that badge," she said. "If my papa was alive and breathing, he'd have laid a sound thrashing on him, just for disgracing the title of sheriff."

"Maybe it's best if North doesn't go after that critter," Jeb replied. "I've seen it up close and its scales are harder than iron. I don't think bullets would hurt it a'tall. Maybe make it madder than sin, if anything."

"You're probably right," agreed Miss Claudine. "And you think maybe the Granny Woman has a way to kill it?"

"That's what I'm hoping," he said.

Miss Claudine sat next to the boy once again. "So, when will you be leaving?"

"Tomorrow morning . . . at first light."

The old woman leaned over and gave the boy a kiss on the forehead. "All I've gotta say, Jeb, is God bless you on your journey. And thank you for what you're aiming to do. Your grandma, she wouldn't like your going, but I'm sure she'd be proud anyway."

At the mention of his grandmother, Jeb glanced at the

ceiling overhead. "Do you mind if I go up and see her? Just to say goodbye before I go?"

"You go on, but don't say nothing to upset her," said Miss Claudine. "I'll go in the kitchen and heat up some supper for you and Mr. Ledbetter."

Jeb laid the .45 and its bullets on the lamp table, then left the parlor. Quietly, he mounted the stairs to the upper floor. A few moments later, he had reached the guest bedroom. The instant he stepped through the door, the smell hit him; that stagnated smell of sickness. The last rays of that day's sun filtered through the lacy curtains over the single window, casting the room in gloomy shadows. Jeb tiptoed his way across the floor, until he reached the side of the big, brass-framed bed.

Grandma lay there beneath a thin layer of cotton sheets, stretched out on her back, her mouth slightly open. Once again, the illusion of death hit Jeb and he had to lean in close to make sure she was still alive. He was relieved when he heard her shallow breath whistling between the gaps of her dentures.

When he reached out and took her bony hand, Grandma jerked in her sleep and opened her eyes, if only slightly. "Who is it?" she muttered softly.

"It's me," said the boy. "Jeb."

Grandma smiled and squeezed his hand. "My baby," was all that she said.

Jeb felt his chest tighten. "Grandma?"

"Yes, dear?"

Jeb thought of telling her about his trip, then figured it was best to keep her in the dark. "I . . . I love you," he said instead.

At first, he was sure that she hadn't heard him. Then, as he released her hand, she smiled again. "I love you, too, Jeb. Don't forget me when I'm gone, okay?"

Tears blossomed in the boy's eyes. "I'd never do that," he promised. "Never."

Grandma nodded softly, then returned to her drug-induced sleep. Jeb stood there beside her bed for a long time. Then, wiping his eyes, he turned and left the upstairs bedroom.

He knew then that he had to succeed. He had to go to Fear County and find the Granny Woman. Miss Claudine was right. He was the last hope that Grandma had left in the world. And, no matter how dangerous his journey turned out to be, it would be worth the trouble just to see her back to her old self once again.

Twenty-two

Stalking

"Watch your step now, Sheriff," warned Skyler Lee. "Get too close to the edge and you'll end up down yonder with the catfish and crappie."

The county constable directed his flashlight past the rocky edge of the limestone cliff. Fifty feet below, the muddy water of the Cumberland River churned. He knew the hermit was right. If a man was to fall in, there would be no saving him. The currents would suck him under and drown him, and wouldn't let the body drift back up to the surface until it was several miles downstream.

It had not been a good day for Ed North. He had awakened at six o'clock that morning with a frantic Charles Rutherford pounding on his door. When he had managed to calm the banker down, he was told of the disappearance of Amanda Rutherford. Charles and his wife hadn't even known she was gone, until the housekeeper checked the child's room a little before six and found her bed empty.

The sheriff had accompanied him back to the Rutherford residence and they had made a thorough search of the house and grounds. It was when they checked the big maple next to Amanda's bedroom window, that they discovered the cat. Queenie had been literally torn apart, half of her left at the base of the tree, while the other half had been flung into a clump of holly bushes, some twenty feet away. Charles Rutherford's panic had soon turned into pompous indignation and it wasn't long before he was demanding immediate action. North had searched the lawn for footprints. He had found some, but not the kind common of a human stalker. Rather, he had found the same sort that he had discovered in the hollow below the Sweeny farm. He had tried to show them to Rutherford, but the banker merely dismissed them as belonging to his neighbor's great dane. North knew better, although he kept his theory to himself.

From eight o'clock to well after noon, the sheriff had been pestered by the townfolk, who wanted to know exactly what had happened to Mandy Rutherford and what he intended to do about it. He hadn't even been able to relax and enjoy his lunch at the cafe. Gladys Hudson and the majority of her patrons had hounded him so badly that he had downed his hotdog with relish and sauerkraut in two huge bites, washed it down with Coca Cola, and stomped out. When he returned to his office around twelve-thirty, his secretary, Alice Piefer, had informed him that he had an unscheduled appointment with Mayor Thorne . . . as soon as possible. With the undigested frankfurter doing somersaults in his stomach, North had gone upstairs to the mayor's office. When he arrived, he found Charles Rutherford there, looking none too pleased. The sheriff had then endured an hour of pointless discussion concerning kidnappers and the possibility of ransom notes. North had almost told them about the snake-critter, but decided that it would only heap more criticism and ridicule upon him.

The sheriff had promised to act on Rutherford's and Thorne's assumptions. But, after leaving the mayor's office, he jumped into his patrol car and headed out of town. He drove the dusty backroads for a long time, trying to sort things out in his head. He recalled what Jeb had tried to tell him about the snake-critter and the cave in the southern cliff along the Cumberland. Around sundown, he had made up his mind on what he had to do, like it or not. He had turned off a rarely used stretch of bumpy road and made his way through the dense backwoods to Skyler Lee's place. They had shared a quart of moonshine that was as clear as rainwater and talked things over. The sheriff had offered the hermit twenty dollars if he would help him track down and kill the creature that was terrorizing Mangrum County. They had haggled over the bounty for a while, drinking while they did, and Skyler had finally settled on fifty dollars. It was well past nine o'clock that night when they had left the front porch of the hermit's tin and tarpaper shack. Skyler had taken his two redbone coonhounds, Slim and Jim, from their pen and loaded them into the back of his old Ford pickup truck. North had driven his own patrol car and, forty-five minutes later, they were at the Cumberland River bridge. They had parked their vehicles behind a "SEE ROCK CITY" billboard, so nobody that passed by would see them and wonder what was going on.

Now the two men made their way along the top of the southern bluff, half drunk, but intent on getting the job done. There was no moon to speak of that night; both the woods to their left and the river to their right was pitch dark. The two hounds sniffed at the ground, but, so far, hadn't caught scent of anything out of the ordinary.

It wasn't long before the sheriff shined his light on the clump of scrubby sycamores that grew above the stone ledge. "What now?" he asked.

Skyler worked a chaw of tobacco between his stubbled jaws and sent a spritz of juice flying off the edge of the bluff. "Well, I reckon the best thing would be for you to climb down and check out that cave."

The idea wasn't very appealing to the constable. "Why me?"

The hermit snorted in disgust. "You are the sheriff, you know! Besides, I can't very well go. Can't leave my dogs up here and can't very well carry 'em down there with me, now can I?"

Although North's mind was cloudy with the effects of the homebrewed liquor, he understood the hermit's logic. "Oh, all right. I'll climb down there and take a look."

Skyler watched as the sheriff slipped his flashlight in the hip pocket of his britches and, taking hold of a sycamore's exposed roots, carefully lowered himself over the edge. "You be careful down there, Sheriff," warned Skyler with a snaggletoothed grin. "If you see that critter, aim for the whites of his eyes. Or yellows or greens . . . whatever the hell color they turn out to be!"

When the constable had disappeared into the darkness beyond the bluff's edge, Skyler lost his grin and turned nervous eyes on the darkness of the woods that lay to the south. A thicket of honeysuckle and blackberry bramble stretched scarcely fifteen feet away. He recalled a story his mother had read him when he was a child; the fable of Brer Rabbit and the Tar Baby. Skyler figured the brier patch that Brer Fox had tossed the clever hare into might have been as dense and thorny as the one he now looked at.

Skyler shifted the heavy weight of his ten-gauge shotgun beneath his armpit and directed the beam of his flashlight toward the wild tangle. Almost immediately, he caught a glimpse of something dark moving through the thicket. The two coonhounds that stood on either side of him suddenly perked up and began to growl deep down in their throats. Skyler smelled the musky scent of snake about the same time that his dogs did.

He looked down and saw the two quivering, waiting for permission to let loose and hunt down the critter that crept through the briar patch. Skyler refrained from giving the command right off. He first cracked open the breech of the scattergun and made sure that the ten-gauge was properly loaded. Twin shells packed with double-aught buckshot sat snugly in their chambers. Satisfied, he closed the breech with a crisp snap.

"All right, boys," he said softly. "It's all yours. Go and get it!"

Like rusty streaks of lightning, the two redbones shot across the fifteen feet of stone and grass, and launched themselves bodily into the midst of the thicket. Skyler watched as Slim and Jim disappeared from sight. He shined his light into the vines and bramble, but all he saw was flashes of red hide as they squeezed their way past sharp briars and clinging vines.

Skyler's heart quickened its beat when a low, throaty growl erupted from the thicket—a growl that definitely did not belong to either one of his dogs. It was followed by a ruckus the likes of which the hermit had never heard before. Slim and Jim had pounced on their share of feisty coons in their time, but never had the scuffle been so violent and furious. It was over a moment later. Skyler listened for a yelp or a cry of pain from his hounds, but he heard none.

He relaxed a little and smiled. "Got that bastard, did you, boys?" he called out. "Well, what're you waiting for. Drag it out here so's I can get me a good look at it."

The thicket remained dark and silent. Skyler listened for the sound of dogs picking their way through the bramble, but heard nothing. Nothing but a strange snuffling sound. It almost sounded like a hoarse laugh; the kind that Old Lucifer might make, just before snaring himself another soul for the sulfur pit.

"Jim?" Skyler called. "Slim? Where are you?"

The stillness of the thicket continued for a moment, then something was flung out of the briar patch, straight at him. Skyler stepped back a couple of paces just as the object hit the ground with a thud. He smelled the rich scent of fresh blood as he directed the beam of the flashlight down at the thing that laid at his feet.

It was the twitching leg of a dog, ripped clean off the hip bone.

"Dammit to hell!" cussed Skyler. He was lifting his flashlight, intending to direct it back at the dark thicket, when something much larger spun from amid the blackberry bramble and honeysuckle. Skyler yelled out as the eviscerated carcass of one of his hounds—Slim from the looks of it—collided with him. The lanky man fell to his back and the flashlight was knocked plumb out of his hand. The battery-powered light bounced across the ground, then careened off the edge of the bluff toward the river below.

Abruptly, Skyler found himself in complete darkness. He pushed the bloody body of his dog off him, then felt along the ground for his shotgun, which he had lost hold of. He heard the rustle of the bramble parting and looked in that direction. Even in the darkness, he could see the slight gleam of glossy black scales and two yellowish-green eyes emerging from the thicket. Skyler Lee had seen many a pair of cruel and merciless eyes across a poker table or the bar of a cutthroat roadhouse, but never had he ever seen a pair as purely evil as the ones he now stared at.

Skyler found his ten-gauge just as the thing shot out of the thicket and leaped toward him. He was swinging the twin barrels into line, when the thing pounced in a snarling whirlwind of slashing fangs and flailing claws. The shotgun dropped to the ground amid the attack, Skyler's left hand—severed at the wrist—still clutching the wooden foregrip of the firearm.

The man fought back, trying to kick the creature off him, but it was much too heavy and strong. He was about to scream out, hoping that the sheriff would hear and come to his rescue, when he looked up at the thing's leering face. Its reptilian jaws opened, exposing long fangs dripping with slaver. Before Skyler could utter a single sound, the critter's massive head dipped down and, with no effort at all, tore his throat completely out.

When Ed North reached the crevice between the two boulders, he paused and turned his flashlight back the way he had come. Only the walls and ceiling of the narrow tunnel shone in the pale light of the beam. The sheriff could've sworn that he'd heard something from beyond the mouth of the cave, but now he wasn't so sure. All he could hear past the entrance way was the roaring rush of the Cumberland River below the stone ledge.

He strained his ears for a moment, but heard nothing else. He then turned and regarded the space between the two stones. The boulders seemed to have been moved several inches both ways, as if something of incredible strength and substantial size had worked its way between them. North noticed something dark and shiny wedged in a crack in one of the boulders. When he pried it loose with his fingers and illuminated it with the flashlight, he found that it was a single, black scale, about the size of a Washington quarter.

So, it ain't a tall-tale after all, he thought to himself. *The son-of-a-bitch is for real!* He tossed the scale away and, unfastening the retaining strap of his side holster, withdrew his

.38 Smith & Wesson. The blued steel revolver felt heavy and cold in his hand. Other than cleaning it on very rare occasions, North had never actually drawn the gun before, particularly not in the line of duty.

He thought about backing out of the tunnel and fetching Skyler Lee, but he knew the hermit wouldn't leave his dogs alone on top of the bluff. Therefore, it was up to him to investigate the rear chamber of the cave. He gulped down a couple of breaths of damp air, then pushed his way through the crevice between the two boulders.

The chamber he found himself in was much darker than the one he had just left behind. He directed the beam of the flashlight around, until it settled on a pile of bones next to the back wall. He saw the hog skull and immediately knew that Jeb Sweeny had been right all along. As he took a couple of steps closer, he discovered that the pile wasn't really a pile after all. Rather, the bones had been neatly stacked, one atop the other, as if forming some odd religious pier or altar of some sort. That spooked the sheriff even more. He began to slowly realize that the thing that roamed Mangrum County was not simply some stupid animal, but a clever beast with a sinister intelligence.

North swept the beam of the flashlight away from the stack of bones, toward the left side of the cave. A moment later, the light located a couple of objects hanging from the bowed wall. It took him a couple of seconds before he realized that the bundles of interlaced snakeskin held children. Living children.

"Good Lord have mercy!" he exclaimed as he walked up to the two captives. Troy Jenkins stared at him with eyes that were glazed and uncomprehending. The boy was pale and drawn, and appeared as though he had lost a good ten or fifteen pounds. The other prisoner, however, seemed to be in much better health. Mandy Rutherford looked disoriented, her long black hair tangled and littered with twigs and leaves, but she seemed much more aware than the boy next to her.

North went to her at once. "Amanda? Are you all right?"

The girl stared at the lawman as if he were an imbecile. "No, of course not," she muttered. "That thing's bitten me on the neck and I can't move a muscle below my shoulders."

The sheriff turned to the twelve-year-old hanging next to her. "Troy? Are you okay, boy?"

The bully didn't reply. He simply mumbled something incoherent, a string of saliva dangling from his lower lip, which was shockingly blue in color.

"I think he's dying, Sheriff North," said Mandy. "That thing . . . it keeps sucking at the side of his neck . . . drinking his blood. It's just about drained all of the life plumb out of him."

North directed his flashlight around, trying to locate a third victim. "The Huff baby . . . is it here?"

Mandy shook her head. "I'm not sure, but I think it's already dead."

Suddenly, from beyond the opening between the boulders, came a low thunderous sound; almost like the growl of a bear who had discovered an intruder on its territory.

The girl saw panic fill the lawman's eyes and knew he was about to turn and run. "Don't leave us here, Sheriff!" she pleaded. "Please, cut us loose."

North stood there in indecision for a moment, then decided that he would catch hell from Charles Rutherford and the citizens of Pikesville if he fled. Knowing that his job was on the line, he holstered his gun and drew a folding knife from his hip pocket. He unleashed the longest and sharpest of the three blades and set to the task of cutting through the thick strands of snakehide.

After a moment, he found that he wasn't making any progress. It was like trying to saw through a hickory tree with a dull nailfile.

"Hurry, please!" urged Mandy. "I think I hear it coming."

"Just hold your horses!" snapped Ed North. "I'm trying, but it's too damned tough!"

Then, behind him, came the shrill scraping of hard scales against gritty stone.

The sheriff yelled out in fright, tossing the knife aside and drawing his revolver. His other hand shuddered, sending the beam of the flashlight jittering toward the opposite end of the cave. At first, the light found nothing but jagged limestone. Then it settled on a horrible, triangular face; a gleaming black face with serpentine eyes and jagged fangs bristling from slavering jaws.

The sheriff lifted his revolver into line and fired. The first shot missed entirely, hitting one of the boulders and ricocheting off with a whine. The second shot hit the creature squarely between the eyes. But, even then, it seemed to have no effect other than stunning it for a second or two. The critter shook its massive head, narrowed its eyes, then came for him with an angry roar.

Hit it in the eye, he told himself. *You can do it. Just steady your aim.*

But the thing that came for him was much swifter than the thoughts in his head. Abruptly, Ed North felt an impact like a runaway freight train slamming into him, knocking him onto his back on the cool stone floor of the cave. Then he felt hot breath scald the side of his neck, as well as something wet and sticky. He looked up and, in the gloom of the lost flashlight, saw two fangs protruding slowly from amid the others. Then they descended swiftly, burrowing into the side of his neck, bringing a creeping paralysis.

"Kill me!" he croaked. "Go on, you bastard! Get it over with."

But the gleam of cruelty that sparkled in the creature's eyes told him he would not be that lucky. Ed North began to scream as he heard a dry rustling and saw strands of snakeskin, dead, yet as strong as iron, began to fall away from the beast's dark body.

Part Three
Crossing the Line

Fear County—The Junkyard—Something Underneath
Brimstone—The Pack—Shadows on a Wall
Trapped—Hungry Brood

Twenty-three

Fear County

They awoke with the first crow of the rooster. The gray light of dawn greeted Jeb, Sam, and Roscoe as they dressed and somberly prepared for the journey ahead of them.

First, they went out to the Sweeny barn and gathered the milk cow and mule, along with the sows from the hog pen, then herded the animals down Mossy Creek Road to Claudine Johnson's farm. They had left the gate to the henhouse open and spread enough hard corn along the ground to keep the chickens satisfied for two or three days.

After the livestock had been attended to, they went to Miss Claudine's house. The elderly woman invited them into the kitchen and, soon, they were sitting down to a feast of a breakfast. Miss Claudine had seemingly left nothing out of the meal. There were eggs, country ham, sausage gravy, grits, big cathead biscuits, freshly churned butter, and sorghum molasses. Quietly, they ate their fill, knowing that it could very well be the last home-cooked meal they would enjoy for several days.

Jeb and Sam went upstairs to kiss Grandma goodbye. The woman was fast asleep, half out of physical exhaustion and half from the deadening effects of the morphine. When they returned downstairs, they met Roscoe and Claudine on the front porch. Miss Claudine hugged Jeb and Sam, then shook the old Negro's hand. "God protect you all," was all she said before going back into the house.

Roscoe picked up his guitar and a knapsack of his belongings, while Sam slung his old army duffle bag over his shoulder. The olive drab bag contained clothing and food, as well as the long-handled flashlight and the Colt revolver that Miss Claudine had lent them. As they stood on the porch, Roscoe pulled a big railroad pocketwatch from his vest pocket and found that it was past seven o'clock. "Well, I reckon we'd best head out, gents," he suggested. "We've got several miles of walking before we even reach the Fear County line."

At the mention of their intended destination, both Jeb and Sam traded glances of nervous apprehension. No one had actually talked about Fear County that morning; everyone had simply woke up knowing where they were bound that day. Roscoe's statement, however, brought back the dreadful realization of the dangerous land they would be crossing during the better part of that week, as well as their purpose for going there.

"Then let's get going," said Jeb with a sigh.

"Not having second thoughts, are you, Jeb?" asked the bluesman.

The farmboy remembered the woman lying in the bedroom upstairs. "No, sir," he said, swallowing his fear. "I told you what I aim to do, and, by God, I'm gonna do it!"

Roscoe couldn't help but admire the ten-year-old's loyalty. "Okay. Let's get to it then."

Leisurely, they headed down the long driveway to the rutted dirt track of Mossy Creek Road. They followed the rural road to the main highway as the coolness of dawn dissipated and the heat of late morning settled in. By the time they reached the stretch of two-laned blacktop, the temperature was already in the lower nineties and climbing steadily.

As they walked along the highway, they heard the faint

jangle of cowbells from the pasture next to York's Dairy, as well as the high-pitched whine of the big circular saw at Benny Saunder's sawmill a half mile farther down the road. Before they knew it, farmland gave way to stretches of dense forest that stood, thick and green, on both sides of the road. Soon, civilization was seemingly left behind. Only the sounds of nature could be heard from the woods; the singing of birds, as well as the occasional chatter of squirrels fighting over nuts and berries.

"Have you ever been this far south in Mangrum County before?" Roscoe asked the tow-headed boy with the freckled face.

Jeb looked around at the unfamiliar walls of oak and pine that towered to the east and west. "Nope. Can't rightly say that I have."

"I ain't never been here either," Sam said, putting in his two cents worth. The squawk of a fussy jaybird echoed from out of the woods, causing the farmer to flinch. "Looks kinda spooky, though. You sure we ain't in Fear County already?"

"No, I'd say we've got two more miles to cover before we get there, maybe three."

Roscoe sensed both the Sweenys' nervousness. He knew it wouldn't do to have them jumping at every little noise before they even reached the county line, so he knew it was up to him to ease the tension, if only a little. He pulled the bandanna from his hip pocket and mopped at his face. "Sure is a scorcher today," he said. "It's so hot you could roast a pig on a flagpole."

"Yeah, it is," replied Jeb. "I sure could go for a cold Coca-Cola right about now."

"Well, you'd best strike that notion right outta your head, boy," Roscoe told him. "Ain't gonna be no soda pops where we're going. All they drink in Fear County is stagnant water and gut-rotting moonshine."

"Oh," muttered Jeb with a frown.

Roscoe knew he'd failed in his first attempt to make idle conversation. He tried another route, flashing a gold and ivory grin and patting his potbelly—the only protruding part of his skinny body. "That was an almighty dee-licious breakfast Miss Claudine fixed for us this morning, wasn't it?"

Jeb pulled his eyes away from the forest and matched the Negro's smile. "Yes, sir, it surely was."

"I particularly hankered for them big ol' buttermilk catheads and that sorghum molasses," said Roscoe.

Sam laughed. "I'll say! You downed eight biscuits and half a jar of molasses all by your lonesome!"

Roscoe's grin grew even wider, seemingly suspended from earlobe to earlobe. "You know, I always had a weakness for molasses. Matter of fact, I wrote me a song about it long years ago. Would ya'll like to hear it?"

"Sure," said Jeb. "Why not?"

"This here song's called the 'Sticky Sorghum Blues,' " he told them. The black man gave his guitar strap a tug and, a second later, it was off his stooped shoulder and in his arms. Roscoe dipped his right hand in a vest pocket and, when he withdrew it, the index finger was magically crowned with the little glass bottle. He didn't stop to sing his song. Rather, he kept right on walking, running the edge of the bottle along the steel strings and conjuring that mournful whine and twang common of his people's style of music.

"Well, she makes that ol' molasses . . . right from the sugar cane . . . the way it taste, Lawd have mercy . . . could drive a po' man insane . . . Well, she serves it up on pancakes . . . on cornbread and on pie . . . to reach that point o' heaven . . . boy, you don't have to die . . . Gotta hankering for that sorghum . . . it's sticky and it's sweet . . .

just thinking of that sorghum . . . makes me tremble to my feet!"

Sam laughed and clapped his hands. "Hey, that was funny, Roscoe!"

"Yeah!" said Jeb. "Sing us another!"

Roscoe grinned and launched into another song, this one about a honky-tonk knife fight where the brawlers literally whittled each other down to the bone. He kept up the medley of his self-written tunes while they walked along the dusty shoulder of the road. Jeb and Sam seemed to brighten up considerably, while Buckshot kept his distance from the trio. He trailed behind a good fifteen or twenty feet, the steely twang of Roscoe's Fender sounding more offensive than pleasurable to the coonhound's sensitive ears.

It was nearly noon when they sensed a gradual curve in the straight stretch of highway. Jeb looked ahead and saw that the road made an almost perfect left turn. The railroad tracks, which ran parallel to the main road a half mile away, also curved toward the east, cutting across the highway with twin steel rails. Jeb found something foreboding about the way they changed direction so abruptly. It was almost as if those responsible for building the highway and railroad had purposely avoided crossing the Mangrum line into the neighboring county.

"Are we close, Roscoe?" the boy asked. The cheerful air that had surrounded them for the past three miles suddenly vanished. In its place, dread descended like an invisible, but heavy weight.

"That's it," said the guitar-picker, leveling a bony, black finger. "Up yonder . . . just beyond the curve."

A moment later, they were there. They stood at the edge of the sharp curve and stared at a godforsaken stretch of dirt road, deeply rutted with a long line of ankle-high crabgrass and weeds separating it down the middle. A rusty, bulletholeridden sign on a wooden post stood a yard to the side, nearly obscured from view by a tangle of ugly purple-black bramble. The inch-long barbs seemed to encircle the sign like Jesus's own crown of thorns. And, in the very center, the words they had dreaded all morning stood out starkly against the pocked steel.

"FEAR COUNTY LINE" was all it said. But that was more than enough.

They simply stood and stared at the sign for a long moment. Then Sam turned toward Jeb and Roscoe, his face confused. "What does it say?" he asked. "Are we here?"

"Yeah, Sam," Roscoe said. "We're here." Suddenly, the eyes behind the thick glasses no longer held the levity they had during the past hour or so. Now they seemed deathly serious and much older than they had before. "All right, boys. We could stand here gawking all afternoon, but we wouldn't be doing what we came here to do, now would we?"

"No, sir," said Jeb. The boy's heart quickened a beat or two.

Sam simply shook his head and swallowed loudly.

"Okay, then let's go," said Roscoe cautiously. "But don't wander off too far from each other, understand? Stick close."

The three almost held a collective breath as they took a couple of steps and, in that one simple act, crossed the line that separated Mangrum and Fear counties.

At first, Jeb could tell no difference between the land he had just left and the one he now stood in. Then, slowly, subtly, it began to dawn on him. There *was* something different about Fear County. He had to study the ground beneath him and the forest that stood around him for a while before those differences became apparent.

The leaves on the trees were a little darker and a little less green than the foliage in Mangrum County, and the bark seemed a little rougher, more complex and convoluted in texture. Likewise, the earth of the road was not of the same clay red color as most of the rural roads in that part of the state. Rather, the earth seemed much darker in hue, almost black in some spots. Even as he stood there, Jeb felt something touch the toe of his bare foot. He looked down and, immediately, jumped away. There, burrowing its way out of the ground, was a long earthworm. But it wasn't like any worm he had ever seen before. Unlike the plump pink earthworms he sometimes used while fishing, this one was the color of a bruise; an ugly mixture of purple and mottled yellow. He didn't see it for long. It was gone almost as quickly as it had appeared, pulling the grainy earth up over it. For the first time in his life, Jeb longed for a pair of shoes to wear, even those torturous patent leathers he was forced to wear on Sunday mornings.

"You okay, boy?" asked Roscoe, placing a dark hand on Jeb's shoulder. "You're looking kinda pale."

"I'm all right," he said. They had taken a couple of steps more, when Jeb sensed that his dog wasn't with them. He turned to see the bluetick hound sitting at the edge of the highway, staring at them as if they were touched in the head.

"Come on, boy!" called Jeb. When the dog refused to follow his master, the farmboy frowned at him in frustration. "What in tarnation is the matter with you, Buckshot?"

The hound dog failed to move a muscle. He simply sat there on his haunches and whimpered pitifully.

"He senses that something ain't right over here," said Roscoe.

"Well, we can't just leave him behind," grumbled Jeb. He turned to Sam. "Give me one of them baloney sandwiches that Miss Claudine packed for us."

Sam opened the duffel bag and handed Jeb one of the sandwiches. The boy peeled away the waxed paper, revealing the slabs of white bread and fatty meat inside. He dangled the sandwich enticingly between thumb and forefinger. "Come on, Buckshot. Here, boy . . . there ain't nothing wrong over here. Come on and I'll let you have this whole sandwich for yourself."

The bluetick whimpered and whined like a puppy, shifting uncomfortably from one speckled haunch to the other. Then, grudgingly, he went against his instincts and made his way across the county line toward his young master. Obviously, his weakness for anything edible overrode any qualms he might feel toward the land on the far side of the highway.

As they proceeded down the dirt road, the woods around them grew wilder and more choked with shadows. The branches of the trees met overhead, forming a dense canopy above them. Jeb looked up, trying to see the sun past the leaves, but only a few speckles of sunlight managed to break through. He noticed something else, too. Something that was almost imperceptible at first.

"It ain't quite so hot on this side of the line," said Jeb. "In fact, it's almost downright cool."

"Yeah," said Roscoe looking a little wary. "I remember that from the last time I was here."

No one attempted to explain the mysterious drop in temperature. They continued on, saying nothing. Gradually, Jeb noticed other things. One was the absence of any sort of noise in the forest. There was no rustle of a breeze through the trees, not even the faintest hint of one. And the sound of songbirds was totally absent. At first, Jeb was sure that there was no animals at all in the stretch of dark woods. At least, not the type that frequented the hills and hollows back home.

They were a half mile down the dirt road, when a cry echoed from somewhere off in the woods. It was a frightening cry; one that Jeb couldn't identify. It almost sounded like a cross between the caw of a carrion crow and the throaty croak of a bullfrog.

"What in Sam Hill was that, Roscoe?" asked the boy.

The black man looked off into the woods, then turned his attention back to the road ahead. "I don't know, son . . . and, frankly, I don't want to know. Just don't pay it any mind and keep on walking."

The strange call came again from the top of a towering black oak tree, but, as much as he tried, Jeb couldn't make out anything up there in the shadows. He glanced over at Buckshot, but the dog seemed to have no interest whatsoever in leaving the road to investigate. Instead, the hound moved away from the weedy thicket and stuck close to his master's heels.

Jeb reached around to his hip pocket. The homemade slingshot was there, but he felt little comfort in knowing that it was there. He listened for the cry to come again, but the treetops remained ominously silent.

As they descended further into the stretch of dark woods, Jeb knew that they had left all familiarity behind. He recalled a verse he'd read in the Bible once concerning the unknown; something about "seeing through a glass darkly." Just walking down the stretch of shadowy backroad, Jeb knew that particular scripture, however cryptic it might seem, described Fear County perfectly.

Twenty-four

The Junkyard

The afternoon drew on. Miles of dark forest and uneven road passed behind them and continued to stretch ahead. Jeb began to wonder if that was all there was to Fear County; tangled thicket choked with shadow and an arrow-straight stretch of rutted rural road.

Around four o'clock, the road began to curve and wind, if only subtly so. The forest remained heavy, though. Above the dark canopy of intertwined leaves, echoed the throaty rumble of far-off thunder. "We'll likely find ourselves in a thunderstorm before long," said Roscoe. "We'd best pick up our pace and try to find some place dry to spend the night."

They did as he suggested. An urgency quickened their walking and they headed down the winding road, searching for something other than trees and thicket at the side of the trail. Several times, Jeb was certain that he heard the snap of a branch no more than twenty yards from the road. But, even though he searched to find something there, the woods seemed to be devoid of living creatures. That didn't make him feel any easier, however. He still had the feeling that something was creeping among the trees out there, matching their progress, step by step.

As the thunder grew louder and closer, they were thankful

to find that the woods were thinning out a little. In some of the open spaces, standing amid tall weeds and pink-headed thistle, were small dwellings scarcely the size of the kitchen back at the Sweeny house. Roscoe and Sam cautiously investigated each one, but found that their roofs were infested with holes or missing entirely.

"This one won't do, either," complained the Negro. "If we tried making it through the night here, we'd be soaking wet before night."

As the two men lingered in the dilapidated shanty, looking around, Jeb surveyed the other buildings that stood in the waist-high weeds along the side of the road. "What was this place, Roscoe? Some kinda town?"

"I don't know, Jeb," said the bluesman. "Might've been . . . a long time ago."

"But what happened to all the folks who lived here?"

Roscoe spotted a stain on the dry-rotted floor of the shack he stood in; a rusty brown stain that looked a lot like old blood. "I couldn't rightly say," was all he said, not mentioning his discovery to the boy.

They left the shanty and headed farther down the road. The canopy of leaves opened up in spots overhead. In the sky above, hung dark storm clouds the color of gray cotton. All three sensed the moisture in the air. The storm was nearly upon them. It wouldn't be long before it let loose with rain and lightning, and they would be stuck right dab in the middle of it.

They had gone a quarter mile farther down the road, when Sam pointed up ahead. "What's that yonder?"

From where Roscoe was he could only make out a tall, wooden fence perhaps eight or nine feet in height. "I don't know. Let's go see."

A few minutes later, they were there. The boarded wall stretched around a good three acres of open land and boasted rusted signs that proclaimed "NO TRESPASSERS!" and "INTRUDERS WILL BE DEALT WITH!" But, when they reached the center of the fence, they found the gate standing wide open. It had been that way for a long time. Weeds grew tall and plentiful along the bottom of the door, and the hinges were frozen with orange rust and entwined with climbing ivy. It appeared as though the gate had not been closed for years.

The roll of thunder was accented by a brittle crack of lightning this time. Knowing they had no place else to go, the three stepped through the gate and took a wary look around. Buckshot lingered outside the doorway for a moment later, then, hearing the slight rustle of weeds from the far side of the road, decided to join the others. He caught a whiff of the critter that lurked in the thicket opposite the fence. It smelled like no animal he'd ever encountered during his rambling romps through the backwoods of Mangrum County.

They found themselves at the entrance of a huge junk-yard. The rusted hulls of automobiles and trucks stood in tall piles, five and six high in some places. None of the vehicles seemed to have been condemned there by a faulty transmission or the inactivity that long years of service tend to bring. Instead, they all seemed to have been the victims of horrible wrecks. Fenders were buckled, front ends were pushed—accordion-style—right up to the firewalls, and most of the glass of the twisted windows were either missing or riddled with spiderweb cracks. Some of the remaining glass was coated with splashes of reddish-brown or speckled with bits of foreign matter. Jeb could picture the crash of impact and imagine heads smacking against windshields, or even going clean through them.

"This is a bad place," said Sam. "A mighty bad place."

Roscoe nodded grimly. "You're right about that. It surely is."

"Couldn't we go on down the road a little further?" asked Jeb. "Maybe we could find somewhere else to camp."

He was answered by a loud thunderclap a couple miles to the north. "Naw, I think this is where we'll stay tonight," said the bluesman. "God knows I don't cotton to the thought of sacking down here, but we ain't got nowhere else to go."

They crossed the weedy earth of the junkyard, stepping over rusted fuel pumps, engine blocks, and bent axles. To the right stood a single structure roughly the size of a storage closet. All the glass of the shed's two windows was broken out and the door stood askew on its hinges. "You boys stay out here for a minute," said Roscoe. "I'll go in and take a look-see."

The black musician stepped through the doorway and found himself standing in a cramped office. Its boarded walls were lined with old fan belts, radiator hoses, and airless innertubes. They hung there like greasy trophies of some sort and were shrouded in cobwebs that had been abandoned by their spidery occupants long years ago.

He stepped gingerly over a couple of wooden crates and rusty gas cans, and walked to a desk at the far side of the office. The mummified remnants of a salami and rye sandwich sat there on a sheet of dusty waxed paper and, beside it, stood a coffee mug, its insides coated with a growth of thick grayish-green mold. Roscoe lifted his eyes from the cluttered desk, to the calendar that hung midway up the back wall. The words "KRULLER'S JUNKYARD" were printed above the month of October and the year of 1934. The picture above the numbered squares was what drew Roscoe's interest the most. It was a black and white photo of a pretty, raven-haired woman dressed in spiked heels, thigh-length stockings, and a bodice of black leather, which did nothing to conceal her perky breasts. The girl wore a devilish expression in her dark eyes and held a braided bullwhip in her right hand. The end of the whip snaked its way down, across the laced belly of the girdle, and disappeared between the junction of her thighs.

"Lordy mercy!" muttered Roscoe. For some reason, just looking at the calendar pinup made him squirm a little. He knew then that he didn't want the boy in there, ogling the obscene picture half the night.

He checked the roof. Like most of the other shacks they had passed along the rural road, its roof was festooned with a dozen or so holes, some big enough to stick your fist through. He stepped back out into the open, relieved to be away from the office. "It's just as bad," he told them, shaking his head.

"Then where're we gonna stay?" asked Sam.

Roscoe felt a droplet of water strike the bridge of his nose. He looked and saw a dark swirl of storm clouds hovering over them. Soon, raindrops were coming down steadily, pitting the dusty earth and rat-tat-tatting on the rusted bodies of the wrecked cars. As the rain grew in intensity and the thunder more vocal, Roscoe searched for a place that would keep them dry for the night. He found it a second later. "Over there!" he called, gathering up his guitar and gear. "Follow me!"

Jeb and Sam did as he said. Sam slung the duffle bag over his shoulder and, at a dead run, followed him through the driving rain toward a long vehicle that had once been painted a bright yellowish-orange color. Now it was covered with a heavy coating of rust and clinging ivy. The front end was torn open, the hood folded up clear to the windshield and the engine block protruding like an exposed organ from the open chassis.

They were nearly soaked to the skin by the time they reached the school bus. Roscoe tried to open the folding door with his fingers, but the hinges were fused together by years of rust. Sam stepped past the black man and pried at the door for a moment. His work-toughened muscles did the job and, soon, the door folded to the side with a squeal of protest.

Quickly, they ducked into the bus, mounting the steel steps to the dark belly of the vehicle. Buckshot caught a whiff of something foul, but reluctantly followed the others when thunder boomed like cannonfire overhead.

Dust and filth coated the windows of the school bus, casting an eerie gloom throughout the long vehicle. The first thing they noticed when they entered was the driver's seat, which had been wrenched from its bolts by some terrible force of impact. Jeb noticed that the steering wheel was twisted and covered with something that might have been dried blood. Clinging to the wheel were fragments of a man's shirt, as well as a few buttons.

Roscoe ushered the boy past the seat. "Come on, Jeb. We'll find us a place on back a ways."

They moved along the narrow center aisle of the school bus. The rain grew more furious, drumming against the roof of the bus and pattering against the small windows on both sides. The darkness of the storm, as well as the shadows inside the vehicle, made it difficult to see. Soon, Sam had to open the duffle bag and dig out the long-handled flashlight. He snapped it on and directed its bright beam around the murky interior.

School books, lunch pails, and Number Two pencils littered the floor of the bus. Jeb looked at several of the seats and saw that the padded seats were covered with something similar to what coated the steering wheel up front. "What do you think happened to this bus, Roscoe?" he asked.

"Head-on collision, more'n likely," replied the black man. "Either that or it ran into a tree or an electric pole."

Even though the accident had obviously taken place years ago, Jeb could detect a nasty odor in the bus; kind of a mixture of hot copper and the high stench of fresh roadkill on a hot summer day. True, the scent was faint, but it was still there . . . and probably always would be.

They had to go all the way to the rear of the bus before they found several seats that were clean enough to sit on. They directed the beam of the flashlight toward the roof of the bus. It seemed intact and watertight except for a few broken seams toward the front, which dribbled only a small amount of rainwater onto the center aisle.

When they were satisfied that the rain had set in and wasn't going to let up for some time, they settled down for the night. Sam opened up the duffle bag and brought out a can of pork and beans, and half a pan of cornbread that Miss Claudine had packed for them. Roscoe took out his Swiss Army knife and opened the can. They considered building a fire in the center aisle, using cotton padding from some of the seats, but Roscoe decided against it. After all, there was no way to tell if there was still any gasoline left in the bus's tank. If there was, the cookfire could burn through the floor and blow the vehicle—and its occupants—to kingdom come.

Their canteen was nearly empty, so Sam pried down one of the side windows and, uncapping the flask, held it outside for a minute or two. It wasn't long before the canteen was filled to the neck with fresh rainwater. While they passed the water, beans, and cornbread around, they talked about one thing or another. Finally, Roscoe knew it was time to talk about a few things concerning Fear County that he'd neglected to tell Jeb and Sam before.

"I want to tell you two about how things are here in Fear County," said the bluesman. "I tried to tell you how bad this godforsaken place is, but I didn't tell you all of it. I want to do that now, before we go any farther."

"All right," agreed Jeb. "Go ahead. We're listening."

"Well, first of all, there ain't no real reason why Fear County is so dadblamed evil," continued Roscoe. "It ain't like the storybooks. There ain't no long-ago Indian curses or anything of the sort to explain why things are the way they are. It's just like this particular patch of land was made naturally bad when God first breathed life into the world. Things are kinda out of kilter here. The folks hereabouts don't act like normal people. They're mean and ornery, and have nary a kind word to say to anyone, even their own kin. Some are drunkards, thieves, and drug fiends, while others are just plain stone-cold murderers."

Jeb recalled that Saturday morning five years ago. "You mean like Jack Gallow?"

Roscoe's eyes narrowed behind his thick glasses. "Lawdy, boy, where'd you ever hear of that son-of-a-bitch?"

"I was there on Main Street the morning they caught him and sent him off to prison," Jeb told him. "He'd kidnapped a baby for some reason."

The Negro nodded grimly. "I recall hearing about that. Bad business, from what I gathered."

"I think he'd done something to the kid's arm, but I don't know what," said Jeb.

Roscoe's eyes told the boy that he knew exactly what had happened, but wasn't about to say it out loud. "Yeah, that Jack Gallow was an evil bastard, that's for sure. But there's others in Fear County that're a shade worse."

Jeb remembered the bearded man with the wild look in his eyes and the butcher knife in his hand, and couldn't fathom anything more evil than that.

The black man went on. "Even nature ain't the same as it is in the neighboring counties. The trees, the plants, even the earth beneath your feet . . . all are dripping with shadow and full of poison. Don't ever eat a nut or apple off a tree in Fear County, 'cause it could very well be the death of you. And the critters here ain't like any you've ever known over in Mangrum County. They don't take the laws of nature to heart. Animals mate with animals they have no business mating with. Birds mate with reptiles and reptiles mate with dogs and cats. That creature that's been terrorizing Pikesville is probably the offspring of some such act of fornication. And there are other critters in Fear County that don't have no link a'tall to God's creatures. Critters that don't have no rightful name and likely never will."

"But there is some good here, ain't it?" asked Jeb. "Like the Granny Woman?"

"That's right, but she's just one person in the entire county. She supposedly lives in a place called Paradise Hollow a good ten miles south of the county seat of Brimstone. I'll be honest with you, Jeb. I've traveled across Fear County before, but it was from south to north, and not north to south. I've never walked this stretch of road before today, but I know where Brimstone is located and, if Paradise Hollow is where it's supposed to be, we shouldn't have no trouble finding it a'tall."

"I sure hope so," said the boy. He thought of his grandmother, dying in the upstairs bedroom of Claudine Johnson's house, as well as Mandy Rutherford trapped in a cocoon of tough snakeskin and at the mercy of the snake-critter in the cliffside cave. If he didn't find the Granny Woman, both would surely be doomed.

"There's something else I forgot to tell you," said Roscoe, his face grim. "We'll have to keep a watch out for the Snake Queen."

Sam's eyes widened with fright. "The Snake Queen? Who is she?"

"Another witch, or so the story goes," explained the musician. "But she ain't a good one like the Granny Woman. She's the curse-flinging, chicken-sacrificing kind. Makes the Wicked Witch of the West look like a dadblamed Sunday school teacher. They say she lives to make misery and chaos, and that she dwells on the far side of Adder Swamp. She lives in a nest of every kind of snake you could think of and thinks of each and every one as her children."

"The snake-critter," said Jeb. "Do you think it came from Adder Swamp?"

"Could have," agreed Roscoe. "I just hope we don't run into the Snake Queen or any of her young'uns before we reach Paradise Hollow."

"Me either," replied the boy, feeling more than a little uneasy.

Fortunately for Jeb's youthful nerves, the conversation shifted away from the subject of Fear County and they began to talk about other things. After the beans and cornbread had been finished off, Roscoe took up his guitar and began to sing a few tunes. He had sang half a dozen songs when he started to play a Roy Acuff song called "Wreck on the Highway," but he neglected to even finish it. The lightning of the thunderstorm flashed outside the school bus windows, revealing glimpses of the wrecked vehicles, stacked one atop the other. Seeing all that devastation and destruction in one place kind of put a damper on the bluesman's singing and picking, and he put the guitar aside, looking a little spooked.

The storm raged on, giving no indication of letting up. Despite the fact that it was the height of summer and they were shut up in a bus whose windows were mostly fused shut, it seemed a little chilly inside the old wreck. Sam brought out several woolen blankets and they each settled upon a seat, turning it into a makeshift bed. The darkness of twilight descended swiftly and, soon, they were asleep, exhausted by the distance they had walked that day.

Jeb's slumber was more restless than that of the others. He kept hopping from one nightmare to the other. One was the recurring dream concerning McHenry's Funeral Home and the three caskets. Others included the murder of Old Jack and his narrow escape from the cave in the bank of the Cumberland River. As one dreamscape dimmed, revealing yet another, Jeb hoped that the next would be something cheerful and pleasant. But that wasn't the case. They always turned out to be even more depressing and horrifying than the nightmare before.

The farmboy was jolted awake by a particularly loud clap of thunder. He muttered a soft cry and propped himself on his elbows, staring into the darkness. The storm was at its pinnacle; lightning cracked wickedly and rain fell in heavy sheets, drumming almost deafeningly upon the roof of the school bus. During one lightning flash, Jeb caught a glimpse of Roscoe and Sam in the two seats opposite his own. The Negro had his dusty fedora down over his eyes and his blanket pulled clean up to his stubbly chin. Sam was sprawled on his back, his mouth wide open and his legs dangling off the edge of the seat. Jeb reached down beside his own seat and felt his dog sleeping on the floor of the bus. Buckshot's ribs rose and fell gently, but every now and then the coonhound would twitch violently, as if enduring a doggy nightmare of his own.

Jeb lay back down and was about to attempt sleep again, when he heard something echo from outside the school bus. It was a long, shrill shriek that he couldn't identify at first. Then, as it came to its climax and ended in a crunch of crumpling metal, he knew what it was. It was the distant sound of tortured brakes, just before a fatal crash.

The noise was followed by a scream—a woman's from the

sound of it—and then the sound of weeping. The urge to sit up and look out the side window almost overcame Jeb, but he resisted it. He simply lay there, staring up at the leaky ceiling of the bus, his ears straining to hear more.

And he did. As the storm grew in intensity, so did the sounds of squealing brakes, buckling steel, and shattering glass. The sounds grew so plentiful that the boy could've sworn he was caught in the middle of a demolition derby. But he knew if he looked out the window, he would see none of the vehicles moving across the cluttered acreage of the junkyard. Rather, they would be right where they had been earlier that day, resting, mangled and beyond use, one atop the other.

The sounds of automotive carnage seemed to grow nearer, causing a dread to settle in the pit of Jeb's stomach. He lay there on the seat, waiting. Then, abruptly, it was the school bus's turn to participate. Jeb heard the shriek of brakes and felt the bus lurch sharply. There was a loud crash of folding metal and breaking glass. For an instant, Jeb had the dizzy sensation of spinning, as if the vehicle was rolling over, time and time again. Then there was a bouncing of struts and springs, and the bus seemed as if it were back on its tires.

Jeb's heart thundered in his chest as he lay there and listened, knowing that it wasn't over yet. He was right. There was a long stretch of silence, then it began; the cries and moans of the injured and dying. The terrible commotion filled the bus, seemingly coming from every seat and the aisleway in between. From the driver's seat, Jeb could detect the deep groaning of a man, as well as a nasty sucking sound. Jeb could picture the terrifying scene in his mind; the school bus driver impaled on the twisted column of the steering wheel, still alive but unable to pry the obstruction from his shattered ribcage.

Jeb clamped his hands over his ears and attempted to drown out the sounds around him. But he couldn't. In fact, they almost seemed to come from *inside* his head, rather than outside.

Then, from the seat directly in front of the one Jeb lay on, came the mournful cry of a child perhaps six or seven years of age. It was a heart-wrenching cry, full of agony and the fear of death. Jeb looked up at the top of the seat and watched, terrified, as something appeared over the edge. It was the pale hand of a small child, glistening with fresh blood. The tiny fingers were curled like the talons of a bird and, through the torn flesh, Jeb could see naked bones, some jagged and splintered.

Jeb clinched his eyes shut, trying to drive away the sight of the mutilated hand. *Go away!* his thoughts pleaded. *Please . . . just go away and leave me alone!*

The crying of the child in the next seat grew louder . . . then faded. Another clap of thunder shook the junkyard and, abruptly, it was over. The school bus returned to an empty hull of a wreck. If the ghosts of its former victims had, indeed, been there, they were gone now, leaving only blood-stained seats and discarded textbooks.

Slowly, Jeb opened his eyes. The mangled hand was no longer creeping into view. Only empty darkness yawned beyond the edge of the seat.

The farmboy released a sigh of relief. He sat up and peered toward the front of the bus, seeing only empty seats and the shattered frame of the windshield. He then turned his attention toward Roscoe and Sam. Both men had slept throughout the horrifying spectacle. He glanced down at Buckshot. The one-eyed bluetick was also fast asleep.

Jeb considered waking them up and telling them about what he had experienced, but he didn't. Instead, he lay back down and closed his eyes. He didn't sleep for a very long time that night. Every time he began to drift off, the apparition of the dying child's hand came back, reaching toward him, and he would wake up, afraid that it might follow him into the inescapable confines of yet another nightmare.

Twenty-five

Something Underneath

They awoke the next morning to find sunlight streaming through the dirty windows of the school bus. Water dripped sluggishly from the broken seams of the roof, but it was the last remnants of the thunderstorm. Jeb sat up and listened for the singing of robins and sparrows, but he heard no such comforting sounds. It took him a moment to realize exactly where he was and, again, that antsy feeling of dread fluttered in the pit of his belly.

"You don't look so good, Jeb," said Roscoe from the seat opposite him. "Did you have a bad night?"

Jeb nodded. He almost told him about what had happened last night, then decided not to. "I had me a passel of nightmares all night long," he said. "Hardly got a wink of sleep."

"I slept like a winter bear, but I had me one hellacious dream, too," replied the bluesman. "Dreamt that I met the Granny Woman and she was my own mother, God rest her soul." The very thought of the dream seemed to unsettle Roscoe a little and he shuddered openly.

"I had a dream, too," added Sam. "But it weren't no nightmare. I was fighting in the war, just like John Wayne or Gary Cooper, and I was shooting at the Nazis from a foxhole. Then somebody threw a tatermasher grenade into the trench and everything went black. Funny dream, wasn't it?"

Jeb and Roscoe traded knowing glances, but said nothing in reply.

"Roscoe?" asked Jeb, tossing off his blanket. "Can we get out of this place now? It gives me the creeps just being here."

"I was just thinking the same thing," agreed the black man. "We'll eat our breakfast somewheres else."

They gathered up their gear and soon were climbing down out of the wrecked bus. As they crossed the junkyard and made their way toward the front gate, they walked around broad puddles left behind by the storm. In one such mudhole, Jeb spied the dark body of a cottonmouth snake. But it was unlike any the boy had ever seen before. When it lifted its neck from the murky water, Jeb was shocked to see that it had two heads. It hissed contemptuously as he passed, both of its fanged mouths yawning wide and exposing the pale white flesh that lined the inner jaws.

Jeb, Roscoe, Sam, and Buckshot made a hasty exit through the open gate, leaving the auto junkyard behind. They walked a mile farther down the road before they sat down beneath a huge oak tree and began to fix breakfast. Roscoe built a small fire out of twigs and dry weeds, then, taking a small cast iron skillet from his knapsack, mixed up a pan of home-made biscuits using flour, butter, and water from the canteen. They ate the biscuits with pear preserves Miss Claudine had sent with them, then put out the fire and continued down the lonely stretch of rural road, their spirits a little lighter than they had been an hour ago.

They passed a couple of wide pastures where only tall weeds and jagged tree trunks grew, then the open land again gave way to forest. Like the woods they had passed through the day before, the upper limbs of these bowed outward and connected, casting a dense canopy of foliage above the road.

Soon, the sunshine was shut out and only speckles of light showed through the shadowy thicket.

"How far is it to Brimstone?" asked Jeb.

Roscoe shrugged his skinny shoulders. "Like I said before, boy, it's been thirty years since I last walked this land, and, even then, I was walking from the other direction. If I had to take a wild guess, I'd say maybe two or three miles."

Jeb didn't know whether to be glad or frightened over the prospect of reaching the Fear County seat by late morning. On one hand, it would be nice to be away from the spooky forests and abandoned shacks, but, on the other, there was the unfriendly folks of Brimstone to consider. He recalled what Roscoe had told him about the citizens of Fear County and how they weren't the most congenial folks on the face of God's green earth. He was wondering exactly what they might find in Brimstone, when he almost tripped on something. He stumbled a couple of steps, then looked behind him. Stretched across the road, was a long, leafy strand of dark green kudzu.

Puzzled, he turned to look ahead. Jeb was surprised to see that the wild ivy criss-crossed the road, growing thicker and thicker until it completely covered the bare earth some fifty feet away. He stared off into the distance, but saw no visible sign of the road reappearing. There was only the heavy carpet of kudzu, stretching as far as the eye could see.

"What the heck is this?" asked Sam.

A guarded look crossed Roscoe's dark face. "I don't know. I can't recollect coming across anything like this the last time I was here."

"What're we gonna do?" asked Jeb. "I can't even see where the road goes . . . if it's even there any more."

"Aw, of course it's there!" barked the Negro. "We'll just keep on walking until this ivy peters out and the road shows itself again."

Roscoe Ledbetter stepped into the kudzu and began to high-step across its leafy growth. Reluctantly, Jeb and Sam did the same. Buckshot stood at the edge of the road and watched them for a moment. Then he tucked his tail between his legs and followed.

Slowly, the kudzu grew wilder and more tangled the further they went. It wasn't long before the road beneath their feet took a sharp dip and they found themselves up to their knees in the thick ivy, rather than up to their ankles. Once or twice, Jeb and Sam had to kick free from vines that got tangled around their lower legs. Roscoe and Buckshot seemed to make better progress. The black man's long strides kept the kudzu from tripping him up and the dog simply jumped from spot to spot, the vegetation reaching clear to the hound's shoulders with each hop he took.

They were halfway through the viney thicket, when Jeb yelled out. "Hey!" he called, his eyes startled.

"What's the matter?" asked Roscoe, turning around.

Jeb looked down at the kudzu around him. "I felt something rub against my ankle. I swear I did."

"Could've been a snake," offered Sam good-naturedly. "Or some kinda furry critter like a weasel or a rat."

"Thanks, Sam," said Jeb with a frown. "That makes me feel a whole lot better!"

"Just forget it and let's go," said Roscoe. "I think I can see the road up ahead."

Jeb craned his neck and saw that the guitar-picker was right. He could see the dusty track of the rural road, emerging from the kudzu a hundred yards ahead.

They took a couple more steps forward. Then it was Roscoe's turn to nearly jump out of his shoes. "I felt it that time!" he said, his eyes wide behind his eyeglasses. "And it sure as hell wasn't no snake or weasel!"

"Then what was it?" asked Sam, looking a little frightened.

"I don't rightly know," said Roscoe. "Felt kinda slick and slimy, and as cold as frost."

Jeb was about to suggest that they head for the road, when Buckshot bared his teeth and began to growl. "What is it, boy?" he asked, his heart beating faster.

"Listen!" whispered Roscoe.

The boy did as he was told. Faintly, he could hear the rustle of something moving under the cover of the kudzu. He stared down at the blanket of heart-shaped leaves and saw them shimmer slightly. Almost immediately, he felt something rub against his ankle again. This time it lingered a little longer. Roscoe had been right. It was slimy, like the body of a slug, and as cold as an iron pump handle on a cold February morning.

Jeb jumped away and stumbled back a few paces. Buckshot growled at the shuddering leaves, his good eye gleaming with menace. Then, before Jeb could stop him, the dog leaped into the thicket, burrowing down under the leaves. Soon, he was totally gone from sight.

"Buckshot!" Jeb yelled. "Boy, come back here this instant!"

If the dog heard him, he gave no intention of obeying his master's command. Jeb heard a muffled bark beneath the ivy a few yards to the west, followed by total silence.

"Jeb?" came Sam's frightened voice from behind him.

"It's all right, Sam," the boy said, trying to soothe his father's fears. "Buckshot'll be back directly. You know how he likes to chase critters."

"Jeb," said the big farmer once again. This time his voice carried more than simple fear.

The ten-year-old turned around and found Sam standing stone still in the middle of the kudzu patch. The man's broad face was as white as baking flour. "What's wrong, Sam?" he asked.

Sam directed terrified eyes downward, to the kudzu around his knees. "It's got me, Jeb. It's got me . . . around the ankle."

"Just stand there," warned Roscoe. "Don't move a muscle. We're coming."

Jeb and Roscoe were starting toward Sam, when the big man was suddenly jerked off his feet. "Help!" screamed Sam. "It's pulling me under!"

"Hang on!" yelled Roscoe. Wildly, he leaped through the kudzu with a pace characteristic of a man half his age.

When they reached Sam, he was up to his waist in the undergrowth. Roscoe grabbed him under his armpits and yanked, trying to pull him free. But there was no give. Whatever had hold of his ankle wasn't about to let go. It yanked back sharply, pulling Sam a couple of inches further beneath the thick ivy.

"Find it, Jeb!" demanded Roscoe frantically. "Dig through that kudzu and see if you can find what's got hold of him!"

Without hesitation, Jeb did as he was told. Tearing handfuls of the leafy vine up and tossing it aside, he worked his way down to where Sam's left leg was. When he saw what had hold of his father's ankle, he could scarcely believe his eyes. "Good God Almighty!" was all he could utter.

Tears of fright and pain rolled down Sam's suntanned cheeks. "What is it, Jeb? What is it?"

Jeb stared down at the thing around Sam's ankle, but, for the life of him, couldn't tell exactly what it was. It was as thick around as a tube of sausage and as gray as wrought iron. He reached out and touched it, then quickly drew his hand away. It was sticky and slimy, and terribly cold.

"You gotta do something, boy!" called out Roscoe. "Whatever it is, it's strong as a bull. Won't be long before it pulls me down under, along with Sam here!"

"I'll try to get it off!" Jeb said. He reached down and tried to grab hold of the gray tentacle, intending to pry it off. But he simply couldn't get a grip. The rubbery flesh of the thing was too slimy. His fingers slid right off.

"It's no good! It's too danged slippery!" Jeb reared back and gave it a kick. But that act seemed to do more harm than good. Sam let out a shrill scream of agony and Jeb saw the tentacle tighten around the man's ankle. It wasn't long before the skin of Sam's leg had lost all color. The thing was cutting off his circulation!

"I don't know what to do!" said Jeb, himself near tears.

"Well, you'd best think of something fast!" wailed Roscoe. " 'Cause both of us is losing ground!"

Jeb looked over at Roscoe and Sam. Inch by inch, the critter beneath the ivy was dragging them under.

Right when Jeb was about to give up, salvation came. It came leaping up out of the kudzu with an angry snarl and sank its teeth into the gray flesh of the mysterious creature.

"Buckshot!" cried Jeb in elation. He watched as the bluetick hound growled deep down in his throat and bit down harder on the tentacle around Sam's ankle. A couple of yards behind Jeb erupted a hoarse cry that sounded like the gurgle of a backed-up toilet. Then the tentacle began to loosen.

"Pull!" he screamed at Roscoe. "Now!"

The black man yanked with all his might and, soon, both he and Sam were stumbling backwards. When the two were out of harm's way, Buckshot released his hold and the slimy, gray coil retreated into the depths of the viney thicket.

"Let's get the hell outta here!" said Roscoe.

Together, they leaped through the kudzu, heading for the road beyond. Buckshot wiggled out of the ivy and had soon outdistanced them. Despite his act of bravery, he was just as scared as the others were.

Behind them came an angry roar and the rustle of leaves. Jeb glanced over his shoulder just long enough to see the kudzu rolling toward them like the waves of an ocean. Whatever was underneath, was coming for them. And it wasn't at all happy.

"Run!" urged Roscoe. "Run like you've never run before!"

Jeb turned on the speed. The kudzu threatened to trip him up several times, but he pulled free before he lost his balance. Then, suddenly, he no longer felt the vegetation around his legs and he was running on dusty earth again. He ran twenty or thirty feet further before he realized that he was out of the thicket and back on the road again.

He turned and looked behind him. Jeb breathed a sigh of relief when he saw that Roscoe, Sam, and Buckshot had also made it to safety. The two men and the boy stood and caught their breath, while the dog coughed and gagged, a nasty coating of silver-gray slime dripping from his canine lips.

"Are you okay, Sam?" asked Jeb, as he reached his father's side.

"I dunno. I think so," replied the farmer.

"Pull up your britches leg and let's take a look," suggested Roscoe.

Tenderly, Sam pulled the hem of his pants leg up to the middle of his shin. Roscoe and Jeb grimaced. There, just above the top of his combat boot, was an ugly pink welt that circled Sam's upper ankle. "Does it hurt, Sam?" Jeb asked.

"Smarts a little," said Sam. "But it ain't all that bad."

Jeb looked back at the stretch of dense undergrowth. The turbulence that had chased them a moment ago was gone. No movement showed amid the tangle of dark green kudzu.

"What was it, Roscoe?" asked Sam.

"I can't rightly say for sure," said the Negro. He thought

to himself and something came to mind; a place up in East Tennessee called Pale Dove Mountain and a creature called the Dark'Un that some folks claimed lived there. He didn't tell Jeb or Sam about the old legend, though. More than likely, it would end up spooking them even more than they were right now.

Roscoe fished his pocketwatch from his vest and checked the time. It was a quarter till nine. "We'd best just forget about this and move on. I'd like to make it to Brimstone by eleven, if at all possible."

"Yeah, let's go," said Jeb. The boy took a bandanna from his pocket and wiped the slime off his dog's mouth. The hound blessed his master with a look of gratitude, then followed the three as they started on down the road.

As they went, Sam Sweeny glanced back at the kudzu that had nearly swallowed him whole. Goosebumps prickled his muscular arms and he shook his head. "I don't like this place," he said. "I don't like it a'tall."

"Amen to that," said Roscoe. Grimly, he eyed the desolate stretch of country road ahead of them and wondered what they would encounter around the next bend.

Twenty-six

Brimstone

By the time mid-morning rolled around, they had left the dark forest and again traveled open ground. The rural road stretched through a desolate expanse of pastureland lined on both sides with barbed-wire fences. From where Jeb walked along the side of the road, he could see that the wire was not the type he and Sam bought in five-hundred yard rolls at Holt's Feed and Farming Equipment. These strands seemed to be homemade; simple chicken wire laced with razor blades, rusted nails, and sewing needles dabbed with cow manure. Jeb pitied anyone who attempted to climb such a wicked barrier, for it was intended to bring nothing but pain and sickness to trespassers, rather than merely discourage them from setting foot on property that wasn't rightfully their own.

Jeb also noticed the animals the fences were meant to protect. To one side stood a herd of Holstein cows, while the other pasture held only a few sway-backed mules. The boy was shocked at the state of the livestock. Both the cattle and the mules were thin and malnourished. Their legs were as skinny as chair legs and their ribs showed clearly through their sides. Hollow eyes stared at them feverishly, almost *hungrily,* but they made no sound or movement as Jeb and the others passed by. Suddenly, the farmboy found himself thankful that those fences were there. If they hadn't been, no telling what the starving animals might have attempted.

As they headed on down the road, Jeb looked for the homes of those who owned the gaunt mules and cows. He only saw one farmhouse at the edge of the cow pasture, but the structure was weathered down to the bare wood. It looked as though no one had lived there for a very long time. That, in itself, made the hollow-eyed cows with their hungry stares seem even more menacing than before.

They continued onward. It wasn't long before the farmland petered out and they again saw trees towering up ahead, this time at the mouth of a valley between two wooded hills. But, unlike the other two stretches of forest, this one wasn't wild and desolate. For, nestled within, were an abundance of brick buildings and high-roofed houses. Even from where they were, Jeb and the others could tell that it was an inhabited township. Unlike the settlement around the auto junkyard, this one was not one that had been abandoned to weather and weeds. The roofs of the buildings seemed well-maintained and the trees looked to have been recently pruned.

"Is this it?" asked Sam.

"Sure is," said Roscoe. He nodded toward a sign standing at the side of the road. It simply said "BRIMSTONE."

Jeb noticed right away that the words "welcome to" were not included like they were on the signs leading to and from his own township of Pikesville.

Quietly, they entered the Brimstone city limits. At first, the place seemed almost inviting. The town was laid out similar to that of Pikesville, with two lines of shops and businesses bordering the long main street, which led to a circular town square and the tall brick structure of the Fear County courthouse.

But, the further they traveled, the more that illusion began to fall away. Most of the store windows were curtained with black drapes and there seemed to be no signs there, advertising wares or services. Some shops seemed to be completely out of business. Withered wreaths garnished with black ribbon hung on their doors and a couple of the broad front windows were riddled with bulletholes. Jeb thought about asking Roscoe what had taken place, then decided that he really didn't want to know.

It wasn't long before he noticed something else that was unusual. They had been walking along Brimstone's main avenue for several minutes, but had not yet come across a living soul. There were a few vehicles parked at the side of the street; a couple of rusty pickup trucks with cracked windows and patched tires that seemed more suitable for Kruller's Junkyard than for the streets of Brimstone.

"Where is everybody?" asked Jeb.

Roscoe shook his head, his eyes suspicious. "I don't know. Seems like we should've come across someone by now."

As they passed a shadowy shop with a sign reading "TEMPLETON'S GROCERY" hanging above the front door, Buckshot headed toward it, seemingly sensing the presence of food. But, by the time he reached the sidewalk, the hound had changed his mind. With a whimper, he moved away from the open doorway and walked back to Jeb's side. The boy breathed in deeply and nearly gagged. The delicious scents of fresh vegetables and fruit wasn't what he smelled at all. Instead, the combined stench of decay and putrefaction drifted from the streetside grocery. He detected the odor of rotten eggs, tainted meat, and spoiled produce, as well as other things he couldn't quite identify.

"Sure ain't nothing like the store at Pikesville," commented Sam, pinching his nostrils between thumb and forefinger.

"There ain't nothing here that's like back home," said Roscoe. "You'll find that out soon enough."

They continued on down the main street, to the circular lawn of the courthouse. Jeb was surprised to find no benches there, or even a single shade tree to sit underneath on a muggy summer day. Instead, there was a concrete platform that held a tall metal statue of a long-bearded man with a stern and unforgiving expression on his face. The bronze monument was tarnished an ugly green and speckled with bird droppings. The man who had been immortalized struck an impressive figure, standing there with a strange-looking book in one hand and a curve-bladed scythe in the other.

"Who is it?" the boy asked.

This time Roscoe knew the answer. "It's Ezekial Gallow, the only man brave enough—or crazy enough—to settle in Fear County when no one else would. Matter of fact, he founded this here town of Brimstone back in 1748, or so I've been told."

Jeb frowned. "Gallow? Was he any kin to Jack Gallow?"

"More than likely," said the bluesman. "The whole county's full of Gallows, on account folks have no morals hereabouts. They tend to interbreed a lot and not give it a second thought."

Jeb noticed something else on the circular platform. In front of the scowling statue was a wooden contraption with one large hole in the center and a smaller one on either side. Jeb knew what it was immediately. It was a stockade, like the ones folks used to imprison criminals in years ago. Jeb knew what one looked like, mainly because he had checked out a copy of *The Count of Monte Cristo* from the school library for a book report and he had seen a drawing of a similar contraption in one of the illustrations.

Jeb wondered what such a device of torture was doing there on the courthouse lawn, when he noticed a sign hanging just below the hole where the head went. It simply read: Children, Obey Your Elders!

Abruptly, the purpose of the stock became apparent. Jeb could picture himself confined in that contraption of heavy wood and iron pins, receiving punishment for some act of defiance or disrespect. The very thought of it made the boy feel a little sick to his stomach.

His attention was drawn from the stockade by Sam. "Sure is an ugly looking courthouse, ain't it, Jeb?" pointed out the slow-witted farmer.

Jeb turned his eyes to the tall building beyond the statue. "Sure enough is," he replied.

The Fear County courthouse stood two stories high. But it was not constructed of red brick and white-washed trim like the one back home in Mangrum. Rather, it was built with slate gray brick and mortared with something that looked like black tar instead of common mortar. And that wasn't the only thing peculiar about the structure. The tall columns out front, the slope of the high-pitched eaves, even the set of the long, thin windows—something about them all seemed disturbingly out of kilter. Jeb tried his best to detect exactly what it was about the building that gave that impression, but, try as he might, he couldn't tell precisely what was the matter. It was just wrong for some reason, he was sure of that.

"Come on," urged Roscoe. "Let's be on our way."

They walked around the town square and started down the street that led southward out of Brimstone. They passed a few homes and vacant lots, before the city limits began to give way to open pastureland once again. They were about to sigh a breath of relief, when a bell tolled to their right. The mournful sound drew their attention to where a single structure stood midway up the western hill.

It was a church; lofty steeple, stained-glass windows, and all. But, like every thing else in the township of Brimstone, it was different from any they had ever seen before.

"It's black," said Jeb, a little confused. "They've painted it completely black."

The boy stared at the dark structure on the hillside and listened as the lonesome ringing of the bell stopped and a new sound came from within the black church. It was the sound of singing . . . or rather chanting. Jeb tried to make out what they were saying, but couldn't. It sounded like they were singing in what his Grandma Sweeny might refer to as "an unknown tongue."

Jeb turned to Roscoe, intending to ask the black man why the citizens of Brimstone were in church on Thursday instead of Sunday morning, when his question froze up in his throat. Roscoe had a funny look on his face; like something had just dawned on him that he would've just as soon not have figured out. Jeb knew that, if it had been physically possible, Roscoe's face would have been as white as a bedsheet at that moment.

"Let's get outta here," said the guitar-picker softly.

"What's the matter, Roscoe?" asked Sam, turning his innocent eyes from the black church house to Roscoe and then back again.

Sam's question was answered a moment later. The chanting stopped and silence filled the structure. Then, from within, came the most godawful sound they had ever heard in their lives. It was the agonized shriek of an animal being viciously slaughtered.

"Come on and let's go!" urged Roscoe, pushing Sam and Jeb ahead of him. "Let's get away from this place before those church doors open up and they see us standing down here."

Jeb felt a shiver run down his spine. "Yeah, you're right," he said. "Let's go."

Quickly, they headed down the road out of town. Jeb didn't have to call for Buckshot to follow like he usually did. The coonhound was just as anxious to leave the town limits of Brimstone as his master was.

They were a half mile away, when they finally sat down to eat lunch. This time they lit no fire to heat their food, afraid that the smoke might make their presence known. Sam dug out several strips of beef jerky and they ate it with biscuits left over from breakfast.

It was a while before Jeb gathered the nerve to ask Roscoe the question that had been pestering him since their departure from Brimstone. "Exactly what were they doing there . . . inside that church?"

Roscoe yanked a hunk off his strip of jerky with his gold and ivory teeth. "Can't say that I really know," he said quietly. "But, whatever it was, it didn't have nothing to do with God, that's for sure."

Jeb let it go at that. He finished his meal of cold meat and bread, and looked over at Buckshot. The dog sat at the edge of the road, staring back the way they came. Jeb knew the hound was thinking about the death cry of that unfortunate animal that had echoed from the altar of the black church.

The boy knew Roscoe was right. Whatever the folks of Brimstone had been up to that morning, it had more to do with the Devil than anything else.

Twenty-seven

The Pack

The long shadows of dusk began to stretch across the rural road heading southward and, still, Jeb and the others could not shed that uneasy feeling the town of Brimstone had cast over them. They tried to put the brief journey through the deserted hamlet out of their minds and think of what lay ahead, but it was difficult to do so. Thoughts of the bullet-ridden store windows, the wooden stock on the town square, and the black church on the hill kept resurfacing time and time again, causing them to wonder just what sort of terrible peril they had narrowly escaped.

They were five miles from Brimstone, when Roscoe fished his railroad watch from his vest pocket and flipped open the engraved lid with a black thumb. "It's going on half past six," said the bluesman. "Won't be long before it's pitch dark. I reckon we'd best look for a good place to bed down for the night."

Jeb looked up at the darkening sky beyond the branches of the encroaching trees. "Thank God there ain't no stormclouds tonight," he said. "We'll be able to sleep out under the stars and not in some stinky old bus."

"Yep," said the black man with a nod. "But it still might be worth our while to rustle up some kindling and build a good-sized campfire."

Sam scratched his head. "It's in the middle of summer, Roscoe. I wouldn't think we'd need one on a night like this."

"Oh, it's bound to be a warm one, that's for sure," agreed the musician. "But we'll fire one up anyhow . . . just to ward off anything that might be creeping out there in the woods in the dead of night."

Jeb and Sam looked at each other. Suddenly, they knew what Roscoe was getting at. They thought of the thing beneath the kudzu and goosebumps prickled the arms of both boy and man.

They continued a little further, searching for a good place to settle down and eat their supper. "There's a spot over yonder," said Sam, pointing to a clearing in the middle of a grove of weeping willow trees.

Roscoe appraised the potential campsite, then directed his gaze farther down the lonesome stretch of dirt road. "What I'm looking for is something near a pond or creek," he told them. "I know I told ya'll that the water here in Fear County ain't fitting to drink, but, as it turns out, we ain't got no choice." He took the canteen from around his neck and shook the container. The slosh of liquid inside told them that it was no more than a quarter full.

"How're we gonna find a waterhole before dark?" asked Jeb, a little discouraged. "We ain't come upon one since we crossed the county line."

Roscoe flashed a gold and ivory grin. "There's our divining rod up yonder in the center of the road," he said, pointing ahead.

Jeb followed his finger, but was confused. "What're you talking about? That's only Ol' Buckshot."

"That's right," said Roscoe. "But just take time to watch him for a minute."

Jeb did as the man instructed. He watched the bluetick hound stop in the middle of the road every so often. The dog would simply stand there for a long moment and raise his head slightly. It took the boy a while before he realized what the coonhound was doing. He was sniffing the air.

"He's smelling for water," said Roscoe. "Critters can do that you know, most particularly dogs and horses. And, from the way Ol' Buckshot's acting, I'd say we're getting mighty close."

The farmboy studied his dog. Buckshot was again in motion, heading down the road before them. This time, however, his pace was a little quicker. It wasn't long before Jeb, Roscoe, and Sam had to speed up, just to keep the hound in sight.

A few minutes later, Buckshot let out a throaty bay, then leaped off into the wooded thicket to the left of the road. When Jeb started to go after him, Roscoe held him back. "Just let him have at it, Jeb," he told him. "He'll let us know where it is when he finds it."

Jeb nodded, although he wasn't all too easy about his dog being out there in the woods by himself. He considered what Roscoe had told him before; about how there were critters within the boundaries of Fear County that were freaks of nature and had no rightful place in God's world. If that was the case, one such creature could jump out of the thicket and grab Buckshot before the dog knew what had hold of him. By the time Jeb and the others reached the hound, it could be maimed or devoured completely.

They continued on down the rural road. The shadows of the surrounding trees stretched across the rutted dirt track, interlacing, turning the forest and its sole pathway even more spooky than before.

They reached the spot where Buckshot had left the road. Jeb stared off into the woods, but could only see a shadowy tangle of trees, kudzu, and blackberry bramble. He strained his ears but heard nothing.

"I don't hear him, Roscoe," said Jeb, worried.

The black man laid a comforting hand on the boy's freckled shoulder. "Aw, he's all right. He's just sniffing out that creek like a bloodhound looking for a chain ganger. He'll call out before long."

They headed on down the road. They had gone fifty yards further, when they heard something behind them. The brittle crack of a branch snapping in half.

"What was that?" asked Sam, his eyes wide.

Roscoe and Jeb turned and regarded the way they had come. All that lay behind them was the stretch of desolate road and the dark woods that crowded in on both sides.

The ten-year-old turned curious eyes to the elderly bluesman. Roscoe merely shrugged his skinny shoulders. "Could be anything. Come on and let's keep going."

They were another twenty yards down the road, when the second sound drew their attention. This time it was the low rumbling of an animal's growl. Again, the three travelers stopped in their tracks and, together, looked behind them.

There was a dog standing in the middle of the road, no more than sixty feet away.

At first, Jeb thought it was Buckshot, who had gone exploring and, having come up empty-handed, returned to join them. But, even in the deepening gloom, Jeb could tell it wasn't the bluetick who stood there. For one thing, the dog was larger than Buckshot, even though it appeared to be much thinner; no more than skin and bones.

A big smile split Sam's face and he squatted and patted his knees. "Here, boy!" he called out.

Roscoe reached down and grasped Sam's shoulder firmly, causing the farmer to look up, puzzled. "No," explained the Negro. "There's something wrong with it."

The three watched as the dog took a couple of staggering

steps closer. Then it growled again. This time the noise had a different quality to it; a gurgling, wet quality.

"What's the matter with it, Roscoe?" asked Jeb softly, afraid to raise his voice.

But, before Roscoe could answer, the dog wagged his head and snarled. It was then that they saw the faint gleam of dampness around the canine's muzzle . . . followed by a long string of foamy slaver that dripped from between the animal's tightly-clenched jaws.

"Lord help us," whispered Roscoe.

"What's wrong?" asked Sam. "Is it sick?"

"It's worse than that," he said. "It's rabid. It's plumb raving mad with the hydrophoby!"

Jeb had grown up around animals all his life and he knew what Roscoe was talking about. He thought of the time when Jimmy Stentson's prized beagle, Pepper, had been bitten by a diseased weasel and caught the rabies. The dog had gone all crazy in the head, foaming at the mouth and snapping at anything that came into view. Pepper had ended up biting Clarence Watson, a worker over at York's Dairy. The dog had been shot dead and its head had been chopped off and sent to a laboratory in Nashville. Poor old Clarence had suffered through two weeks of daily shots smack-dab in the stomach. Although he had recovered from the ordeal, the dairyman's nerves were never quite as steady after that.

Sam suddenly seemed to understand, too. His smile faded immediately. "Are you sure, Roscoe?"

Roscoe watched as more foam dripped from between the dog's teeth and landed, in a thick pool, at its feet. "Oh, I'm pretty damned sure. Now, let's just turn ourselves around real slowlike and keep walking. Maybe it'll think we're not worth the trouble and leave us be."

The three turned and continued down the shadowy road. They hadn't gotten twenty feet when they heard another growl . . . and another. With lumps in their throats, they glanced over their shoulders as they walked.

There were now three dogs behind them. And, like the first dog, the other two seemed to be infected with the same dreaded virus.

"What now?" Jeb asked in desperation.

"Just keep walking," said Roscoe. "A little faster."

Jeb and Sam followed the black man's example, quickening their pace. They had covered a dozen feet more, when the sound of growling and snarling seemed to multiply once again.

They looked around and felt a cold fear run through them, from head to heels. The number of dogs in the middle of the road had increased from three to eight. All were unsteady in their gait and possessed the same feverish eyes and slavering jaws as those who had appeared before them.

Roscoe looked at Jeb and, in turn, Jeb looked at Sam. All three knew what confronted them. There was a pack of dogs stalking them . . . a pack of *rabid* dogs.

The bluesman increased his pace a little and Jeb and Sam matched it, step by step. They had gone only a few more yards, when a tormented howl the likes of which they'd never heard in their lives echoed from behind. They heard the sound of feet padding swiftly along the dusty road, as well as the moist racket of dogs attempting to breathe through foam-choked muzzles.

Jeb chanced a glance over his shoulder, but he already knew what was going on. The pack of mad dogs was coming toward them, as fast as their unsteady feet would carry them.

"Into the woods!" bellowed Roscoe. "Quickly!"

A moment later, Jeb and Sam had left the dirt road and followed Roscoe, plunging into the thicket at the left of the trail. As they descended down the steep slope of a backwoods hollow, tearing through thorny bramble and clinging strands of honeysuckle and kudzu, they could hear the rustle of vegetation behind them. It was the pack, dogging their heels in pursuit.

Blindly, Jeb tore through the shadowy thicket, his heart racing and his mind imagining the dire outcome in the event that the pack overtook them. The thought of being dragged down and eaten alive wasn't as frightening as that of actually being bitten by one of the rabid mutts. Jeb could imagine the sting of teeth ripping open his flesh and injecting the horrible disease into his bloodstream. Even if he escaped alive, there would be no hope for him. In Fear County there were no caring doctors or fourteen shots of vaccine in the stomach. There was only miles of unfamiliar terrain between him and his hometown of Pikesville. And such a great distance spelled nothing but doom and disaster to someone who was cursed with hydrophobia.

They were halfway down the hollow, when Jeb heard the distant baying of a dog. But it didn't come from behind them. Instead, it came from the bottom of the valley.

"It's Buckshot!" said Sam. "He's found the creek."

Jeb strained his ears. Yes, now he could hear it. The gentle rush of a branch that snaked its way along the basin of the wooded hollow.

"Hallelujah!" yelled Roscoe, a shade of hope in his gravelly voice. "Don't slow down, gents! Run straight for that creekbed and don't let up till you get there!"

"But that won't help us," protested Jeb. The strength in his legs began to flag and he almost fell flat on his face a couple of times.

"You're wrong about that, boy!" laughed Roscoe. "You just wait and see!"

The confidence in Roscoe's voice lifted the boy's spirits. Jeb suddenly called upon a reserve of energy he didn't know he had and it wasn't long before he had outdistanced even

Roscoe and Sam. The slope of the hollow seemed to level out a little and, before he knew it, he was running, ankle-deep, in cool, clear water.

He slowed down and looked around. He was standing in the middle of a wide stream. Buckshot was there, too, wading up to his belly in the rush of the current. Jeb heard two tremendous splashes and turned to find Roscoe and Sam jumping into the creek. They joined him in the middle, breathing hard from their wild dash down the slope of the hollow.

"Look!" gasped Sam. "Here they come!"

They looked toward the far bank of the creek and saw the pack of mad dogs approaching, snapping and snarling and flinging thick droplets of diseased foam into the evening air.

Jeb and Sam took a couple of steps back in anticipation of the attack. Then the boy remembered something. He took his slingshot out of his hip pocket and began to dig around in his side pocket for ammunition.

"No," said Roscoe, standing in the middle of the creek as if he didn't have a care in the world. "I don't think we'll have need of that. Watch!"

Jeb watched as the pack made their way down the steep slope and reached the floor of the hollow. But when they came to the edge of the stream, they reacted completely different from what Jeb expected them to. They stopped dead still in their tracks and glared at the three travelers from the creekbank. Although it was growing darker by the moment, Jeb recognized the emotion that burned in their crazy eyes. It wasn't hunger or even insanity. Rather, it was a mixture of agony and frustration that showed there. Their muscles seemed to lock up and begin to quiver, then, one by one, the rabid dogs began to howl. It was a heart-rending, mournful howl, like tormented souls condemned to a hell from which there was no escape.

"What's the matter with 'em?" asked Sam, perplexed. "Why don't they come after us?"

"They can't," said Roscoe. "That's as far as they can go. A mad dog can't stand water, especially the sound of it. The hydrophoby clenches up their throat, makes 'em thirst for water they can't possibly swallow. It's a sorrowful thing, to be sure, but, in our case, it just saved our hides."

Jeb looked back at the dogs who stood trembling on the bank of the coolwater branch. He could tell they wanted to jump into the creek and tear them to shreds, but something deep down in their feverish brains wouldn't let them. It was as if the sound of water over smooth stones had raised an invisible barrier between the dogs and those they had chased down the face of the wooded hollow, keeping them completely at bay.

"Now what do we do?" asked Jeb.

Roscoe kept his eyes glued to the dogs on the bank as he took a couple of steps down the middle of the creek, the current pushing at the calves of his legs. Slowly, the dogs lost their immobility and started southward along the bank, as if intending to keep him from escaping by the same direction he had come. "Didn't think that would work," said the bluesman.

Jeb turned toward the opposite side of the stream, but immediately found that there was no escape route to be found there. Where he expected to find the other slope of the hollow towered only sheer bluffs of smooth sandstone. He studied the cliffs, which ran the entire length of the creek as far as the eye could see, but he could detect no handholds with which to scale the thirty foot walls.

"I reckon the only way we'll get away from these confounded dogs is to head downstream and see where it leads us," said Roscoe.

Jeb and Sam nodded in agreement. They turned southward

and found that Buckshot was already heading down the center of the creek. Jeb heard growling come from the western bank, but he paid it no mind. He knew there was no immediate threat in the grumbling of the mad dogs, at least as long as they stayed in the water and off dry earth.

They walked a hundred yards downstream, hoping to leave the pack behind. But the animals were stubborn in their lunacy. They dogged the three from the creekbank, preventing them from leaving the stream.

"What's that up ahead?" asked Sam, pointing southward.

Jeb and Roscoe turned their attention to where the creek rounded a sharp bend. The stream ran square into the side of a tall hill, or, more precisely, into an opening at the bottom of it. As they rounded the bend and grew closer, they discovered that the stream disappeared into the mouth of a cave.

When they reached the entrance, Roscoe peered inside. "Sam, hand me that flashlight, will you?" he called back to the big farmer.

Sam opened the bag and, finding the flashlight, handed it to the black man. Roscoe snapped on the switch and directed its beam into the mouth of the cave. The light revealed only smooth, dank walls and nothing more. "Mighty dark in there," he said, searching the shadowy ceiling for bats.

"What're we gonna do?" asked Jeb.

Roscoe thought about it for a moment, then swung around and shined the light on the western bank of the creek. The slavering pack sat there, patiently watching them as they growled and twitched.

"Well, I reckon there ain't much else we can do," he told the boy. "We'll just have to keep going and take our chances."

Jeb sighed. Roscoe was right. They had no choice but to proceed.

"Just stick close and don't talk unless I tell you to," instructed Roscoe. Then, together, Jeb, Sam, Roscoe, and Buck-shot stepped through the rocky portal and, wading through water up to their knees, began to make their way into the dark depths of the cave beneath the hill.

Twenty-eight

Shadows on a Wall

It seemed like they traveled the underground stream for miles before they finally found a place to rest. The tunnel was dark and wet, and the water around their legs grew increasingly colder the further they traveled, making their legs feel numb and heavy.

Eventually, though, they reached the heart of the hill and stepped through a second entranceway. All of a sudden, Jeb and the others found themselves standing in a cavern thirty feet across and fifty feet high. Roscoe flashed the beam of the battery-powered light upward and revealed row upon row of jagged stalactites dangling from overhead. The glittering eyes of tiny animals—maybe bats and maybe not—reflected back at them, but made no move to drop down upon their heads.

"We'd best get outta this cold water before we catch our deaths," said Roscoe. He directed the flashlight toward the eastern wall and smiled. "There! That oughta do for the night."

Jeb and Sam looked to where the beam illuminated the far wall. A narrow ledge of rock ran along the left side of the underground stream. When they reached it, they found that it was barely wide enough to accommodate one person, let alone three and a dog.

"Can we all fit on there?" asked Jeb doubtfully.

"I reckon we'll have to," said Roscoe. "Unless you want to walk some more and take your chances further on."

Jeb looked toward the southern end of the cavern and saw the stream disappear into a tunnel identical to the one they had just traveled. Nothing but pitch darkness could be seen beyond the craggy exitway. Jeb wiggled his toes and was shocked to find that he could hardly feel them. He reached down and tested the water with his fingertips. It was as cold as ice.

"No," said the boy. "I reckon we oughta stay right here."

"Glad you agree," said the old bluesman looking more than a little weary. "I'm plumb tuckered out and, truthfully, I don't believe I could make it to that hole over yonder, let alone out the other side of this hill."

"Yeah," replied the boy with a nod. "It'd be better if we camped out here and went the rest of the way in the morning."

Sluggishly, they helped each other onto the ledge, then hauled Buckshot—who dog-paddled in the cold water—up with them. Roscoe shined the flashlight around. The ledge was littered with broken fragments of clay pottery, flint arrowheads, and pieces of driftwood that had washed up there by chance. It was the wall that stretched above the ledge that fascinated Jeb. It was adorned with numerous drawings; ancient figures of Indians brandishing tomahawks and bows, fighting off beasts that Jeb couldn't rightly identify. Some appeared to be a cross between a mountain lion and a buffalo, while one painting depicted a group of braves defending themselves against something lean and black and scaly. Something that looked an awful lot like the snake-critter they had left behind in Mangrum County.

"Hand me that wood over there, Jeb," said Roscoe. "We'll build us a fire and heat us up some vittles."

Jeb was gathering up the driftwood and tossing it into a pile next to the black man, when he looked around and saw that Sam was sitting, stone-still, with his back against the cave wall. "Sam?" the boy asked. "Sam, why don't you help us here?"

When his father refused to answer, Jeb felt his stomach clench. Sam's face was cloaked in shadow, but the boy could hear the man's breathing. It was shallow and uneven.

"Roscoe," said Jeb. "Shine that light over here, will you? I think there's something the matter with Sam."

The guitar-picker directed the beam of the flashlight on the man sitting against the wall. When his face came into view, Jeb's heart skipped a beat. Sam's skin was an ugly shade of reddish-purple and swollen. The farmer's eyes were clenched tightly and thin streams of blood trickled from both nostrils, dribbling past his lips and clefted chin.

"Good God Almighty!" declared Roscoe, his eyes filling the thick lenses of his spectacles. "What's wrong with him?"

"He's having one of his seizures," Jeb explained. "His brain is swelling up inside his skull."

"Can we do anything for him?" asked the black man, his voice small and helpless.

Strangely enough, the ten-year-old found himself calm instead of in a fit of panic. He looked around and discovered that Sam's seizure couldn't have happened at a better time, or in a better place. Jeb grabbed up the duffle bag and began to pull out its contents, until he found several towels they had brought along for drying off in case they decided to take a bath along the way. "Here!" he instructed, tossing a couple to Roscoe. "Douse 'em with cold water!"

A moment later, the towels had been soaked in the frigid water of the underground spring. Roscoe watched in amazement as Jeb went to work. The boy laid his slow-witted father down on the ledge, then gently began to wrap the man's swollen head in the wet towels. By the time the last one was in place, Sam's color was slowly returning to normal and the flow of blood from his nose had stopped completely.

Jeb turned and found a question in Roscoe's eyes. "It causes the swelling to go down," he said. The boy took his bandanna from his pocket and, dipping it in the water of the stream, dabbed the blood from beneath his father's nose. "How're you feeling, Sam?" he asked.

Sam opened his eyes slightly. "It hurts, Jeb . . . but not as bad as before."

"You just lay back and relax," Jeb told him. "Sleep if you want to."

It wasn't long before the man did just that. Sam drifted off, his breathing easier and his face much more at peace.

"Well, I'll be damned," said Roscoe, shaking his head. "You oughta plan on being a doctor, Jeb. I've come across my share of sawbones in my time, and none could've done any better than what you just did."

Jeb blushed in embarrassment. "Aw, it weren't nothing to it. I just did the way Grandma does whenever the seizures hit him."

Roscoe smiled. "Well, I'd say that your papa's mighty lucky to have you around, that's for sure."

Jeb glanced over to see if Sam had overheard. The man snoozed deeply, giving no indication that he was even conscious of what the discussion was about.

Quietly, Roscoe and Jeb finished building the fire. Soon, it was crackling into life, providing light and heat. Roscoe snapped off the flashlight and returned it to the duffle bag, not wanting to waste the batteries. They opened a can of corned beef and ate it with some fried cornbread that Roscoe mixed up and cooked over the flames of the fire. They fed Buckshot his share, then laid a portion aside for Sam, to eat whenever he woke up.

Jeb lay on his side at the edge of the ledge and studied the Indian paintings on the wall. Roscoe sat against the wall, strumming his guitar and writing a new song in his head. The boy pulled his attention away from the strange drawings and studied the elderly Negro instead.

"You know something, Roscoe?" he asked quietly.

"What's that, boy?" asked the bluesman, looking up from his guitar.

"It just came to me that I don't know much of anything about you," he said.

"Oh, like what?"

The boy shrugged. He picked up a broken arrowhead and examined it in the light of the campfire. "I don't know. Maybe where you're from and what you've done all the years you've been on the road."

Roscoe laid his Fender aside. "Well, now, if you don't mind me bending your ear for a while, I'll tell you."

Jeb smiled and sat up attentively. "All right."

Roscoe Ledbetter leaned back and rested his bald head against the cool stone wall. His eyes grew dreamy behind the thick glass of his spectacles as he reminisced about years past. "Well, let's see. I was born way back in the year of 1886 in a little one-horse town called White Bluff over in Dickson County, right here in the state of Tennessee. My mammy and pappy were freed slaves who'd taken to tobacco farming. They raised sixteen young'uns in all, me being the seventh of the bunch."

Jeb frowned. "Then what you told Troy Jenkins and the Boones about being the son of a Louisiana mojo man was just a fib?"

" 'Fraid so, boy," said Roscoe with a grin. "I just tell that story when I come across white folks who are too damned stupid to back down when trouble's stirred up. And all three of them bully boys were about as thick-headed as they come."

The ten-year-old laughed. "I'll say," he said, then waited for Roscoe to continue.

"Well, I'd probably been content to live out my life there in White Bluff, farming and raising a family of my own, but there were a couple things that kept me from doing that," said the black man. "One was my love for the blues. I could play half a dozen musical instruments by the time I was ten years old; everything from Jew's harp to fiddle. But my instrument of choice was the guitar here. I started singing and writing songs of my own and it wasn't long before I got the urge to go to Memphis, where I'd heard tell folks of my own race had the freedom to pick and sing along a place called Beale Street. I was thirteen when I packed my traveling bag, slung my git-box over my shoulder, and kissed my mammy goodbye. I walked clear to Memphis and played my music in the gin joints and nightclubs down there for two or three years. Then I just up and left."

"Why'd you do that?" asked Jeb.

"Remember I told you I had two reasons for not sticking around home?" pointed out Roscoe. "Well the other one was my love for rambling. When my feet hit the open road, well something just comes over me and I start walking. I've been from one end of Tennessee to the other five or six times over, and wandered as far north as Maine and as far south as Texas. Lord knows I've tried to settle down. Been married three times, but every time I thought I was there to stay, I'd hear the whistle of that southbound train and it put the itch to ramble back into these lanky bones. I'd pack my bag in the dead of night, leave a note on the kitchen table, and hit the road again. And never once did I ever look back."

"But don't you get lonesome sometimes?" asked the boy.

"Sure," said the bluesman. "But I try to look at it in a

good way. I have my music and my health, thank the Lord, so I take one mile at a time and try not to think about what tomorrow might bring. This rambling, Jeb . . . it's like being addicted to a drug of some sort."

"Like that morphine Grandma takes for her pain?" asked Jeb.

"In a way, yes."

Jeb stared up at the dark crevices of the cave ceiling. "I wonder how Grandma's doing?" he said to himself, more than anyone else. "I wonder if she's awake or sleeping, or if she's hurting. Sometimes just thinking about her makes me hurt way down inside."

Roscoe nodded. "I know, boy. I recall when my mammy withered away from the tuberculosis, it was like I had it, too. I guess when you love someone strong enough, you feel the hurt right along with 'em."

"Yeah," said Jeb softly. "I reckon you're right about that."

The boy lay back down on the cool stone ledge and closed his eyes. He thought of his Grandma Sweeny stretched out in that bed at Claudine Johnson's house and he found himself wondering if he was being selfish for coming to Fear County and trying to locate the Granny Woman. Maybe it was better if Grandma just went ahead and died in her sleep. Maybe Jeb wasn't doing what he was doing just to save Grandma's life. Maybe he was doing it to ease the pain and fear he'd felt ever since he'd discovered that the elderly woman was dying.

Jeb put the thoughts out of his mind, afraid of examining the truth too closely. The fluid rush of the stream, as well as the exhaustion of walking so far in a single day, lulled him into a light slumber. It wasn't long before he surrendered to it completely and was soon fast asleep.

* * *

He was awakened by the touch of someone's hand on his shoulder.

"Jeb!" whispered an excited voice. "Jeb, wake up! Quick!"

Startled, the boy opened his eyes and sat up. At first, he thought he was still in the midst of a particularly disturbing nightmare he was having. He had dreamt that he had separated from the others and was being chased down an endless country road by a rusty school bus packed with rabid dogs and rustling clumps of kudzu. The driver of the bus was old Ezekial Gallow himself, yelling out in unknown tongues, his stern eyes blazing red like hellfire. But, just before the tires of the school bus could crush Jeb, he had been saved from such a fate by the urgent hand that had roused him.

The campfire had burned down a little, so it took a moment for Jeb's eyes to grow accustomed to the gloom. When they finally did, he realized it was Sam who had awakened him. The big man sat with his back to the creek, his head still wrapped in a turban of damp towels. Sam would have almost looked comical, if it hadn't been for the expression of wonderment in his blue eyes.

"What's the matter?" asked Jeb with a yawn.

Sam raised a beefy hand and pointed toward the stone wall. "Look, Jeb," he said softly. "Look at 'em dance."

Jeb turned and looked at the wall that stretched no more than a yard away. At first, the boy saw nothing out of the ordinary. Then, in the flickering light of the campfire, he noticed something. The drawings on the wall were gone. The brown stone was completely barren.

But then, at second glance, Jeb knew that he was wrong. There was something on the broad wall; something that shouldn't have been there.

Jeb watched breathlessly as shadows danced upon the backdrop of eroded stone. They were the shadows of Indians—as thin as skeletons and clad in loincloths and feathered headdresses—leaping and dancing, swinging tomahawks and pounding drums of taut deerskin. Jeb listened, expecting to hear chanting or the rhythm of the tom-toms, but he heard nothing except the roar of the water behind him.

"Should I wake up Roscoe?" asked Sam, his eyes glued to the shadows on the wall.

Jeb looked over at the bluesman. Roscoe was stretched out on his back, his knapsack serving as a makeshift pillow behind his head and his dusty fedora tilted over his eyes. "No," the boy whispered. "Let him sleep."

When Jeb again turned his attention to the firelit wall, he found that the scene had changed. The forms no longer danced. Now they fought, their lanky arms lashing out with a fury that was more akin to terror than bravery. Suddenly, a huge shadow came into view, filling half the wall. It was a hulking, wooly beast with clawed feet, a toothy snout, and two long horns protruding from its sloped brow. Horrified, Jeb watched as the creature attacked the gallant braves, shrugging off arrows, knives, and tomahawks as if they held no danger whatsoever.

Then the mysterious scenario on the wall turned even more violent. The shadows of the Indian warriors turned and began to run. The horned beast snarled and leapt, reaching them before they could escape. Terrified, Jeb watched as the creature tore into the Indians, tearing them limb from limb, casting them aside like limp rag dolls. One was even devoured, drawn into the beast's fanged maw and swallowed whole.

"Jeb," said Sam. The boy looked over and saw that the wonder in his father's eyes had changed to mortification. "Jeb . . . I'm getting scared."

"It ain't real," Jeb assured him. "It's just make-believe, that's all."

Sam's eyes widened. "No, it ain't. Look!"

Jeb looked back at the wall. The shadow of the beast had finished its slaughter and was now turning, as if it had just noticed them sitting there. Jeb heard a low roar echo throughout the cave at the same time the shadow turned its wooly head and stared straight at them.

Sam began to back toward the edge of the stone ledge. "It's seen us, Jeb! It's coming to get us!"

"That's foolishness, Sam!" said Jeb. "It's just a shadow. It ain't real."

But, as the shadow began to grow larger, and the roar of some great beast grew louder in his ears, Jeb began to wonder if he was wrong about that. He found himself easing toward the lip of the ledge himself. Suddenly, he caught a strong odor; the musky scent of some hideous animal he wasn't at all familiar with.

"What'll we do, Jeb?" whimpered Sam.

Jeb knew his father was on the verge of turning and jumping into the stream. He thought for a moment, then turned to Sam. "Close your eyes, " he said. "Close your eyes and tell yourself it ain't real."

"But—" protested Sam.

"Just do as I say!" ordered the boy.

Frightened, Sam closed his eyes. "It ain't real," he said softly. "It ain't real."

Jeb did the same. "It ain't real," he told himself, his eyes tightly clinched.

The farmboy felt a warm breeze hit his face . . . or rather a warm *breath*. Above the rush of the creek, he heard a coarse snort and, abruptly, smelled a stench like decayed meat. Jeb knew that, whatever the shadowy beast was, it was there . . . right in front of them.

"It ain't real," Jeb said firmly.

"Yeah," added Sam, his voice frightened. "Just make-believe, that's all."

Then, just when Jeb was certain that the beast from the past would break through the barrier of stone and shadow, the warmth and stench of its breath abruptly vanished. Jeb listened for the coarse huff of its breathing, but that, too, was no longer present.

Slowly, the boy opened his eyes. The monstrous shadow was gone. Only the smooth stone wall with its profusion of crude drawings yawned before them, looking the same as it had several hours before.

"It's okay, Sam," Jeb said softly. "It's gone now."

The big farmer gradually opened his eyes and regarded the painted wall. "What was it, Jeb?" he asked.

Jeb was at a loss for an answer. "I don't know. A ghost maybe. Whatever it was, it can't hurt us now."

Sam seemed to take Jeb's assurance as gospel. He nodded his towel-wrapped head and lay back down. "Good night, Jeb."

"Good night, Sam," replied the boy. He sat there staring at the painted wall, puzzling over what had just taken place, until he heard the sound of Sam's soft snoring. Then he lay back down himself.

Before he closed his eyes, Jeb stared at Buckshot, who had made his bed between the duffle bag and Roscoe's lanky frame. He couldn't understand why the dog hadn't been awakened by the apparition he and Sam had just witnessed. Even if the coonhound hadn't heard the rumbling growl, the musky scent of the beast should have roused him. But, oddly enough, the dog hadn't budged an inch.

Jeb tired of trying to figure it out and curled up into a ball next to the campfire. He gave the cave wall one last glance. Then, finding it devoid of any unexplained shadows, he closed his eyes and drifted back to sleep.

Twenty-nine

Trapped

The next time Jeb was roused from his sleep, it was by Roscoe.

"Rise and shine, boy," he said, the light of the flashlight gleaming on the thick lenses of his spectacles. "It's six o'clock."

Jeb sat up and yawned, and instantly thought of the sinister shadow on the wall of the cave. He glanced over at Sam, who was removing the damp towels from his head, but his slow-witted father seemed to have completely forgotten the incident of the night before. Sam was like that. He could remember something one day and totally fail to recall it the next.

They ate a quick breakfast consisting of a quartered apple, beef jerky, and leftover cornbread. When they were through, Roscoe gathered up his knapsack and guitar, and slung them high across his shoulders. "Reckon we'd best get going," he told them.

One by one, they left the ledge and eased themselves down into the knee-deep water. Buckshot was a little skittish about plunging back into the icy creek, so Sam took the dog and slung him around the back of his neck. When the coonhound had relaxed and settled down for the ride, Sam laughed. "Now, don't you go and get too comfortable," he told the dog. "I ain't gonna tote you clear across Fear County like this."

In the darkness of the underground spring, with only the beam of the flashlight to light the way, they began the cold, wet walk forward. They left the roomy chamber of the cavern and again entered a cramped tunnel. No one said much of anything. Their attention was directed southward, searching for the first glimpse of outside light. Several times, they heard the flapping of leathery wings overhead, but the flying creatures—whatever they might have been—retreated into the shadows whenever Roscoe directed the flashlight upward, toward the ceiling of the tunnel.

They had walked nearly twenty minutes when they noticed that the stream had changed, disturbingly enough. Slowly, the water began to rise in level. Soon they found it up around their waists, instead of around their kneecaps. Also, the strength of the currents had increased. A powerful undertow began to form, until it became increasingly difficult for them to keep their footing.

"There it is!" Sam finally called out. "Up ahead!"

Jeb and Roscoe saw the mouth of the tunnel at about the same time Sam did. "Thank God!" exclaimed the black man. "This cold water was making my old pecker more wrinkled than it already was!"

Jeb was about to laugh at Roscoe's statement, when he felt his feet suddenly slip out from underneath him. Abruptly, he fell backwards and was swallowed whole by the stream. For a second, Jeb felt as if he were drowning. Water snaked into his nostrils and down his throat, cutting off his air. Then he was bobbing back up to the surface again, coughing and sputtering. But, when he tried to plant his feet firmly on the rocky bottom once again, he found that he couldn't. The current had him in its grasp and was carrying him away.

"Grab him, Sam!" called Roscoe.

The big farmer tried, but the added bulk of the bluetick hound across his shoulders thwarted his attempt to reach the boy in time. It wasn't long before Jeb was shooting downstream, the distance between him and the others widening with each moment.

"Sam! Roscoe!" the boy cried out. "Somebody help me!"

The bluesman's voice echoed distantly behind him. "We're trying, Jeb! When you get outside, look for something to grab onto!"

Suddenly, Jeb found himself past the shadowy passageway and out into the open. The early morning sunlight blinded the boy at first and he squinted to see what lay ahead. The stream stretched for a couple hundred feet, much wider and deeper than it had been on the other side of the hill. Then Jeb saw something that threw him into a panic. The creek simply seemed to drop off the face of the earth. Blue sky yawned above the torrid surface of the branch, framed on both sides by rocky banks and leaning trees.

Jeb listened and heard a roar that grew louder and louder the further he drifted downstream. He knew at once what it was. It was a waterfall.

Dear Lord, don't let it be a bad one! he prayed. Then, before he knew it, he was being swept over the edge of the falls and into the open air.

Jeb screamed out. His arms flailed, grabbing for something to break his fall, but there was nothing within reach. He spun head over heels, catching quick glimpses of cascading water, blue sky, and green treetops. Then, after what seemed an eternity, the boy hit water so hard that it nearly shucked the straps of his overalls clean off his shoulders.

Stunned, he sank into the depths of a pool so deep and dark that it seemed nearly bottomless. Jeb felt himself almost black out, but fought to regain his senses. He swam toward the surface, bubbles exploding from his nose and mouth.

Right when he was sure that his last ounce of air would run out, he broke the surface and was blessed with a precious lungfull of life-giving oxygen.

He treaded water and stared back toward the north. What he saw made him a little queasy in the stomach. The waterfall that he had just dropped over was well over sixty feet tall, surrounded on both sides by towering cliffs of smooth, marbled sandstone. It was a miracle that he had even survived such a fall, let alone uninjured.

As he floated in the still water of the falls' reservoir, Jeb saw Sam, Roscoe, and Buckshot appear at the top of one of the bluffs. Their faces were frantic and scared, but once they spotted him swimming below, their anxiety was replaced by relief.

"Jeb!" yelled down Roscoe, cupping his dark hands around his mouth. "Are you all right, boy?"

"Yeah," Jeb called back. "I think so."

"Didn't break no bones, did you?"

Jeb shook his wet head. "No, sir. Just shook me up a little."

Roscoe and Sam seemed to discuss something for a moment, then the black man turned back to the edge of the cliff. "You swim to that far bank over yonder and wait for us!" he instructed. "I don't know how we're gonna get down there just yet, but we'll find a way."

Jeb looked to the east and west of the waterfall. The sixty-foot bluffs stretched as far as he could see. He reckoned that was another peculiar feature of the land known as Fear County; the way the earth just seemed to start and end wherever it had a mind to.

The boy waved to them and began to swim toward the far side of the pool. He heard Buckshot bark out a couple of times before Roscoe and Sam headed eastward along the top of the bluff, looking for a safe way down to the valley below.

When Jeb reached dry ground, he sat there for a long moment, spitting up creekwater he'd swallowed and trying to warm himself. The cold water had leached the heat right out of him and goosebumps covered every inch of his body. As the sunshine drove away the chill, he checked the pockets of his overalls. Amazingly enough, everything was still there, including the homemade slingshot.

Shakily, he got to his feet. He was staring up at the top of the bluff, trying to find the others, when he heard a sound behind him. He jumped at first, but relaxed when he recognized it as the curious meowing of a cat.

He turned and regarded the animal. For some reason, Jeb expected it to be different from any cat he'd ever seen back home in Mangrum County and, oddly enough, he wasn't disappointed. The cat was jet black and possessed one emerald green eye and one baby blue one. The feline was also missing a front leg and its tail. It looked like someone had deliberately chopped them off for some perverse reason.

"Howdy, puss!" said the boy. He was about to call the cat to him, when he saw that its black coat was speckled with patches of raw, pink skin. It had the mange and a bad case of it to boot.

The cat didn't seem as if it had any of intention of drawing any closer than it already was. In fact, it seemed a little leery of him. Jeb ignored the cat as it circled around him and went to take a drink from the edge of the waterhole. That was when Jeb spotted a well-worn pathway cutting through the thicket, heading eastward.

Figuring it would take him to his friends, Jeb started down the trail, the denim of his overalls clinging uncomfortably to his lean body. The grass at the side of the path was high and he kept an eye open for snakes hiding there. If there were, Jeb didn't see any. He listened for the sound of Roscoe and Sam calling, but he didn't hear that either. The woods that surrounded him on all sides were shadowy and still . . . a little more so than he would have liked. In fact, he felt as if something—or someone—was watching him from just out of view.

He heard a soft purr behind him and cast a glance over his shoulder. The three-legged cat was following him, hopping its way up the wooded path. He walked a little faster, wanting to put as much distance between him and the animal as possible. He didn't know exactly why, but its missing parts bothered him

Jeb rounded a bend in the trail and came upon a stretch of pathway that was covered by the dried husks of dead leaves, something that was odd in the middle of summer. As he approached the scattering of leaves, he heard something up ahead. It sounded like the mischievous snicker of a child, followed by a harsh "Shhh!" from someone else.

"Hey!" called Jeb, seeing nothing but trees and thicket around him. "Is somebody there?"

When he heard nothing else, he continued. He was halfway across the ankle-deep blanket of leaves, when he knew he had made a mistake. Jeb felt something beneath the leaves grab hold of his ankle and jerk him off balance. At first, he thought a critter similar to the one in the kudzu patch had nabbed him, but a second later he dismissed that idea. He suddenly found himself being pulled upward by his right foot until he hung upside down.

Dizzily, Jeb realized what had happened. He had stepped into a snare of strong hemp rope. He now dangled from the sturdy limb of a black oak tree, swinging to and fro, his blond head scarcely a foot from solid ground.

Desperately, he tried to pull himself up and loosen the noose around his ankle, but the rope was much too tight. He reached into his pocket, but the three-bladed Case knife wasn't there. It had fallen from his pocket when the snare had jerked him upside down, along with the slingshot and most of the pebbles and coins he carried for ammunition.

Suddenly, he realized his predicament. He was trapped and there was absolutely nothing he could do to set himself free.

"Help!" he began to yell, unable to keep a cool head. "Somebody let me down from here!"

Then, from a clump of honeysuckle a few yards away, emerged two boys. One looked to be around Jeb's age, while the other was thirteen or fourteen. Both boys held a resemblance to one another—oily black hair and equally oily eyes—and both were overweight to the point of being downright fat. When he saw the two brothers, Jeb instantly thought of Tweedle-Dee and Tweedle-Dum in *Alice in Wonderland.*

"Well, will you look at what we got us here!" said the elder boy with a snaggle-toothed grin. "Better than some danged ol' jackrabbit or possum, I'd say."

The younger one matched his brother's smirking smile, tooth by crooked tooth. "Didn't I tell you that you'd bag something interesting if you rigged that snare just a tad bigger?"

Jeb stared at the boys, his panic turning into annoyance. "Okay, so now you know it works! Just get me down outta this thing, will you?"

"Not so fast," said the older boy. He walked up and felt the biceps of one of Jeb's arms. "Ain't the best catch we ever had, Randy. Matter of fact, he's downright puny, if'n you ask me."

Randy shrugged his chubby shoulders. "You remember what Papa used to say, Jasper? Beggars can't be choosers."

"I reckon not," agreed Jasper. He then pulled a wicked stag-handled hunting knife from his belt and took a step toward the snared boy.

Jeb's eyes widened in fright and he was about to scream bloody murder, when someone else appeared in the pathway.

"Randy! Jasper! What're you boys up to? I heard the most godawful hollering down here. Now what the hell's going on?"

Jeb turned his eyes to the one who had brought Jasper to a halt. It was a huge woman dressed in a billowy calico dress, a white apron, and an old-timey sunbonnet. The woman had the same dark hair and eyes as the two boys, and probably weighed a good three or four hundred pounds in her stocking feet. Jeb wondered if the big scales at Holt's feed store could have handled such a big woman without busting a spring or sprocket.

The woman wasn't alone. Tagging along behind her was a brood of young'uns ranging from about age five to nine. All seemed as well-nourished as their mother and just as eager to find out what was going on at the pathway in the woods.

When the rotund woman saw Jeb dangling there, she planted her hamlike hands on her hips. "Jasper! What in the devil's name have you done now?"

The expression of menace left Jasper's homely face and he reddened in embarrassment, as if he'd been caught with his hand in the cookie jar. "Nothing, Ma. I swear! This kid just walked by and stepped in our snare, that's all. I was just about to cut him down."

"Well, you'd best do that!" demanded the husky woman. "This very moment!"

Jasper swallowed nervously. "Yes, ma'am!" he replied. Then he reached up and sawed through the length of sturdy hemp with the hunting knife. A second later, Jeb was released from the trap. He fell to his back on the ground, the blanket of leaves beneath him cushioning the impact, if only a little.

It wasn't long before Jeb was being helped to his feet by the big woman. "I'm mighty sorry for what Randy and Jasper did to you," she said sweetly. "They're all the time stirring up trouble, for one reason or another." She shot a withering glare at the two boys. "But don't you worry none. They'll get a stripe or two from a hickory switch for their shenanigans!"

Jeb saw the terrified looks on the brothers' faces, and immediately understood their predicament. He'd suffered a whipping at the end of a switch himself, from time to time. "Wasn't no harm done, ma'am," he told the woman. "Just scared me a little."

"Well, I reckon so!" declared Ma. She eyed him curiously. "You ain't from around these parts, are you?"

"No, ma'am," he replied. "Name's Jeb Sweeny and I'm from over Mangrum County way."

The woman's eyes seemed to harden a little at the mention of his home county, then softened once again. "Well, I'm mighty glad to meet you, Jeb." She looked him up and down. "How'd you get so wet? You look like a drowned rat."

"The creek washed me over the waterfall," he said.

Ma seemed amazed. "I do declare! You are a lucky one then, ain't you? Known men to break every last bone in their body going over that fall, but you look like you scarcely have a scratch on you."

"A little bruised, that's all," agreed Jeb.

The woman studied him for a moment. Then she placed a plump hand on his bare shoulder. "Well, even if it is summertime, it won't do you a speck of good standing there dripping wet. A person can catch the pneumonia now just as quick as they could in the dead of winter. You'd best come on back up to the house and get outta them wet clothes."

"I really can't, ma'am," Jeb began, intending to tell her about how Roscoe and Sam were probably looking for him at that very moment.

"Nonsense!" she said. Ma grabbed his hand in hers and

began to drag him up the pathway. "Now come along and don't make no fuss about it!"

Jeb really had no choice but to tag along. "Yes, ma'am," he said obediently.

They walked for five minutes before they finally reached their destination. It was a simple wood-frame house, unpainted and roofed with rusty sheets of corrugated tin. The front yard was full of weeds and discarded junk, and the sagging front porch boasted a broken swing, a wringer washing machine that was no longer in use, and half a rick of firewood stacked against one wall. Green-tailed flies seemed to swarm about the place in abundance, and for good reason. The place stunk to the high heavens. Jeb wrinkled his nose at the stench of mildew, dirty clothes, and something else he couldn't quite put his finger on. It reminded him of that smell that drifted from Templeton's Grocery back in Brimstone . . . only two times worse.

"Hope you'll excuse the clutter," apologized Ma. "Ain't much to look at, but it's home."

"Yes, ma'am," was all that Jeb said, trying to be polite.

The boy followed the big woman and her brood across the creaking porch and through the front door, which was propped open to let in the fresh air. The interior of the house certainly needed as much fresh air as possible. The smell Jeb had detected upon approaching the house was nothing compared to the reeking stench that filled the rooms inside.

He soon found himself standing in a huge kitchen. The room was furnished with a large Franklin cookstove, a table with straight-backed chairs, and a tall cupboard boasting Blue Willow china behind its glass-paned doors. There was a stone fireplace at the far end of the kitchen that looked sooty and neglected. Above it was a mantel of heavy oak, displaying knick-knacks and framed photographs.

"Shuck off them overalls and I'll hang 'em out on the line

to dry," Ma told him. "Pretty warm this morning, so it shouldn't take long."

Jeb hesitated for a moment, then began to unhook the straps of the suspenders. He was about to let the wet garment drop so he could step out of it, when he looked around and saw two of the woman's rotund daughters—twins by the looks of them—staring at him with dimpled smiles. Jeb shifted uncomfortably from foot to foot, hanging onto those suspenders, doubtful about letting them go.

Ma laughed, sensing the boy's embarrassment. "Aw, don't pay Peggie and Pauline no mind," she said. "They've seen their share of naked boys. You don't have nothing they ain't already seen before."

Jeb turned around, his cheeks blushing bright red. He considered keeping the wet overalls on, but a violent sneeze and a fit of the shivers told him it would be best to surrender his modesty and shed the clothing. If he caught the pneumonia, he might not be able to reach Paradise Hollow and help Grandma and Mandy the way he'd set out to do.

The boy let the overalls fall. They hit the dusty wooden floor with a wet slap. Jeb immediately heard the twin girls begin to giggle. Annoyed, he glanced over his shoulder and found their tiny black eyes staring at his bare butt. Jeb didn't think his face could turn any redder, but he was mistaken.

"Here," said Ma, tossing him a dish towel from out of the cupboard. "You can cover yourself with that, if you're too proud to show your pecker."

Jeb snatched up the towel quickly and held it in front of his privates. It dangled around his hips like Tarzan's loincloth.

Ma bent down and picked up Jeb's sopping overalls. "I'll be back directly and we'll cook us up some dinner." On the way to the back door, she turned to her children and winked. "Are you young'uns hungry?"

The boys and girls that were gathered around the eating

table grinned their identical, snaggle-toothed grins. "Yes,
ma'am!" they rang out cheerfully.

Jeb looked at the family and, the way they looked back
at him, gave the ten-year-old the heebie-jeebies, although for
what reason he really couldn't determine.

"Sit down, Jeb," said Jasper, who stood next to the front
door like a sentry on guard. "Make yourself to home."

Jeb was about to sit down, when he noticed something
about the chair at the head of the table. Unlike most kitchen
chairs, the back and seat of this one wasn't made of interlaced wicker. Instead, it was upholstered with tanned hide,
stretched tautly across the frame.

At first, Jeb didn't find anything too peculiar about it.
After all, this was a backwoods family and folks such as
these tended to hunt and trap a lot. Then, the more he looked
at the hide that covered the back of his chair, the more Jeb
began to realize that it hadn't come from a deer or coon.
No, it hadn't come from any type of animal at all. At least,
not the four-legged kind.

The skin held a scattering of imperfections—some that
looked disturbingly like freckles and moles—as well as one
particular mark that had not been made by nature. His heart
pounding, Jeb stepped closer and studied it.

It was a blue and red tattoo of a ship's anchor with "U.S.
NAVY" etched across the top and the word "MOTHER" underneath.

"He was a good'un," said Randy, licking his lips in re-
membrance. "A little tough and salty, but filling."

Jeb backed away from the chair, feeling more frightened
than he had been since first entering Fear County. He recalled
something he had seen atop the fireplace mantel; something
he had only given a fleeting glance. Now he whirled and
studied the object more closely.

It was a framed photograph of the children's absent father;

a lanky man with wild eyes and a maniacal grin on his heavily whiskered face.

Jeb recognized that face at once, although it had been five long years since he'd last seen it.

It was the face of Jack Gallow.

Thirty

Hungry Brood

Suddenly, it all came back to him again. The roadblock in the middle of Main Street, the black sedan slamming into Sheriff Anderson's patrol car, and the crazy man with the cackling laugh and the butcher knife in his hand. And the terrible cry of that poor baby wrapped in the bloodsoaked blanket.

"The dirty son of a bitch," one of the sheriff's deputies had said. "He's done taken the young'un's arm!"

That statement had always been a mystery to young Jeb. But now, standing inside the Gallow house, he knew exactly what it meant.

Jeb turned toward the front door, but there was no escaping that way. Jasper had already shut and locked it. He stood there with ravenous eyes and the hunting knife in his right hand.

That meant the back door was the only way out. Jeb turned around, but he was plumb out of luck. Ma Gallow's massive bulk filled the doorframe. Jeb saw stern eyes glitter from the shade of the woman's bonnet. The humor and compassion that had been there moments before were completely gone now.

The woman turned toward her patient children, her hands planted on her hips. "Well, don't just sit there like lumps on a log! If you're gonna eat, you're gonna have to help skin and clean him."

"Yes, ma'am!" said the Gallow brood in unison. Suddenly, they were out their chairs and storming across the hardwood floor toward him.

Jeb froze, unable to think of a way out of his predicament. The slingshot came instantly to mind, but it was back on the leaf-strewn pathway. He had forgotten to pick up the sling-shot and its ammunition when Jasper had cut him down from the snare.

A moment later, they were upon him. Jeb found his nerve and tried to fight them off, but there were too many. The sheer weight of them dragged him down to the floor. He felt someone wrapping a rope around his ankles and looked past those leering faces at the kitchen ceiling. Anchored in the stud of a rafter was a pulley. Horrified, Jeb watched as three youngsters, sitting one atop the others' shoulders, threaded the rope through the wheel. Then, together, the brood hauled Jeb upward, feet-first, until he hung upside down.

Ma nodded in approval when they finally had the boy se-cured. "Jasper, you go fetch the bleeding bucket," she or-dered as she walked over to the cupboard. "Randy, you and the others get that big iron kettle out. I think we'll fix us up a pot of soup today."

"Oh, boy!" yipped a little one who was barely five years old. "Can I lick the spoon this time, Ma? Can I?"

Jeb felt his stomach roll. He'd asked the same favor of Grandma Sweeny countless times before, but it had never sounded quite so sinister.

"Peggie, go to the pantry and get out those canned to-maters and shelly beans," Ma said as she opened a cupboard drawer and rummaged through its contents. "Billy, you and Ben fetch some kindling outta the woodbox. Stoke up that stove good and hot."

In shock, Jeb watched as the children went about their chores eagerly. When he looked back toward the cupboard, he saw that Ma Gallow had turned around. His heart thundered in his chest and a low, whimpering moan passed his lips. The woman stood there with a hungry look of her own, a broad-bladed meat cleaver in one hand and a sharply-honed skinning knife in the other.

"Don't worry, boy," she assured as she started toward him. "I'll cut your throat before we get to work. I may be a cannibal, but I'm a decent one."

As Jeb watched the morning sunlight from the kitchen window gleam on the edges of the carving implements, he suddenly knew that his journey across Fear County had come to an end. Sure, he feared for his own life, but what disappointed him the most was the fact that Grandma and Mandy would suffer as well.

Jeb felt tears well up as he clenched his eyes tight. He mouthed a silent prayer as he heard the hollow clang of the bleeding bucket being placed beneath him, as well as the heavy footsteps of Ma Gallow growing nearer. Then, abruptly, he felt the chill of honed steel against his throat.

"Hold still, Jeb Sweeny," said Ma Gallow almost tenderly, "and you won't feel a thing."

The boy finished his prayer, but felt little comfort. If God was ready to take him, why didn't He do it in some way natural for boys his age? Like falling headfirst out of a tree or drowning in a swimming hole? Jeb would've preferred either fate to being skinned and used for stock in someone's stew.

The pressure of the knife on his throat increased and he prepared himself for the fatal slice that would open his gullet from ear to ear. But, miraculously, that never happened.

Jeb heard a tremendous crash. Startled, he opened his eyes. The front door had been kicked in. It hung askew on its hinges like Samson himself had been responsible. Jeb stared at the man who stood there, fists clenched, a look of childish rage on his broad face. It was his father.

"You get away from Jeb!" bellowed the big farmer. "You get away from him . . . *right now!*"

Jeb hadn't seen such a look of boundless anger on Sam's face since his tangle with Harvey Holt. The boy didn't mind it this time, however. He was just glad to see his father standing there, madder than hell.

"I don't know who you are, mister," scolded Ma Gallow, the knife in her hand never wavering from Jeb's throat. "But you ain't welcomed here. This is our catch and nobody's gonna steal it away from us!"

"I'll chase him off, Ma!" boasted Jasper. The teenaged boy brandished his knife and leapt toward the man in the doorway.

Jeb gasped, sure that Jasper would run Sam through with the hunting blade. But he was pleasantly surprised. When the boy came within reach, Sam ducked the slash of the knife and lashed out with a work-hardened fist. The farmer's knuckles collided with Jasper's face with an ugly sound like a melon being split open. Jasper lost his knife and fell flat on his back, most of his crooked teeth gone from his bleeding mouth.

"Pick up that knife and step aside," came a gravelly voice that Jeb recognized immediately. He watched as Sam bent down and grabbed the knife, then moved away from the doorway. Behind him stood Roscoe Ledbetter, tall and bony, but looking as dangerous as any roadhouse brawler. Jeb dropped his gaze to Roscoe's right hand and was stunned at what he held there. It was Miss Claudine's Colt .45 revolver, cocked and ready to fire.

"Step away from him, woman!" demanded Roscoe. "Step away and throw down them knives!"

Jeb felt the skinning knife move away from his throat, but it hadn't been removed out of fear. The boy craned his neck and looked up at Ma Gallow's pudgy face. Outrage shone in her beady, little eyes. Clutching the knife and cleaver even more tightly than before, she left Jeb's side and started toward Sam and Roscoe.

"How dare you barge in here and scare my young'uns like this!" she hissed from between clenched teeth. "You got no right to be here. You're trespassing!"

Roscoe laughed. It was a cold laugh, totally devoid of humor. "We're preventing a killing, that's what we're doing. Now, you throw them knives aside and let Jeb down. He's going with us."

"Oh, I see now!" said Ma venomously. "You're friends of the boy. From over in Mangrum County, more'n likely! Lowdown trash! Arresting my man like that and sending him off to the state pen to be fried in the electric chair! You had no right! Took him away from his wife and young'uns, you did! Made us fend for every damned mouthful of food we could find!" A cruel grin crossed the woman's face and she turned back toward Jeb. "Well, we ain't gonna give up this one! Just knowing he's a bastard from Mangrum County will make him taste that much sweeter!"

Jeb watched dumbfounded as Ma Gallow brought the knife up, aiming its point for the side of his neck.

The boy waited for the pain of the blade when the kitchen was filled with a thunderous boom. Ma Gallow cried out, clutching her bloody elbow. The skinning knife went spinning out of her hand. It landed with a clatter in the iron kettle that sat atop the Franklin stove.

Jeb turned his eyes toward Roscoe. The gun in the black man's hand smoked from the barrel. Jeb saw a shade of regret in Roscoe's magnified eyes, but his aim failed to waver.

"You listen to me and listen good!" warned the guitar-picker. "Toss down that cleaver and step aside. Do it now!"

But, despite the bullet in her arm, Ma Gallow wasn't about to back down an inch. "Filthy nigger! Coming in here and threatening a woman and her young'uns like this! Well, I'll show you! I've just gotten me a hankering for some dark meat and, by God, I'm gonna have it!"

Roscoe braced himself and, lifting the peacemaker, cocked back the hammer. "Stay back, woman!" he yelled. "Stay back or I'll shoot you again!"

Ma Gallow was listening to none of it, however. With a hoarse bellow, she stormed across the kitchen, one arm hanging limply at her side, while the other swung the heavy blade of the meat cleaver back and forth. Jeb knew then that there was no reasoning with her. The woman was hellbent on carving Roscoe clean down to the bone.

She was scarcely a dozen feet away from the black man when something flashed past Roscoe's open legs and launched itself unerringly at Ma Gallow. It was Buckshot, snapping and snarling, once again protecting those he loved. Before Roscoe could fire another shot from the forty-five, the coonhound had his fangs buried deeply into the chubby ankle of Ma's left leg.

The woman cried out and, surprised by the attack, lost her balance. She fell to the floor with a thunderous crash . . . landing smack-dab on the wicked blade of the cleaver she held in her outstretched hand.

For a moment, no one said a word. Everyone in the kitchen stared down at the woman who moaned and writhed on the floor. Then Ma rolled over and everyone saw that the fall had been a fatal one. The meat cleaver protruded from the center of her chest, heaving and bucking with each beat of her heart.

That was when the children began to cry. "Ma!" they

screamed, running to her side. The Gallow brood congregated around their dying mother, squawling and bawling like babies. Jasper was the only one excluded from the mourning, but that was only because he was still on floor, knocked cold by Sam's devastating haymaker.

"Good Lord have mercy!" said Roscoe with a sigh. All the menace seemed to drain out of him and he let the gun sag until the barrel pointed at the floor. He pulled his sorrowful eyes from the dying woman and looked at Jeb, hanging from his heels at the far side of the room. "Sam, you go cut Jeb down, will you?"

Sam side-stepped the brood of crying children, his rage having burned itself out. He rushed to Jeb and, taking the naked boy in the crook of a brawny arm, reached up with the other and cut the rope. After Jeb's ankles were untied, the boy turned pale and nearly fainted. "Are you all right, Jeb?" Sam asked in concern.

"Yeah," replied Jeb, taking a couple of deep breaths. "I reckon it scared me more than I thought." He steadied himself and looked around. "My overalls . . . she took 'em out the back door with her."

Jeb and Sam stepped outside. There was no clothes line for hanging damp laundry. Instead, there was a fifty-gallon drum that had been made into a trash bin. The drum was filled to the brim with the discarded clothing of countless men, women, and children. Jeb's denim overalls were laying on the very top.

Hurriedly, Jeb stepped into his britches, which were still a little damp. When he hooked the clasps of his suspenders, he turned to find Sam holding something out to him.

"Here," he said. "I found these laying in that path a ways back."

It was his slingshot, Case knife, and some of the rocks and coins he carried everywhere he went. "Thanks, Sam," he said gratefully. He took the possessions and put them back where they belonged.

They went back inside the house in time to see Ma Gallow breathe her last. The handle of the meat cleaver rose one final time, then failed to move again.

"Shouldn't we call the sheriff or somebody?" asked Sam, looking scared.

"Ain't no telephones in Fear County," Roscoe told him. "And, as far as I know, there ain't no law hereabouts, either."

"Ya'll killed her!" screamed Randy Gallow, leveling a fat finger at Roscoe and Sam. "All she was doing was rustling up some grub for us!"

Roscoe opened his mouth, but could find nothing to say. He simply shook his head, looking sadder than Jeb had ever seen him before.

The farmboy walked over and took the black man's bony hand. "Come on," he said. "Let's get outta here."

"Yeah," said Roscoe, turning away from the grieving orphans. "Let's go."

Soon, they had left the Gallow house and were making their way back down the pathway through the woods. Buckshot took the lead and it wasn't long before they skirted the pool beneath the waterfall and reached its opposite side. They found another trail through an equally dense stretch of pine forest and followed that for a good half hour. Then, all of a sudden, they found themselves back on the dirt road again, as if they had never strayed from it.

"Well, I reckon we'd best start walking," suggested Jeb. "You did say you wanted to get to Paradise Hollow before dark."

"That's right," said Roscoe almost absently. He turned and stared back the way they had come. Somewhere to the east was the Gallow house.

"What's wrong?" asked the boy.

"Them young'uns," said Roscoe with a pained expression on his dark face. "Just can't seem to get 'em outta my head."

Jeb took the Negro's hand and squeezed it. "It wasn't your fault. She was tetched in the head . . . just like Jack Gallow was."

"Maybe," said Roscoe. "Or maybe it wasn't her fault after all. Maybe she was just raised differently than me or you."

"Try not to think about it, okay?"

Roscoe squeezed the boy's hand back and attempted a lame smile. "I'll surely try. But it's gonna be hard."

Jeb nodded. "Yeah. For me, too."

Then, together, they turned southward and followed Sam and Buckshot down the road that, hopefully, would lead them to the place they had been in search of since crossing the Fear County line.

Part Four
Paradise and Purgatory

Thirty-one

The Granny Woman

Late afternoon was darkening into evening when the forest around them started to thin out and the rural road began to rise sharply. Seeing the rutted trail seemingly vanish into the brilliant crimson and purple sunset, Jeb felt the same sensation of dread he'd experienced just before reaching the edge of the waterfall earlier that day. He recalled all they had encountered during their strange journey and wondered what would be next.

But, when they topped the rise and stood there for a moment, bathed in the colorful glow of the sunset, Jeb felt all the tension drain from his body. He looked over at Roscoe and found the same expression of relief on his dark face. The sadness that had dogged the old man following the grisly death of Ma Gallow seemed to suddenly disappear.

"We're here, boy," he said with a big grin. "Praise the Lord, we're finally here."

Jeb stared down at the valley that lay within the basin of three tall hills. "You mean—?"

"That's right," replied the bluesman. "Paradise Hollow."

As they left the rise and descended into the hollow, Jeb began to marvel at how different the spot was from the rest of Fear County. In fact, it was like the difference between summer and winter. Or, more precisely, between life and death.

Where weeds, thistle, and thorny thicket had dominated the land before, the gentle slope of Paradise Hollow was blanketed with soft grass, green clover, and a multitude of wildflowers. The trees were also different here. Black oak and spiny pine had grown heavily, almost oppressively so, along the road through Fear County. But the hollow they now traveled through was plentiful with blooming dogwood, silver poplar, and lilac bush. Jeb breathed in and felt as if he were using his lungs for the very first time. Unlike the rest of the county, with its unfamiliar scents and underlying stench of decay, the air here was fresh and sweet. Jeb was sure that it was untainted by manmade inventions like smokestacks and automobiles, and that the air smelled the same as the day God had first breathed life into the Earth.

Jeb also noticed something else. Paradise Hollow was full of wildlife; the kind he was totally familiar with. Colorful songbirds darted from tree to tree, warbling happily. There were also butterflies, something else Jeb hadn't seen since entering Fear County. The winged insects fluttered playfully around the boy's blond head like the runaway colors of a rainbow.

As they reached the bottom of the hollow, a strange euphoria seemed to overcome them. All the dread and apprehension that had sat like a weight upon their shoulders for the last three days now seemed to lift away. Roscoe took the Fender guitar off his back and began to play a cheerful tune, while Jeb and Sam smiled and picked up their pace. Even Buckshot appeared to notice the difference. The coonhound no longer looked at the forest bordering the road as a place of suspicion and potential dangers. Instead, the dog began to leap and play, his tail wagging happily.

"Sure is pretty here, ain't it, Jeb?" asked Sam. He bent

down and picked a buttercup, then sniffed the blossom so vigorously that the boy was sure it would go right up his nose.

"Yep, it surely is," said Jeb. "Ain't at all like the rest of Fear County. If you ask me, I don't think there's one bad thing here in this hollow."

"Let's don't go jumping the fence just yet, Jeb," Roscoe told him. "Sometimes things have a way of changing right fast, particularly in this county."

Jeb considered the gamut of strange places and things they had encountered since stepping across the county line. "Yeah, I know what you mean."

They continued on until they came to a rounded bridge made of stone and sturdy timber. When they stopped at the middle, they looked down at the stream that passed underneath. The water was as clear as glass, its currents trickling almost musically over the rocks that lay along the bottom. Under the surface, Jeb could see all manner of fish; trout, bass, crappie, and catfish. The boy was a fair hand with a fishing pole, but he didn't think of the sport when he looked at the fish in the clearwater creek. In fact, he knew it would be a downright sin to hook and eat such creatures. The same went for the squirrels that chattered and played along the railing of the bridge. Even Buckshot seemed to sense it. The coonhound could have easily jumped up and snatched one of the squirrels off the railing, but he didn't. He seemed more content watching them dance and wrestle with one another.

"I wish Grandma could see this place," said Sam. "She'd sure like it here."

Jeb nodded. "Wouldn't she, though?"

Roscoe regarded the two. "Speaking of your grandmother, I reckon we'd best get on to finding the person we came here to find. It'll be dark before long."

They left the bridge and headed southward along the country road. As he walked, Jeb wiggled his toes in the dirt of the road. The soil was soft and powdery, not dark and coarse like the earth he had trod for the last three days. Just the feeling of it against the soles of his bare feet helped to relax him. Even though the sky was darkening and the shadows of the surrounding woods were deepening, he felt none of the creeping dread that he had felt elsewhere in Fear County. In the peaceful cradle of Paradise Hollow, Jeb felt safe, as if no harm could come to them there.

They walked a half mile further. The sky turned to black velvet and, soon, the only light they traveled by came from the moon and a scattering of stars. The songbirds nested down for the night and, in their place, sounded the chirring of crickets and the lonesome call of a whippoorwill from high off the hillside to the east. Jeb kept straining his ears, listening for spooky sounds in the woods or the noise of some nocturnal critter stalking them. Fortunately, such sounds didn't seem to exist in the basin of Paradise Hollow. All was quiet and without a hint of menace.

They were passing through a dense grove of towering magnolia trees whose leather-leafed branches were decorated with pale and fragrant blossoms, when Sam sniffed at the air. "I smell woodsmoke," he told the others.

Roscoe drew in a breath. "So do I." He squinted through the thick lenses of his spectacles and stared ahead through the magnolias. "Believe I see a light up yonder, too."

Jeb followed the old man's gaze. He could also detect the faint glow of lantern light a hundred yards or so away. "Do you think it might be where the Granny Woman lives?" he asked hopefully.

"Could very well be," replied Roscoe.

"Then let's go see her!" piped the boy, getting ready to run.

Roscoe reached out and stopped Jeb before he got two steps. "Hold up there, boy! If it is her, she ain't going nowhere. Anyhow, there's a couple of things I want to say to you before we get there."

Jeb was a little annoyed by Roscoe's call for patience. "Like what?"

"Well, first of all, I think it'd be best if you didn't just barge in on the old lady and start calling off a list of things you want her to do for you," he explained. "It ain't good manners and makes you out to be selfish. Just take your time and talk to her for a bit, then ask when the time is right. Do you understand what I'm saying?"

Jeb looked a little puzzled. "You mean kinda like praying to God without seeming too pushy?"

Roscoe grinned to himself. "Well, now, I wouldn't put the Granny Woman up there on the same level as the Almighty, but . . . yeah, kinda like that."

"Okay," said Jeb. "I reckon I can hold my horses that long."

"Good," said the Negro with a nod. "And there's something else. I know you're counting on her to do some difficult things for you, but, please, don't get your hopes up too high. Especially where your grandmother is concerned. The Granny Woman is supposed to be able to work some powerful magic, but miracles, well, that's something else entirely."

Jeb felt disappointment threaten to dampen his good spirits, but he refused to let it. "Aw, I know that, Roscoe. But she'll help me, just you wait and see."

The old bluesman squeezed the boy's shoulder gently. "Just don't let it hit you too hard if she can't, that's all I'm saying."

"All right," agreed Jeb, although he didn't want to dwell on that possibility. "I'll try not to."

Together, they continued farther down the dark road, toward the light in the middle of the magnolia grove. A few minutes later, they heard the sound of someone singing. Jeb recognized the song at once. It was "Rock of Ages," and the ten-year-old had never heard it sung any better. In fact, it sounded as if an angel was singing the old-time hymn, so wondrous and youthful was the voice that breathed life into each soulful verse.

Then they came through a tall stand of yellow-headed sunflowers and, abruptly, found themselves standing before a small cabin constructed of dove-tailed logs, clay mud chinking, and cedar shingles. Rose bushes grew rampant along the eaves of the roof and the four posts of the front porch, the soft-petaled blooms glowing red, white, and yellow, even in the gloom of night.

Jeb looked at the porch and saw that it was barren, except for a single rocking chair. Sitting in the rocker, with a patchwork quilt draped over her knees, was an elderly black woman. She looked incredibly old—perhaps even past a hundred years of age—but her brown eyes held a spark of youth that was almost startling to look at. She looked to be under five feet tall, as skinny as a beanpole, and her wrinkled head was crowned with a wreath of cotton white hair. It took Jeb a moment before he realized that it was she who sang the gospel hymn with the voice of an angel.

By the time she finished the ending chorus, Jeb, Roscoe, and Sam were walking up the pathway to the steps of the porch. The old woman grew silent and eyed the three thoughtfully, as well as the bluetick hound. Then she grinned, showing only three yellowed teeth set in shiny blue-veined gums. "Howdy," she finally greeted.

"Howdy," said Jeb back, his heart suddenly beating faster.

The old woman smacked her gums, looking a little amused. "Knew you were coming," she told them. "Known since late this afternoon." She breathed in deeply and frowned, as if she'd caught wind of something offensive. "This young'un here smells freshly scrubbed, but you two stink like a couple of ol' polecats. When was the last time ya'll had a bath?"

Roscoe and Sam seemed embarrassed. "It's been a few days, ma'am," said the bluesman. "Sorry about that."

The old lady waved a bony hand at them. "Aw, that's all right. I've smelled worse before. I was just picking fun at you, that's all."

Jeb stepped forward. "Ma'am?"

"Yes, child?" she replied, her eyes twinkling.

"Are you the Granny Woman?" he asked.

The woman grinned at the boy benevolently. "Well, that weren't my given name, but, yes, that's what some folks tend to call me." She appraised the ten-year-old, from head to toe. "And who might you be?"

"Name's Jeb Sweeny, ma'am," he replied. "I'm from Pikesville over in Mangrum County."

"Well, it's nice meeting you, Jeb," said the Granny Woman. "And who are your friends?"

"This here's Sam Sweeny and Roscoe Ledbetter," Jeb said in introduction. "Oh, and the dog is Buckshot. Best coonhound this side of Tennessee."

The Granny Woman turned her eyes to the dog, who lay on the bottom step of the porch, already fast asleep. "Oh, I bet he is," she said. She turned her eyes to the lanky, black man. "Can you play that git-box you've got slung across your back?"

Roscoe removed his dusty hat out of respect. "Yes'm. I can pick well enough to make folks laugh or cry, bring a smile to their faces every once in a while."

The Granny Woman nodded her head and smiled. "Good.

I like a man with music in his soul. And, just looking at you, I can tell you've got a heap of it in yours."

They stood there awkwardly for a long moment, as if at a loss of what to say next. Then the Granny Woman spoke again. "I can tell ya'll have walked a far piece and seen some queer things along the way, too, I bet."

"Yes, ma'am," said Jeb. "We certainly have."

"And are you just passing through . . . or did you have some other purpose in setting foot in Fear County?" she asked. "Maybe to find me, perhaps."

Jeb and the others simply nodded.

"Well, you've done that," she said. "Won't ask you why you'd want to; we'll get to that directly. I reckon ya'll ain't had supper yet, have you?"

"No, ma'am," said Sam. His stomach growled like a thunderstorm was taking place inside his innards.

The Granny Woman shed the quilt from off her legs and stood up more spryly than Jeb and the others would have expected. "Well, come on in the house then and I'll feed ya'll. You can play me a tune or two on that git-box, Mr. Ledbetter, and then young Jeb here can tell me what led ya'll to seek me out."

Silently, Jeb, Roscoe, and Sam mounted the porch, stepping over the sleeping hound as they went. Soon, they were following the elderly woman through the door and into the cabin's single room.

Before Jeb entered the home of the Granny Woman, the boy couldn't help but feel a twinge of disappointment nag at him. For some reason, he'd expected more than a skinny, toothless woman who was old enough to be his great grandmother. He had come to Fear County expecting to find someone much more powerful and more threatening than the Negro woman they'd found rocking on the front porch. Maybe he was wrong, but he simply couldn't help but feel that the legend of the Granny Woman was more tall-tale than truth and that their journey across Fear County had, unfortunately, been in vain.

Thirty-two

Three Wishes

"Ya'll come on in," beckoned the Granny Woman with a forefinger as skinny as a chicken bone. "Pull up a chair and make yourselves to home."

Jeb, Roscoe, and Sam stood within the doorway for a moment, allowing their eyes to grow accustomed to the gloom of the cabin's only room. A fire blazed in a hearth of rounded gray stones, but, despite the fact that it was mid-July, it seemed more comforting and cozy, than stifling hot. A kettle of black iron hung over the flames. The lid over it rattled as its contents bubbled and boiled, unleashing a burst of steam every so often.

The room was sparsely furnished. In front of the fireplace sat a long wooden bench. To one side of the room sat a crude table with four chairs and an ancient cupboard bearing a multitude of wormholes and no glass in its twin doors. In the place of china dishes and teacups, bottles and mason jars lined the shelves of the cupboard, each bearing pale powders, finely ground herbs, or syrupy liquids. From the rafters overhead hung bundles of dried leaves, earthy roots, and tanned animal hides, some of which Jeb couldn't rightly identify. The only furnishings that occupied the opposite side of the room was a bed with a cornhusk mattress, an ancient cedar chest for storing clothes, and a picture of Jesus and his lambs hanging on the wall.

The boy and his friends took their places at the eating table, while the Granny Woman went to the iron pot and lifted the lid. The cabin's interior was suddenly filled with an aroma so delicious that it nearly made their bellies launch into a chorus of hungry growling.

The old woman laughed. "I can tell ya'll are ready to eat," she said. "Got possum stew and corn pone for supper tonight. Hope ya'll weren't expecting fried chicken and dumplings or some such delicacy, 'cause I'm afraid that possum was all ol' Midnight could rustle up this morning."

"Midnight?" asked Jeb. "Who's that?"

"She's up there," replied the Granny Woman pointing to the mantel above her head.

Jeb turned his eyes to the wooden shelf over the hearth and was startled to find a jet black cat stretched out there, staring back at him with pea-green eyes. "A cat?" said Jeb incredulously. "I ain't never heard tell of no cat bagging a possum before."

"Don't believe me, eh?" asked the old woman, amused. "Well, truth of the matter is, ol' Midnight is the best hunter I ever did see in all my born days. Possums are easy for her to catch. It's the wild boars and deer that give her the most trouble, but she drags 'em home, too. Bet she could give that bluetick of yours a run for his money if'n they were to hunt the woods together."

"Hah!" Sam said, shaking his head. "No old cat's gonna out-hunt Buckshot. Anyhow, he'd likely tear that cat in half if it got in his way."

"I doubt that," said the Granny Woman.

Midnight purred deep in her throat, as if seconding her mistress's remark.

The Granny Woman took a knife and a white onion from

her apron pocket. After peeling the vegetable, she began shaving slivers into the bubbling stew. "It'll be a few minutes more before it's fitting to eat. Why don't you play us a song or two while we wait, Mr. Ledbetter?"

"I can surely do that," agreed Roscoe. He took his guitar from where he'd leaned it against the wall and fiddled with the tuning knobs for a bit. "Here's a song I've been writing in my head for a few days now." Then he slipped the little glass bottle on his finger and began to play.

"Well, there's a county that lays smack-dab . . . in the land called Tennessee . . . It's evil and it's ugly . . . just as mean as it can be . . . Folks, they call it Fear County . . . and they stay clear of its line . . . If a man goes crossing over . . . he might not leave alive."

Roscoe made the Fender squeal and squall like a child frightened of the dark, then continued. *"There be things down in that county . . . that have no rightful place . . . Crazy folks and critters . . . that's never known God's grace . . . The land, it's filled with shadows . . . and dangers of every kind . . . Lawd, things go on in Fear County . . . that'd make the Devil lose his mind!"*

When the bluesman finished, he looked around the room. "That's all I've come up with so far. What do you think?"

The Granny Woman nodded sagely as she returned her stirring spoon to the iron pot. "Never heard a song more true," she said. "You hit the nail right on the head with that one, Mr. Ledbetter."

"Then you ain't offended by it?" asked Roscoe.

"Why, good heavens, no!" she said. "I've never had a speck of pride for Fear County and the evil that goes on within its borders. I live here in Paradise Hollow, which is like a patch of healthy flesh surrounded by a cancer. I've spent all my adult life doing good for folks and trying to show 'em that everything here ain't all piss and vinegar. The light of God does shine upon this county, if only within this hollow here."

"Folks say you're a witch," blurted Jeb, before he realized what he was saying. He glanced over at Roscoe and saw a warning look in the black man's magnified eyes.

The Granny Woman turned from her pot, her eyes not angry, but full of good humor. "Well, child, there's a good reason for folks saying such a thing. And that's 'cause it's true. I am a witch."

"But a good one, ain't that right?" added Jeb.

"Just as right as rain," she replied with a gummy grin.

A few minutes later, the Granny Woman ladled hot stew into clay bowls and brought them to the table, along with an iron skillet full of corn pone. Jeb wrinkled his nose at the stew, with its mixture of potatoes, onions, beans, and hunks of greasy possum meat floating on the surface. But, once he spooned some into his mouth, the boy swiftly changed his opinion. It was the most delicious stew he'd ever eaten. Of course, he wasn't sure if that was because it was actually good or because he had walked a long way that day and he was starved half to death.

He heard a coarse sniffing sound and turned to see Buckshot standing in the open doorway, his nostrils flaring hungrily. At the sight of the dog, Midnight stood up on the mantel and hissed hatefully, the black hairs on her back turning as stiff as those of a porcupine.

"You just settle down there, Midnight!" scolded the Granny Woman. "You ain't got no cause to be pitching a fit. The dog ain't gonna hurt you none. He's just visiting. So you treat him as a guest and quit your bitching and moaning."

The black cat eyed the coonhound contemptuously, then lay back down on the mantel again. A few seconds later, Midnight had drifted into a lazy sleep, the one-eyed dog the furthest thing from her feline mind.

The Granny Woman filled a bowl full of stew and set it on the floor next to Jeb's chair. "Here you go, boy," she called sweetly. "Hope you enjoy it and, if'n you're in need of seconds, just let me know." She turned her eyes to the three who chowed down at her table. "That goes for ya'll, too, of course."

Jeb, Roscoe, and Sam certainly didn't disappoint the old lady. Before they were done, they'd downed three bowlfulls of possum stew each, a whole skillet of corn pone, and a gallon jug of apple cider. When they were finished, they pushed themselves away from the table a few inches, allowing ample space for their swollen bellies.

The Granny Woman smiled at the satisfied looks that graced the faces of the two men and the boy. "Well, now since your guts are full, let's get down to brass tacks. Or, more precisely, the reason you're here."

Jeb looked over at Roscoe, who sent a nod of approval his way. The boy swallowed, his mouth suddenly as dry as cotton, but, at first, couldn't find the right words to use.

"No need to be scared of me, child," the old woman said softly. "I know you've been chomping at the bit to ask me something since you first got here. Now, you just take your time and speak your mind."

The ten-year-old took a deep breath and nodded. He didn't know what he was so frightened of. After all, he hadn't traveled all that way just to turn tongue-tied and shy. "I've had some troubles lately . . . bad troubles. And I was wondering if you could help me out with some things."

"Things?" asked the Granny Woman. "How many things are you talking about, boy?"

"Three," replied Jeb.

The old lady's eyes widened a bit. "You came here with a truckload of wants, didn't you? Kinda like ol' Aladdin and that genie in the lamp?"

"Kinda like that," said Jeb, afraid that he'd asked for too much. "But I don't want money or nothing like that. These things I want you to help me with . . . they're mighty important."

"All right," allowed the Granny Woman, crossing her bony arms. "Let's hear 'em."

Jeb was about to tell her, when he suddenly remembered that Sam was sitting at the table. He wasn't even sure whether or not Sam remembered exactly why they had come to Paradise Hollow, but Jeb did know that one of his wishes had to do with his father and he really didn't want to discuss it in front of the man.

Roscoe seemed to sense Jeb's hesitancy and immediately understood. "Uh, Sam, why don't you take Buckshot and sit out on the porch. We'll be out in a little while."

Sam didn't seem offended by Roscoe's suggestion. In fact, he didn't seem to care about what was being said between Jeb and the Granny Woman to begin with. "Come on, boy," he said, heading for the front door. "Let's go outside and look for shooting stars."

The dog left his spot next to the table and followed Sam outside. Before he left, he cast a baleful glance at the black cat on the fireplace mantel. Apparently, Buckshot didn't care much for Midnight and vice versa.

After Sam was out of earshot, the Granny Woman turned her eyes back to Jeb. "I assume one of these wishes of yours has to do with your simple-minded friend out there," she said.

"It does," agreed Jeb. "Sam, he was one of the cleverest men in all of Mangrum County. That was, before he went off to fight in the War. He was over in Germany, fighting Hitler's army, when one of them krauts tossed a Nazi grenade into the trench he was in. Killed all the men in his outfit and gave him what they call 'shell shock.' Addled his brain and made him where he was more like a child than a man. He didn't even remember his family or friends once he got back home."

"But that ain't the worse of it, is it?" asked the Granny Woman.

"No, ma'am," said Jeb. "You see, Sam's my daddy . . . and he don't even know it."

"I could tell you were son and father the first time I saw you standing side by side," said the elderly lady. "The hair color's different, but you look alike in the face." The Granny Woman sat in her chair and thought to herself for a moment. "Does he have fits of pain in his head?"

"Yes, ma'am, he does," replied Jeb.

"Swelling and a bleeding from the nose?"

"That's right," added Roscoe.

The Granny Woman nodded to herself. "I think I might just be able to help you on that count, but it could take a while for the medicine to sink in and work proper. When a man's mind gets separated from his soul like that, it's like a nasty clog of hair in a backed-up drain. It takes some patience and know-how just to get it unblocked. But we'll certainly give it a try. First, tell me about your other two wishes, though."

Again, Jeb hesitated, trying to find the right words. "The second has to do with my grandmother," said the boy.

"She's dying," the old witch told him.

Jeb was startled. "How did you know that?"

"Death or the coming of death leaves scars on one's soul, Jeb Sweeny," said the Granny Woman. "You've got your fair share of 'em. Exactly what is she dying of?"

The word didn't come easily for the boy. "Cancer."

The old woman grunted and shook her head. "That's a tough one. How far gone is she?"

Jeb began to feel dread creep into him. "Well, she's bed-ridden right now and taking medicine for her pain."

"Morphine?" asked the Granny Woman.

"Yes, ma'am."

Again, the old lady gave a grim shake of the head. "Then there might not be much I can do for her. A cancer is like a swarm of termites in an old house. Once it chews away a body's foundation, there ain't much left to save."

The boy wouldn't hear it, though. "Couldn't we at least try to do something for her?"

The Granny Woman could see the desperation in the child's tormented eyes. She reached out and took his hand in hers. "Sure we can," she said. "And I have just the thing . . . if you can get back to Mangrum County in time, that is."

"What's that?" asked Jeb.

"I'll go fetch it," she told him. The Granny Woman left her chair and went to the cupboard that stood against the wall. She opened one of the glassless doors and rummaged through the bottles and jars that lined an upper shelf. A moment later, she returned. "Here," she said. "Hold out your hand."

Jeb did as she requested. Soon, he found a small silver snuffbox lying in the palm of his hand. Jeb unscrewed the top and found the little container half full of tiny, brown seeds. "What are they?" he asked.

"Seeds from a plant that no longer lives on this earth," she told him. "You plant two or three in a plot of land and, the very next day, there will be a full-grown plant in that very spot. It'll look like a mess of poke sallet, but the leaves will be fuller and the stalk will be a dark purple in color. You strip the leaves and cook 'em and feed 'em to your grandma and *maybe* it'll kill that cancer down in her. But if the sickness is bad enough, it won't help her much. Might keep her alive a few days longer, but that's all."

"I see," said the boy quietly. He screwed the cap back on the silver box, feeling more than a little disappointed.

"One more thing," said the Granny Woman, her eyes serious. "Never . . . I say *never* . . . plant them seeds on the mound of a freshly covered grave."

"Why?" Jeb asked, puzzled.

"'Cause that's powerful medicine you hold in your hand there," she told him. "If the roots of one them plants burrows through the lid of a casket and touches the one inside, it'll bring the dead back to life. But they won't be the way they were before. It'd be a sin against God and nature. Always remember that, Jeb."

"Yes, ma'am," agreed the farmboy. "I will."

The Granny Woman nodded as Jeb tucked the snuffbox deep into a side pocket of his overalls. "All right, two down and one to go. What's your third want?"

At first, Jeb felt foolish even mentioning his last concern. Then he recalled that he was in the dark heart of Fear County, a land full of the hellish and bizarre. "There's a critter that's been roaming around Mangrum County," he told her. "A terrible critter that, more than likely, came from right here in this county."

The Granny Woman's eyes narrowed. "What sort of critter?"

"Kinda half snake, half dog."

The old witch nodded. "Long and lanky with raven black scales all over its body? Almond-shaped eyes and fangs as long as my middle finger?"

"Yes, ma'am," replied Jeb, surprised by the accuracy of her description.

"I know the critter you speak of," she finally said with a sigh. "And you're right. It did come from hereabouts." She leaned forward, her eyes full of interest. "Exactly what has this snake-critter been up to over in Pikesville?"

"At first it just killed some cows and chickens, along with my prized hog, Old Jack," explained Jeb. "Then, several days ago, it got a hankering for young'uns. It started taking 'em and holding 'em prisoner in a cave on a bluff of the Cumberland River." He studied the old woman's face, trying to determine what she was thinking. "Do you believe me so far?"

"I've seen the thing with my own eyes, too, if that'll help any," offered Roscoe Ledbetter.

"Oh, don't worry," said the Granny Woman. "I believe every word you're saying. And I know why this critter is doing what it's doing."

"Just what is it doing?" asked the boy eagerly.

"She's preparing to hibernate," said the old woman. "She's gathering up food before the fall comes and getting ready to bed down for the winter."

Jeb's eyes grew as wide as pie plates. *"She?"* he blurted. "You mean to tell me that monster's a *girl?"*

"That's right," she told him. "And that ain't all. If she's feeding off them young'uns now, before autumn's even started, then she's doing it for a reason. And that reason is 'cause she's in the family way."

"She's gonna have babies?" asked Jeb, the thought sending a shiver throughout him.

"Yep. She'll lay a whole nest of eggs and keep 'em warm till hatching time next spring," said the Granny Woman. "Here in Fear County it wouldn't be such a disastrous thing. But anywhere else, well, that'd be like opening a door to hell and inviting ol' Lucifer to sit down to Sunday dinner."

"Can you help us get rid of it?" asked Jeb. "Can you help us kill it?"

A look of regret filled the Granny Woman's eyes. "No, son, I can't. Them things have more lives than ol' Midnight over yonder. Their innards are nearly as tough as their scaly hide. It could swallow a stick of pure dynamite and, more'n likely, not suffer more than a bad case of indigestion."

Jeb's spirits dropped. He thought of Mandy Rutherford trapped in the snake-critter's lair and, suddenly, felt as if his failure had condemned her to death. "But ain't there nothing you can do to stop it?"

The Granny Woman considered the problem for a long moment. Then a sparkle of hope replaced the grim resignation in her ancient eyes. "I can't . . . but there is someone who can. The only person I know of who has a hand over them damned critters."

Abruptly, it came to Jeb like a bolt out of the blue. "The Snake Queen," he muttered softly.

Their hostess seemed surprised. "Seems like you know a shade more about Fear County than I first suspected."

"Roscoe told me about her, just like he told me about you," said Jeb.

The Granny Woman turned her eyes to the lanky bluesman. "Then I reckon you told the boy about Adder Swamp and its dangers, too?"

"Yes'm, I did," said Roscoe.

She turned back to the ten-year-old. "Jeb, nothing you've come across north of here can hold a candle to what you'll see out yonder in Adder Swamp," she said. "You might not even make it outta there alive."

Jeb squared his freckled shoulders. "I don't care. If I don't at least try, a lot of folks in Mangrum County are gonna end up dying."

The old woman seemed to admire the boy's spunk. "If ya'll go by yourselves, it's likely you'll never make it to the far side of Adder Swamp in one piece. But if *I* show you the way, then maybe you'll have a fair chance."

"You?" said Jeb. "But you can't go. You're too—" The

boy shut his mouth before he could say the word that instantly came to mind.

The Granny Woman laughed. "Too *old?* True, I might be getting on in years, but I ain't all that feeble. I'll make it there and back with no trouble a'tall, just you watch me! Besides, the Snake Queen, she can be a contrary sort most of the time. She might not give you the time of day, but she *will* talk to me. I'm one of the few folks in Fear County she's actually afraid of."

"And if you do take us across Adder Swamp?" asked Roscoe. "What then?"

"Them snake-critters, they're what you might call the Snake Queen's *familiars,*" said the Granny Woman. "She created them by her own brand of black magic. That means she can destroy them, too, if she has a mind to. If we can talk her into giving up the secret, you can go back and deal with that beast with an ace in your pocket."

"But how long will it take us to get there?" asked Jeb. "We've been gone three days already and we ain't got much time left."

"It ain't but two or three miles south from here," assured the old woman. "We'll be in and out of there by dusk tomorrow."

"Okay," agreed Jeb. He didn't know why, but it almost seemed as though the Granny Woman had insisted on accompanying them on their journey to Adder Swamp for some reason other than simply to help them out. It was almost as if she had a score to set straight with the Snake Queen; a score that was long overdue.

"Then it's settled," said the old woman. "We'll leave at first light." She left the table and stepped to the cupboard once again. Soon, she was taking out jars of green river mud and taking down sprigs of dried leaves from off the rafters overhead. "But, before we bed down for the night, we'll see to your papa out there. It's gonna take several days for this medicine to work its magic and now's as good a time as any to start."

Jeb and Roscoe watched as the Granny Woman produced a large mixing bowl and began to combine mud and herbs until a thick paste was concocted. Jeb couldn't help but hold his nose. The odor of the poultice was horrendous, smelling like a combination of sulfur, rotten potatoes, and horse manure. "Pretty rank, ain't it?" grinned the old witch as she went to the cedar chest at the foot of the cornshuck bed. She opened the trunk and, finding an old bedsheet, began to rip it up into narrow strips.

Taking the bowl and the bandages, she left the cabin and stepped out onto the front porch. The night was calm and peaceful and fragrant with the scent of honeysuckle and magnolia blossoms. Sam sat on the edge of the porch with Buckshot, scratching the snoozing dog behind its one good ear.

"Sam," said the Granny Woman, sitting down next to him. "They tell me you have some awful fits of pain in your head from time to time."

The big farmer wrinkled his nose at the bowl full of greenish-brown paste. "Yes, ma'am, I do."

"Well, this here's some medicine that'll help stop all that," she told him as if talking to a small child. "All we have to do is put it on your head and keep it there for two or three days."

Sam shook his head in protest. "That stinky stuff? Uh-uh! You ain't gonna put it on me!"

Jeb stepped up and patted the brawny man on the shoulder. "Aw, come on, Sam! Don't be such a big baby! Sure, it stinks to the high heavens, but it'll do you some good. Remember how bad them seizures hurt? Wouldn't it be nice not to feel that hurt ever again?"

Sam thought it over for a moment, then nodded reluctantly. "Okay, go ahead. But I ain't gonna like it none!"

With Sam's blessing—more or less—the Granny Woman set to work. She first smeared the odorous paste on the crown, temples, and base of Sam's head, massaging it deep into his scalp and the nape of his neck. When she had applied a thick coating of the sludge, she then took the strips of bedsheet and began to tenderly wrap them around the man's skull. Fifteen minutes later, Sam's head was encased in a cocoon of damp cloth. All that was left visible was the farmer's face, from eyebrows to chin.

"I don't like this one bit!" pouted the man. "I can't hardly hear nothing and it stinks like horse apples!" His face began to turn a sickly shade of green. "I think I'm gonna puke, too!"

The Granny Woman reached into her apron pocket and took out bundle of cut tree bark held together by a rubberband. She took one of the strips and handed it to Sam. "You chew on that for a spell," she told him. "It'll keep you from losing your supper."

Sam stared at the piece of gray bark skeptically, then bit it in half. Jeb was sure his father was going to send possum stew all over the Granny Woman's front yard, but he didn't. The bark he chewed seemed to quell his nausea almost immediately.

The old black woman wiped her hands on her apron and got up. "Well, I reckon we'd best get us some shut-eye if we're gonna leave for Adder Swamp first thing in the morning," she said. "Ya'll can sack out on the porch here. Looks like a mighty fine night for sleeping out."

"Yes, ma'am, it does," replied Jeb. He looked out into the darkness and saw a swarm of fireflies in the magnolia grove, their taillights winking on and off. The boy drew in a lungful of air and savored the smell of the garden around them. In comparison to the rest of Fear County, the place he was now in truly seemed like Paradise. It was just a shame that he only had one night to enjoy it before they left the peaceful hollow and entered Purgatory once again.

After the Granny Woman had bid them good night and retired to her cornshuck bed inside, Jeb sat for a moment while Roscoe and Sam prepared their spots on the front porch. He reached into his overall pocket and took out the silver snuff box. Shaking it, he heard the rattle of the tiny seeds inside.

"Roscoe?" he asked. "Do you really think all this is gonna work? These seeds and that poultice she put on Sam's head?"

The bluesman shrugged his skinny shoulders. "Who knows? But I'll tell you this. If you have enough faith, there's a good chance that it will."

Jeb studied the snuffbox a while longer, feeling as if he were holding his grandmother's life in his hands. Carefully, he wrapped the tin in his bandanna and returned it to his pocket. Then he followed the others' example and prepared to settle down for the night.

Thirty-three

Adder Swamp

Jeb awoke from a wonderful dream.

He had been sitting in the kitchen of the Sweeny house on a bright spring morning. Robins and mockingbirds sang happily outside the open window, and bees buzzed around the lilies and irises of his grandmother's flower garden. The kitchen table was laid out with a breakfast fit for a king. Steaming bowls and platters of scrambled eggs, sausage gravy, juicy slabs of country ham, crispy bacon, flapjacks, and big cathead biscuits crowded the checkered tablecloth, along with jars of every sort of jelly, jam, and preserves imaginable.

But the feast wasn't the best thing about the dream. It was the state of those around him that pleased Jeb the most. Grandma was standing next to the cookstove, robust and healthy, looking like she would be around for a thousand years. And his father was no longer the stranger Jeb had known since his return from the War. Sam Sweeny sat at the table across from his son, cracking jokes and discussing the chores that needed to be done that day.

Jeb looked at that wry, good-natured gleam in the farmer's eyes and it made his heart sing as cheerfully as the birds outside. It was as if his father had never left him.

But, unfortunately, dreams never last forever. Jeb felt a

spidery hand shake him gently by the shoulder and, sleepily, he opened his eyes.

He peered through the gloom of early dawn and saw a frail, stooped form standing over him. It was a moment before he realized that it was the Granny Woman who had roused him.

"Rise and shine, child," she said softly. "Breakfast is ready and waiting on the table."

Sluggishly, Jeb sat up. He yawned and stretched, then followed Roscoe and Sam into the cabin. The instant Jeb stepped through the doorway, echoes of his dream came back to him. The aroma of eggs, fried hog jowl, and buttermilk biscuits filled the single room. For a moment, the boy felt as if he was standing in his grandmother's kitchen once again.

"Ya'll sit down and dig in," the Granny Woman directed. "We got us a long walk this morning, so you're gonna need all you can stomach."

The three needed no further urging. They sat down and began to heap their plates full. When they had finished with their eggs and jowl, they set to work on the mountain of golden biscuits. Jeb and Sam smeared theirs with goat butter and blackberry preserves, while Roscoe poured a lake of molasses in the middle of his plate and went to sopping. After the bluesman had finished, he cracked a big gold and ivory grin and, grabbing up his guitar, sang a few verses of his "Sticky Sorghum Blues." Just listening to it, the Granny Woman rocked back in her chair and laughed so hard that Jeb was certain that she would suffer a fatal stroke at any moment.

After breakfast, their light spirits began to grow heavy again as the purpose of that day's journey came to mind. "Well, I reckon we'd best get going," suggested the old lady with the head of cotton hair and the youthful eyes.

Jeb, Sam, and Roscoe went out on the porch and began to gather up their belongings. The boy had to scold Sam for picking at the poultice around his head. It didn't stink half as bad as it had the night before, but it still had a pungent air about it. When Jeb had convinced him that the dressing was for his own good, the big farmer grumbled beneath his breath and slung the duffle bag over his broad shoulder, looking none too happy.

When the Granny Woman appeared, she was wearing ankle-high walking shoes and a straw sun hat upon her head; the type Grandma Sweeny sometimes wore while she was out hoeing her vegetable garden. She also had an old carpetbag hanging from her stooped shoulder, packed full of charms and potions. The bag was unfastened and, from the open top, poked the green-eyed head of Midnight.

"You gonna take that ol' cat with you?" asked Sam skeptically. He stooped down and petted Buckshot, who eyed the animal in the bag as if it were a poisonous snake instead of a simple black cat.

"Midnight, she goes anywhere I do," the Granny Woman told him. "Anyway, where we're going, she's bound to come in handy. She ain't afraid of nothing that walks, swims, or slithers on its belly."

By the time first light broke over the peak of the eastern hill, they were already on their way down the dirt road, heading south. They left the magnolia grove and crossed a sprawling field full of wildflowers, clover, and tall stands of Queen Anne's Lace. Butterflies and junebugs filled the morning air, stirred into motion by the warm rays of the sun. Jeb and Sam watched them play, flying figure-eights over the sea of colorful flowers.

When they reached the far side of the pasture, however, they found themselves gradually mounting a rise in the clay road. As the trail topped and left the beautiful valley, they

once again found themselves in a dense stretch of forest that
was choked with ominous shadows. There were no songbirds
or butterflies here. There was only a noticeable absence of
such innocent creatures, as well as a silence that was almost
unnerving to the human senses.

Immediately, Jeb knew. "We ain't in Paradise Hollow any
more, are we?" asked the boy. "We're back out in Fear
County."

"That's right, boy," said the Granny Woman. "So watch
your step and stick close to each other."

Jeb did just that, moving nearer to Roscoe and the Granny
Woman. In turn, Sam and Buckshot shied away from the far
side of the road with its dense border of tall weeds, afraid
of what might be lurking there just out of sight.

They walked along the rutted road, leaving the early
hours of the morning behind. The sun rose higher in the
sky, but they could barely see it. Like the stretch of road
Jeb and the others had traveled a couple of days ago, this
one was shaded overhead by a canopy of interlacing limbs
and branches. Slivers of sunlight broke through the foliage
every so often, speckling the pathway before them. At first,
Jeb wished there was more sunshine to see by. But, on
second thought, he figured it was better that there wasn't.
If there had been, it was likely he would've seen some
things out there in the woods that he would have rather
been mercifully ignorant of.

One such creature made an appearance when they had traveled a couple of miles down the shadowy road. The Granny
Woman motioned them to halt and they stood on the trail
as the weeds at the side of the road parted noisily. Jeb
watched in a mixture of horror and fascination as a tiny
critter scarcely the size of his hand scuttled across the road.
The boy had never seen such an animal in his life, but it
resembled an albino mole with nimble feet and a longer head.

Its eyes—which were shiny black and as tiny as the head of a pin—glittered at them contemptuously and it snorted out loud.

Buckshot growled between his teeth and was creeping forward to investigate, when the Granny Woman reached out with a skinny hand and grabbed hold of his collar. "Whoa there, boy!" she said softly. "You'd best not tangle with that critter. I've seen 'em rip a dog's nose right off its face with one bite."

"That little ol' thing?" asked Jeb, about to laugh. But, before he even had the chance, the molelike creature turned its head and snarled at them like an angry badger, displaying a mouthful of wicked fangs. Satisfied that those in the roadway had no intention of coming closer, the critter continued on its way. Soon, it was back in the weeds and out of sight again.

Even more cautious than before, they resumed their journey down the dark stretch of rural backroad. Midway through the morning, they stopped to drink water from a hollow gourd the Granny Woman had brought along, as well as snack on peaches she had picked from a tree that grew out back of her log cabin. Jeb savored the meat and nectar of the peach, knowing that it might be the last piece of fruit he would enjoy until he made it back home to Mangrum County.

It was nearing noon when they came to a sudden bend in the road. It curved to the east, entering another stretch of wooded thicket, while directly to the south lay a stand of young saplings and tall cattails. Jeb smelled the familiar stench of rotted vegetation and algae, and knew that they had reached their destination.

"Is that it yonder?" he asked. "Adder Swamp?"

"It is," the Granny Woman simply said. She reached down and opened the top of her bag, allowing her cat room to

move. "Take a look-see, Midnight. Blaze the trail and make
sure it's safe enough."

In response, the lean black cat leaped from the bag and
darted into the bramble that grew thick along the water's
edge. They stood at the side of the road for a long moment,
watching as the cat disappeared from sight. For a while, they
heard nothing. Then came a fit of hissing and snarling that
would make the hairs on the back of your neck stand on
end. It wasn't long before the cat emerged from the thicket,
dragging a copperhead snake along behind her. Jeb was startled by the size of the serpent. It was as big around as his
wrist and a good six feet long, much bigger than any copperhead he'd ever come across in the woods along Mossy
Creek.

"I told you ol' Midnight was a hunter," said the Granny
Woman proudly. She bent down and, taking a long-bladed
knife from her carpetbag, cut the snake's head clean off.
Jeb was surprised when she deposited the head in a mason
jar and left the still-twitching body of the copperhead behind.

Carefully, they made their way through the thicket to the
edge of Adder Swamp. The body of water was muddy and
murky, and covered with a thick blanket of green algae the
consistency of phlegm. Jagged stumps broke the surface here
and there, looking like mossy tombstones sitting atop a watery grave. A nasty stench permeated the swamp that made
the poultice on Sam's head smell like a bouquet of roses in
comparison.

"Well, here it is," said the Granny Woman. "Right ugly,
if I do say so myself."

"Sure is," said Jeb. He peered off across the stretch of
stagnant water and saw the dark bodies of snakes swimming
through the algae every so often. "But how're we gonna get
across it?"

The Granny Woman already had that figured out. She dipped into her carpetbag and brought out a sturdy hatchet with an iron blade and a handle of seasoned hickory wood. "We'll have to build us a raft to take us to the far side," she said. The old lady turned to the brawny farmer. "Sam, you look to have the arms for the job. How's about going over to that grove yonder and cutting me down eleven or twelve good-sized saplings?"

"Yes, ma'am," replied Sam. He took the axe and headed toward the stand of young trees. Buckshot tagged along, his nostrils flared for the smell of snake, ready to pounce on anything that might try to strike out at them.

The elderly woman then turned to Jeb. "We're gonna need some vines, too," she told him. "To tie the saplings together with. Grapevine would be best, but honeysuckle will do if you can't find it."

Like his father, Jeb set out in search of the materials they would need for the raft. A half hour later, they were again gathered on the bank of the swamp. Jeb had returned with several coils of thick grapevine that he'd found growing in a wild briarpatch a hundred or so feet away. Sam had done his part, too. Soon they had laid out ten saplings that the farmer had chopped down and stripped of their branches. Roscoe helped lash the saplings together tightly with the grapevine, while the Granny Woman cut a deep notch in a sour gum tree nearby and, sticking a piece of hollow cane into the notch, let the sap flow into an empty tin can. Soon, she was kneeling over the raft, pouring the sap into the cracks. When they were finished, they laid the raft upon the water and watched it for a moment. It floated there, showing no evidence of leaking. Apparently, the sap had served its purpose well.

They ate a quick lunch of leftover possum stew and corn pone, then carefully mounted the raft. It creaked beneath their combined weight and, at first, Jeb was sure it would cave in and sink. But it proved to be more sturdy than he expected. Once they had spread out on the crude platform, the raft found its balance and complained no more.

"Ya'll ready?" called the Granny Woman, who sat at the front of the raft.

The others nodded silently. The old woman motioned to Sam, who stood at the rear of the raft, holding a long pole he had fashioned from one of the spare saplings. The big man stuck the pole into the murky water and, touching the muddy bottom with the end, pushed them away from the shore of tall reeds and cattails. Soon, they were gliding smoothly across the swamp, the front of the raft parting the covering of algae like the bow of a ship.

For a half hour, they traveled the length of Adder Swamp without incident. Once or twice, cottonmouth snakes approached the raft, their pale mouths gaping, eager to bite those who stood or sat upon the platform. But Buckshot and Midnight discouraged their intentions and they passed the raft by, looking for less troublesome prey.

The sun was high in the sky and the air was sticky and humid around them, when the first sign of menace showed itself. Jeb was talking to Roscoe, when he heard a loud buzzing near his ear and felt a sharp sting at the back of his neck. "Ouch!" he yelled and slapped at his nape, which was already sprouting hair in defiance of the shearing Mr. Drewer had given him a couple of weeks ago.

"What is it, son?" asked the Granny Woman, turning concerned eyes toward the boy.

"I don't know," said Jeb. "Something bit the fire outta me." Then he looked at the palm of his hand and his eyes widened at what he found there. It was the crumpled body of a mosquito, but not like any he had ever encountered before. This one was a good three-inches in length and its body was an ugly bluish-black color.

Before Jeb could yell out a single word of warning, they found themselves in the middle of a full-scale attack. A heavy swarm of the huge mosquitoes dive-bombed them, stinging them upon necks, faces, and arms, then rising back into the stagnant air. The four on the raft cussed and slapped at the vicious insects, while Buckshot and Midnight howled and yowled, nearly driven mad by the merciless assault.

It wasn't long before Jeb was covered with the wicked things. He could hardly see or breathe, they were so thick on him. Then, when he was certain that they would smother the very life out of him, he smelled an odor like burning cedar. One by one, the mosquitoes began to leave his body and take flight. A minute later, he stood up and looked around. The buzzing swarm was high-tailing it toward the west as fast as their wings could take them.

"What happened?" he asked. "What made 'em leave?"

He turned his eyes to the center of the raft and saw that the Granny Woman had set a small cloth bag on fire. A plume of thick black smoke rose from the flaming bag, filling the air above the raft.

"They can't stand the smell of it," the old woman told him. "Just some cedar shavings, dried moss, and skunk hair, but it's like a poison to them skeeters. That's why they left so fast."

Once they were sure that the mosquitoes were gone for sure, the Granny Woman kicked the burning bag into the water and, taking her satchel, attended to the others. She took out a jar of strong-smelling salve and began to spread it on the inflamed bites left by the giant blood-suckers. "This'll take down the swelling and kill any sicknesses them skeeters might've been carrying. Wouldn't want any of us to come down with typhoid or malaria, that's for sure."

After the Granny Woman had doctored them all—the dog and cat included—she returned to her place at the head of the raft. Sam continued to work the pole, propelling them forward across the still water.

They had traveled a good mile farther into the swamp, when they reached an open stretch of water that was totally devoid of algae or dead stumps. Jeb stared ahead and saw— or *thought* he saw—the ripple of a current in the water. But, just as quickly, it was gone and the surface grew completely motionless again.

Roscoe failed to see the shimmer on the water, but still he seemed to sense that something was amiss. "We've got trouble coming," he said softly. "I can feel it in my bones."

"So can I," replied the Granny Woman, her ancient eyes staring across the water. "Just keep your wits about you and stay calm."

"What's wrong?" asked Jeb. "What is it?"

Before anyone could answer, the ripple in the water came again, but much larger than before. Jeb's eyes widened as a small wave flowed their way and bucked the raft underneath them. The force of the ripple was so strong and unexpected that Sam nearly lost his balance and fell over the side. But, before he could, Roscoe reached over and, grabbing his britches' leg, corrected his footing.

"What was that?" asked the simple-minded farmer, looking more than a little scared.

"There's something under the water," said the Granny Woman. "Something mighty *big.*"

Jeb was about to speak up, when he was interrupted by a loud noise. A noise that he could actually *feel.* It was the sound of something coarse and scaly grating against the bottom of the makeshift raft.

The ten-year-old's heart began to pound as the platform of saplings and grapevine began to sway back and forth, growing more unstable with each passing moment.

Whatever lurked beneath the muddy waters of the swamp, it was directly underneath the raft now. And it seemed none too happy about them being there.

Thirty-four

Treacherous Waters

Jeb listened. The grating beneath the raft had stopped and the water around them grew suddenly still. "Is it gone?" asked the boy.

"No," said the Granny Woman.

Without warning, the raft was abruptly lifted several feet out of the water. Jeb caught a glimpse of something black and covered with slime and barnacles just beneath the raft, then it descended back into the depths of the swamp again. Its departure was so quick that the raft was left in midair for a split second. It hit the surface with a splash an instant later, striking the water with such force that it jarred everyone clear down to their bones.

"Lordy Mercy!" declared Roscoe, his eyes filling the thick lenses of his spectacles. "What was that thing? Some kinda sea monster?"

"Maybe," replied the Granny Woman, searching across Adder Swamp for a sign of the creature. "There be critters that live in this here swamp that should've gone the way of the dinosaur millions of years ago, but are just too danged ornery to give up the ghost. This might be one of 'em."

Suddenly, a froth of surfacing bubbles exploded to the rear of the raft, followed by a muffled sound. It was sort of like the roar of a lion, but softened by the water beneath them.

"It's coming up again," warned the Granny Woman. "Everybody grab hold of a grapevine. Hurry!"

Jeb and Roscoe did as she suggested. Even Sam crouched, grabbing one of the thick vines with one hand, while keeping a firm hold on the pole with the other. They waited for a long moment. Then it happened.

The raft began to buck and lurch like a wild bronco in a western rodeo. They had to hold on tightly to avoid being tossed off the platform and into the murky water. At one point, Buckshot nearly lost his footing and slid into the swamp, but Midnight came to the rescue. She anchored her claws into the floor of cut saplings and, grabbing the bluetick's tail in her teeth, prevented him from falling in.

When the raft finally came to a rest, the water around the raft rose and fell in turbulent waves, washing mud and debris over the sides. "It ain't through just yet," the Granny Woman told them. "It still wants to play with us a mite."

The old lady was right. A second later, something long and dark broke the surface—the tail of some huge creature from the look of it—and passed blindly over the raft.

"Look out, Sam!" cried Jeb as the tail swung dangerously close to his father.

Sam saw the tail just in time. He ducked just before it approached him. Its scaly tip missed the crown of the farmer's bandaged head by less than an inch, coming so close that it could have almost parted Sam's hair down the center.

A moment later, the tail was withdrawn from its search and pulled back into the depths of the swamp. Fearfully, Jeb watched the water around the raft, looking for tell-tale ripples and bubbles. "What'll it do after it gets tired of playing with us?" he asked.

The Granny Woman shrugged her scrawny shoulders. "Tip this here raft over and swallow us one by one, more'n likely," she said.

Jeb didn't like that answer at all. "Don't you have nothing in that bag of yours that can stop it?"

The elderly woman shook her head. "Sorry, child, but I ain't never crossed paths with this manner of critter before. Did you see them scales that covered its back and tail? I'd say it'd be harder to kill than that snake-critter you left back yonder in Mangrum County."

That was even more discouraging to hear. But Jeb was determined not to end up in the swamp monster's belly. He let go of his grapevine and stood up in the middle of the raft.

"What in tarnation are you doing, boy?" scolded Roscoe. "Get back down, right now!"

But the ten-year-old ignored his friend's request. He reached around to his hip pocket and withdrew the slingshot, then rummaged through his side pocket until he found what he was looking for. He placed a single steel jack in the slingshot's pocket and waited for the thing to reappear.

It did just that a moment later. But this time, neither its tail or its back broke the surface. Instead, a great horned head covered with dead vegetation and algae emerged from the water. He only saw the upper half of it; the nose and mouth were hidden from view. Milky yellow eyes full of contempt glared at them, and Jeb could imagine a huge maw of long fangs grinding eagerly, one against the other, just below the water's surface.

The boy knew then that it was time for him to act. He lifted the slingshot into line and stretched the innertube to its limit. Just before he took aim and released the spiky projectile, he knew that his action would either save them or send them to their doom.

He knew he must take that chance, however. He steadied his trembling hand and put the homemade catapult to use. The jack shot from its sling with the force of a rifle bullet and hit the critter square in the left eye. The projectile burrowed its way past the thing's pupil and settled deep in the center of its milky orb.

A jet of black jelly erupted from the wound and the creature unleashed a shrill scream, thrashing its head wildly. Jeb prayed to God that the critter would not go into a mad frenzy and crush them and their raft with its long, black tail. Fortunately, it appeared as though the Almighty was listening. The swamp beast was too concerned with its own agony to inflict chaos on the one who had caused the blinding injury. With a howling moan, it descended into the depths of the swamp and did not show itself again.

"Well, I'll be damned," said Roscoe, amazed. "You went and did it, Jeb!"

The Granny Woman flashed a gummy grin and laughed. "That critter won't be back no time soon. You showed him who's boss, Jeb, just like David did to ol' Goliath."

Jeb returned his slingshot to his back pocket, exhilarated and mortified at the same time. "Yeah, I reckon I did."

The black witch surveyed the swamp around them. "No sign of him a'tall," she said. "But it'd be best if we'd not tempt the fates. Let's get going, Sam. We've still got a ways to go before we reach the far side."

"Yes, ma'am," replied the brawny farmer. He took his place at the end of the raft once again and, dropping the end of the pole into the water, began to propel them across the still water toward the south.

An hour later, they left the open expanse of the swamp and entered a treacherous stand of water-logged cypress trees. The twisted trunks and their gnarled roots protruded from the muddy water and the sky overhead was shut out by a canopy of leafed branches and long, whisker like growths of stringy gray moss.

They traveled into the dark heart of the cypress swamp, taking a narrow channel that ran through its center. The oppressive heat they had suffered on the open water was gone now. The air around them grew cooler and the shadows much darker than before. Roscoe caught glimpses of black loons flying through the treetops and the pebbled backs of gators floating just below the surface of the water. Both were sights that the guitar-picker had seen in southern Mississippi and Louisiana, but ones he would never have considered encountering there in the heart of Tennessee.

They were a half hour into the cypress swamp, when something fell from above and landed on the raft directly in front of Jeb. He eyed the thing closely. It was about as long as his index finger, slimy and black.

"What is it?" he asked, wrinkling his nose in disgust.

The Granny Woman glanced behind her. "It's a nasty ol' leech," she told him. "Sometimes they shimmy up the trees and cling to the limbs above, waiting to drop down on whatever passes underneath."

Jeb turned his attention back to the leech, but it was already gone. In its place was Midnight, sitting there licking her lips and looking satisfied.

A moment later, another leech fell from the treetops, this time striking Sam on the back of the neck. "Yeeech!" cried the big farmer, pinching at the thing. "It's grabbed hold of me and it won't let go!"

"Don't yank it off, Sam," said the Granny Woman. "Lean over and I'll take care of it." The old witch took a jar of pure, white salt from her carpetbag and, walking over to him, spread a handful upon the leech and the skin around it. The parasite jerked at the touch of the salt and fell away, leaving an angry pink welt.

The Granny Woman picked up the blood-sucker and flung it off into the swamp. "Don't you fret no more," she told him. "It's gone now."

Sam was about to thank her, when a sound echoed from the cypress branches high overhead. It was a laugh, but not like any you would expect from such a place. It was the giggling coo of an infant, drifting from twenty or thirty feet directly over their heads.

"What the hell was that?" asked Roscoe, looking spooked.

"I don't know," said Jeb. He peered up into the treetops, but it was like searching for something in the starry expanse of the heavens.

The Granny Woman was about to reply, when a rain of leeches began to fall around them. It took a moment before they realized that the parasites weren't dropping by their own choice, but were being *flung* down at the passengers of the makeshift raft. And, after each leech hit the raft or its intended victim, there came the playful laugh of a baby.

"What's up there?" asked Sam, his face as pale as baking flour. "Ghosts?"

"No," said the Granny, her eyes gleaming with interest. "That ain't it. But I've heard tell of this part of Adder Swamp before. I thought it was all a lot of foolish talk, but I ain't so sure now."

"What do you mean?" asked Jeb. A leech landed on his bare shoulder, but the boy flicked it off before it could latch onto him.

The Granny Woman's face grew grim. "Do ya'll know what the folks of Fear County do with a baby who's born a runt? One that's born before its rightful time?"

"No," said Jeb. "What?"

"They take a canoe out to the middle of this here swamp and toss 'em in," she said. "They figure a runt wouldn't have a fighting chance in an evil place like this."

Sam seemed horrified. "You mean, they *drown* their little babies to death?"

"Well, some of 'em drown," the old woman told him. "Others are pulled outta the swamp by the Snake Queen her ownself. She raises 'em, teaches them how to survive in the wild, then sets them loose again. Or that's the story I've heard."

A shiver ran down Jeb's spine. "Do you think that's who's up there now?"

The Granny Woman was about to answer, when a rock the size of a walnut hit the elderly woman across the back of the skull. She lost her balance and dropped to her knees, looking dazed.

"Good Lord!" cried out Jeb. He made his way to her and found a good-sized dent in the crown of her straw hat. "Are you all right?"

Suddenly, before they knew it, a hail of stones began to rain upon the raft and its passengers. They yelled out as the rocks struck them more often than not. And, in the treetops overhead, the shadowy branches were alive with the noise of infantile giggling.

"Get us outta here, Sam!" called Roscoe, grimacing as rocks hit the guitar on his back, giving it more scrapes and scratches than it already had. "They'll stone us plumb to death if we stick around!"

Sam ignored the projectiles and, putting his muscular arms to work, moved the pole back and forth, propelling the raft forward at a quicker pace. It took a few minutes, but finally they left the stretch of dark cypress trees and turned a bend in the channel. The rock-throwing began to peter out, until it stopped completely.

When they were out of harm's way, they gathered around the Granny Woman. "Are you hurt bad?" asked Roscoe, his magnified eyes full of concern.

The Granny Woman shucked off her caved-in hat and rubbed the back of her head. "One little ol' crack on the skullbone ain't gonna do an old buzzard like me in," she said, displaying a broad smile. "I'll be just fine."

When he was sure that the elderly woman was okay, Jeb glanced down the shadowy channel of the swamp. "So, how long till we reach the far side of Adder Swamp?" he asked. "I don't mind telling you that I'm good and ready to be away from this place just as soon as possible."

"Oh, shouldn't be more than a half hour more," she promised. "But, take it from me, boy. It ain't gonna be no safer once we reach solid ground. If anything, it'll be even more perilous than what we've come across so far."

Jeb stared at the deepening shadows of the swamp, knowing that late afternoon was already upon them. Soon, the sun would set and the shadows would grow even darker. And, although he couldn't really say why, he had the feeling that was when all hell would break loose.

Thirty-five

The Canebrake

"There it is," called the Granny Woman. "Up yonder."

Jeb and the others looked toward the southern end of the channel and found that it widened into a boggy pool fifty yards away. When they reached the spot, they found that the channel had reached its end. They had finally made it to the other side of Adder Swamp.

"What now?" asked Jeb as Sam poled them toward the marshy shore of tall reeds and thicket.

"We go the rest of the way by foot," she told him. "Ain't a far walk, just a mile or so."

When they made their landing, Jeb jumped off the raft, anxious to be away from the water and the dangers that lurked above and below it. But he was startled when his foot touched ground. The earth was not solid, but unpleasantly soft and damp, like soil that had been rained upon for several days. Jeb had a feeling that it was like that all year round, whether the weather was rainy or not.

As they disembarked, the Granny Woman peered past an opening in the treetops and gauged the position of the sun. "It'll be getting dark in an hour or so," she said. "Ya'll watch your step. There's sinkholes and quicksand pits aplenty here in Adder Swamp. And a trainload of snakes, too. Just look yonder."

Jeb and the others looked to where she pointed. A squirming den of snakes could be seen in the open trunk of a hollow oak tree. The sight of all those snakes—cottonmouths from the looks of them—made Jeb want to jump back on the raft and hightail it out of there. But he knew now was no time to become a coward. He had made it that far across Adder Swamp and he was determined to make it the rest of the way, if only for the sake of Mandy and whoever else the snake-critter might have captured since Jeb's departure from Mangrum County.

"Just keep your step light and your eyes peeled and you'll do just fine," the old woman assured them. They gathered up their gear and, with Midnight and Buckshot blazing the trail, descended into the thicket that lay south of the swamp.

It was a little after four in the afternoon and, already, the shadows of the undergrowth were dark and spooky. Several times, snakes appeared in the weedy pathway ahead of them. Copperheads, timber rattlers, and brightly banded coral snakes slithered across the trail and clung to the limbs of nearby trees. They hissed and buzzed their rattles menacingly, but steered clear of the travelers for the most part. At one point, a copperhead that was coiled next to a clump of toadstools almost struck the Granny Woman on the ankle, but her loyal cat was upon its back before it could do her harm. With a single swipe of a clawed paw, Midnight decapitated the amber serpent, knocking its triangular head off into the brush at the side of the pathway.

They walked a good thirty minutes more before they came to a tall canebrake. Walls of dense sugarcane towered on both sides of the trail, standing ten feet tall in some places. Between the stalks lay tangles of thorny bramble and patches of deep shadow.

"Exactly where does the Snake Queen live?" asked Roscoe. He glanced down at his feet and, seeing the head of a snake poking from a hole in the ground, jumped out of the way.

"It's on ahead, past this canebrake," said the Granny Woman. "When we get there, I'd suggest ya'll keep quiet and let me do the jawing. She'd likely listen to me more'n she would you."

They continued through the dense grove of cane, watching their step as they went. Once, Sam stepped into a quicksand pit and was nearly sucked under. Jeb and Roscoe reached the farmer in time, however, and yanked him free before it could get a good hold on him.

As the sun began to set, the shadows of the canebrake grew longer and darker. Soon, it became too gloomy to see the path ahead of them without some sort of help. Sam opened the duffle bag and brought out the long-handled flashlight, directing its beam along the shadowy trail. The light reflected off the reptilian eyes of the snakes up ahead, driving them into the thicket and away from the pathway they traveled.

Jeb was about to ask the Granny Woman about their route out of Adder Swamp, when he heard a brittle crack echo from the canebrake to his left. He turned and peered into the grove of close-grown stalks. He didn't see anything at first, just wild vegetation and shadows. Then a form—black and lean—came into view, if only briefly.

"Something's out there," he said. "Yonder in the canebrake."

The Granny Woman motioned for them to stop. They stood on the path for a long moment, listening. Then the crunch of weight upon dead cane came again, but this time from the right instead of the left.

"There's more than one, that's for sure," said the old woman softly.

Then, from somewhere behind them echoed a low growl.

Sam whirled and shone the flashlight to their rear. Something black and shiny left the trail swiftly, diving into the canebrake before it could be identified. "Right big, whatever it was," said the slow-witted farmer. "Pert near the size of a year old calf from the looks of it."

Suddenly, a thrill of terror shot through Jeb. The boy lifted his head and drew in a deep breath. Yes, it was there, just as he suspected. The musky odor of snake, twice as strong than it should have been.

"I know what it is," he whispered. "It's some of them snake-critters . . . and they're dogging us from all sides."

"It *is* them," agreed the Granny Woman, her eyes wary. "I can tell by that godawful smell."

They took a few steps forward, but stopped in their tracks when a crash came from thirty feet ahead. Sam directed the beam of the flashlight toward the noise and illuminated a huge snake-critter that was a good twelve feet long from snout to tail. The creature hissed menacingly beneath its breath, its yellow-green eyes glowing in the battery-powered light. Its black lips curled into a hellish grin, showing off rows of sharp teeth that could rip through sheet metal if put to the test.

"Good God Almighty!" groaned Roscoe Ledbetter. The bluesman simply stood there and stared at the thing that blocked their way. It was twice as big as the one he had encountered at his campsite on the outskirts of Pikesville.

Again a growl came from behind them, but it was much closer this time. His hand trembling, Sam turned and flashed the light the way they had come. Another snake-critter, just as big as the other, was standing on the pathway no more than twenty feet behind them. It gnashed its teeth together, making a wicked clicking noise and drooling heavily. The gleam in its oval eyes was instantly recognizable. The thing was hungry, pure and simple.

"What're we gonna do?" asked Jeb, his voice small and full of lost hope. He looked ahead of them and saw the other beast starting toward them, as quiet and sure-footed as a mountain lion, but three times more dangerous.

"Do something!" Sam called to the Granny Woman, his eyes pleading.

The elderly woman looked uncertain. "I ain't sure there's anything I can do," she said. Her dark brow grew more wrinkled than it already was as she tried to think of some way of escaping the pack of hungry creatures.

Jeb looked down at Buckshot and Midnight. The animals no longer showed the bravado they had displayed during most of the journey. The dog and cat now clung close to the legs of their masters, whimpering and whining, their eyes full of fear.

Growling came from the right and left now. The boy looked around and saw serpentine eyes appraising them from just beyond the canebrake. It would take only a short leap on their part to leave their concealment and pounce upon him and the others.

They're gonna kill us! Jeb thought to himself. *We came all this way for nothing.* He thought of Grandma and Mandy and wondered if they could forgive him for being so careless and dying so stupidly.

Then, as the creatures began to close in on them, Roscoe threw his head back and laughed out loud. A big grin split his dark face and his eyes sparkled with a triumph that Jeb failed to understand at first. Then the Negro grabbed his guitar from off his back and, suddenly, Jeb knew what he had in mind.

The next moment, Roscoe was playing that guitar with all the feeling he could muster and belting out an old hymn called "Leaning on the Everlasting Arms." He sang with such

a depth of soul that veins popped out on his temples and he
swayed back and forth like a scarecrow in a high wind.

Jeb looked behind him. The critter that was stalking them
from the rear had backed up a few paces. The beast in front
of them had done likewise. It snapped and snarled, but advanced no further. Instead, it was steadily backtracking up
the pathway.

"Come on!" yelled Roscoe, his fingers still strumming the
strings of the battered Fender. "Join in with me on this one.
Ya'll know the words, so sing it long and loud!"

The bluesman launched into a passionate rendition of "Onward, Christian Soldiers." Immediately, Jeb, Sam, and the
Granny Woman joined him, wailing the old gospel hymn to
the top of their lungs. The throaty snarls of the snake-critters
grew less defiant and more uncertain. They retreated into the
canebrake, their eyes shining with a mixture of disgust and
mounting panic.

"It's working!" said Jeb. "They're leaving!"

"Don't talk, boy," said the Granny Woman. "Just sing!
Sing with all the goodness that's deep down in your heart."

Jeb did as she said and continued to sing, loud and slightly
off-key. They began to make their way slowly up the pathway,
reeling off every hymn that popped into their heads. They
went from "Jesus Loves Me" to "Standing On The Promises"
and "Nearer My God to Thee." And, with the completion of
each song, the sounds of stalking and snarling grew more
and more distant.

They didn't stop singing until they emerged from the canebrake. A stretch of dark woods lay ahead of them and, from
the far side, flickered the light of a fire. Exhausted, the band
of travelers made their way toward the beacon, ready to
launch back into chorus the moment they heard a menacing
snarl or the sound of a clawed foot behind them.

Eventually, they reached the source of the light. It was a

crackling fire with a great iron pot hanging over the flames. A writhing tangle of snakes squirmed in a thick circle around the cauldron, knotting and unknotting in a frenzy Jeb couldn't comprehend at first. Then the boy, having been raised on a farm, recognized their urgency for what it truly was. The serpents were in the midst of some grotesque mating ritual. Just watching them, Jeb found their motions much more sensual and hypnotic than the crude ruttings of cattle and hogs that the ten-year-old was accustomed to witnessing.

Then, from the porch of a weathered shanty that stood a few yards beyond the fire, came a thin, reedy voice; a voice that was as sharp as a shaving razor and dripping with venom.

"So, *you're* the ones!" growled the hateful voice. "Crossing my territory uninvited and singing them damned songs of heavenly rewards and redemption!"

Startled, Jeb looked past the vapor of the boiling pot to the sagging porch of the old shanty and, for the first time in his young life, laid eyes on the one known as the Snake Queen.

Thirty-six

A Favor Owed

When Jeb Sweeny had gotten his first glimpse of the Granny Woman, he had been a little disappointed. The elderly Negro had looked more like someone's sweet old grandmother than the snaggle-toothed, wart-infested witches portrayed in stories like *Hansel & Gretal* or *The Wizard of Oz*. But he felt no such dismay upon meeting the Snake Queen. It was plain to see that she was a witch if there ever was one.

The Snake Queen was black like the Granny Woman, but that was where their similarities ended. The one who stood on the porch of the shanty was tall—a good six feet at least—and looked as if she would be afraid of no man, like those Amazon women who showed up in Tarzan movies or Flash Gordon serials from time to time. She had a dark bandanna wrapped tightly around her skull and wore a tattered dress sewn from coarse burlap. Her eyes were an odd hazel green color and her dark face was set into the most hateful scowl Jeb had seen in his life. But her attire and demeanor wasn't what surprised the boy the most. It was her jewelry that gave him the cold shivers. At first he thought the woman was wearing a necklace and bracelets made of tanned snakeskin. But, upon further inspection, Jeb discovered that it was live serpents that were around her lean neck and wrists. She also wore black widow spiders from her lobes, like living earrings.

"What're you gawking at, you little bastard?" snarled the Snake Queen, looking as though she were ready to strike the boy down with a bolt of pure lightning, if she had possessed such a deadly power. "Is that why you came sneaking into my swamp unannounced? So you could lay your beady little eyes upon the almighty Snake Queen? Speak up, boy! Is that it?"

"Uh," stuttered Jeb at first. "Yeah, kinda, in a way."

"You've got no cause to bully the child, Lucretia," spoke up the Granny Woman. Her head was held high and there was nary a speck of fear in her soft brown eyes. "The reason he had for crossing Adder Swamp is sound enough."

The venom in the Snake Queen's eyes lost its potency when her true name was spoken out loud. Startled, she stepped down off the porch and walked closer, studying the old black woman more closely. "Well, I'll be damned to hell and back again! Lucinda . . . is that you?"

"It is," said the Granny Woman, her face not in the least bit friendly. "It's been a while, ain't it?"

"Going on twenty years, I'd hazard to say," agreed the Snake Queen. "Never though I'd see you set a self-righteous foot on my side of Fear County again. No, ma'am, never thought I'd live to see the day!"

"Neither did I," said the Granny Woman. "But I'm here just the same."

Jeb shifted his gaze from good witch to bad, surprised that they knew each other by their rightful names. It was plain to see that they had been acquainted, if uneasily so, during their younger days.

"So, Lucinda," continued the Snake Queen, her green eyes full of suspicion. "What business do you have coming here? And why have you brought these white devils with you?"

She stared at Jeb and Sam as if they were something that should've been shoveled up and dumped down the seat of an outhouse.

"They've come here to ask your help," said the Granny Woman. "But, knowing how dadblamed ornery and hateful you are, I took it upon myself to accompany them here, just to make sure you didn't go and do something crazy."

The Snake Queen laughed and turned her eerie green eyes to Jeb. "What did you come here to ask me, boy? Do you need a potion or a spell? Want to kill somebody you hate or paralyze 'em where they can't move a muscle in their body? You want to make an enemy so sick that they'll pray for death? I can do that, too, if you want. I can give 'em any disease imaginable, as well as a few nobody's ever heard of. I got a bottle of the Black Plague back yonder in the shack that'll put an entire town in their graves, if that be your desire."

"The boy don't desire no such thing," said the Granny Woman sternly. "We'll tell you the reason for our visit, if'n you'll invite us inside."

"I ain't doing no such thing until I get a few things straight," said the Snake Queen defiantly. "Like how'd you get here in the first place? Even if you made it past the swamp itself, just how did you manage to get past my children? They should've had ya'll for supper with no trouble a'tall."

"You mean them damned snake-critters?" asked the Granny Woman, her eyes amused. "We sang our way past 'em."

The Snake Queen turned toward Roscoe Ledbetter. "So you were the one who was strumming that git-box and cat-erwauling about Jesus and salvation! Well, I'll tell you right here and now that I don't appreciate such blasphemy in my domain. So you'd best keep that instrument slung across your back and the name of God off your tongue whilst you're in my presence."

Roscoe simply nodded his head, a deep dislike for the swamp witch showing in his magnified eyes.

The Snake Queen then turned her attention to Sam. "What's ailing this one? Why's he got his head all cinched up tight?"

"He's got a brain sickness," the Granny Woman simply said. "I put a poultice on to heal him up. It'll be a day or so before it does its magic, though."

The woman dressed in burlap and snakes sneered with contempt. "Yeah, I know what kinda magic you pedal, Lucinda!"

"That's right, you do," said the Granny Woman, her jaw set firmly. "Mine is the witchcraft of heaven, whilst yours is from the depths of hell. I've dedicated my life to helping folks and making 'em happy, while the only magic you concoct is the kind that brings pain, misery, and death. Well, I ain't ashamed of what I do, but you surely oughta be!"

Anger flared in the Snake Queen's eyes. "Don't rile me up, Lucinda," she warned. "You know what I'm capable of conjuring up."

"I know," said the Granny Woman. "That's mainly why we came here in the first place. Jeb here has trouble back in Mangrum County and it has to do with one of your confounded snake-critters."

A wicked grin crossed the witch's face. "Aw, is one of my darlings over yonder, reeking havoc across the county line? So what do you expect me to do about it?"

"He wants you to give him a potion or charm," replied the Granny Woman. "To kill the dadblamed beast."

"Kill it!" exclaimed the Snake Queen in outrage. "Why, I'd just as soon cut off my own right arm with a rusty saw than harm a scale on one of my children's heads. If'n that's

your reason for coming here to Adder Swamp, then you'd best just turn around and head on back from where you came. 'Cause I'll take no part in helping do such a thing."

Jeb saw the stubborn defiance in the Snake Queen's eyes and knew that no amount of talking would change the swamp witch's mind. He looked toward the Granny Woman, his eyes pleading.

The Granny Woman nodded to the boy, then turned back to her nemesis. She regarded the Snake Queen for a long moment, then a mischievous grin crossed the elderly woman's face. "Well now, Lucretia, it might turn out that you've got no choice in the matter. You might be beholden to helping us, whether you like it or not."

"Beholden?" scoffed the Snake Queen. "To this white boy here?"

"No," replied the Granny Woman. "It's me I'm talking about. Seems that I recall that you owe me a favor, Lucretia . . . and a mighty big 'un at that. Or has twenty years made you forgetful?"

The scowl on the Snake Queen's ugly face told Jeb that she hadn't forgotten. In fact, from the look of hateful disgust in the swamp witch's eyes, the ten-year-old could tell that, whatever the favor was, it was not to be taken lightly.

"All right," she finally replied. "I do owe you, Lucinda. But what you're asking is just too much. I mean, destroying one of my poor little babies . . . ?"

"I'm ready to collect on that favor," the Granny Woman told her sternly, with no intention of backing down. "Now, are you gonna help my young friend here defeat that snake-critter . . . or do you want *me* to get riled up?"

Jeb wasn't sure, but he thought he saw raw fear sparkle in the Snake Queen's green eyes. She considered it for a long moment, then finally nodded her head. "I reckon I'll just have to betray my wayward young'un and do the dirty deed you're asking of me. But it's only to repay the debt I owe. After that, we're square, you and me. Understand?"

"I do," replied the Granny Woman, satisfied.

"Ya'll just stay put," the Snake Queen said grudgingly. "I'll go inside and fetch what you need. Then I want you outta my swamp and outta my sight!"

"We'll go," assured the elder witch. "You just keep your end of the bargain."

Cussing beneath her breath, the Snake Queen turned and disappeared through the open door of the ramshackle shanty.

"Do you think she'll really do it?" asked Jeb quietly. "She won't try to pull the wool over our eyes, will she?"

The Granny Woman grinned. "Lucretia's a tricky ol' gal, to be sure. But she ain't gonna deceive me, of all people. She knows better than to try that."

A few moments later, the Snake Queen stepped out onto the front porch, looking none too happy about what she was being forced to do. "Here!" she said, tossing a mason jar to the tow-headed farmboy.

Jeb caught the glass container and studied what was inside. It was an egg the size of a plum, floating around in a pint of cloudy vinegar. The egg was as black as coal and looked to have a leathery texture to it. "What is it?" asked the boy, fascinated and repulsed at the same time.

"It's a snake-critter egg," the Granny Woman told him. "Been a while since I laid eyes on one, but that's what it is."

Jeb turned to the Snake Queen, a question in his young eyes. "And this here egg is gonna kill that critter back in Mangrum County? How?"

The gloomy look on the swamp witch's face vanished and, in its place, bloomed a nasty grin. "The only thing that'll kill one of my young'uns is to force it to eat its own kind.

All you gotta do is make it swallow that egg there and it'll curl up and die right fast."

Jeb's eyes widened. "But how in Sam Hill am I supposed to do that?"

The Snake Queen laughed wickedly. "That ain't none of my concern, boy. You've got what you need to do the job. Whether you can do it or not, well, that's up to you."

Jeb stared at the egg in the pint jar skeptically, but said nothing. If getting the snake-critter to swallow the egg was the only way to defeat it, then he would have to figure out a way to do it.

"All right, I've given you what you came here for," snapped the Snake Queen. She looked over at the Granny Woman. "And I've paid back the favor owed you, Lucinda. Now get the hell outta my swamp before I cast a spell upon you all. Take away your singing voices and sic my young'uns on you. I'll do it, too, if'n ya'll don't hightail it outta here."

Sam turned and looked back the way they had come, his eyes frightened. "You mean we gotta go back across that swamp . . . *tonight?*"

Jeb swallowed nervously. Sam was right. It would be suicide traveling back across Adder Swamp in the dead of night. The dangers they had encountered there had been bad enough in broad daylight. They would be twice as treacherous in pitch darkness.

"Naw, we ain't stupid enough to do a thing like that," said the Granny Woman. She eyed the Snake Queen slyly. "Lucretia, is that pathway to the east still in the thicket out back of your house?"

The Snake Queen scowled sourly, looking as though she had hoped her nemesis would forget about the easy route out of the swamp. "It's back there. Just take it and git!"

"Come on, gentlemen," called the Granny Woman, reaching down and picking up her carpetbag. "Let's leave this evil place."

Jeb and the others wasted no time. They gathered up their gear and followed the elderly woman around the back of the dilapidated shack. Sam retrieved the flashlight from out of the duffle bag and handed it to the Granny Woman. She had to search for a while before she found the pathway that she was looking for. After years of neglect, the path was scarcely there at all. It was choked with tall weeds and was crowded on both sides by tangles of thorny bramble, their barbs long and sharp.

"Ya'll stay quiet and stick close," she warned. "It'll be a while before we're away from Adder Swamp. That means there's still a chance we might come across some badness on our way out."

Sam's stomach growled loudly. "I'm hungry," he pouted. "Can't we have a bite of supper before we go?"

"We'd best wait and eat later," the Granny Woman told him. She cast a suspicious glance back at the Snake Queen's shack. "We made ol' Lucretia do something she purely hated to do and I figure it won't set well with her. If she thinks about it long enough, she might just try to cast a hex upon us. When my sister forms a grudge, she'll hold it till her dying day."

"Your *sister?*" piped Jeb, his jaw hanging open. "I didn't know ya'll was kin to one another!"

"Yeah, we be kin," said the Granny Woman, her face grim. "But only by blood and not by spirit. That tie was severed when we chose our separate masters."

"You mean God and the Devil?" asked Jeb.

The old woman nodded. "That's what I'm saying."

Without another word, the four, along with Buckshot and Midnight, entered the thicket out back of the Snake Queen's home and began to make their way along the weedy pathway.

The bramble that stood to either side of them was dark and
full of strange sounds, but they did their best to ignore what
might be lurking there. Silently, they began the journey eastward, hoping to be far away from Adder Swamp before long.

Thirty-seven

Parting Company

They walked nearly five miles through the pitch darkness, the beam of the flashlight being their only source of illumination. The sky above them was dark and choked with stormclouds. The thunderheads were so thick that nary a beam of moonlight could break through.

Once, they took a breather, sitting down on the path and eating a meal of stale cornpone and muskrat jerky, a delicacy that the Granny Woman had brought along. While they relaxed—or tried to, at least—they heard something fly over their heads several times. From the sound of its wings and the breeze it generated, it was apparent that the critter, whatever it might be, was a mighty big one. But, no matter how hard they tried, they couldn't distinguish the winged creature from the rumbling clouds overhead. Sam tried to pinpoint the thing with the beam of the flashlight several times, but it eluded detection every time, remaining an uncomfortable mystery to them all.

Halfway through their nocturnal journey, they left the briar patch and entered a stand of dense pines. The smell of the evergreens was cloyingly pungent and possessed an underlying odor that was unfamiliar to Jeb and the others. The Granny Woman told them that a band of settlers had been slaughtered by hostile Indians in the grove in the early 1700's and that their life's blood had been absorbed by the roots of the pines. Jeb took in a deep breath and identified the scent as the rich coppery stench of blood. Combined with the sharp odor of pine, it was a stink that nearly made him lose his supper.

They left the grove and continued through an equally thick stretch of woods. They found a clearing midway through it and slept for an hour or two, leaving Buckshot and Midnight awake to stand watch. Several times, distant cries or growls echoed from far off in the forest, putting the animals on edge and waking Jeb and the others up. The Granny Woman took several stubby candles from her carpetbag and, placing them in a circle around their camp, lit them with a sulfur match. The candles put out a scent much like burning sandlewood and soon filled the woods around them with the peculiar smell. It seemed to drive the restless critters away. Their calls soon died and silence reigned throughout the rural wilderness.

Having rested, the band of travelers rose and continued on their way. After what seemed an eternity, daylight broke and lifted the uncertainty of darkness from their path. They reached a fork in the trail and, taking the northeastern route, walked for several miles more. It was nearly seven in the morning, when they reached a break in the forest and came upon something that was totally unexpected to Jeb and the others.

An ancient set of railroad tracks cut through the dense woods, tall weeds and thistle growing from the spaces between rusted rails and weathered ties.

Jeb looked over at the Granny Woman. "But I thought the railroad didn't run through Fear County," he said, puzzled.

"The one built by the L&N doesn't," explained the old woman. "But this here stretch of tracks was laid by the folks of Fear County themselves. In the late 1800's, Jeremiah Gallow, the grandson of ol' Ezekial, heard that the Louisville and Nashville Railroad was being extended clear down to Florida. Being the impetuous businessman that he was, Jeremiah ended up jumping the gun a mite. He hired a hundred able-bodied men to lay forty miles of track from the southern border of Fear County to the northern border, and even bought a big coal-burning locomotive from a train-builder way over in England. They had nearly thirty miles of track done, when Jeremiah got the word that the L&N had decided to bypass Fear County, mainly because of its reputation. Jeremiah went kinda crazy in the head when he got the bad news. He loaded all hundred of his workers on that train and pushed it to the limit, heading north as fast as that steam engine would go. And he didn't let up when they reached the end of the line, either. He crossed the trestle over Beelzebub Creek and kept right on going, till they ran plumb outta tracks. Needless to say, the locomotive derailed and every last one of them hundred men, ol' Jeremiah included, died in the crash."

"That's horrible," said Roscoe. "You mean to say that none of 'em survived?"

The Granny Woman shook her head. "Nary a one."

They all stood there for a while, staring silently at the long stretch of abandoned track. Each pictured that long-ago train roaring through the forest, carrying a hundred and one doomed men to their eventual deaths.

"Well," said the Granny Woman with a sigh. "I reckon this is where we part company."

Jeb and the others were startled. "Ain't you going on a ways further with us?" asked the boy, disappointment showing in his eyes.

"Ain't no need," said the woman. She pointed toward the northwest. "You see that tall hill a couple miles yonder? On the other side is Paradise Hollow. Won't be but an hour hike till me and Midnight are back home again."

Jeb, Roscoe, and Sam looked a little sad. They had gone through a lot with the Granny Woman in the span of a day and a night, and were a little reluctant about leaving her behind.

The old woman sensed their sorrow and laughed. "Aw, don't ya'll go sulling up over me now! Ya'll got what you came for and now it's time for you to get on back to Mangrum County." She directed a gnarled finger toward the railroad tracks, which curved around a bend and off into the woods. "Ya'll can't get lost. Just walk due north along these tracks and it'll take you within four or five miles of the county line. Just heed my warning about two things before you go."

"What's that?" asked Jeb.

"Steer clear of the town of Lynching Springs just before you reach Beelzebub Creek, particularly for Roscoe's sake," she told them. "They ain't nothing but sorry white trash and don't hate nothing more in this world than a man with black skin."

Roscoe nodded in understanding. "And the other thing?"

"When you're crossing that bridge over the creek, keep your ears keen. If you hear the scream of a train whistle or the chugging of an engine at full tilt, you either get to the other side as fast as you can . . . or jump off into the creek. Hopefully, you won't encounter nothing outta the ordinary, but I just wanted to give you fair warning in case you do."

When the old woman was certain that her words had been taken to heart, she walked over to Jeb. "Farewell, Jeb Sweeny," she said, embracing the boy and kissing him gently atop the forehead. "I wish you much luck with the things you gotta do once you get back home again."

"Thank you," said the boy, his voice cracking. "Thanks for everything you've done."

The Granny Woman released the boy and went to Roscoe

next. "Goodbye, Mr. Ledbetter. It was surely a rare pleasure to meet a minstrel as full of soul as you. You keep on playing that there git-box and, remember, watch yourself near Lynching Springs."

Roscoe shook her hand and tipped his hat politely. "Yes, ma'am. I'll do that . . . and thank you."

The elderly witch then turned to the brawny farmer. "Take care of yourself, Sam," she said, standing up on tiptoe and giving him a kiss on his broad chin. "You keep that poultice on a day or two more and it oughta end up working wonders for that poor head of yours."

"Yes'm," replied Sam with a dumb grin. "It stinks awful bad and feels heavier than an anvil, but I'll keep it on a while longer if you want me to."

"You do that," she said, her eyes looking a little watery around the rims.

Jeb turned and saw that Buckshot was sniffing at Midnight's hindquarters. "Looks like they're saying their goodbyes, too," he said.

The Granny Woman picked up her black cat and put it back in her carpetbag. Then she waved goodbye and, stepping into the forest, soon vanished from view.

After she was gone, Jeb turned to the lanky bluesman. "We ain't ever gonna see her again, are we, Roscoe?"

"No, boy, I don't believe we ever will," he replied. He looked off into the woods, his eyes searching for a glimpse of knitted shawl or straw hat. "But I ain't never gonna forget her. Been a long time since I've met a lady as fine as that one."

"Yeah," said Jeb. "Me, too." Absently, he reached inside his overall pocket. He felt the snuff tin of seeds and thought of the jar with the pickled monster egg swimming in its juice, which was nestled amid clothes in Sam's duffle bag.

"That stuff I was given . . . do you think it'll really do what it's supposed to?"

Roscoe shrugged his skinny shoulders. "I reckon we'll just have to wait till we get back to Mangrum County to find out."

"I reckon so," said Jeb with a sigh.

And, with that, they set off down the weedy railroad tracks, heading for the northern region of Fear County.

Five
The Long Walk Home

The Boxcar—Lynching Springs—The Ghost Train
Farewell to a Friend—Sacred Ground

Thirty-eight

The Boxcar

They walked along the abandoned tracks for most of the day. Their conversation was sparse, their thoughts mostly occupied with the visit they had made to Adder Swamp the day before. Jeb found himself walking faster than the others several times, feeling an urgency to get back home and administer the magic that the Granny Woman and the Snake Queen had given him. But Roscoe slowed him down, explaining that they would cover less miles if they hurried and tuckered themselves out. Grudgingly, Jeb agreed to pace himself, although his impatience showed with every step he took.

Shortly after noon, they stopped and ate a bite of lunch next to the tracks. As they feasted on the dwindling remnants of jerky and cornpone, something odd took place. Buckshot was taking a nap next to Jeb, when, abruptly, the bluetick hound jerked awake and shot to his feet. The dog walked to the center of the railroad tracks and stared back the way they had come, his body as tense as a coiled spring. Jeb, Sam, and Roscoe watched the coonhound for a breathless moment, wondering what it was that the dog sensed from the south end of the track. They strained their ears for sound, perhaps expecting to hear a distant whistle or the grinding wheels of a ghostly locomotive. But, after a moment, Buckshot relaxed and turned his attention from the south. With a puzzled look in his one good eye, the dog stepped off the tracks and made his way back to his master's side. Jeb and the others traded equally perplexed glances, then quickly finished their lunch, eager to leave the spot and continue on their way.

When the last rays of the sun began to fade into dusk, Roscoe suggested that they set up camp for the night. They found a good spot in a clearing at the right side of the tracks; an oval patch of grass surrounded by tall pines. As they dumped their gear on the ground and began to settle down for the evening, they spotted something unexpected on the opposite side of the tracks.

It was an old, abandoned boxcar. The wheels had been removed for salvage and the long, wooden hull was weathered a dull gray by countless years of sun, snow, and rain. Clinging ivy covered the walls of the structure and the metal tracks of its sliding cargo doors were coated with thick, orange rust.

"Do you think it was one of Jeremiah Gallow's?" asked Jeb, eyeing the boxcar with interest.

"More'n likely," said Roscoe. He finished unpacking his knapsack, then turned to Jeb and Sam. "Ya'll go gather some wood for the stove. I'm gonna fix us some hot grub tonight. I'm getting kinda tired of cold jerky and stale bread, and I know you are, too."

The two agreed that they were. Sam began gathering dead branches from the pine grove around the clearing, while Jeb crossed the tracks to do his searching. As he gathered up twigs and rotten slivers of old railroad ties, he made his way through the knee-high weeds to the boxcar. He didn't know exactly why, but the abandoned car nagged at his boyish curiosity. He studied the front of the structure for a moment, then made his way around back, Buckshot tagging along behind him.

When he reached the other side, he was surprised to find the rear door to be partially open. He peered through the crack, but, at first, could only see pitch darkness inside. Jeb looked around. The sun had nearly set now; the sky was growing blacker by the minute. He wished that he had brought the big flashlight, so he could explore the car's shadowy interior further.

Jeb tried to push the door back on its track, but the metal seemed to be fused together by decades of rust. With a shrug of his shoulders, the ten-year-old turned and went back to the task of gathering kindling for the campfire.

He was only a couple yards from the boxcar, when he heard a loud grating sound behind him. Startled, he whirled and saw that the door of the boxcar had been slid open . . . from the inside.

Jeb watched, frozen to the spot, as a pale form stepped from the shadows within and stood just inside the frame of the open door. The farmboy expected it to be a haint or some such thing, but he was wrong. Instead, it was only a boy not much older than himself—perhaps fourteen or fifteen—dressed in ragged, hand-me-down clothes.

"Howdy!" called the boy, lifting a hand that was as white as lard.

"Howdy," said Jeb, trying to be friendly. "Who're you?"

"Name's Mickey," said the teenager. "And yours?"

"Jeb," replied the farmboy. He took a couple of steps closer. "What're you doing in that old boxcar there?"

"Aw, we kinda make it our home here," said Mickey. The nearer Jeb came, the more distinctive the boy's features became. He was kind of skinny in the face, possessed a thick crop of bright red hair, and dark freckles speckled his forehead, nose, and cheeks.

"We?" asked Jeb, puzzled. "Who're you talking about?"

"Come on in and I'll introduce you to the gang," said Mickey.

Normally, Jeb would have declined such an invitation, but there was something in the teenager's eyes that put him at ease. Jeb could find nothing threatening about the boy with the freckles and the red hair, so he walked through the weeds toward the open door of the boxcar.

Just as he was about to climb inside, Jeb heard a familiar whine behind him. He turned to see Buckshot standing there, looking a little upset. "Come on, boy," he called. "I'm sure they won't mind you coming in, too."

But the coonhound would have no part of it. He whined down deep in his throat once more, than took off around the side of the boxcar toward the railroad tracks.

"Come on in," called Mickey, his voice a hollow echo from inside. "My pals sure would like to meet you."

"I'm a-coming," said Jeb. The boy climbed up through the open door and stepped inside.

At first he could see nothing. Then his eyes grew accustomed to the dim glow of an old coal oil lantern, which hung from a nail in one of the car's ceiling studs. When the boy's vision sharpened, he found that Mickey wasn't the only one in the boxcar.

Standing around the inner walls of the structure, was the most ragtag bunch of hoboes and tramps that Jeb had ever seen. They were lean and hungry-looking, much like the bums who hung out at the Pikesville depot on occasion. But, then again, there was something else about them that wasn't like those rambling hoboes at all. This gang—consisting mostly of men, but including a few women and children—had a tragic air about them, as if they were condemned to some horrible fate that no amount of walking or train-hopping could leave behind.

"Howdy," called Jeb, raising his hand.

The hoboes simply stared at him and said nothing. Jeb didn't rightly like the way they looked at him. He studied their lean faces, which possessed the waxy pallor of melted tallow, and their hollow, bloodshot eyes, and Jeb felt the impulse to turn and leave that place as fast as his feet could carry him. But he found that to be impossible. Their feverish stares seemed to pull at him, drawing him closer.

"Are you hungry?" asked the boy named Mickey. "You look it, Jeb. You look like you're starved half to death."

"I am hungry," agreed Jeb. He took a couple of steps forward and felt something firm, yet pliant beneath his feet. He looked down. Raw earth covered the floor of the boxcar, instead of the hard wood of two-by-fours.

"Then come on over here and eat your fill," invited Mickey. He waved at a spot where a dark-eyed woman and her brood of silent children sat.

Jeb couldn't believe his eyes. He had failed to notice it before, but there was a blanket spread out on the earthen floor of the boxcar. And, laid out on that wrap was a meal that made Jeb's mouth water. Bowls of steaming vegetables, yeast rolls, and crispy fried chicken sat there, as well as a wooden bucket chocked full of Coca Cola and Orange Crush on ice.

"Go on, Jeb," urged Mickey, his smile growing broader. "Help yourself."

Jeb could smell the rich scent of the fried chicken in his nostrils and he could restrain himself no longer. He was about to take a step forward, when he felt a strong hand on his shoulder, holding him back. Almost dreamily, he looked back and was surprised to see Roscoe Ledbetter standing there.

"Let's get back to camp, Jeb," Roscoe said, his eyes grim.

"But look at all these nice folks I've found over here,"

protested Jeb. "And will you take a gander at that spread? Look at all that food!"

"There ain't no food, son," said Roscoe firmly. "Look again."

Jeb turned his eyes back to the floor of the boxcar. The blanket and its wondrous feast were gone. In their place was only bare earth.

"What's going on, Roscoe?" asked Jeb, feeling a little dizzy in the head. "I don't understand."

Roscoe glared at the hoboes who stood there with sly grins on their pale faces. "I'll explain it to you when we get back to camp. Right now, let's just back outta here right slow and easy."

"Don't go, Jeb," called Mickey as the two began to ease toward the open door. "Stay a spell and make yourself to home."

Jeb felt the urge to walk forward, but Roscoe's dark hand clamped down hard on the boy's shoulder, almost painfully so. "Don't look at his eyes," he told him sternly.

The farmboy did as Roscoe requested and, suddenly, felt the dazed sensation begin to fade. The feeling of warmth and welcome he had experienced a moment before began to turn into gradual alarm. Jeb began to realize that danger lurked there inside the boxcar, and the source of that menace was those gaunt, malnourished souls who stood before him.

It seemed like an eternity, but they finally made it outside. Frantically, Roscoe tugged at the old door and slid it back into place. Then he grabbed Jeb's hand and ran, pulling the boy behind him.

A moment later, they were across the tracks and back in the clearing. Sam stood there with an armload of wood and Buckshot sat on his haunches, whimpering like a frightened puppy. "What's going on?" asked Sam, dumping the wood in the center of the clearing. "Where'd ya'll run off to?"

"Over beyond that boxcar," said Roscoe. Nervously, he fumbled through his knapsack and found a box of sulfur matches. He lit one and tossed it on the kindling, but not before he separated a number of long sticks from the stack. Soon, the campfire was blazing strong and hot. "Ya'll sit over here on this side of the fire," he instructed. "Away from the railroad tracks."

Jeb and Sam complied. The farmboy sat down on a fallen log next to Roscoe and watched as the black man took out his pocket knife and began to whittle at the ends of the sticks. As the shavings fell away, Jeb saw that Roscoe was cutting them down to sharp points.

"What's wrong, Roscoe?" asked the boy. "What's got you so spooked?"

"It's them folks over yonder in that boxcar," he said. His eyes moved from his whittling to the darkness beyond the railroad tracks, and then back again.

"What about 'em?" Jeb wanted to know. "And what in tarnation are you doing with them sticks?"

Roscoe finished one and held it up. In less than a minute's time, he had whittled himself a stake with a wicked point. "This is one of the few things that'll stop their kind, Jeb."

"What do you mean . . . *their kind?*"

Jeb had never seen the old bluesman look so scared before. "The undead, son. That's what I mean."

The boy had to wrestle with the word for a while, before it suddenly dawned on him. He recalled the term being used in that Bela Lugosi movie he'd seen at the picture show in Nashville. "You mean *vampires?* Aw, come on, Roscoe, are you joshing me?"

"No, son," said Roscoe, his eyes bright with fear. "I ain't never been more serious in my life."

Jeb was about to ask another question, when Sam spoke

up. "Who's that there?" he asked, pointing past the flames of the fire.

The ten-year-old turned and looked toward the far side of the clearing. There, standing on the railroad tracks, was Mickey.

"Come on, Jeb," he called out, his voice echoing strangely in Jeb's ears, almost as if it were snaking its way clear down into his brain. Mickey extended a long-fingered hand. "Come on over and meet my family."

"Look away!" yelled Roscoe harshly. The Negro leapt to his feet and, clutching two sharpened sticks, held them together like a cross. "You'd best just git outta here!" he warned the red-haired boy. "Git back yonder to that boxcar where you belong and stay there!"

At the sight of the cross, Mickey's friendly face changed into a visage of hatred and disgust. With an angry cry, the hobo leapt off the tracks and back into the darkness.

"Hold these!" Roscoe told Sam, handing him the two crossed sticks. The bluesman rummaged through his pack and found a brown paper sack that held the spices he used for cooking. He found a small glass jar and, unscrewing the cap, made a complete circle of the campsite, sprinkling white powder upon the ground as he went.

"What's that?" asked Jeb. He kept looking toward the railroad tracks, but, so far, the tramp named Mickey had failed to reappear.

"Garlic powder," said Roscoe. "Hopefully, it'll keep 'em at bay."

After the circle of garlic had been completed and more crosses and stakes had been made, Roscoe seemed to calm down a bit. They fixed themselves a supper of hot beans and cornbread, but none of them enjoyed it. Their attention was directed more toward the darkness beyond the campsite, than their grumbling bellies.

Several times, Jeb glanced toward the train tracks and the dark grove of pines around them and swore that he saw pale faces staring at them from out of the night. Bloodless faces with ravenous eyes and teeth much longer than they should have been.

They made it through the night, restlessly, but with no further visits from those who dwelled across the tracks. Jeb and the others waited until the sun was well over the eastern hills, then ventured across the railroad tracks. They went around to the far side of the boxcar, but found the door closed. When Sam tried to pry the door open, they found that it wouldn't budge an inch. It was as if the rusted door hadn't been opened for countless years, let alone the previous evening.

Before they left, Jeb pressed his ear to the side of the boxcar. But, no matter how hard he listened, he could hear nothing inside. No stirring of sleeping forms, no snores or breathing. Just complete silence and nothing more.

As they gathered their gear and started north along the tracks, Jeb couldn't help but think that his senses had deceived him. He knew that Mickey and the others were there, behind that closed door. He could imagine them laying on their beds of earth, motionless and cold, waiting until the darkness of night arrived to awaken them once again.

Thirty-nine

Lynching Springs

Several miles further down the tracks, the forest began to thin out. Tall stands of pine, oak, and maple dwindled down to scrubby thickets of thistle and blackberry bramble. Soon, that too had petered out, giving way to weedy lots littered with broken bottles, tin cans, and the rusty hulls of abandoned automobiles. Little by little, they began to realize that they were leaving the rural wilderness and approaching a town of some sort.

"Do you think it's that place the Granny Woman warned us about?" asked Jeb. "Lynching Springs?"

"Probably so," replied Roscoe, looking a little uncomfortable. He looked up ahead and saw several houses and buildings standing a few yards east of the railroad tracks. "If it is, it'd be in our best interest to pass by unseen."

Jeb nodded. He and Roscoe left the bed of the railroad track and descended down a steep embankment that dropped sharply to the left. "Come on, Sam," called the boy.

The brawny farmer failed to hear Jeb at first. He simply stood there, staring up ahead at the little town that bordered the tracks. Jeb shook his head, feeling a bit uneasy. This wasn't the first time since they had awakened that morning that Sam had acted strangely. The boy had noticed his father behaving in a manner that was odd for the man. Sometimes he would pause and stand on the tracks for a moment or two, his eyes glazed, as if he were attempting to look *inward* rather than outward. Other times, Jeb would ask Sam a question and his father would answer him in a voice that was devoid of the naive, slow-witted tone Jeb had known for the past couple of years. It was then that the boy heard echoes of his true father in Sam's voice. Jeb had crossed his fingers during such instances, hoping that the poultice the Granny Woman had applied was finally doing its magic.

"Sam," he called again, trying not to talk too loudly. "Are you coming?"

The farmer pulled his gaze from the buildings and turned to the boy. "Uh, sure, Jeb," he said, looking a little confused. Soon, he was off the tracks and heading down the embankment to where they waited in the cover of a honeysuckle thicket below.

"Are you okay, Sam?" asked Roscoe, having also noticed the way the big man had been acting that day. "How's your head feeling?"

Sam shrugged his broad shoulders. "Fine, I reckon. It ain't hurting none, if that's what you mean."

"Good," said the bluesman. He motioned for them to follow him. "Let's be as quiet as a mouse when we pass by that place. If we draw somebody's attention, it might bring us some trouble we could do without . . . especially me."

Jeb nodded. He recalled what the Granny Woman had said about the folks of Lynching Springs and how they hated the sight of a black man. Jeb couldn't rightly understand why someone would feel such a way toward a person purely on account of their skin color, but he wasn't quite innocent enough to believe that such feelings didn't exist. He knew a few people back in Mangrum County who felt the same way and didn't care who knew it, either.

Quietly, they started through the underbrush, heading north

along the side of the embankment. When they had entered the town limits, they could see the peaks of roofs over the edge of the railroad tracks. Every now and then, they heard people's voices, mostly cussing and arguing, from somewhere just beyond. Midway through Lynching Springs, they heard the distant sounds of a roadhouse; the dirty laughter of liquored rednecks and the fast-paced music of a jukebox blaring a country-western tune about cheating men and wanton women.

It was at that moment that Roscoe raised his hand, motioning them to stop. "There's a creek down yonder," he said, pointing toward the base of a deep hollow. He shook the canteen that hung around his scrawny neck. It sounded as if it were less than a quarter full. "Ya'll stay put for a minute," he told them. "I'm gonna go down and fetch us some water."

"Hurry back," whispered Jeb. He didn't much like hiding there in the honeysuckle patch with the hostile burg of Lynching Springs no more than a stone's throw away.

"I will," promised the guitar-picker. Then, with Buckshot close behind him, Roscoe stepped into the thicket and was gone from sight.

Jeb and Sam sat there in the underbrush, waiting for their friend to complete his chore and return. The boy looked up at the sun and noted that it was well past one o'clock in the afternoon. When he turned back to Sam, he noticed that odd expression in the big man's eyes again. Sam looked distracted, as if the music from the honky-tonk overhead was triggering something deep down in his brain.

"What's wrong, Sam?" asked Jeb, his voice hopeful. "That music up yonder . . . does it remind you of anything?"

"Yeah," mumbled Sam with a frown. "But I can't rightly put my finger on it. Not yet anyway."

"Well, just keep listening," said Jeb. "Maybe it'll help you remember."

Jeb felt elated at the possibility of his father recalling

something from his past. But his excitement turned into alarm when Sam suddenly stood up, like something had kicked him in the seat of the pants. "Sit back down, Sam!" the boy warned. "Somebody might see us down here!"

But the farmer didn't seem to be listening. He ignored the boy and, turning toward the bank, began to climb his way back up to the railroad tracks. "What in tarnation are you *doing?*" asked the boy, his eyes wide. "Get back here, right now! Do you hear me?"

But if Sam did hear Jeb, he gave no indication of obeying the boy's order. As if in a daze, the big man reached the mound of the railroad bed and disappeared from view.

"Good Lord!" said Jeb, his heart beating a mile a minute. He debated on what to do about Sam's strange behavior. Should he follow his father, or get some help? It took him a moment, but he finally decided. He left the honeysuckle patch and headed down the slope of the hollow to find Roscoe.

Sam felt as if he were in the middle of a dream.

The weight and tightness of the bandages around his skull seemed to have disappeared. Instead, he felt strangely light-headed, as if he had ridden the roller coaster at the county fair one time too many.

Absently, he stepped off the railroad tracks and began to walk across a vacant lot choked with ragweed and spiny cockleburr. With each step he took, the music that had drawn him out into the open grew louder and more distinct. For some reason he couldn't fully comprehend, the shriek of a fiddle and the moan of a steel guitar stirred something inside him. He began to experience fragments of sights and sensations; the feeling of a cold mug in the palm of his hand, the warm comradery of old friends trading tall tales and dirty jokes over a poker table, and the sight of a pretty gal whirling across a dance floor, a smile on her face and a wink in her eye.

The music drew Sam like a magnet, past the edge of the lot and into a dusty dirt road that served as the town's main street. As he crossed over, he was oblivious to everything around him. All his attention was focused on one place and one place only; the building from where the music originated.

The honky-tonk was a low building of weathered boards and a tarpaper roof that had been patched many times over. Its outer walls were decorated with old tobacco and liquor advertisements and, above the front door, hung a crudely painted sign that proclaimed "THE DEVIL'S JUKEBOX."

Anyone in a sensible frame of mind would have avoided the roadhouse like the plague, but Sam felt no such hesitancy. Without a second thought, he walked up to the open door and stepped inside.

The barroom was dark and smoky, its only illumination coming from a few neon signs over the long bar at the far side. Sawdust covered the floor and the only furnishings in the place consisted of several tables with chairs, a pool table, and, of course, the jukebox in the corner. Its volume was cranked higher than any Sam had ever heard before, filling the room with foot-stomping music from ceiling to floor.

Dazed, Sam crossed the barroom and stopped in front of the bar. Standing on the other side was a short fellow with scars on his face and a maze of tattoos on his brawny arms. He spat into a shotglass, wiped it out with a filthy bar rag, and eyed the big farmer with a scowl. "What do ya want?" he snapped, not sounding the least bit friendly.

Sam thought for a moment. A thirst that he hadn't felt for a very long time suddenly hit him. "Beer," he said.

With a grumble, the bartender took a spotted mug from off a shelf behind him and positioned it beneath a tap. A minute later, he pushed the drink across the bar to the man.

There was more foamy head in the glass than beer, but Sam didn't seem to mind. He lifted the mug to his mouth and drank deeply.

"That'll be a quarter," said the bartender. But his customer failed to hear him. Sam turned around and studied the barroom with that dreamy look on his broad face.

His attention was drawn by three burly, rawboned fellows who congregated around the pool table with sticks in their calloused hands. They wore torn T-shirts and threadbare overalls, and smelled as if they hadn't taken a bath in a month of Sundays. They were an ugly bunch, to be sure. Their brows were bushy and low, and their stubbled jaws protruded slightly. Sam was instantly reminded of apes he had seen at the fair; the kind that grunted within their wire cages, scratching themselves and picking the lice from each other's fur.

But that wasn't the only thing that Sam noticed. It was a flag that hung on the wall on the far side of the billiard table that sent a strange jolt of contempt through the big farmer. It was a brilliant red flag with a white circle smack dab in the center. And, inside that circle, was a crooked black cross; the familiar symbol of the Nazi swastika.

Suddenly, the pleasant feeling that had engulfed Sam was gone. In its place boiled a rage that started at the base of his brain and burned, slowly, toward the back of his eyes. His knuckles tightened around the handle of the beer mug as he stood there for a long moment, listening to the talk being bantered about at the far side of the room.

"Yes, sir, I'm sorry them Krauts lost the War," said a lumbering fellow with mats of hair on his long arms and a matchstick clinched between half-rotten teeth. "They sure could've taught us a few things over here in the States. Could've took control and set things straight."

"You're right, Travis," agreed the one who leaned over the

table, knocking balls into pockets with the end of his stick. "Take them there concentration camps for instance. Why they killed 'em millions upon millions of jew-boys in just the matter of a year or two. Gassed 'em right good and baked 'em in ovens till they were no more'n dust. Some of 'em they skinned and made into lampshades and such."

"Aw, go on!" scoffed a shorter fellow with a bum eye and a slight hump in his back. "They didn't do nothing of the sort!"

"Sure they did, Jimmy," said the one named Travis. "Homer and me, we were over there in the thick of it all. That's where we got those dishonorable discharges we've got hanging on our walls at home. We wouldn't fight the Krauts along with the other doughboys. We just couldn't bring ourselves to go against folks who believed in the same things we do right here in Fear County. So they booted us out, lickity-split."

"You know," said Homer, "Sometimes I wish I'd stayed over there a while longer and studied their ways of killing. Then maybe we could've done the same thing over here. Do you know how much better life would be if we'd rid ourselves of all the niggers hereabouts, just like the German's did the Jews? That ol' Adolf Hitler was a genius, I tell you. A frigging genius!"

Suddenly, the rage that mounted within Sam Sweeny finally reached its pinnacle. He took a long draw on the beer and set it down on an empty table. Then he took a few steps forward and opened his mouth. The single word that he uttered was one that hadn't crossed his lips for a very long time, but it summed up his opinion of the rednecks' conversation rather bluntly.

"Bullshit," he said.

Travis, Homer, and Jimmy looked up from their pool game, as if they hadn't noticed the man until that very moment. Homer narrowed his eyes slightly. "What did you say?"

"I said that's a load of bullshit," repeated Sam. He took a couple more steps closer, clenching and unclenching his ham-sized fists. "Hitler wasn't nothing but a sick-minded son-of-a-bitch with a lot of hatred in his soul. I was over there, the same as you. But what I saw was evil, pure and simple. Wasn't no good to it a'tall."

Travis laid his pool cue down and slowly started around the table. "Who the hell do you think you are, coming in here and talking such a way?"

"Yeah," said the one named Jimmy. "It's clear that you ain't from Fear County. Just where are you from, anyhow?"

Sam thought for a moment, his thoughts sluggishly rising to the surface like debris from the bottom of a muddy pool. "Mangrum County," he finally said.

"Hah!" laughed Homer, his eyes turning mean. "I should've known. Ain't nothing over in Mangrum County but queers and nigger-lovers. Which one are you, sodbuster? Or are you both?"

Sam said nothing in reply. He simply stood there, anger boiling in his brain as the three men crossed the barroom and began to circle him. Homer and Travis had laid down their pool sticks, but one-eyed Jimmy still had his fisted in his right hand.

"You didn't answer my question, boy!" growled Homer. Raw hatred burned in the redneck's eyes; a hatred as hot as the furnaces of Auschwitz and Treblinka.

"Maybe the fella didn't hear you," said Travis. "Be kinda hard, what with all that shit wrapped around his head."

"Yeah," said Homer. He stepped up to Sam and regarded the bandages around the farmer's head. "Maybe you're right. I reckon I'll just have to unwind this thing and see if I can't pound some sense into this sodbuster's thick head." Then the redneck reached out with his right hand, ready to rip the first strand of cloth away.

His fingers never quite reached their destination, though. When they were scarcely an inch away, Sam's rage could be contained no longer. The farmer grabbed Homer by the wrist and began to squeeze. The redneck tried to break free from the grasp that held him, but it was as unyielding as a shop vise. Then a cruel grin crossed Sam's broad face and, with a wrenching twist to the side, he broke the bones of Homer's wrist with a crack as loud as a gunshot.

Abruptly, the contempt in Homer's eyes gave way to agony and fear. He opened his mouth to scream, but Sam's other fist went to work, delivering an uppercut underneath the redneck's stubbled jaw. The blow slammed Homer's tobacco-stained teeth together, cutting off his painful cry, as well as the tip of his tongue.

Sam released the redneck and watched him drop, groaning and moaning, to the sawdust floor of the Devil's Jukebox. He turned just as Jimmy swung his pool cue. Sam dodged the stick, then reached out and wrenched it from Jimmy's hands. With an angry growl, the big farmer took the stick in both hands and snapped it across his knee as if it were no more than a strand of milkweed. Then, flinging the shattered ends of the cue away, he went for Jimmy. He grabbed up a handful of the man's shirtfront, as well as the crotch of his overalls, and hoisted him high over his head. Jimmy lost his gumption and began to plead for Sam to let him down. A second later, the farmer did just that. With a strength that would have shamed Hercules, Sam tossed the hunch-backed cracker completely across the barroom. Jimmy landed smack dab in the front of the jukebox, his head shattering the glass and joining the machinery and records that occupied its lighted dome.

Travis came next. Sam whirled as he heard the third man's

footsteps coming up behind him fast. He saw a glint of honed steel in the redneck's hand and knew that he'd pulled a knife from his back pocket. For one instant, panic froze Sam in his tracks. But then he recalled something he'd been taught in the army, something he had thought was long since forgotten. As Travis slashed out, aiming for his belly, Sam sidestepped the pig-sticker and grabbed the man's wrist. He jabbed his thumb in the soft underbelly of Travis's wrist and his fingers popped open, pretty as you please. The knife fell away, spinning to the sawdust floor and sticking there, like in a game of mumbly-peg.

The last remaining pool-player looked into the farmer's wild eyes and knew that he had made a terrible mistake. He tried to run, but Sam had a hold of his arm and he wasn't about to let go. In desperation, Travis kicked out, aiming the toe of his boot for the farmer's balls. Again, Sam blocked the attack and, in turn, delivered a devastating assault of his own. Time after time, Sam's fist crashed into Travis's head, rocking it back and forth on his unwashed neck. Soon, there wasn't much left of Travis's face except for bruises, swollen eyes, and split lips. Finally, the farmer seemed to run out of steam. He let go of the redneck's wrist and let him fall to the floor next to Homer.

The fight over, Sam stood there for a long moment, breathing heavily. A peculiar sensation filled his head and the room began to spin around him. The lightness he had felt before entering the honky-tonk was gone now. The bandages around his head seemed to grow ten-times heavier than they had before and he found that he could hardly keep his head up.

Dazed, he dropped to his knees and closed his eyes. Deep down at the back of his skull, a pain began to form. It grew larger and more intense as it filled his brain and pressed on the back of his eyeballs. He cried out and clamped his hands around the sides of his head, as if trying to push the hurt

back to where it originated. But it did no good. It just kept
on mounting, growing more intense with each beat of his
heart.

Sam was so preoccupied with the pain in his head, that
he didn't hear the fall of steady footsteps approaching him
from behind. Neither did he see the tattooed bartender with
a tire iron clutched in his right hand, ready to bring it down
and lay the back of the farmer's skull wide open.

But someone else did notice.

Just as the bartender was about to bring the club down
and send Sam's brains splattering across the sawdust floor,
he heard a brittle click. The owner of the roadhouse knew
that noise by heart. It was the sound of a gun's hammer
being pulled to full cock.

"You'd best drop that jack handle, before I drop you,"
warned a voice from the front door.

The bartender did as he was told. The tire iron slid from
his grasp and struck the sawdust floor with a muted clang.
When he gathered the nerve to turn and look at the one who
had the drop on him, he was shocked to find that it was a
lanky black man wearing thick spectacles and a dusty fedora
hat. In the Negro's hand was a long-barreled Colt .45.

"You got some nerve, nigger!" said the bartender, his
scarred face growing beet red with rage. "Pulling a pistol
on a white man . . . and right here in Lynching Springs to
boot! You'll pay dearly for that, I do declare!"

"Why don't you just shut up," said Roscoe as he crossed
the barroom and came within a few feet of the quaking bar-
keep.

"The hell I will!" spat the man. "Just one whistle from
me and everyone in town'll be here. And then you and that
sodbuster'll wish you'd never been born!"

The bartender was raising two fingers to his mouth, intending to alert the other citizens of Lynching Springs with an ear-piercing whistle, when Roscoe acted. He eased down the peacemaker's hammer, then, raising the gun high, brought the barrel down hard. It hit the bartender's skull with a loud crack, splitting his scalp and bringing blood. The burly man dropped like a sack of potatoes, knocking over a bar table and a couple of chairs as he went.

As soon as the bartender hit the floor, Jeb and Buckshot came through the door. They ran across the barroom, reaching the farmer's kneeling form a second later. "Sam?" asked Jeb frantically. "What's wrong? Did they hurt you?"

Sam found the wits to shake his head "no." He tried to mouth words to express the agony in his head, but he couldn't. He simply stared at the boy helplessly, his palms pressing firmly against his bandaged temples.

"I'm sorry, Sam," said Jeb. "I don't know what to do for you." Then he looked closer at the farmer's tormented eyes and something odd struck him about them. They no longer held that dull-witted expression that had possessed Sam Sweeny's eyes for the past two years. No, that veil almost seemed to be lifting, if only gradually.

"Roscoe!" screamed Jeb excitedly. "Come quick!"

A moment later, the bluesman was crouching next to the boy and his dog. "What is it, boy?"

"Take a look at his eyes, Roscoe!" said Jeb with a grin. "He's coming back. I just know he is."

Roscoe stared into the big man's eyes and, suddenly, knew that the boy was right. He could detect a trace of adult intelligence beyond the man's childlike innocence. He grasped Sam's shoulders in his dark hands and shook him gently. "Sam, this is Roscoe Ledbetter talking. Can you hear me?"

Slowly, the big man nodded his bandaged head.

Roscoe decided to go a step further. "Listen to me, Sam.

Do you know who I am? I mean *really* know? Remember how you used to come around and shake my hand and fill me in on all the gab and gossip whenever I first rolled into Pikesville? Remember how I'd lend you my guitar and you'd pick that thing and sing long and loud like ol' Roy Acuff himself?"

Sam stared back at the black man, his eyes searching and his face screwed into a mask of pure frustration. Finally, he shook his head, unable to dredge the memory of Roscoe from the deepest recesses of his injured mind.

"You give it a try, Jeb," said Roscoe.

Eagerly, Jeb crouched in front of Sam and gently took one of the farmer's huge hands in his own. "Papa?" he asked, his voice trembling. "Papa, it's me . . . Jeb. You remember me, don't you? I'm Jeb . . . your boy."

Sam studied the boy's face as if it were some torturous mystery he was unable to solve. His lips trembled as his eyes grew sharper, registering the faintest gleam of recognition. "Jeb?" he asked in a whisper.

Jeb's heart soared. "That's right! It's me . . . Jeb! Remember? You used to take me and Grandma to town on a Saturday morning and you'd buy me an ice cream or an RC and a moonpie at the store. Then later that night, after we'd listen to the Grand Ole Opry on the radio, we'd take ol' Buckshot here and go coonhunting till early the next morning. We'd drag in, dog-tired, an hour or so before churchtime and Grandma would be madder than a hornet. You remember that, don't you?"

Jeb held his breath and watched as Sam's eyes widened a bit and a faint smile came to his face. Then, an instant later, that expression was gone. The farmer's eyes clenched tightly shut as a new spasm of pain racked his brain. When he opened them again, that tiny hint of dawning recognition was nowhere to be seen.

"No!" yelled Jeb, clutching his father's hand tightly. Don't go! Don't leave me again! Please, Papa!" Tears loomed in the boy's eyes and rolled down his freckled cheeks.

Roscoe laid a hand on the boy's shoulder. "I'm sorry, Jeb."

"But it almost happened, didn't it?" he asked. "He almost came back."

The bluesman nodded. "Yes, son . . . almost."

Jeb tried to hide his dejection. "It could still work, though, couldn't it? The Granny Woman's magic?"

"There is a chance, I reckon," allowed Roscoe, although he seemed doubtful.

A moment later, the seizure Sam had suffered seemed to pass. His face regained its normal color and the pain in his features seemed to slowly subside. It wasn't long before that peaceful, slightly befuddled expression of his was back in place.

"What's wrong, Jeb?" Sam asked when he saw the tears trickling down the boy's face. "Whatcha crying for?"

Jeb quickly wiped the wetness away with the back of his hand and tried to smile. "Nothing," he said. "Wasn't nothing 'tall."

They helped Sam to his feet. He was dusting the sawdust off the knees of his britches, when he suddenly noticed those who lay on the floor around them. Jimmy, Travis, and the bartender were all out cold, while poor Homer was still drawn up into a ball, clutching his shattered wrist and moaning.

"What happened here?" asked Sam curiously.

"There was a fight," Roscoe told him.

"But who won?"

Roscoe and Jeb looked uneasily at one another. "I ain't sure anybody did," the boy finally said.

The bluesman stared down at the revolver he still held in

his hand, then stuck it back in Sam's duffle bag, which they'd brought along with the guitar and knapsack. "I believe we'd best get back over to them railroad tracks and hightail it outta this town," he suggested. "'Cause, sooner or later, one of these gentlemen are gonna wake up and, when they do, all hell's gonna break loose. They'll be coming after us like a pack of bloodhounds."

Carefully, they left the Devil's Jukebox through the front door. Just as before, the town's main street was completely deserted. Fortunately, they made it across the road and the vacant lot unseen.

Once they hit the railroad tracks, they didn't stop walking. It wasn't very long before they were on their way, leaving the evil honky-tonk and the town of Lynching Springs behind.

Forty

The Ghost Train

Afternoon had passed and evening was upon them when they reached the trestle that spanned the winding channel of Beelzebub Creek.

After leaving the roadhouse, they had covered twice as much ground as normal, traveling three or four miles in only a few hours time. Their urgency was lost on Sam, but Jeb and Roscoe were aware of the potential for disaster that lay behind them. The Negro most of all seemed on edge and anxious to put as many miles as possible between himself and Lynching Springs.

But, as the sky began to darken and the shadows deepened in the forest on both sides of the tracks, it appeared as though their fears might be pointless. Either the men at the beer joint had been unsure of which direction Roscoe and the others were heading, or, for some reason, they had decided their assailants weren't worth the fuss and bother of tracking down. The latter seemed unlikely, given the threat made by the bartender just before Roscoe had knocked him senseless.

Jeb, on the other hand, was more concerned with what had happened with his father than anything else. He still felt let down by the apparent failure of the Granny Woman's poultice. For one brief moment, Jeb had been certain that

Sam Sweeny was on the verge of returning, just as strong-willed and intelligent as he had been before the War. But that opportunity seemingly had been lost and Jeb wasn't at all sure that it would ever come back. Sam had asked if he could remove the smelly poultice, but Jeb had denied his wish, thinking maybe there might be another chance. Secretly, the boy knew he was clutching at straws. If the Granny Woman's medicine was going to work, it would have worked its wonders there in the barroom of the Devil's Jukebox.

They reached the southern end of the bridge just as the last rays of day painted the sky a brilliant mixture of violet, gold, and crimson. The sunset cast an eerie light over them, increasing their unease even more.

Roscoe stopped in the middle of the tracks, bracing his hands on his knees and breathing hard. "We're gonna have to set up camp as soon as we reach the other side," he told them. "I don't think I could go much further."

"Do you think we'll be safe?" asked Jeb, looking back at the dark stretch of tracks behind them.

"I think so," said Roscoe. "I don't rightly know how we did it, but it looks like we managed to shake that trash. Hopefully, we'll be rid of 'em entirely, once we're on the other side."

They approached the edge of the bridge and peered off the bluff on the southern side. The murky waters of Beelzebub Creek lay twenty feet below, peppered with boulders and dead logs that protruded partly from the muddy surface. If someone were to fall off the bridge—or were forced to jump for some reason—they had a better chance of hitting a rock or stump than actual water.

Roscoe gauged the distance between one side to the other. A good two hundred feet of bridge lay between them and the opposite bank. That seemed to be a short distance, considering that the bridge crossing the Cumberland River back

in Mangrum County was eight hundred or more feet in
length. But there in a place like Fear County, even the short-
est of distances could seem like a trip through eternity.

"Well, we'd best get to it before it gets too dark to see
where we're going," said Roscoe. "And watch your step. The
tracks are on sturdy timber, but between the ties there's nothing but open air. If you don't look where you're going, you
could end up down in that creek with a broken leg or worse."

"What about Buckshot?" asked Jeb. "How's he gonna get
across?"

"I reckon I'll just have to tote him on my shoulders, like
I did back at that creek near the Indian cave," said Sam.

Jeb eyed the farmer peculiarly. It was odd that Sam would
remember that at all. Normally, his father had a difficult time
remembering events that happened from one hour to the next,
let alone from one day to another.

They waited until Sam had slung the squirming dog around
his broad shoulders. Then, one by one, they started across
the bridge, stepping from one railroad tie to the next. It was
tedious, especially for Jeb, since the space between each tie
was a good two feet. Sam and Roscoe seemed to make the
distance with little trouble at all, but Jeb sometimes felt as
if he would split completely in half just trying to step across.

Carefully, they made their way toward the northern end of
the trestle. When they were a fourth of the way across, the
sunset reached its end and darkness began to close in around
them. It grew increasingly difficult to tell the ties from the
open air that lay in between. "Ya'll take your time," called
Roscoe, who was ahead of the rest. "Wouldn't wanna lose
nobody before we get there."

Several more minutes passed. The creek below them turned
as black as the sky overhead. They were halfway across the
bridge, when Buckshot suddenly perked his ears and began
to whine.

"Don't worry, boy," Sam whispered soothingly. "We'll be there directly."

Roscoe suddenly stopped and turned around. "No," he said. "That ain't what's got him riled. It's something else."

"What?" asked Jeb. He stood atop a railroad tie, trying to keep his balance.

"I ain't sure yet." The bluesman stood stone still for a long moment, then held up a hand that was barely visible in the darkening dusk. "Listen," he said.

Jeb strained his ears. At first, he heard nothing but the rush of the creek below. Then, far off to the south, echoed a sound so soft that it was almost nonexistent; a low moan that lasted for only a few seconds, then stopped.

"It's the wind, ain't it?" asked the boy.

Even in the darkness, Roscoe's eyes looked whiter and wider than usual. "No, I don't believe so," he said. "Look yonder."

Carefully, Jeb turned and stared back down the tracks. Far off, nearly a mile away, gleamed a single light. But it was no ordinary light. It wasn't white, but an odd blue that pulsed and shimmered like sunlight reflecting on a pool of water. He watched it for a moment before he realized that the tiny circle of light was growing gradually *larger.* Whatever it was, it was getting closer.

Then the strange sound came again, a little clearer than before. It was then that they all recognized it for what it truly was.

It was the high-pitched shriek of a train whistle, heralding its swift approach.

Jeb suddenly turned cold. "It's the train," he said. "The ghost train!"

"Over to the far side of the bridge!" yelled Roscoe. "Quick!"

One tie at a time, they began their frantic journey to the

other side of the Beelzebub Creek bridge. Jeb nearly fell through several times, for the dusk had darkened so deeply that it was next to impossible to see where he was going.

Behind them, the shrill cry of the whistle was joined by the chugging roar of a coal-driven engine pushed to the very brink of its endurance. Beneath their feet, the bridge began to tremble ever so slightly.

"It's coming for us!" yelled Sam. "We gotta get across!"

"Just be careful!" warned Roscoe. "You could end up killing yourself before it even gets here!"

Jeb hopped from one tie to the next, nearly losing his footing as he went. He looked ahead and barely made out the end of the bridge, fifty feet away. If he had been on solid ground, the farmboy could have covered that distance in a matter of seconds. But, on the treacherous trestle, it was impossible to apply such speed. Even one misstep could turn out to be a fatal one.

Jeb was ten feet closer, when the trembling of the bridge suddenly turned into a bone-jarring shake. The boy's ears began to roar and he realized that it came from some external source, rather than the pounding of his heart. He was turning to look behind him, when the whistle screamed loudly, and not from very far away. In fact, it sounded as if the train had already mounted the southern end of the trestle.

He resisted the urge to look and concentrated on safely reaching the far side. Roscoe, Sam, and Buckshot had already made it there. They stood on the bluff, waving and calling out to him.

"You're almost there, boy!" yelled Roscoe. "Just thirty more feet and you'll be home free!"

"You can do it, Jeb!" cheered Sam. "Just take it one step at a time!"

Jeb decided to follow Sam's advice. He stared down at the tracks at his feet and was suddenly amazed that he could see them. And that wasn't all. Jeb could see his shadow, too, stretching long and thin to the northern end of the bridge. At first, he was comforted by the sudden illumination. But then, in one horrifying instant, he realized where the light was originating from.

Even though he was afraid to, Jeb looked over his shoulder.

No more than a hundred and fifty feet away, was the ghost train. It was a sight both magnificent and terrifying; a fire-breathing locomotive etched in black shadow and lightning blue. From the top of its smoking stack to the wicked tip of its iron cow-catcher, the engine was an impressive fifteen feet tall. And, beyond the Cyclops eye of a headlight, Jeb could see the cab of the runaway train. It was the apparition he saw there that froze him in his tracks, rather than the locomotive itself.

For, standing at the helm of that ghostly engine, was the glowing form of a tall, bearded man with the fire of pure lunacy burning in his eyes. Jeb knew him at once, although the man had lived a good seventy years before the boy had even been born.

It was the spectre of Jeremiah Gallow, driving himself and a hundred others to their doom.

Jeb fought his fearful paralysis and turned back to the bridge in front of him. He leapt, taking two ties in a single bound. Jeb knew that it was only a matter of seconds before the train caught up with him. He recalled the ghostly beast on the wall of the Indian cave and the way he had willed it away. But he knew willpower would do nothing to banish this apparition. There was too much tragedy, too much needless death and suffering powering the spectral vehicle that bore down on him. There simply was no stopping such a hellish machine.

"Come on, Jeb!" urged Roscoe. "Just twenty feet more!"

Jeb jumped twice, spanning two ties with each leap. The bridge beneath him was shaking so badly that he could hardly keep his balance. He looked ahead. A dozen feet was all that lay between him and his friends.

"You're almost there!" called Sam, but his voice was nearly lost amid the deafening roar of the engine.

Five more ties stretched between himself and safety. He leaped.

The cackle of the crazed engineer sounded no more than fifty feet behind him.

Three more ties.

Jeb heard the collective screams of a hundred damned souls, crying out for a salvation they knew would never come in time.

One more tie.

The headlight of the locomotive burned like a comet scarcely twenty feet away, bathing him with blinding blue light.

He knew he had only a few seconds left to act. Although his legs quivered with fright and exhaustion, he summoned the strength to jump one last time. He crouched, threw his weight forward, and prayed for solid ground.

Suddenly, all Jeb Sweeny knew was light, noise, and the scorched stench of metal heated far past its limits. He clenched his eyes shut and waited for the cow-catcher to drag him underneath the locomotive's grinding wheels.

But it didn't happen. A moment before his doom was sealed, Jeb felt a strong hand close around his wrist and he was yanked swiftly to the side. When he opened his eyes, he found himself in Sam's brawny arms, a good six feet from the bed of steel rails and hewn ties.

They turned and watched the ghost train as it reached the northern end of the trestle. Like a beast straight from Hades, it roared past them in a dizzy blur of billowing black smoke and sparkling electricity. Jeb caught a glimpse of a long, flatbed car hooked directly behind the locomotive. Perched upon that car was the helpless team of laborers who had unknowingly slaved with pick and hammer to pave their way to death. Their faces were pale with terror and their eyes pleaded for a deliverance that was beyond their grasp. At that moment, Jeb felt a tremendous sadness engulf him. He felt sorry for those men who had died at the hand of Jeremiah Gallow so many years ago.

Then, a hundred feet further on, the apparition came to its climactic conclusion. The tracks abruptly came to an end, but the train kept right on going. Jeb watched as the wheels dug deeply into soft earth and the cars began to fishtail and tumble. Death screams merged with the tortured shriek of mangled steel. Then, with a gradual fading of light, it was over. Darkness reigned once more and the night was full of silence.

Stunned, Jeb, Sam, and Roscoe stared at the spot for a long moment, the noise and fury of the derailment still lingering in their ears. Then Roscoe started forward. "Come on," he said. "Let's take a look."

"Are you sure it's safe?" asked Sam, returning Jeb to his feet.

The black man nodded. "It's over now."

Together, they made their way to the end of the railroad tracks. Two huge ruts the size of drainage ditches furrowed the earth and, beyond them, lay the rusted hulls of old railroad cars covered with decades of honeysuckle and wild kudzu. Further on lay the ruins of the locomotive and its flatbed, which had been melded into a twisted mass of pig iron and steel. And, in the gloom, they could barely make out the pale gleam of sun-bleached bones scattered here and there; the remnants of victims long since dead and forgotten.

"It's a shame, ain't it?" asked Jeb. "A graveyard worth of death, all in one spot."

Roscoe shuddered in spite of himself. "Come on. Let's find a place to camp for the night."

Jeb looked back at the opposite side of the Beelzebub Creek bridge. "But what about them folks back in Lynching Springs?"

"Don't worry about them," assured the bluesman. "Nobody in their right mind would cross that bridge in the dead of night. No, sir, it'd be flat-out suicide for sure."

They walked back to the end of the bridge and gathered up their gear. Then they made their way into the woods, using the flashlight to search for a suitable place to bed down for the night.

Forty-one

Farewell to a Friend

They made their camp in a clearing a few yards east of the railroad tracks. Tall oaks and heavy thicket enclosed the clearing on all sides. Jeb didn't mind the isolation, though. The image of that ghost train was still fresh in his mind and at least the site of the tragedy couldn't be seen from where they chose to settle down for the night.

Jeb and Sam gathered wood and built a fire, while Roscoe dug a big can of pork and beans out of his knapsack and began to open it with his Swiss Army knife.

As he and Sam lit the mound of twigs and branches, Jeb looked over at the lanky bluesman. Roscoe had been acting oddly ever since they'd left the Devil's Jukebox. He seemed jumpy and nervous, like Lucifer himself was dogging his heels. Jeb didn't rightly understand what had taken place between Sam and those rednecks at the honky-tonk, but Roscoe seemed to know. The black man seemed to know their kind well and, although he acted otherwise, seemed to fear them and the hatred they carried around inside.

The fire was ablaze and Roscoe was emptying the beans into an iron skillet, when the Negro paused for a long moment. His eyes narrowed a little behind his thick-lensed glasses. He froze as still as a statue, scarcely drawing a breath of air for a second or two.

"What's wrong?" asked Jeb.

Roscoe failed to answer the boy at first. Then he shook his head. "Weren't nothing," he finally said. "Thought I heard something, that's all."

The bluesman set the skillet on top of the fire and let the beans simmer. A minute hadn't passed, when that strange look crossed Roscoe's face again. "Jeb?" he said.

"Yes, sir?"

"Why don't you and Sam go down yonder to the creek and fill up this canteen here with water." He picked up the canteen and tossed it to the boy.

Jeb shook the container and frowned. "But it's still more'n half full."

"Then fill it up all the way," said Roscoe. "Don't argue with me now. Ya'll go on down to the creek . . . and take Buckshot with you."

A little puzzled, Jeb stood up and motioned for Sam and the bluetick to follow. "We'll be back in a minute."

"Just take your time," said Roscoe. "It'll take a while for these beans to cook."

Taking the flashlight, they left the bluesman beside the fire and picked their way through the woods until they reached the northern bank of Beelzebub Creek. Jeb searched until he found a pathway that led to the stream below. The boy left Sam and Buckshot standing at the edge of the bluff, while he carefully made his way down. As he went, Jeb ignored the dark framework of the train trestle, not wanting to dwell on the close call he had experienced there only a short time ago.

Jeb reached the bottom and filled the canteen clear to the spout, even though the water was a little too muddy for his taste. On his way back up, he thought he heard the faint sound of voices, although he couldn't tell where they originated from or exactly what they were saying. He also swore that he heard the soft snort of a horse or two.

When he finally reached the top of the bluff, Sam met him there, his face full of worry. "Jeb, I heard somebody talking," he whispered. "I think they're back yonder in the clearing with Roscoe."

Jeb's heart began to pound. "Let's go see," he said. "But be quiet."

They were making their way silently through the woods, when the drumming of horse hooves sounded from up ahead. Gradually, they faded, crossing the railroad tracks and heading toward the west.

A minute later, they reached the clearing. It was empty. The skillet was smoking on the campfire and the contents of Roscoe's knapsack were scattered across the ground. The black man was nowhere to be found.

Stunned, Jeb walked over to an object laying at the far edge of the clearing. It was Roscoe's guitar. The neck of the Fender had been broken completely off and its body was caved in, as if by the stomp of a heavy boot.

"Look here, Jeb," called Sam.

The boy went to where the farmer crouched. He directed the beam of the flashlight at the ground and picked out a number of deep horseshoe tracks. "Looks like it was three or four men on horses," he said. "And they took Roscoe with 'em."

"But where'd they go?" asked Sam.

Frantically, the boy peered through the dense woods. At first, he saw nothing but pitch darkness. Then, to the west, he made out the distant flicker of torches.

"Where's the duffle bag?" he asked, looking around in alarm.

"I set it against that tree over yonder," said Sam.

Jeb breathed easier when he saw the olive drab bag leaning

gainst the base of a black oak tree. Apparently, the intruders
ad overlooked it during their raid of the campsite. Jeb ran
> the bag and quickly loosened its drawstrings. He groped
1rough its contents, past the clothing and the pint mason jar
ontaining the snake-critter egg. Finally, he found what he
`as looking for.

The ten-year-old withdrew the Colt .45 and checked its
ylinder. The revolver was fully loaded.

"What are you gonna do with that?" asked Sam.

"I don't know," said the boy truthfully. "But I can't let
:m hurt Roscoe. I just can't."

Sam stared at the tow-headed boy, then nodded in under-
:anding. Together, they left the clearing and headed west.

They left the forest, crossed the railroad tracks, then en-
:red the heavy woods on the other side, hearing a strange
racking sound as they went. They didn't have to walk far
ntil they found the spot they were looking for. It was a
learing much larger than the one they had just left, and in
s very center stood a lightning-struck oak that stood a good
1irty or forty feet in height.

Jeb crouched in the thicket at the edge of the clearing, the
un in his hand feeling incredibly heavy. His heart beat even
1ster than before and every last drop of spit dried up in his
1outh as he watched what was taking place only a few yards
way.

Three men in white robes and hoods sat on the backs of
>al-black horses. One held only a torch in one hand, while
1e other two sported both torches and double-barreled shot-
uns. Another man—who was dressed in the same garb as
1e others—stood in the clearing with a long whip of braided
:ather in his right hand. At first the eyeholes of their linen
1asks seemed dark and empty. Then the light of the torches
:vealed the cruel glint of pure hatred that lurked within
1ose shadowy pits.

Jeb then turned his eyes to the tree and the horse tha
stood next to it. On the back of the black gelding sat Rosco
Ledbetter. It hurt the boy to even look at the old bluesman
Roscoe had been stripped from the waist up, bound with hi
hands behind his back, and sat in the saddle. Blood bathe
his back and Jeb could see the pink of raw flesh peekin
from long slashes in the Negro's black skin. Jeb recalled th
brittle cracks they had heard and suddenly knew they ha
been the ugly slap of the bullwhip against Roscoe's bar
back.

But that wasn't the thing that scared Jeb the most. Rathe
it was the noose of a rope that had been slipped around th
black man's neck that sent a jolt of horror through th
farmboy. A rope that had been slung over the lowest lim
of the dead oak, a good fifteen feet up.

"Thought you could outsmart us, didn't you, nigger?"
asked the one with the whip. Jeb instantly recognized th
voice as belonging to the bartender at the Devil's Jukebox
"Thought you could brain me with that hogleg Colt an
make it across that railroad bridge scott free! Well, we sur
fooled you, didn't we? Didn't know there was another bridg
that crossed the creek a mile or so to the east. One that ou
horses could cross without falling through."

Roscoe said nothing in reply. He simply glared down a
the man with the whip, his eyes full of contempt.

"Now you tell us again!" said the rider who held only
torch, his other hand cinched up in bandages. "Where's tha
damned sodbuster who crippled me? Tell me, or I swear I'
stick this here torch to your pecker and burn it clean off!'

Jeb looked over his shoulder at Sam. The big farmer stare
at the man on the horse, that familiar spark of mountin
anger growing in his eyes. Jeb knew it was only a matter o
time before Sam lost his temper and stepped into the clearin
to confront the clan of nightriders.

He turned his attention back to what was taking place beneath the tree. "That won't do no good," came the voice of the one named Travis. "That lashing Joe gave him would've done the trick if'n he was gonna talk. No, he's too damned stubborn to give up his buddy. Either that or too stupid."

"Then I reckon we're just wasting our time here," said Joe the bartender. "Goodbye, nigger," he said, bringing his open palm back over his shoulder. "And good riddance!"

Suddenly, Jeb knew what the man was about to do. A great fear welled up inside him and, without a second thought, he stepped out of the thicket. "No!" he scream at the top of his lungs.

But he was too late. The man slapped the horse sharply on the flank of its rump, sending the animal lurching forward with a startled whinny. Unfortunately, Roscoe stayed precisely where he was. The rope grew taut and the noose tightened round the Negro's neck. As the horse fled to the far side of the clearing, Roscoe dropped through open air for a second, then halted with an abrupt jerk. The bluesman strangled and kicked, his feet a good four feet from the ground.

At first, Jeb could only stand there and stare. Then an anger he never knew he had inside him began to fill his brain. "You lousy son-of-a-bitch!" he screamed. He cocked the hammer of the Colt back with both thumbs, then lifted the big gun at armslength.

The one named Joe whirled and, seeing the boy standing across the clearing, brandished his whip and took a step forward. He didn't take another. There came a thunderous boom and a cloud of gunsmoke left the muzzle of the .45 revolver. The bartender staggered back a few feet, then dumbly looked down at his chest. There was a hole square in the center of his breastbone. Amazed, he watched as a crimson stain began to spread, dying his white robe bright red.

"Oh shit," he muttered softly. "I've been shot."

Jeb turned to a rider who was reining his horse around. The man lowered his shotgun, aiming both barrels at the ten-year-old. Nervously, the boy attempted to cock the six-shooter again, but his hands were drenched with sweat and his thumbs slipped off the spur of the hammer. Jeb stared into the dark muzzles of the twelve-gauge. It was like looking Death square in the face.

Right when he was certain the barrels would go off, blowing him to kingdom come, something whistled over his head. It was a rock the size of a baseball. The stone struck the rider in the side of the skull, rocking him back in his saddle. The shotgun wavered from its aim and discharged, sending twin loads of double-aught buck flying skyward. Another rock, smaller than the one before, cracked the man across his elbow and he lost hold of the smoking scattergun. It spun from his grasp and hit the ground with a clank.

Jeb looked around to see Sam standing there, holding another rock in his pitching hand, ready to let loose once more.

The farmboy turned back to find the other armed rider preparing to finish the job his buddy had failed at. He tossed down the torch and was bringing the butt of his shotgun to his shoulder, when Jeb's thumbs finally found their grip. He cocked the gun and fired almost as quickly. The barrel was aimed at the ground, but, fortunately, it did the trick. The .45 slug kicked up dirt at the horse's feet, causing it to buck wildly. The rider had to discard his gun just to keep hold of the reins. Another shot from the Colt sent the skittish horse bolting for the dark forest, taking its frightened passenger with it.

"Let's get the hell outta here before that young' un shoots us all!" yelled the one with the bandaged hand.

"I've been shot!" moaned the bartender, staggering around and clutching his bleeding chest. "The little bastard's done killed me."

The one named Homer galloped over and held out his good arm. "Aw, quit your belly-aching, Joe, and jump on. Do it or I swear I'll leave you here!"

The wounded man did as he was told. Soon, he was perched on the rump of the horse and the two were close behind the others, heading east the way they had come.

After the lynchmen had vanished into the forest, Jeb turned back to Roscoe. The Negro was still dangling at the end of the rope, his kicking and struggling growing weaker by the moment.

"Quick!" he screamed. "We gotta get him down from there!"

He and Sam ran to the tree, looking for some way to release Roscoe from his noose. It was Sam who reacted first. He grabbed the bluesman around the knees and lifted him up a foot, easing the tension on the rope. "Climb up on my shoulders and cut it!" he told the boy.

Jeb followed his instructions and, soon, was balanced on his father's broad shoulders. He fumbled through his overall pocket and found his folding knife. He released the longest and sharpest of the blades and went to work. It took some sawing, but finally the rope parted, strand by strand, and Roscoe's bald head lolled limply to the side. "Okay, I got it!" he called down to the man beneath him.

Gently, Sam lowered Roscoe to the ground. Jeb jumped from the farmer's back and was soon crouching next to the old man. Roscoe's wire-rimmed spectacles dangled from one ear and his eyes were nearly bugged from their sockets. The bluesman gasped and wheezed, as if his lungs fought to draw the tiniest breath of air.

"What's wrong?" asked Jeb, tears forming in his eyes.

"Can't . . ." struggled Roscoe, his mouth working like a fish out of water. "Can't . . . breath. Can't find . . . no air."

With a trembling hand, Jeb laid his hand on Roscoe's

throat. The man's Adam's apple—which had once protruded so prominently—was gone now. His windpipe had been completely crushed by the lynching noose.

"Oh, Roscoe," moaned Jeb. "I don't know what to do!"

Roscoe's voice was scarcely more than a harsh whisper. "Nothing much . . . you can do. That rope they hung me with . . . it's cut off my wind. I'm suffocating . . . to death."

"No!" cried Jeb. Tears rolled down his cheeks and dripped off his chin. "We can fetch a doctor. We can get you some help."

Roscoe's ragged gasping turned into a tiny wheezing as his injured throat began to swell. "Ain't a doctor . . . within ten mile . . . of here, boy. And . . . even if there was . . . they wouldn't be able . . . to do nothing. Them nightriders . . . they've done gone . . . and killed me."

Jeb wanted to deny the truth of Roscoe's words, but he simply couldn't. It didn't take a trained physician to tell that the black man was fading away fast. "I shot one of 'em, Roscoe," Jeb told him. "That one that tended bar back at the beer joint. I shot him smack-dab in the chest."

"Did you . . . kill him?" Roscoe managed.

"I don't rightfully know for sure," Jeb had to admit.

Helplessly, Jeb and Sam knelt next to the dying man, tearfully watching as his breathing grew more and more shallow. Blindly, the bluesman reached out with both hands. The boy and his father quickly took the man's hands in their own and held on tight.

"Some kinds of evil . . ." muttered Roscoe so softly they could hardly hear him. "They're the same . . . no matter where you go."

Jeb nodded, trying to fight down the sobs that shook him from head to toe. The boy looked over at Sam. The brawny farmer was blubbering like a big baby. Even Buckshot sensed that something was terribly wrong. The dog laid his speckled head on Roscoe's belly and whimpered pitifully.

"I want . . . ya'll . . . to promise me . . . something," said Roscoe. "Please . . . don't bury me here . . : in this wicked place. Lay my bones to rest . . . when you get to Mangrum. It's only . . . a mile or two further. Will you . . . grant me that?"

"We promise," said Jeb. Sam simply nodded, unable to speak.

"You're good boys," said Roscoe, closing his eyes. "Both of you. And I . . . was proud . . . to have known you."

Jeb wept, his throat growing sore from crying. "Roscoe?" he whispered.

"Yes?" asked the Negro. The rise and fall of his chest was so shallow that it was almost nonexistent.

"I love you, Roscoe."

The bluesman grasped the youngster's hand tightly. "I love you, too, Jeb."

Then, with a gentle smile and a sigh, he was gone.

For a long time, they knelt there and grieved the passing of their friend. Jeb, most of all, seemed to have difficulty accepting the death of the rambling musician. For he knew, if anyone was responsible for the success of his trip to Fear County, it was Roscoe Ledbetter. The old bluesman had risked his neck many times over to help Jeb locate the magic he had gone there to find. And, before it was over, he had paid for that loyalty with his life.

Forty-two

Sacred Ground

The sun of a new day was only a couple of hours high in the cloudless Tennessee sky when Jeb and Sam reached the line that separated Mangrum and Fear counties. The moment the farmboy stepped across the invisible border, he knew he was home again. The forest of shadowy thicket and dark earth abruptly gave way to colorful wildflowers, soft grass, and dusty red clay. He closed his eyes and listened. The warbling of songbirds echoed from the treetops, as well as the reedy call of cicadas and grasshoppers hidden from view. The noises that greeted him failed to cheer the boy, however. He still had a job to do, and it wasn't one he was looking forward to.

He turned and looked at the man behind him. Sam Sweeny followed a few yards away, the limp body of Roscoe Ledbetter slung over his shoulder. They had taken a wool blanket from the bluesman's knapsack and wrapped him up, cinching it tightly with a pair of Roscoe's old suspenders. Sam wore the Negro's brown fedora as if it were a timeworn crown. Jeb hadn't protested the farmer's inheritance of the battered hat. It seemed to relieve some of the hurt Sam felt at the old man's loss. Jeb wished he had a similar balm for his grief, but he didn't.

"Are we here, Jeb?" asked Sam, his eyes hopeful.

The boy breathed deeply. That stench of underlying decay that had permeated the air of Fear County was no longer present. Now there was only the warm scents of July; the fragrance of goldenrod and dandelion, as well as the dry odor of clay dirt stirred by walking feet. "Yeah," he finally said. "We're here. We're home again."

"So," said Sam, shifting the weight of Roscoe across his right shoulder. "Where are we gonna do it?"

Jeb looked around and spotted a bed of soft clover beneath the shade of a hickory tree. "There," he said, pointing. "I think he'd like to be over there, outta the sun."

Together, Jeb and Sam walked to the patch of clover, followed by Buckshot. Sam gently laid the man on the ground, careful not to disturb the blanket around him. They searched for something to break earth with and found a rusted hubcap that had fallen off the wheel of someone's Studebaker. Just finding the object told them that they were only a short distance from a road or highway.

It took some elbow grease, but they finally managed to chisel a hole from the earth, three feet deep and twice as long. Sam tenderly rolled the body of their friend into the grave, a solemn expression on his broad face. Then, both boy and man covered his remains over, packing the earth down firm.

When they were finished, Jeb took something from the duffle bag. It was the broken neck of Roscoe's flattop guitar. The boy put his weight against the length of inlaid wood and ivory tuning keys, driving it into the ground and turning it into a makeshift headstone.

They stared at the mound of earth for a long moment, unsure of what to do next. "I reckon we oughta say some words," said Jeb. "Pray or something."

Sam removed the fedora from his head and, closing his eyes, bowed his head. "Jesus . . . this here's Sam talking.

We've just buried our friend Roscoe in this earth of yours. He was a mighty good man. We'd be obliged if you'd look after him up there in heaven, the same as he looked after us down here. Amen."

"Amen," echoed the boy, staring at his father in amazement.

With nothing more to be said or done, they left the grave and walked toward the north. They stepped through a thicket a few yards further on and found themselves standing on the shoulder of the main highway. Jeb looked to the west and was surprised to see where the railroad crossed paths with the main road. He didn't exactly know how, but they were only a few yards away from where they had first begun their journey into Fear County,

They were about to head down the highway, in the direction of Pikesville, when Jeb noticed several objects scattered around his feet. The trash consisted of an empty Coca-Cola bottle, an apple core stripped clean down to the seeds, and the greasy page of a newspaper someone had wrapped their lunch in, a baloney and mustard sandwich from the smell of it.

The bottle and apple core didn't interest Jeb in the least. It was the page of newsprint that caught the boy's eye. Slowly, Jeb bent down and picked it up. It was the front page of the *Pikesville Gazette,* dated only two days ago. His heart began to pound when he noticed a boldfaced headline at the right side of the page. It read: "TWO MORE CHILDREN ABDUCTED—COUNTY SHERIFF STILL MISSING."

Jeb stood there for a moment, feeling a cold chill run down his spine. "It's gotten worse," he whispered, more to himself than anyone else.

"Where're we going first?" asked Sam. "To see Grandma?"

Jeb knew then that he had a decision to make. He thought

f his grandmother in the upstairs room of Claudine
ohnson's house, suffering from the cancer inside her. She
as safe there and well taken care of. He couldn't say as
uch for the prisoners of the riverside cave, though. Jeb
ould picture the walls of the cavern, decorated with children
cked in cocoons of tough snakeskin. He could imagine their
rror, too, as the snake-critter awoke from her slumber, that
satiable hunger for blood shining in her reptilian eyes. He
uld also picture Mandy Rutherford, pale and nearly drained
f life, clinging to one last shred of hope . . . and that was
eb's promise to come back for her.

Finally, he turned toward Sam, his eyes determined.
No," he said. "I think we oughta go to the cave first.
randma'll be all right for a while, but those young'uns
the cave, they ain't got much time. Do you understand
hat I'm saying?"

Disappointment showed in Sam's eyes, but he reluctantly
odded his bandaged head. "Yeah, I reckon you're right. That
nake-critter, it's had 'em long enough."

"That's right," said Jeb. He set down the duffle bag he
ad been carrying since they left the hanging tree and dug
rough its contents. After a moment, he found what he was
oking for.

He held up the pint jar that the Snake Queen had given
im. Sunlight played through the vinegar that sloshed around
side, making the leathery egg appear much blacker than
efore. It resembled a nasty pill of some sort; a poisonous
ill, or so Jeb hoped.

The boy returned the jar to the bag and closed the draw-
trings with a tug. "Are you ready?" he asked.

The farmer didn't look too sure. "I reckon so."

"Then let's go kill us a monster," said Jeb.

Together, the two started along the highway, heading to-
ard Pikesville and the bridge that spanned the Cumberland

River. In the shade of that bridge, they would find a hol in the side of a bluff. A hole that housed terror and despair as well as an evil that was almost too horrible to comprehend.

Part Six
Slaying the Dragon

Den of Darkness—Reunion—The Bitter Pill

Forty-three

Den of Darkness

"I'm scared," said Sam.

Jeb swallowed nervously. "Yeah, so am I."

It was high noon when they finally reached their destination. They stood on the lip of the bluff that towered along the Cumberland's southern bank, knowing what they had to do, but hesitant to do it. Jeb recalled the two times he had crossed paths with the snake-critter—in the hollow out back of the Sweeny property and in the cave below their feet little more than five days ago—and he was surprised that he had escaped with his life then. Now they were going to deliberately confront the beast with the intention of doing it in. It would be a wonder if they survived their self-appointed task, but Jeb knew they had to at least try.

Both man and boy steeled their nerves and began to make preparations. Jeb opened the duffle bag and took out the mason jar that contained the ebony egg. He studied it for a moment, then stuck it in the side pocket of his overalls. He checked to make sure he had other articles that might come in handy; his Case knife, slingshot, and lucky buckeye.

When Sam took out the flashlight, the boy shook his head. "I took the flashlight the last time I went in there and it didn't shed light worth spit," he told him. "That cave's mighty dark. I think we oughta try something else this time."

He went to the sycamore tree that grew at the edge of the bluff and yanked off a good-sized branch. Then he took one of Sam's old chambray shirts from the duffle bag, along with the can of lighter fluid Roscoe had carried in his knapsack. The ten-year-old stripped the branch of its leaves, wound the shirt tightly around the end, then saturated the cloth with fluid. When he was done, he slipped a box of matches in his pocket and looked over at Sam. "Well, I reckon it's time to do it," he said.

"But what about the gun?" asked the farmer. "Ain't we gonna take it with us?"

"No, it wouldn't do us no good." Jeb patted the bulge in his side pocket. "This here egg is the only thing that's gonna destroy it . . . or at least I hope so."

Sam nodded solemnly. As they made their way to the lip of the cliff and began to let themselves down, holding on to the roots of the sycamore as they went, Buckshot stood there and whined. "I'm sorry, boy," called Jeb. "But we can't take you with us this time. You're just gonna have to stay put and wait for us."

The coonhound seemed to understand, even though he didn't like it. He peeked over the edge as the two dropped to the narrow ledge below, then lay down with his head on his paws, waiting for his master's return.

Jeb and Sam stood on the ledge for a long moment, eyeing the dark entrance of the cave. It was pitch black within and gave nary a hint of the danger that lurked inside. Jeb recalled the last time he had stood on that ledge. The snake-critter had glared at him from the shadows and laughed at him. Actually laughed at him! The very thought diminished Jeb's fear and stoked an anger inside the boy. He swore that the creature wouldn't laugh at him this time. All Jeb wanted to hear from the snake-critter this time were screams of pain and defeat.

"Hold that branch by its end there," Jeb instructed. After Sam held it at armslength, Jeb struck a sulfur match and touched it to its head. The bundle of damp cloth caught fire immediately. Satisfied with the handmade torch, Jeb took it and held it in front of him. Then he turned to Sam, who looked even more scared than he was. "Follow me, but keep your head low," Jeb told him.

They entered the front tunnel, leaving the outer ledge of rock behind. The torch illuminated the narrow corridor of dank stone, casting much more light than a flashlight ever could. The additional light should have comforted them, but it didn't. The fact that the snake-critter was there, at the far end of the tunnel, prevented them from feeling anything but anxiety.

As the tunnel widened, Sam pointed to the side wall and whispered. "What's that yonder?"

Jeb looked over and saw the cigar box and the stack of girlie magazines. "Nothing that concerns us," he whispered back. The boy then turned to the entrance of the main chamber. He was shocked to find that the narrow passageway between the two boulders was three times wider than before. The huge rocks had been pushed aside by some tremendous strength and their edges were cracked and crumbling. Jeb spotted claw marks on the stone and knew that the snake-critter had been responsible. Apparently, she had grown so large that the additional space had been necessary to allow her to come and go as she pleased.

"They're in here," indicated Jeb. "In this back room."

Sam looked at the boy, his face a picture of fear amid a frame of yellowed bandages. "How're you gonna do it, Jeb? How're you gonna make it swallow that egg?"

Dread laid heavy in the pit of Jeb's stomach. "I don't rightly know," he said. "At least, not yet." He turned and handed the torch to Sam. "Are you ready to go in?"

Sam looked like he was ready to turn around and run from the cave, but he stuck out his jaw and nodded. "I'm shaking in my boots, but I ain't gonna let that critter know that. Let's get it over and done with."

Jeb took the pint jar from his pocket and swallowed dryly. Nervously, he unscrewed the top just enough to loosen it a bit. Holding it ready in his right hand he looked back at the farmer who held the torch. "Okay, let's go."

One at a time, they passed through the crevice between the two boulders. The air of the rear cavern was cool and tainted with the coppery scent of blood and the musky odor of snake. The flames of the torch cast an eerie glow on the craggy walls and the jagged ceiling of layered stalactites. Jeb looked around, searching for a glimpse of the snake-critter but he failed to locate it. Despite the additional light of the torch, there were still dense patches of shadow around the walls and across the boulder-strewn floor.

"Come on, but be quiet," he whispered to Sam. Slowly he started across the cavern, toward the far side.

When they reached the wall opposite the entrance, Jeb found that his worst fears had been justified. Where the wall of dank stone had once held only the cocooned forms of Mandy Rutherford and Troy Jenkins, it now boasted five prisoners, each trapped in their own coats of interwoven snake skin. Jeb recognized two children as Russell Miller, a boy in Mrs. Martin's second grade class at Pikesville Elementary and Effie Mae Fleming, the two-year-old daughter of James Fleming, the pastor of the local Methodist church.

The fifth prisoner on the wall was two times larger than the others and a good deal older. As Sam brought the torch closer, Jeb was surprised to see that it was Ed North who hung suspended from the wall, his boots dangling two feet from the stone floor. The county sheriff stared at Jeb and Sam, his eyes glassy and dull with shock. Several days worth

of stubble peppered his pale face and dried blood coated the
entire length of his neck. Looking closer, Jeb found two ugly
holes, puckered and blue, on the right side of the lawman's
throat, just beneath his ear.

More scared now than when he had first entered the cave,
Jeb tightened his fingers around the mason jar and went to
the second bundle on the wall. He was shocked to find
Mandy looking almost as ghastly as the sheriff. Her skin was
as white as baking soda and her eyes were half-closed and
glazed. Jeb could tell by the blood on her neck, that the creature had fed off her as well. The very thought both sickened
and frightened Jeb. Had he been away too long? Had he
arrived too late to save her?

"Mandy?" whispered the farmboy. "Mandy, can you hear
me? It's Jeb. I've come back."

The raven-haired girl opened her eyes a bit. Feebly, she
lifted her head and stared at him for a long moment. "Who?"
she asked, her voice barely audible.

"Jeb," repeated the boy. He felt the dread triple in his
stomach. "Jeb Sweeny. I've come to set you free."

The faintest of smiles crossed Mandy's gray lips. "Free,"
she muttered, then closed her eyes.

Jeb reached out and laid the palm of his hand against the
side of her bloodstained neck. Her pulse was weak, but it
was there. "Bring the torch over here," he told Sam. "I want
to check on Troy."

Sam did as he was told. As he brought the burning branch
closer, Jeb stepped to the left and regarded the boy who had
been the monster's first human victim. Jeb felt a jolt of terror
shoot through him and he nearly yelled out in fright.

For Troy Jenkins was no longer a boy. Instead, he was
nothing more than a sunken husk of mummified flesh and
bone. The smirking face that had once reveled in cruelty and
insolence was now frozen in a rictus of eternal horror. The

boy's eyes had fallen back into their deep pits and his mou
gaped wide, displaying cracked, yellow teeth and a tong
that was withered and black. Troy's skin was as brown a
clay dirt and fissured with a thousand wrinkles. It was as
the snake-critter had drained every last drop of blood an
moisture from the bully's body, before moving on to fea
upon the others.

"Oh God, Jeb!" gasped Sam, the torch shuddering in h
calloused hand. "What's wrong with him?"

"He's dead," was all that Jeb said.

For a long moment, silence stretched between the tw
Then Sam spoke again. "How're we gonna get them loos
Cut that hide off?"

"I tried that before," Jeb whispered. "It's too dang
tough. It'd take more than my ol' Case to set them free."

Sam was about to say something else, when a sound cam
from behind them. It took a moment to identify it and loca
its origin, but when they did, they both knew that the tim
of reckoning had come.

It was the soft rasping of scales against stone . . . and
echoed from a thick pool of shadow, no more than twen
feet away.

Startled, they turned. From the darkness emerged th
snake-critter, her scales gleaming like black diamonds an
her eyes blazing greenish-yellow in the light of the torc
Jeb was shocked by just how large the beast had grown. Sh
was a good fifteen feet in length now and her triangular hea
was nearly the size of that of a full-grown mule. The b
stared at her teeth and claws. Both were much longer an
sharper than they had been before.

Before he could say a word, the snake-critter was leapi
across the cavern toward them. Jeb expected Sam to screa

and run, but he didn't. Instead, the brawny farmer stepped
forward, waving the torch before him. The fire failed to ward
off the creature, however. It uttered that guttural laugh and
kept right on coming.

"Look out, Sam!" screamed Jeb.

The warning came too late. The creature landed in front
of the big man and, whirling like a black tornado, lashed out
with its scaly tail. It curled around Sam's waist and flung
him bodily across the underground room, causing him to
drop the torch. Jeb watched in horror as Sam hit the far wall
with a loud thud, then fell to his knees.

The tail came for Jeb next. The boy saw it sweeping toward him with enough force to knock his head clean from
his shoulders. Jeb ducked at the last instant, though, and the
scaly appendage passed over his head. He stumbled backward, hopping over the fallen torch and trying to put some
distance between him and the creature. With a hiss, the
snake-critter flailed out again, this time aiming toward the
boy's ankles. Jeb dodged the second attack, jumping up as
the tail flashed underneath, much like jumping a rope on the
playground at school.

When the boy's feet touched ground, he lost his balance.
His hands were slick with sweat and so was the mason jar
he held. Jeb cried out as the glass container slipped from
his grasp. He fumbled with it, trying to regain his hold, but
it was no use. The jar dropped to the stone floor, shattering
in an explosion of broken glass and vinegar as it hit.

"No!" screamed the boy. Terrified, he watched as the black
egg bounced twice across the cave floor and rolled toward
the base of a boulder. Jeb ran after it and reached the rock
a second later. When he reached down, he found the egg
mercifully intact. He cradled it in the palm of his hand. The
black orb was repulsive to the touch. The shell was thick
and leathery, and, as he tightened his grasp, he could feel

something soft and pliant swimming in the inner fluid. It was the undeveloped embryo of a snake-critter baby, tucked neatly inside the shell.

As Jeb straightened up and turned, a deep growl sounded in Jeb's ears. He suddenly found the creature standing before him, no more than ten feet away. Her reptilian eyes blazed cruelly and her jaws worked hungrily, allowing a phlegmy mixture of saliva and venom to dribble from its lower jaw. Jeb stared at the grinning maw with its six-inch fangs and he abruptly felt as if his entire crusade across the dark length of Fear County had been in vain. Deep down in his soul, the boy knew there was no chance of him getting the egg in his hand past that barrier of bristling teeth.

The snake-critter seemed to also sense that defeat was close at hand. With that rattling laugh of hers, she slowly started toward the boy, her razored claws clicking against the stone floor.

Jeb felt no fear, but rather a shame so intense that it made his heart ache. "I'm sorry, Mandy," he muttered bitterly. "Sorry, Grandma."

Then, when the beast was scarcely eight feet away, Jeb saw the creature stagger slightly, her eyes registering something akin to surprise. At first, the boy didn't understand what was happening. Then, a second later, the glow of the torch revealed the source of the monster's dilemma.

It was Sam. The big man had recovered from the snake-critter's assault and jumped upon her back. He rode the creature like a cowboy on the back of a brahma bull, his legs locked tightly around her scaly torso. Jeb looked past the snake-critter's huge head and saw Sam hanging on for dear life. But he didn't look as frightened as the boy expected him to. Instead, there seemed to be a strong sense of purpose in the farmer's eyes.

"What are you doing, Sam?" yelled Jeb. "Get off her before she ends up killing you!"

Sam ignored the boy. If anything, he tightened his legs around the monster even more and locked his ankles firmly together. The snake-critter lurched forward, ready to sink her fangs into Jeb, but Sam grabbed the beast by the head and jerked it backward. With a deafening roar, the creature bucked and reared, trying to pitch the big man off. But Sam was there for the duration. He wasn't about to let go.

Then Jeb saw Sam snake his hands around the creature's head and, hooking his strong fingers between her upper and lower teeth, began to slowly work the fanged jaws apart. It took some doing, but eventually he had them pried completely open. It reminded Jeb of that scene in *King Kong* when the mighty ape wrenched open the jaws of the Tyrannosaurus rex.

"Get ready, Jeb!" called Sam. "Now's your chance. You can do it!"

As the jaws trembled in the big man's fists, threatening to snap close and sever his fingers at the knuckles, Jeb stared at the dark gullet that lay beyond the fangs. He glanced down at the black egg in his hand and considered throwing it into the horrid mouth. But he knew his pitching arm was not strong enough to send it where it needed to go. No, he needed something with a little more punch to it.

"Hurry!" said Sam, his face red with exertion. "I can't hold 'em open much longer, son!"

Quickly, Jeb shucked the slingshot from his hip pocket and unfurled the length of cut innertube. He placed the egg in the cradle of the sling, then, taking aim at the opening just beyond the creature's slimy black tongue, pulled back and let go.

Jeb was trembling so badly that, at first, he was certain he would miss his target completely. But his marksmanship proved to be as keen as always. The black egg spun past the jagged fangs, traveled the length of her slavery jaws, and neatly popped into the dark hole of her gullet. For a second, it lodged there and Jeb was certain that the creature would cough it back up. Then Sam gave the snake-critter a sharp kick in the belly with the heel of his boot and the egg disappeared from sight. Jeb heard an audible gulp as the monster swallowed it whole.

Sam leapt from the critter's back and dropped to the stone floor a few yards away. Jeb stood perfectly still and watched, the slingshot still fisted in his hands so tightly that his knuckles were white with strain.

The snake-critter belched a couple of times, then appeared to recover. She took a step toward the boy, that glint of pure evil shining in her serpentine eyes. Then something began to happen. The expression of malice faded from the creature's eyes and a look of confusion replaced it. Slowly, a blackish-blue vapor began to seep from between the gaps of the monster's teeth and the tiny pits of her nostrils. A low groan sounded deep down in her throat as the eyes of brilliant yellow-green gradually changed to an ugly reddish-orange, the color of stove embers before they grow cold and turn to ashen gray.

Amazed, Jeb watched as the snake-critter took another step forward, then abruptly crashed to her knees. She attempted to get up, but was unable to. The muscles beneath her shiny black skin appeared to shrink and melt away. The vapor that spewed from her bodily orifices grew denser, reeking of sulfur and decay. A mournful moan like that of a dying cow wailed from the creature's throat as her eyes sank back in her head and her fangs began to drop from her jaws, one by one. The teeth struck the floor and shattered, as brittle as finely blown glass.

Then, from within the lean body, echoed a bubbling and

a popping as organs and bones began to slowly disintegrate. The snake-critter tried to focus her receding eyes on the boy, but it was no use. She was already blind. Sightlessly, she crawled a couple of feet in his general direction, but could go no further. A spasm of tremendous agony seemed to shudder through the beast's body and she rolled over, her sides heaving, attempting to draw a few last breaths of air. Strangely enough, it pained Jeb to see the creature in such a state. It was kind of like watching Roscoe suffocate to death all over again, the way she gasped and wheezed.

The snake-critter clung to life for a minute more. Then a loud, hollow boom sounded in her chest—the muffled report of her black heart exploding from within—and her eyes grew dark and glassy in the sockets of her eyes. The strong scent of snake slowly disappeared and was, instead, replaced by an ancient, dusty odor much like the yellowed pages of old books or boxes that have stood in an upstairs attic for too many years.

A long sigh whistled through the few teeth that remained in the creature's jaws. Then, with one last shudder, the monster relaxed and grew still.

Jeb waited a full minute before gathering the nerve to draw closer. When he finally did, he poked at the snake-critter's ribcage with his foot. His toe broke the skin, punching through brittle scales and flesh as thin as old cobwebs. A fart of cold air escaped from the hole and the creature's entire body suddenly caved in, leaving only a flattened shell of the demon that had once thrived within.

Shakily, Jeb stepped away, the slingshot falling from his aching fingers. It was over. He had accomplished what he had come there to do that day.

The horror that had once stalked Mangrum County was no more.

Forty-four

Reunion

As Jeb stared at the ruins of the snake-critter, something slowly dawned on him. He thought back to the moment before he shot the black egg down the creature's throat and the words that Sam had spoken as he had struggled with those monstrous jaws.

"Hurry! I can't hold 'em own much longer, son."

In the heat of battle, Jeb hadn't even noticed it. But now, with the danger past and his thoughts unburdened, he realized what had actually taken place. His heart began to beat faster and he turned toward the big farmer. Sam stood there, the matted cloth of the poultice draped around his shoulders and a hauntingly familiar smile on his face.

"You . . ." stammered the boy, "You called me . . . son."

Sam Sweeny nodded, his smile growing even broader. "That's right, Jeb. I remember now."

Tears began to bloom in the ten-year-old's eyes. "You mean—?"

"Yes," replied his father, his voice cracking. "I'm back."

For a moment, the two simply stared at each other. Then, an instant later, the boy was across the cave and in his father's arms. He buried his face against the man's broad shoulder and wept. "Oh, Papa! I've missed you. I've missed you so much."

Sam wrapped his brawny arms tenderly around his only child, tears of joy rolling down his own face. "I'm sorry it took so long, son," he said. "I tried. God knows I tried to come back, but it was like I was locked away somewhere in my head. That poultice the Granny Woman put on me did the trick. It took a while, but it finally broke down the wall between us."

"But you're back, ain't you?" asked the boy hopefully.

"I'm back, Jeb," assured the farmer. "And I'm here to stay."

For a few moments, they simply stood there and embraced, reluctant to let go. The years that had been lost between them seemed to roll away and it was like they had never been separated. "I love you, Papa," said Jeb.

Sam Sweeny flashed that hearty smile that used to grace his face so often. "I love you, too, son. More than you'll ever know."

When they finally let go, the reality of what had taken place in the cave came back to them. They turned toward the far side of the cavern. Surprisingly enough, those who had been bound to the stone wall were no longer there. Upon the creature's death, their cocoons of interwoven snakehide had disintegrated and fallen away, releasing them from their bonds. They lay on the hard floor, disoriented, paper-thin strands of snakeskin clinging to their arms and legs.

Jeb and Sam quickly went to them. They helped the three children and the county sheriff to their feet. Each was pale and thin from the draining the snake-critter had inflicted upon them. Russell and Effie Mae began to sniffle and cry, their senses more intact than those who had been captured before them.

Mandy Rutherford and Ed North were a different matter. "Mandy?" Jeb said softly, taking her hand in his. "It's me. It's Jeb."

"Who?" she muttered. Her glassy eyes focused on the boy's face, attempting to identify it.

"Jeb Sweeny," he said, feeling a dreadful ache down deep in his heart. "Don't you remember me?"

"No," she said, bewildered. "I'm sorry, but I don't."

Sam tried the same thing with North, but the county constable was just as ignorant of who they were as the girl was. "What's wrong with 'em?" asked Jeb, disappointment showing in his young eyes. "Why don't they remember us?"

The farmer studied on the problem for a moment. "Could be that it's the shock of what they've been through," he said. "Either that or something in that snake-critter's venom has poisoned their brains, caused 'em to forget a few things."

"Will they ever remember?"

Sam shrugged his big shoulders. "I couldn't say for sure, son. But there's always a chance. I'm living proof of that."

Together, they herded the four through the tunnel, leaving the remains of the snake-critter and Troy Jenkins in the darkness of the adjoining cavern. It took some doing to help them to the top of the bluff, as weakened and unsteady as they were, but eventually Jeb and Sam managed to get them there.

Upon their return, Buckshot shot up from where he lay beneath the sycamore tree. He jumped up and down like a happy puppy, relieved to see that they were okay. Jeb bent down and gave the hound a big hug. "I'm glad to see you, too, boy."

Single file, they led the monster's victims along the steep bluff to the Cumberland River bridge. When they reached the main road, Sam put the hands of Russell and Effie Mae in those of Sheriff North. The lawman simply stared down at the two, as if he had never seen children before in his life.

"Okay, this is what you need to do, Ed," said Sam, looking

the haggard constable squarely in the eyes. "Pikesville is a couple miles straight ahead. You take these young'uns with you. Their folks'll be mighty happy to see 'em. And, when you get there, you tell them that Troy Jenkins's body is back yonder in that cave you just left. They'll come get it and give it a decent burial. Did you understand all that?"

North nodded slowly. "Yes, sir," he said. "I reckon I can remember that."

"Good," replied Sam. "Now, ya'll get going."

Jeb and Sam watched as the sheriff and the two children started across the bridge and headed for town. Reluctantly, Mandy Rutherford followed, turning to look back at the two, her eyes uncertain. "You go on with 'em, girl," urged Sam gently. "I know your mama and daddy'll be right glad to see you."

"So long, Mandy," called Jeb with a wave of his hand. "See you later."

The dark-haired girl simply stared at him, then turned and walked across the bridge with the others. Jeb shook his head and tried hard to conceal the hurt he felt inside, but it was difficult to do so. He had a bad feeling that the girl would never think of him in the same way as she had during the Fourth of July celebration. He recalled the kiss they had shared at the top of the oak tree, surrounded by flashing fireworks and a sky full of stars, and that made him feel even sadder than before.

But then he remembered the third matter that had prompted him to cross the treacherous region known as Fear County, and his spirits began to lift. "Papa," he said, a big grin splitting his freckled face. "We gotta get home. We've got something else we've gotta do today."

Sam nodded, knowing what the boy was referring to. "Let's go then."

Together, father and son headed south in the direction of

Mossy Creek Road and the farmstead of Claudine Johnson. As he walked, Jeb reached down in his side pocket and found the snuffbox wrapped safely in its bandanna. He just hoped that the magic inside that tin would prove to be as powerful as the rest he had brought back from the dark heart of Fear County.

Forty-five

The Bitter Pill

Jeb ran the length of the dirt driveway as fast as his bare feet could carry him. Up ahead stood the two-story farmhouse owned by Claudine Johnson. He looked up at the second window from the right, knowing that his grandmother slept there in the big feather bed of Miss Claudine's guest room. As he kicked up dust and jumped over uneven stones in the drive, Jeb could hear the rattle of the seeds in the snuffbox. The sound drove him onward, increasing his urgency to see Grandma Sweeny and tell her of the cure he had brought back home with him.

As he neared the house, Jeb turned and saw his father walking up the drive, his pace unhurried and his hands stuck in his pockets. Jeb couldn't understand why his father wasn't running, too. After all, it was his mother who lay up there in the upstairs bedroom. There was bound to be a joyous reunion between them, what with Sam having been mentally absent for so long. That was why Jeb had a hard time figuring out why the farmer poked so far behind. For some reason, Sam Sweeny wasn't quite as excited about arriving home as Jeb was, that was plain enough to see.

"Come on, Papa!" he called as he reached the end of the drive. As he reached the green grass of the front lawn, he saw Miss Claudine standing in the flower garden at the opposite end of the house, working among her lilies and gardenias. "Howdy, Miss Claudine!" he called out happily. "We're back!"

He expected the elderly woman to greet him, but she simply stood there staring at him, looking a little startled.

Jeb was in too much of a hurry to stop and talk. He flung open the screen door and entered the house. "Grandma!" he yelled as he crossed the foyer and bounded up the staircase. "Grandma, I'm back!"

As he took the risers two at a time, he dug the snuffbox from his pocket and unwrapped the bandanna from around it. He knew the contents inside weren't much to look at—if anything, they looked like sunflower seeds, only a little bit smaller. But it wasn't how they looked or what size they were that counted. It was the promise of the magic within them that mattered most of all. He ached to tell his grandmother about those seeds and the miracle they would bring once they sprouted from the earth.

A moment later, he had reached the landing of the upper floor. With a big grin on his face, Jeb ran down the hallway until he reached the door of the guest bedroom. He turned the shiny brass knob with one hand, while the other clutched the box of seeds.

Jeb flung the door open. He knew she might be sleeping, but what he had to tell her was important. He wanted to see the peace that filled those tormented eyes when she discovered that a cure was so close at hand.

"Grandma!" he said, stepping through the doorway. "Wait till you—"

Jeb came to a stumbling halt in the center of the room, his smile suddenly faltering. His eyes swept the room, searching, but unable to comprehend what he found there. Or rather, what he did not.

The feather bed was empty. The covers and quilt weren't

even pulled down. And the little lamp table that had once held medicine bottles and the pouch with the syringe inside was bare. It looked as if no one had spent the night in that room for a very long time.

The only odd thing that Jeb could find in the room was a single, long-stemmed red rose that lay atop the bed's pillow. Something about the presence of that flower sent a chill down the young boy's spine.

Stunned, he turned and left the room. He walked back down the hallway to the head of the stairs. When he reached it and took a couple steps down, he saw Claudine Johnson and his father standing in the foyer. At the sound of his footfalls, they turned and looked up at him. Their faces were grim and their eyes were full of pity.

Jeb felt as if all the strength was about to drain from his legs. Slowly, he descended the stairway, one step at a time. "Miss Claudine?" he asked. "Where is my grandmother?"

The woman simply stared up at him, her eyes red and on the verge of fresh tears. She looked as if she had already been crying, and for a lengthy period of time.

"Please, Miss Claudine," he pleaded. "Tell me where she is."

When the woman brought a trembling hand to her face and turned away, Jeb knew that it was bad. He watched, his heart thundering in his chest, as his father walked across the foyer and stopped at the foot of the stairs.

"Jeb," he said, his face full of pain, "Son, I have some bad news."

But his father didn't even have to tell him. "Oh God," he breathed. "She's dead, ain't she?"

Sam nodded slowly. "Yes, son. She is."

Jeb stopped on the stairs and stood there for a moment. He closed his eyes, seeing images of his grandmother behind the lids of his eyes; baking pies in the kitchen, hanging the

wash on the line with wooden pins, and sitting in her favorite
pew at church, hanging on every word the preacher had to
utter.

"When . . . when did it happen?" he asked, his voice
small.

Miss Claudine turned toward the staircase. Tears trickled
freely down her wrinkled face. "She took a turn for the
worse, right after you left. Just fell asleep and never woke
up. We buried her three days after ya'll left for Fear County.
I wanted to wait, but I had no earthly idea where you were
or how I could get in touch with you. There was nothing
else to be done, what with it being the heat of summer and
all."

As Jeb reached the bottom of the stairs, he stared his father in the face. "She ain't dead," he said firmly.

"Yes, she is, son," said Sam Sweeny. He reached out to
take the boy in his arms, aiming to comfort him.

Jeb dodged his embrace, however. "Not for long, though,"
he said.

The farmer watched as his son started for the front door.
"No, Jeb," he said, alarm registering in his eyes. "Don't."

But the boy wouldn't listen. He rushed past Miss Claudine,
pushed open the screen door, and, leaping off the porch, began to run back the way he had come.

The shadows of late afternoon were deepening by the time
Jeb Sweeny reached his destination. Even though he was exhausted by his long run, he managed to hop the iron gate
of the Pikesville Cemetery next to the Baptist church with
no trouble at all.

Breathing hard, the boy searched the field of marble and
granite, looking for the raw red of clay dirt among them. He
spotted it a moment later, surrounded by a semicircle of col-

rful flower arrangements, most of them roses and carnations,
ll of them wilted by the sweltering July sun.

Jeb ran through the graveyard and collapsed atop the
lound of earth. There was no stone at its head to tell who
belonged to, but he knew. Grandpa Sweeny's modest gran-
e marker stood only a few feet to the left.

The boy sobbed as he opened his fist and released the
nuffbox he had held since his arrival at the Johnson house.
Vith trembling fingers, he lifted the lid and stared at the
ny seeds inside. There were perhaps forty or fifty there,
oking blandly unremarkable for such a miraculous cure.

Silently, he reached out and scooped up a handful of clay
irt, then tossed it away. The impression he left in the earthen
lound was only a few inches deep, but he prayed that it
vas enough.

Jeb was gathering up five or six of the tiny brown seeds
etween his fingers, when he felt a strong hand on his shoul-
er. He didn't even have to turn around to see who it was.

"What are you doing, Jeb?" asked the voice of his father.

"I'm gonna work the magic, that's what," Jeb sobbed. "I'm
onna bring her back."

"But you can't," said Sam firmly. "Remember what the
Granny Woman told you?"

Jeb recalled what the old woman had said; about how the
oots of the seeds would touch the lid of a casket and bring
he one inside back to life. He also remembered something
lse she had warned him of. Something about how the dead
vould return, but not the same as before.

"I don't care!" he cried. "I want her back. I want every-
hing to be the way it was before!"

"But that just can't be, son," Sam said gently. "The Lord
as a plan for us all. He's called your grandma home to Him
nd that's all there is to it. If you were to go against His

wishes and plant them seeds, well, it'd be sin. A sin you likely regret for the rest of your life."

Through a prism of tears, Jeb stared at the seeds betwee his fingertips. It would be so very easy to plant them in th hole and cover them over with dirt. But he didn't. The trut of his father's words rung in his ears and, little by little, th hurt in his soul began to ease, if not entirely. He opened hi fingers and let the seeds fall back into the tin where the belonged.

"Come on, son," said his father, wrapping a strong arr around his shoulders. "Let's go home."

Jeb failed to budge from the spot, however. "Can't we sta for a while longer?" he asked his father. "Maybe say a praye or two and let her know we're down here thinking of her?

Sam Sweeny smiled sadly and gathered his son close t his side. "Sure we can," he replied.

They sat at the foot of Grandma's grave until the sky dark ened into evening and the crickets began to sing their nightl chorus. While they were there, they reminisced about goo times and things that had been said and done. But, most c all, they came to the realization that magic, no matter how powerful it might be, did not always work. Sometimes on had to accept the fact that some illnesses were beyond curin and some events beyond altering.

It was a bitter pill for Jeb to swallow, but he swallowe it nevertheless and grieved about the unfairness of it n more.

Epilogue

Howard Drewer flapped the striped cloth, sending hair trimmings falling to the barber shop floor. "Next?" he called, like a prizefighter calling for his next opponent.

Jeb Sweeny pried his attention from a Blue Beetle comic book and, reluctantly laying it aside unfinished, left his chair and headed for that throne of torment he visited the last of every month.

As the boy settled against the black leather cushions, Mr. Drewer tied the cloth around his neck, pulling the strings a little too snugly. "Haven't seen you around town in two or three weeks, Jeb," he said, appraising the boy's head sagely. "Heavy off the sides and light on the top?"

Jeb grinned. "Right as usual, Mr. Drewer."

The boy heard a grunt of satisfaction, followed by the rattle of a glass lid and the crackle of cellophane. He opened his mouth wide and waited for his prize. The sucker was grape, just as he had hoped.

Cy Newman and Bill Brownwell were over by the window, trading conversation and dirty looks over their checkerboard. "How're you and your daddy doing, Jeb?" asked Bill. "Are ya'll getting along pretty well? Must be kinda hard trying to make do without your grandma, God rest her soul."

"Yes, sir," said Jeb. "But we're managing."

"It was a miracle, your papa regaining his senses like he did," said Cy. "A flat-out miracle."

"Aw!" barked Drewer, going to work on the boy's tousled head with comb and scissors. "I knew Sam Sweeny was too smart a fella to stay simple-minded for the rest of his life. I figured he'd come back good as new, sooner or later."

Jeb sat and listened as the men bantered opinions and bits of gossip back and forth. He was quiet when they discussed the return of the missing children and the discovery of Troy Jenkin's mummified body, and he smiled to himself when Bill and Cy got into a quarrel over whether the culprit had been a bear, a wild dog, or a black mountain lion. Mr. Drewer, who had been one of the men who had investigated the riverside cave, claimed that it was some kind of hideous monster that had abducted the youngsters. The barber regretted saying so, though. The two checker-players laughed so hard, that Drewer grew red in the face and silently went back to the haircut he was giving.

It was toward the end of Jeb's time in the chair that an interesting bit of news surfaced. "Have ya'll heard about Lester Odell?" asked Cy Newman, searching for a way to win a hopelessly lost game.

"Heard he was sick with a cancer in his lungs," said Bill. "Also heard that he had one foot in his grave."

"Well, that was last week," the old man informed him. "John Redding told me this morning that Lester ain't dying after all. He went to his doctor a couple days ago and they did an X-ray. Didn't find nothing a'tall, where they'd found him nearly eaten up a month ago."

"Is that so?" asked Drewer, interested. "And how did that happen?"

Cy chuckled. "Well, John told me that Lester claims it was some collard greens he found growing in his garden. He dug 'em up, cooked up a mess, and ate 'em for two or three days. After that, the pain in his chest stopped and that confounded cough of his simply disappeared."

"And collard greens was what cured him?" asked Bill. "Bullsh—" He cast a glance Jeb's way. "—shovels!"

"Speaking of cancer, I heard that Thelma Martin's got it," said Mr. Drewer.

"The teacher over at the elementary school?" asked Cy, raising his bushy gray eyebrows.

"Yep," said the barber. "Heard they found it in her titties. Both of 'em."

"Now ain't that a shame," said Bill Brownwell. "And I know for a fact she ain't over forty years of age."

"I reckon it can hit you anytime, no matter how old you are," said Mr. Drewer. He finished up with the electric clippers, then brushed the fine hairs off the nape of the boy's neck with a talcumed brush. "There you go, Jeb," he said, unloosening the stranglehold of the cloth with an experienced jerk of a string.

Jeb hopped down out of the chair and dug three quarters from his pocket. "There you go, Mr. Drewer," he said, dropping the change in the man's waiting hand.

"See you next month, Jeb," said the barber. "And tell your daddy I said howdy. He don't stop by and chew the fat as much as we'd like him to."

"He's been working a lot lately," Jeb told him. "He's plowing today. Says he's going to plant tobacco and corn next season."

"Well, much luck to him," said Mr. Drewer. He turned his attention back to the line of chairs around the walls of the barber shop. "Next?"

Jeb stepped out in the bright July sun and shielded his eyes with his hand. The day was sweltering hot and he knew it would be even hotter once August kicked in next week. The sidewalk scorched the soles of his feet and he quickly jumped into a pool of shade in the mouth of the alley.

The boy looked across Main Street and saw his dog

stretched out in his favorite sleeping spot beneath the apple bin. "Buckshot!" he called. "Let's go, boy."

The hound opened an eye, then closed it again, acting as if he hadn't heard his master's command.

Jeb considered going over and dragging him from beneath the bin by his collar, but dismissed the notion. He had a few things to do there in town, so he'd come back and get the dog before he started the long drive home.

As he stepped out of the shade and hopped up on the seat of the Sweenys' mule-drawn wagon, Jeb saw Mandy Rutherford and her mother leaving Thompson's Shoe Store across the street. He summoned a big grin and waved. "Hi, Mandy!" he yelled out.

The girl looked his way, but didn't answer. She clung close to her mother and followed her down the sidewalk to the drugstore.

Jeb tried not to be discouraged, but it was difficult. Mandy still didn't remember him or the feelings they had felt toward each other that week of the Fourth of July. None of the snake-critter's victims seemed to recall much about their former lives. Ed North had suffered more than any of them. Due to his forgetfulness, he had been relieved of his position as Mangrum County sheriff. These days, he made his living sweeping sidewalks and doing odd jobs around town.

The farmboy finished his sucker and tossed the stick into the street, which would soon be paved, thanks to a vote made by the city council a few days ago. For a moment, he sat on the wooden seat of the wagon and thought about what Mr. Drewer had said concerning Mrs. Martin.

But, strangely enough, the news didn't make him feel as sad as it should have. A sly grin crossed his freckled face and he stuck his hand in the side pocket of his overalls. His fingers groped through the clutter of junk until he found what he was searching for. He shook the silver snuffbox and smiled even more when he heard the rattle of magic inside.

As Jeb headed for Holt's feed store to pick up a load of supplies, he figured he would take a moment and stop by Thelma Martin's house on his way home. And, while he was there visiting, he might just sneak out back to her vegetable patch and plant a few seeds.

*YOU'D BETTER SLEEP WITH THE LIGHTS TURNED ON!
BONE CHILLING HORROR BY*

RUBY JEAN JENSEN

ANNABELLE	(2011-2, $3.95/$4.95)
BABY DOLLY	(3598-5, $4.99/$5.99)
CELIA	(3446-6, $4.50/$5.50)
CHAIN LETTER	(2162-3, $3.95/$4.95)
DEATH STONE	(2785-0, $3.95/$4.95)
HOUSE OF ILLUSIONS	(2324-3, $4.95/$5.95)
LOST AND FOUND	(3040-1, $3.95/$4.95)
MAMA	(2950-0, $3.95/$4.95)
PENDULUM	(2621-8, $3.95/$4.95)
VAMPIRE CHILD	(2867-9, $3.95/$4.95)
VICTORIA	(3235-8, $4.50/$5.50)

Available wherever paperbacks are sold, or order direct from the Publisher. Send cover price plus 50¢ per copy for mailing and handling to Penguin USA, P.O. Box 999, c/o Dept. 17109, Bergenfield, NJ 07621. Residents of New York and Tennessee must include sales tax. DO NOT SEND CASH.

MAKE THE CONNECTION

WITH

Come talk to your favorite authors and get the inside scoop on everything that's going on in the world of publishing, from the only online service that's designed exclusively for the publishing industry.

With Z-Talk Online Information Service, the most innovative and exciting computer bulletin board around, you can:

- ✔ CHAT "LIVE" WITH AUTHORS, FELLOW READERS, AND OTHER MEMBERS OF THE PUBLISHING COMMUNITY.
- ✔ FIND OUT ABOUT UPCOMING TITLES BEFORE THEY'RE RELEASED.
- ✔ DOWNLOAD THOUSANDS OF FILES AND GAMES.
- ✔ READ REVIEWS OF TITLES.
- ✔ HAVE UNLIMITED USE OF E-MAIL.
- ✔ POST MESSAGES ON OUR DOZENS OF TOPIC BOARDS.

All it takes is a computer and a modem to get online with Z-Talk. Set your modem to 8/N/1, and dial 212-935-0270. If you need help, call the System Operator, at 212-407-1533. There's a two week free trial period. After that, annual membership is only $ 60.00.

See you online!